THREE FANTASIES

(Levity, Flight, Angel Undone)

Leta Blake

Other Books by Leta Blake

Contemporary

Will & Patrick Wake Up Married
Will & Patrick's Endless Honeymoon
Cowboy Seeks Husband
The Difference Between
Bring on Forever
Stay Lucky

Sports

The River Leith

The Training Season Series
Training Season
Training Complex

Musicians

Smoky Mountain Dreams
Vespertine

New Adult

Punching the V-Card

Winter Holidays

The Home for the Holidays Series
Mr. Frosty Pants
Mr. Naughty List
Mr. Jingle Bells

Fantasy

Any Given Lifetime

Re-imagined Fairy Tales

Flight
Levity

Paranormal & Shifters

Angel Undone
Omega Mine

Horror

Raise Up Heart

Omegaverse

Heat of Love Series
Slow Heat
Alpha Heat
Slow Birth
Bitter Heat

For Sale Series
Heat for Sale

Coming of Age

'90s Coming of Age Series
Pictures of You
You Are Not Me

Audiobooks

Leta Blake at Audible

Discover more about the author online

Leta Blake
letablake.com

Gay Romance Newsletter

Leta's newsletter will keep you up to date on her latest releases and news from the world of M/M romance. Join the mailing list today and you're automatically entered into future giveaways.
letablake.com

Leta Blake on Patreon

Become part of Leta Blake's Patreon community in order to access exclusive content, deleted scenes, extras, bonus stories, rewards, prizes, interviews, and more.
www.patreon.com/letablake

LEVITY

A Gay Fairy Tale

Leta Blake

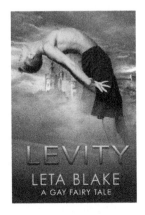

Cursed as an infant with a lack of physical and emotional gravity, Prince Efrosin can't keep his feet on the ground or his head out of the clouds. Laughing his way through life, he's never been weighed down by love and lust.

Then one fateful day, his tenuous tie to the earth is severed and he blows away on the wind. He's rescued by Dmitri, a handsome young woodsman who suffers from a mysterious curse of his own, and the two strangers are irresistibly drawn together. Experiencing sex and love for the first time, they dive into a delightfully sensual and passionate affair.

But the evil witch who cursed them is planning her ultimate revenge. Efrosin and Dmitri must fight to find their fairy tale ending and live happily ever after.

Prologue

O NCE UPON A time, there was a kingdom at the edge of what was and what could never be. At the center of this kingdom was a castle, and within this castle was a king. Inside this king was a terribly selfish heart.

One summer day, as the river ran, the birds flew and the flowers bloomed, King Leo paced by his queen's chamber door, listening as she labored. After three bastard daughters and one bastard son, King Leo was impatient for his queen to present him with an heir to the crown.

He banged a fist against the door, raging at her to hurry, so that he might hold the babe aloft for the gathered crowds to see. "And God help you if it isn't the son I deserve."

But the birth was hard going.

Finally, he heard the midwife shout, "I see the head, my queen."

The king flung open the door, strode into the room and pushed aside the old crone attending to his wife. His wife lay back against the pillows, golden hair spilling around her, and her grey as dust. She rested quietly in a damp circle of sweat and blood.

Her pale face shone from prior effort, but still he cursed her laziness. "Push, or find out what it is to defy me!"

She struggled up to her elbows to obey. As the queen gave another great cry, the child burst forth into the king's waiting palms.

He gripped the small body under its armpits and raised it up. There, before his eager eyes, dangled the child's penis. The king turned away from his sobbing wife, ignoring her outstretched hands and whimpers for her son.

He strode across the room and flung open the shutters to lean out of the queen's high tower chambers. His hands gripped the baby's body firmly as he thrust it into the light of the day. He yelled, "Kneel before your prince! Kneel before my son!"

The sun illuminated the wailing infant until he appeared to fairly glow, and the gathered crowd let out a wild cheer, collapsing to their knees.

As the news of the child spread, joy cascaded through the kingdom. Perhaps this prince would be good and handsome and wise. Perhaps he would be different from his father. And, as with every birth across endless time, hope was reborn.

Chapter One

"IT'S MY BIRTHDAY," Efrosin sang, bobbing in the air near the ceiling of his bedroom, as was his wont. He was wearing his usual silk pajamas, and Geoffry felt a prick of concern regarding his chances of convincing his charge to change into more appropriate finery.

"Indeed it is, Your Highness. Many happy returns to you," Geoffry said.

Efrosin pushed off the stone wall with his bare feet and skimmed through the air. "As my manservant, Geoffry, it is your duty to help me get what I want."

His short golden hair was still wet and disheveled from his usual morning routine—several hours spent swimming in the embrace of the river. Geoffry imagined that if it were not for the traditional wreath-laying ceremony upon the late queen's grave, Efrosin would soon be ready to leave to further frolic in the depths and shallows of the river.

Not that Geoffry could blame his charge for his obsessive love of water. Due to the misfortune of having been cursed soundly by a vengeful witch when he was but an infant, in the water was the only place where Efrosin had any weight at all.

Obviously feeling anything but unfortunate, Efrosin spun about mid-air without a care in the world. Geoffry turned from him and began to set out the proper outfit—including a specially designed coat with many long, colorful ribbons sewn firmly to the hem. Each ribbon would be held by a knight to prevent Efrosin from floating into the great, blue sky. Geoffry straightened the collar on the coat and pondered how best to persuade Efrosin to put it on.

"I hope that what you want, sire, is an afternoon ceremony beside your mother's grave," Geoffry said. "For that is what you shall have. Come now, we should hurry. There isn't much time."

Efrosin pushed off the ceiling and took the white, silver and gold embroidered shirt from Geoffry's hand. "If I must do something quite so dull, then you must entertain me with one of your fine tales first, Geoffry."

"Put on these clothes, sire, and I'll consent. What tale would you like to hear?"

"The one of my birth would be rather appropriate, don't you agree?"

"You know that one by heart, sire. I've no doubt you could tell it yourself quite well enough."

But Geoffry knew it wasn't true. Due to his cursed condition, Efrosin lacked emotional gravity and could never pitch his voice to the right note sof grief, having never felt anything close to the emotion himself. Geoffry had often noted that Efrosin, in his unwitting callousness, best liked tales that evoked great sadness in others. He clearly found their unhappiness fascinating and even amusing.

Pulling the shirt over his head, and taking the pants Geoffry offered, Efrosin took Geoffry up on his suggestion. "Once upon a time, a beautiful queen—my mother—gave birth to a handsome and blessed son." Efrosin frowned. "Hmm, maybe if I skip to the good part?" He cleared his throat and tried again, "Sadly, she was overcome with fever and never recovered from childbed. The country went into great mourning over the loss of her grace and kindness. The kingdom truly suffered when she died."

Efrosin dove down through the air to grab hold of Geoffry, and, with his help, put on the heavy, beribboned coat. "It's much better when you tell it," Efrosin said, a haze of dissatisfaction almost clouding his face before evaporating. "It's my birthday," he repeated, and this time there was a note of determination that set off a warning bell in Geoffry. "And, as I was saying, a prince should have what he desires on his birthday."

"Yes, your eighteenth," Geoffry said warily. "You're a man now, sire." Geoffry hoped, even though he knew it was useless, that by saying it aloud Efrosin might feel even a small portion of the burden associated with his upcoming responsibilities as Crown Prince. "And as for what you desire, well, you should take that up with your father."

The king had decided the time had come to make a strong alliance with one of several neighboring kingdoms, in order to strengthen his position for another war. To that end, Geoffry knew the king intended as his birthday gift to present his son with a selection of several princesses and princes—one of whom was to become Efrosin's spouse.

Being fair of face and having grown into the lean, strong body of a man, Efrosin should have been an ideal husband. Yet because of his cursed condition, his temperament and urges were still very much those of a boy. And, understanding Efrosin better than anyone, Geoffry knew the marriage would be doomed to misery and unhappiness for whomever was chosen.

"Truly, I would rather not go. It's so terribly boring."

Geoffry said, "It is important that your people see how much you honor the woman who died giving life to you."

Efrosin seemed to ponder this. "Well, I am very happy to be alive. It would be awfully dreary to be dead."

"Yes, quite. Now come, let me call Sir Carlisle and the others."

Geoffry was greatly relieved when Efrosin consented. He watched Efrosin closely during the ceremony, though, and noted that beneath Efrosin's expression of cheerful boredom, there was an unmistakable glimmer of excitement. A hard knot grew in Geoffry's stomach. The king, who could barely be bothered to look anything but bored himself, didn't seem to notice. But then, that was nothing new.

Back in Efrosin's room, the sun glowed bright in the early afternoon sky, and Geoffry's fingers shook as he undid the buttons of Efrosin's coat while Efrosin bobbed low to the ground where the knights held him fast with the ribbons.

As soon as the coat was off and the knights dismissed, Efrosin's smile grew so big that Geoffry felt his middle-aged heart might fail him. It was never a good sign when Efrosin looked quite that delighted.

"I am no longer a child, you realize," Efrosin began. "And you must follow my orders. You will tie a rope to my ankle—this one here, the right one, because the left is much too pretty for rope burn, you see— and fly me like a kite, high, high above the tallest tree. So, it must be quite a long rope."

Geoffry's mouth went dry. His eyes went to his time piece and he noted the king would be having his afternoon nap. The punishment for waking him was death or dismemberment, or sometimes both. He cleared his throat.

"Indeed, sire, and while I'm sure it would be a great adventure for you, it would be terrifying for me. What if I were to stumble, drop the rope, and you were to blow away? It isn't as though you're a balloon. We couldn't simply have a good marksman on hand to shoot you down again." He set about needlessly polishing the prince's shoes. How could they be scuffed when they never touched the ground? "And I'm equally sure that we do not have a rope of such a length." This, surely, would be enough to dissuade the young daredevil.

The prince may not have understood the gravity of the proposal, but Geoffry certainly did. He would never forget the violent lashing he'd received when Efrosin was but twelve and had managed to make a rope from lengths of sheets and float himself out the window while Geoffry slept. Though the boy claimed it was an unplanned, impulsive adventure, Geoffry had seen the glint of mischief and glee in the child's face as he'd read the bedtime story that night, and he'd suspected that Efrosin might take his closed eyes as an invitation to adventure.

But could Geoffry be blamed for falling asleep despite his best ef- forts? He was no longer such a young man, with his dark hair graying at the temples and aches in his bones when he did not rest. Besides, who impulsively tied together ten lengths of bed sheets? At some point, one must begin to recognize what one is doing and it then becomes a plan.

"As it happens," Efrosin said, pushing his foot against the ceiling to propel himself downward and drifting weightlessly toward the tall post at the foot end of the bed, "I have requisitioned such a one from the ropemaker. I summoned him last week while you were at market. Surprise! Now you have no excuse."

Geoffry wished to call his prince a scamp and beat his tail with a birch rod, as he would his own child for such foolishness, but he knew it would do no good. He remembered well a day during Efrosin's tenth year when the king decided to forcibly instill some gravity in his free-floating son, declaring that boy would indeed be sobered by the time he was done.

The screams of pained laughter Efrosin had let out as his father had beat him still haunted Geoffry's worst nightmares. At times, sweating from dreams of it, he wished he had interceded—his own beating be damned—for he had known it would change nothing.

And it had not. The king had left Efrosin's chambers with a rare look of humiliated defeat, abandoning Efrosin naked on his stomach, with his back, buttocks and thighs striped from the switch, and delirious, broken laughter drifting from his smiling mouth.

Geoffry's own eyes had filled with tears when Efrosin had giggled, "That rather hurt a lot, Geoffry. I do so wish that I could cry. Tell me, would that make it feel better?"

"No," Geoffry had said. "It would not." Though, he'd thought, perhaps it would.

"Oh, well then, if only I could cry then at least Father would not be so cross." Then he'd laughed some more. "Usually, he is so funny when he is cross."

But something told Geoffry that, despite Efrosin's laughter, he did not find his father so very funny at that moment. It had been a difficult night for Geoffry, applying salve to his princeling's wounds and crying tears in Efrosin's stead. The king had never tried such a thing again, and now seemed resigned to his son's flighty ways.

"You requisitioned a rope so that I may fly you as a kite," Geoffry repeated slowly.

"Indeed. And it shall be jolly and grand. Just think, Geoffry, I'll see the top of the castle. I'll see where the river flows. Perhaps I'll even see—"

"You saw the top of the castle the time you broke free of your handler and floated up to the top of the highest turret. And poor Michaelson nearly fell and died trying to fetch you down."

Efrosin's lips curved up into a wide smile. "Oh yes, that was a brilliant day. But that was not quite the same. That was a mistake, you see, and I was a bit frightened, which made it an ever so sharp joy to float that high. This will be more sedate, and you are always imploring me to be sedate."

"Sire…"

"Come," Efrosin called, gripping the poster of the bed firmly and shoving himself toward the door with the effortless grace of a balloon drifting through the air. "Let us begin."

Geoffry's heart sank. There was nothing to be done for it. He hoped it didn't hurt too badly when he was hanged. And that would be a just punishment if he got caught holding onto the end of Efrosin's rope while the boy floated in the heavens. If Efrosin should float away…well, there was no telling what would happen to Geoffry, or his wife and five children.

Geoffry crossed himself and followed Efrosin as he slowly bounced through the hallway, his feet always at least three feet above the ground.

EFROSIN HAD NEVER been so high before. Well, not on purpose. Well, not lately. And then he was even higher. He gazed down at dear Geoffry, who looked so tiny on the ground, both hands clenched around the end of the rope as though it took effort to keep Efrosin from floating away, when he was as light as air itself.

He could see the preparations for his birthday feast being made on the other side of the line of trees separating the field from the castle garden. He laughed as he imagined the great fright the servants would have if they would but look up and see him there in the sky like an angel of the ether.

"I should have Geoffry construct wings," he declared, his eyes shining at the thought.

He felt a stab of high-spirited annoyance that he had not thought of it before. "It would have been the most divine entrance to my party."

If he'd had it in him to mourn that this idea had come to him much too late, he'd have mourned. As it was, he turned to count the clouds, and called down to Geoffry the many wonders of their beauty. Then he spent a few minutes casting about for a sound other than the whistling of wind in his ears, which was so much sharper than the burble and rush of water.

"Lo, but it is lonely up here," he said at last, his eyes following the green of the fields cutting a swath down to the path taken by the blue river.

Geoffry had argued admirably that Efrosin celebrate his birthday with another swim instead of a flight, and Efrosin had been tempted. The river, much more than the air, was his best friend. It alone held him in a snug and secure embrace, with just the right amount of gravity to prevent him from floating away.

He'd spent much of his life in the water, bobbing in his own world, splashing and laughing, and sunning for endless summer days. The river calmed him, and was the only place he could be persuaded to listen long enough to have learned his letters and numbers. Efrosin remembered his tutor in a boat, umbrella held over his bald head, teaching Efrosin to conjugate verbs as he swam in circles or floated dreamily on his back, his ears below the water, and the professor's rumbling words lost in the tumble of the current.

In comparison, the air was an ocean of risk, at once compelling and terrifying. It was godless, empty, full of distance and height, and Efrosin could vanish into it entirely, never to be seen again.

He sometimes dreamed he'd floated as high as the constellations and the endless, cold horror of it would startle him, laughing, from his sleep. "Oh what a wondrous thing," he'd exclaim, his blood coursing in his veins. "What a terrible thrill."

And yet he was drawn to it like a moth to a flame.

He'd never told anyone—not even Geoffry—that it frightened him so, and that perhaps it wouldn't be quite so very bad to have his gravity returned to him. He'd been told he was born with it, but couldn't remember ever possessing an ounce of substance.

As fate would have it, Efrosin had no sooner decided that he'd had enough of the thin air for the day and that a swim would, indeed, be a better way to pass the time until his birthday celebration, than a black-winged bird flew past his face. It reared around and beat its wings like cupped hands scooping the air to pause mid-flight before him, and screeched.

The bird seemed to smile, something eerie and white, as red flashed in its eyes. Then it dove for the rope tied securely around Efrosin's ankle, landed on it like a sideways clothes line, and tore into the rugged material with a razor-sharp beak.

"Stop! Whyever are you doing that?" Efrosin asked, a giddy burst of fear shaking him, and he started to laugh hysterically. "I shall float away if you break the rope."

Panicked, he looked down toward Geoffry, who had noticed the bird's quick work at severing the prince from his tenuous link to the earth. Efrosin descended through the air rapidly in quick, desperate jerks as Geoffry attempted to reel him in before the damage was done.

"Shoo!" Geoffry screamed. "Sire, kick him away."

Efrosin tried, he truly did, but could not move downward through the air that wished to suck him up into its deadly embrace. Then in one dizzy moment he felt it—the moment the rope broke, and he flew free.

The wind made off with him, rushing him away from the field where Geoffry stood with the long rope coming down on his head, yelling helplessly for Efrosin. Efrosin was pierced with agonizing exhilaration.

His destiny was at hand. He could feel it. The sky that had been his nightmare and fascination since youth would bear him away to his end.

The clouds whispered across his face, and he laughed in mad, spasmodic hiccups until it became quite hard to breathe. It was all so very funny. The Light Prince met his end as an escaped human kite, the people would say. Efrosin could not stop his wild laughter.

Dmitri walked the familiar path through the woods to check the traps again. It had been a full week since he'd caught anything, though he wasn't concerned. Fishing had been plentiful, and he looked forward to harvesting fresh berries and vegetables from his garden later in the month. Still, he did need meat to cure and put aside for winter.

There was only himself to provide for, but he never knew when there might be another drought, as there had been the year Queen Inna died. He had no memory of it himself, having been just a toddler at the time, but his father had told him often of the hunger that gripped the people and animals, and of the scarcity that had ended many lives. It was one of the more exciting stories in Dmitri's father's repertoire, and he'd asked to hear the tale often as a boy.

There were many important lessons in the stories Dmitri's father told, of course, but one of the most important had been to think well in advance on matters of survival. So Dmitri did just that, always putting away more than enough meat to weather any famine or provide for an unexpected visitor. Not that a visitor happened by very often. Yet when one did, Dmitri wanted to make a good impression, in case they could be prevailed upon to stay longer, or, at the very least, return for a visit.

As he rounded the bend that would take him to the boundary, a limit he could sense from several yards in advance, he happened to look up. As he did, his mouth fell open and he dropped his sack.

There, tangled in the tree limbs above him, was an angel. It had to be an angel because his face was inhumanly beautiful with rosy cheeks and lips, and his hair was such a color that it was surely made of gold itself. His white garments were covered with fine silver detail that glittered in the sunlight. He hung there as though weightless, defying the earth's pull, actually tugging the branches up, instead of causing them to droop with the burden of holding him.

Dmitri fell to his knees, and as he stared, the angel's eyes opened, taking him in. A tremulous laugh reached him, and Dmitri blinked in confusion.

"Blessed be the west wind," the angel called out. "Or I should have surely been lost forever. And that would have been entirely unfortunate, because it's my birthday, you see, and no one should be lost forever on their birthday."

Dmitri shook his head, trying to clear the strange vision. Had he fallen asleep in the cabin and dreamed of checking the traps? Was he dreaming still? What an odd thing for an angel to say. Dmitri had never given thought to whether or not angels had birthdays. He supposed they very well might.

"So—you will fetch me down, of course."

"But how will you go back up?" Dmitri asked, noticing now the angel's distinct lack of wings. Had he been injured and lost them in the fall? Or had they been removed? Was he a bad sort? Tossed from heaven like Lucifer? Would God expel an angel on his birthday? If so, he must have done something especially wicked.

"Go back up." The angel chuckled. "Well, that would be easy enough if I wanted to go up, but I assure you that I've had quite enough of up to last forever." The angel shook with mirth again. "Or until tomorrow. Or whenever I'm overcome with the lust for it once more. It's quite delightful, except that it's terrifying. Which is, of course, how so many of the best things are."

Was that any way to speak of heaven? Dmitri tilted his head; he took in the angel's bare feet and the short rope tied to one ankle. "Are you an angel?" he said, deciding it was best to get that part out of the way at once.

"No. I'm a prince. Surely you've heard of me? The Light Prince. Efrosin? Son of Leo, King of Goldenthal? We're truly quite famous in these parts, given that it's our kingdom." The peals of laughter should have been insulting, but seemed without malice to Dmitri's ears.

Of course he'd heard of the Light Prince. But he'd thought the tales told by the old crones and beggars passing through were exaggerated, as most tales are. Yet the man hung there before Dmitri in a tree, as though he were a kite, still being tugged by the breeze.

"Truly, it is life or death," the Light Prince said. "I know it must not seem very serious given my disposition and inability to stop laughing—because it is incredibly funny—but I assure you that I cannot help that, and should you leave me here much longer, the wind will have its way and I'll be cast upon the mercy of the heavens again."

Dmitri took in his blinding smile and tried to reconcile the chipper tone of voice with the professed circumstances. Hadn't the travelers who'd told him stories of the Light Prince said that the malady extended to his manner and personality, resulting in a perpetual lack of depth to any grave feeling?

"If it's a hope for reward money that has you dallying about, let me assure—"

"No! Of course not. Certainly I'll help you, my good prince, but I must admit I've never fished a weightless man from a tree before. How do I start, sire?"

"Start by calling me Efrosin, or I will laugh myself into a stupor with your 'good prince' here and 'sire' there, and general attitude of obeisance. I am not my father, and it will only make me piss myself with giggles to have you bend and jump at my every breath. So I beg of you to take pity, and not make me laugh any harder than I already am."

"Yes, my…Efrosin."

"Quite right. Now, your Efrosin believes that Geoffry usually fetches a rope—truly, he always has one handy since I must be tied down so very often. Then he climbs the tree, ties the rope to my wrist or ankle before also tying it to his own, lest he lose his grip on me. The rest I'll tell you when we are face-to-face."

He sounded coy and Dmitri wondered at that but only long enough for Efrosin to burst into gales of laughter. "You should have seen your expression," he cried. "So shocked! So very funny!" And as his body shook, the branches seemed to loosen their grip on Efrosin's body. There was no time to waste.

Dmitri grabbed his sack, ripped the cord from the drawstring closure and started up the tree. He scaled it as quickly as possible, glad the boundary only applied to the land and that the sky had no power to confine him. As he reached the limbs beneath the prince, he grabbed hold of Efrosin's ankle, the one with a length of rope still dangling from it, and tied the rope to his own ankle.

When it was fastened, he quickly bound Efrosin's wrist to his own with the cord and worked to unhook the prince's silky clothes from the twigs and small branches. Then he grabbed Efrosin's outstretched hand, jerked, and was shocked when the man flew without any resistance toward him, weighing less than a puff of cotton.

As their bodies collided, Dmitri gripped Efrosin around the waist, and he stared into Efrosin's handsome face. Endless laughter filled Efrosin's blue eyes, and his lush mouth was shiny with an abused look about his open lips, as though he'd been biting them in an unsuccessful attempt to stop his mirth. Dmitri had never seen a human being so beautiful.

Dmitri didn't understand it, but he felt a heretofore unfamiliar, and yet compelling surge of need pulse through him, and before he could stop himself, he leaned forward to kiss those lips. The answering gasp, followed by more laughter that seemed to fill his own mouth and tickle against his palate, did not discourage him at all.

Efrosin's lips were soft and his tongue was slick and he didn't pull away from Dmitri's clumsy attempt, but rather deepened the kiss in a way that made Dmitri's toes curl and blood rush to his cock. For a confused moment he thought he was kissing an angel before he remembered that he was only kissing a prince. A free-floating, beautiful, powerful, laughing prince. Perhaps "only" was not quite the proper word.

"Lovely," Efrosin exclaimed, pulling away and licking his lips. "I hope you intend to ravish me, because I have always imagined it would be quite fun to be ravished. No one's ever tried it with me, alas." Efrosin frowned a little and licked his mouth. "You taste like dirt. It's delicious, though I've never enjoyed the taste of dirt before. How odd."

"You taste like clouds," Dmitri said, hoping it was a compliment.

"I ate quite a few during my journey to this tree," Efrosin said. "I…feel a bit strange. Quick. Kiss me again."

Dmitri, reminded of Efrosin's perilous flight, came to his senses, and while he was not willing to say that he would not kiss the prince again, he did think there were just a few things that should be accomplished first. "We must get you down."

Efrosin frowned, seeming much less intent on getting back to the earth now that he had company in the tree. "But you will kiss me again?"

"Once we're safe." Dmitri looked down to choose which limbs they should try, and immediately wished he hadn't. His head swirled with the distance between his body and the earth below. He'd never before climbed so high.

"Safe is such a thrilling state of being. I can't remember the last time I felt safe. Grip my hands," Efrosin said. "Don't let go."

Dmitri took Efrosin's smooth hands into his own, and Efrosin began to shake with amusement again. "Your calluses tickle. Now hold tight. It will be fun."

"What will be?" Dmitri asked.

"Jump."

"What?"

"We are tied hand and foot, and you have hold of my hands. All will be well. Trust me."

It was surprisingly hard to trust laughing royalty. "We'll die. It's too far."

"Too far? What a silly notion."

DMITRI'S LAST THOUGHT when Efrosin kicked his feet out from under him with a strong swipe was, *At least I got to kiss him.* They tumbled into the air, crashing into branches below until Efrosin pushed off against the tree trunk, thrusting them both clear. It was only then Dmitri realized how slowly the ground rose up to meet them.

"Your weight to bring us down," Efrosin sang in his ear. "My levity to keep us from being quite smashed." There was more laughter, and then a curl of words in his ear, which, coupled with the rush of adrenaline coursing through his veins, made Dmitri's cock stiffen against the hard bone of Efrosin's hip. "And you will ravish me, won't you? Once we're on the ground. You promised. You're so handsome, and your hands are so big. I'm aquiver at the thought of you on me, in me, touching me—"

"Oh my God," Dmitri choked. "Do you speak to everyone who gets you down from trees this way?"

Efrosin's face twisted in horror. "Heavens no! Geoffry is nearly fifty years old. And the knights have never kissed me." The merriment was back, though, as Dmitri's feet alighted on the earth, and Efrosin's floated an inch above it. "But I would if the knights ever tried. Especially Sir Carlisle with that beard." Efrosin eyed him. "You are quite clean-shaven; have you ever thought of growing a beard?"

"I can't say I have."

"Beards are nice. Scratchy along the skin. I've noticed this quite often when Sir Carlisle has carried me, of course." Efrosin sighed dreamily, causing a strange, unpleasant feeling to twist in Dmitri's stomach.

So he kissed Efrosin again.

"Oh forget about beards," Efrosin breathed against Dmitri's lips. "The idiot never kissed me. Unlike very handsome, very," here Efrosin moved his hips against the length of Dmitri's cock, "hard you. This is rather lovely. Such a grand adventure. What a good birthday this is turning out to be."

Chapter Two

"YOU COULD ROPE me to that tree," Efrosin argued, bobbing along just above the woodland path beside the dark-haired, dark-eyed man. The man who had saved him from certain death and—better yet—had kissed him. "I wouldn't complain. It would be amusing, I'm sure, especially if you'll kiss me more and harder, and then do things to make the great pleasure descend."

The man gritted his teeth. "I said no." Still bound ankle to ankle, and wrist to wrist, so that Efrosin remained upright and floated along beside him not too far off the ground, the stranger pulled Efrosin with him down the path. Gnarled, ancient trees rose above them, twisted branches and thick leaves arching overhead and, in some places, blotting out the sky altogether.

"Whyever not?"

"I'm not about to tie you to a tree and pleasure you. We've known each other minutes. Is this how it's usually done in the royal court?"

"Perhaps? It seems quite likely."

"Well, don't you prefer it to be a little more...I don't know...romantic?"

Efrosin had never felt anything like this before. His body seemed to burn for the man's touch. Even his prick had woken from its slumber, and Efrosin chuckled over how odd it felt, heavy and aching in his trousers. What did his tutor tell him it was called? Ah yes. Lust. It was a rather divine and entertaining sensation, now that he knew it. He thought of how silly and desperate men behaved when consumed by it, and he hoped to be just as silly and desperate, indeed.

He licked his mouth to taste the man's spit still on his lips and stood up as straight as he could considering he was floating. "I am not a woman and nor are you. I do not need to be treated with kid gloves. Besides, what on earth could be more romantic than being taken in a hard and desperate manner by my rescuing prince?"

"I'm not a prince." His eyes were on Efrosin's mouth, and he stumbled a little over a tree root in his distraction. Efrosin licked his lips again with a slow swipe of his tongue. The man sighed. "Do stop that."

Efrosin knew that the man wanted to get back to the relative safety of his home, where there would be no risk of Efrosin floating into the sky. But Efrosin could tell that resolve was weakening. "You can have me in your house too," Efrosin said. "In fact, I insist upon it."

His rescuer appeared flustered. "Would you not like to get back to your castle?"

"But why? I'm having a great deal of fun imagining what pleasures you're going to give me."

The man frowned, a wonderful little line forming between his eyes, and Efrosin marveled at his urge to lick it. He'd never understood the term "wanton" until now. This delirium was lovely.

"This is all very confusing. I left my house an hour ago to check my traps, and now I'm tied to a floating prince who is trying to get me to bugger him, and doesn't even know my name."

"Sir, must we exchange names? It seems too amusing to think that I might never know what you are called. Don't tell me."

"Dmitri," he said, frowning. "My name is Dmitri, and the idea of you not knowing does not amuse me at all."

Efrosin's mouth formed the name silently, and then he said it aloud. "Dmitri." The strangest thing happened—his toe dragged on the ground.

He tried it again. "Dmitri." And again his toe brushed over roots and rocks as he was pulled along, tied as he was to Dmitri's wrist and ankle. He found he didn't want to laugh about it. That alone frightened him more than his brush with the earth. But then it passed, and he felt as free of weight as ever.

"Yes, that's my name. You say it like you've never heard it before. Is there no one else named Dmitri in all your kingdom?"

"Oh yes, quite a few. There's a stable hand, and a footman and a little snotty-nosed chimney sweep who coughs all the time. I rather dislike them all, actually. They always seem…wrong."

Dmitri listened to these revelations with a flat expression.

"Do you think it comes with the name?" Efrosin asked. "Are you a bit wrong?"

His lips curved into a small, rueful smile. "I should say so."

Efrosin said, "I don't know. You seem quite entirely right to me."

Dmitri ignored his appraisal. "Smoke signals would be an option were the woods not so dangerously dry this spring. But a single spark could set the forest alight. No one comes by this way again until late summer. Even the river flows in the wrong direction, but perhaps we could send a note downstream anyway."

"Oh do end with all this worry. They will find me by and by. The wind could not have blown me too very far. What is the distance to Castle Goldenthal? Two leagues? Five?" How delightful the thought was of being such a long way from home.

"More like ten, sire, or so I hear. I'm afraid I don't know firsthand."

"Thrilling! My birthday party starts at seven. It seems that I will miss it, which is a shame. There were to be elephants and singers, and a brilliant cake made to look like a river. It was to be quite long and very blue."

Dmitri stared at him slack-jawed.

"But never mind. You can make it up to me with kisses." Efrosin leaned forward and took one. Dmitri's mouth was better than cake or elephants or singers. It was so good Efrosin didn't know how to categorize it or contain it. So, of course, he laughed, and Dmitri jerked away.

"But your people will be worried, surely. You wouldn't want them to think you're dead."

Efrosin waved his hand, dismissing that dull concern. "They are all quite funny when they're scared and cross, and they will search for me until they find me. Truly, there are likely knights looking for me even now. My dear Geoffry will probably be hanged if I am not found before nightfall, and judging by the sun, that is not so very long hence. Alas. He was a good servant. But let us think, ten leagues on horseback...they could be here any moment, could they not? You must hurry. If you're to ravish me, there is no time to lose."

Dmitri stared at him with an unfathomable emotion in his deep brown eyes, which were fringed with lashes so thick they would tickle wonderfully, Efrosin was quite sure, if applied to his neck, or wrist, or nether region.

"Geoffry—the man who pulls you from trees—shall be hanged?"

"Indeed he will, for the sin of losing me."

"And 'alas' is all you can say? You do not care for him at all?"

"Did I sound too blithe?" He concentrated on a somber expression. "It is a pity and if I could regret it, I most certainly would, but I can't. It's how I am." Efrosin tried hard not to sound so cheerful, but it was an impossible task. Perhaps he should apologize again? Sometimes that did the trick. "You have lovely eyes," he said instead. "And a beautiful mouth. Have you ever sucked a man's prick?"

Dmitri's sigh was unmistakably wistful before he seemed to remember himself. He cleared his throat. "No."

"Really? Am I the first to ask? In that case, will you please be so kind as to suck mine?"

"Do you think of nothing else?" Dmitri asked, sounding frustrated, which was charming indeed.

"Oh quite. I truly never think of this at all. But you see, it is only now, with you, that I have ever felt quite exactly like this before. You are so very handsome."

"Am I?" He seemed surprised at this information, which made Efrosin's cock throb in delight.

"You are. Now, will you make good the promise of your lips on mine? That tree over there looks sturdy, and if you have more rope in your bag, then—"

"I have no more rope. Are all princes as brazen as you?"

"I haven't the faintest clue." Being jerked through the air was giving Efrosin rope burn, and if he was going to have rope burn, then he'd prefer it was from struggling to take Dmitri's dick whilst strapped to a tree, or perhaps a rock to hold him down. So he said as much.

"Listen, I am not going to screw your royal highness on the forest floor, nor bent over a boulder, nor tied to a tree. What you need is to get back to the castle."

Here in the mossy dim of the forest, with wood and moist earth filling his senses, Efrosin had never felt so far from home. But instead of fear, he felt a strange, warm comfort. "I think I'd quite like to stay here. For the time being, at least."

"Stay? Here?" Dmitri sputtered. "This is madness."

"It's my birthday after all. I've decided what I want. How much farther until we get to where you'll consent to kiss me again?"

Dmitri sighed as though he really wasn't eager to kiss him now, and that rather stung. "There. Just ahead."

Efrosin finally pulled his eyes from Dmitri's face and saw before them a tiny log cabin. It could not be more than one room. Efrosin had never been inside a structure so small in his life. Just contemplating it set off peals of laughter.

Dmitri clenched his jaw. "Didn't your mother teach you manners?"

"I didn't have a mother."

Dmitri looked a bit shame-faced. "Of course. I'd forgotten the tales of your birth. I was...unkind. Forgive me."

Efrosin cast a glance from under his eyelashes. "Get me inside your hovel and do what you will with me, and I'll forgive you any unkindness."

Efrosin's dick had been hard since their first kiss, and as that was a sensation wholly unfamiliar to him—and thus utterly delightful—he was eager for his life-long chastity to come to an end. He summoned his straightest face, though he could feel it was softened with mirth, and said, "As your prince, I command you, take me into your home and defile me."

Despite his laughter, he thought it must have done the trick, because Dmitri grabbed hold of his waist and quickly led him to the cabin.

As DMITRI THRUST open the door to his home, he wondered again if this was some bizarre dream he'd fallen into. The lurid turn it had taken was not unusual, for he was but twenty and quite lonely. He often dreamed of beautiful men coming to his cabin for the sole purpose of bending over for him.

Perhaps if he did as Prince Efrosin asked, the dream would end and he'd wake the same way he always did—physically sated but utterly alone. He wavered between pinching himself awake, and tossing Efrosin on the bed to fuck him silly the way he'd been begging for the whole walk home.

Did Dmitri really want to risk that he might never dream this partic-ular dream again? Efrosin was beautiful, and pulling at him impatiently where they were attached ankle-to-ankle and wrist-to-wrist. The prince wanted it—wanted him. Dmitri's cock throbbed in answer. But if it wasn't a dream, what of the king's search party? How would it look to be found buggering the prince? Would they execute him on the spot for such an offense?

Efrosin clapped his hands, his eyes glowing with amusement. "This is smaller than my old dollhouse."

Dmitri shut the door behind them and took in the room with its wood stove and the square table his father had built to the right. A rocking chair sat next to the only window on the left. In the middle, a trap door led down to the root cellar where he stored his cured meats and vegetables. With a critical eye, he gazed at the far wall and the shelf full of his most treasured items—books—and the rather threadbare mattress atop the wooden bed with tall, smooth, sanded posts, in which his mother had conceived Dmitri.

Was it truly so small? To Dmitri it was the world. Who could have need for more? "Well, it's only me."

"You're alone here?" Efrosin seemed enlivened by such a concept. "How incredibly novel."

"Rather old hat, actually."

Dmitri started every day alone, went to bed every night alone, and spent all but fourteen or fifteen hours a year completely on his own. To say that he was lonely did not fully capture the immensity of his situation. It suddenly hit him that if this was not a dream—and he was rather convinced that it was not—then he only had a few hours of Efrosin's company. Who knew when someone might visit again? Much less someone like Efrosin. He should make the most of it.

"I'm generally not allowed to be alone," Efrosin said, tugging at the links between them, urging Dmitri deeper into the room.

"Why?"

"I might float away, of course. All it takes is someone leaving a window open, and an inopportune waft of air from, say, a lady passing by the door waving a fan, and *voila*, I'm off on an adventure that could end in death."

Dmitri believed that Efrosin sounded much too cheerful about that, but then he sounded cheerful about everything.

"Have you ever imagined what it might be like to see the stars in their own dark habitat?" Efrosin said. "I suspect it is my destiny to do so. For I could float that high, I'm quite sure. The problem is suffocating before I get there. The air gets so very thin." Efrosin looked around again, his babbling ceasing for a moment. "The bed will do, I suppose. Do be romantic: tie me to the posts and cut off my clothes."

Dmitri was sorely tempted as he imagined what the prince's naked body might look like. "Won't you need them for the trip home?"

"They can wrap me in blankets until they reach the river, at which point I'll happily swim the rest of the way."

"Ten leagues is much too far to swim."

"Says who? Go on now, tie me up and cut my clothes off. I feel as though I'll burst if I'm forced to wait a moment longer."

Frowning, Dmitri reached for the knife he had tucked in his boot and quickly cut the rope that had lashed them ankle-to-ankle. He watched in awe as Efrosin giggled and floated feet-first toward the low ceiling, still attached at Dmitri's wrist.

Dmitri didn't know if he should try to pull him back down again or not, but Efrosin jerked on their attached arms and said, "Cut that one too then. Or the blood will all go to my head, and that gives me such a terribly funny headache."

Dmitri cut him free and stared as Efrosin spun round, twirling until his feet touched the ceiling, and then pushed off again, sliding through the air like an eel in water. He reached out with his hands to run his fingers over the walls and the shelf of books before rising back to the ceiling again, where he repeated the push-off and continued his exploration.

Efrosin gripped the edge of the book shelf to read the titles. "Science, science, history, farming, history. Yawn, yawn, yawn, each yawnier than the last. Where are the novels? Where are the torrid stories of illicit coupling? Your mind must be sorely lacking in key areas. No wonder you didn't understand the romance of our situation in the woods." Efrosin's laughter took the sting from his words, and he pushed off the shelf with enough force to catapult through the air until he grabbed the post at the foot of the bed. He held on with one hand, and with the other began to remove his clothes. "Such a silly Dmitri."

Efrosin's body sank about a foot suddenly, and his brow furrowed, but then he was back to floating near the ceiling as his hand gripped the post. He kicked off again, and he hooked a leg around the post, so that it appeared as though he was standing upright in mid-air on one pointed toe.

"Shall we then?" he asked.

Chapter Three

D MITRI'S MOUTH WENT dry as he watched Efrosin's long, lovely fingers open the buttons of his shirt, revealing creamy skin and small, budded nipples. Dmitri could not tear his eyes away from the light golden hair on Efrosin's chest that was followed by a thicker patch leading from his navel down to where his hand was now working to open the drawstring of his white and silver-edged pants.

Dmitri licked his lips at the sight of the wet spot staining the silk. *Are you really going to bugger him?* Incredulity and common sense threatened to overpower his lust. *It's a dream. A strange but powerful dream. Whyever not? When you wake, you'll be quite sorry if you don't.*

But he was not convinced. There was nothing aside from the unlikeliness of it all that spoke to it being a dream.

"Dmitri," Efrosin said, and he sank down the bed post a bit. "I order you under penalty of death to rid me of my cursed virginity." His laughter and inability to say it with a straight face didn't impress anything upon Dmitri other than Prince Efrosin was not afraid to be debauched.

It's what he wants. And you're his subject—of course you'll obey.

But being Efrosin's subject was less of a consideration to Dmitri than the knowledge that he might never get a chance to screw someone again, much less someone as beautiful as Efrosin. And for some unknown reason, Efrosin seemed to feel the same way, given how desperate he was to be plowed immediately and in any way possible, and that need pulled at Dmitri, winding through him like siren song, impossible to ignore.

Dumbstruck, Dmitri watched as Efrosin kicked his pants free, and his body—too masculine to be called delicate, but still supple and slender—was exposed in its considerable beauty. Dmitri's blood thundered at the vision of Efrosin's cock, gorgeous and nothing like Dmitri's own. It was flushed and long, with a rosy, thick head and a slimmer girth. His thighs were sprinkled with that same golden hair from his chest, and his arms and legs were muscular but lean.

"Don't you—do you not think we should—" Dmitri didn't get any more words out, his cock aching and pushing against his breeches painfully. "Oh God forgive me," he muttered, tearing his shirt over his head and casting it aside, his eyes greedily raking over Efrosin's form, taking in every inch of him that was on offer. He ripped open his pants, kicked them off and lunged at Efrosin.

"Forget God," Efrosin said, eyes alight with excitement, and deep laughter rumbling up from his chest. "What has He got to do with anything?"

Dmitri had no thought left in his mind to be appalled at the blasphemy as he grabbed hold of Efrosin's floating ankle and jerked him effortlessly down. He gasped, finding Efrosin quite firm and solid in his arms. His skin was softer than he'd thought possible, but his muscles and bones stronger than expected. Efrosin's laughter was intoxicating against Dmitri's mouth, bubbling into his throat and filling him with a giddy need that felt too good to bear.

"Brilliant," Efrosin cried, as Dmitri threw Efrosin to the bed and captured him there beneath his own body.

Bloody brilliant indeed. He attached his mouth to Efrosin's neck, biting gently, and smoothed his palms over every bit of skin he could. Now, if only he wouldn't lose his mind and shoot his seed too soon. His skin tingled and his prick throbbed with his heartbeat as desperation drove him onward, overcome with a need to fulfill Efrosin's urgent lust, dimly aware beneath his own screaming desire that he would only be truly content again upon Efrosin's satisfaction.

EFROSIN HAD NEVER felt such a delicious sense of weight. Even when he'd been held down forcibly in the past, it had not been like this. Of course it hadn't. He'd never been naked, hard and rutting together with another man in desperate, grasping need. Dmitri was bigger than he was. Taller, and could cover him with his entire body, which made Efrosin feel that most delightful thing of all—safe.

As lust-soaked moans filled the tiny room, Dmitri pinned him, their arms and legs tangled, mouths open and tasting everything in reach. Efrosin quickly lost track of whether his mouth was on Dmitri's arm, neck, cheek, ear or chest, only knowing that Dmitri tasted of earth and skin. It was good—so very good—that Efrosin wasn't even laughing. But before he could fully realize that oddity, he was again enraptured by the intense sensation of flesh sliding on flesh, cock against cock.

Efrosin had never had a moment of modesty in his life, but rocking beneath Dmitri, he suddenly felt shy and hid his face in the crook of Dmitri's neck. He tingled, aware of where his body rubbed against Dmitri's, and he swallowed against the strange thickness in his throat that felt like trapped laughter. Why did it not come out? Usually, no sooner did it bubble up in him than it spilled free.

Dmitri was also clearly overwhelmed, moaning most delightfully as his hands ran everywhere over Efrosin's body, his mouth following, wet and hot, kissing Efrosin's neck and sucking his collar bone before biting down against Efrosin's pink, tight nipple. Dmitri's mouth came back to fit against Efrosin's own, his tongue licking lightly at his lips, until Efrosin grabbed him by the nape of his neck, and forced him into a harder, deeper kiss.

Dmitri groaned and gasped, clasping Efrosin tighter, his fingers digging into Efrosin's buttocks, pulling their hips flush. Efrosin threw his legs around Dmitri's heaving back, hooking his ankles and holding on as best he could as they writhed together.

His tutor had educated him on the theory, but the reality was beyond Efrosin's imagining. There was no space between them at all, and Efrosin's world narrowed down to their desperate grappling, the scent of their lust permeating the air between them as they grunted and whimpered. Efrosin's pulse beat in his ears, and he quivered as he felt their cocks throb against each other, foreshadowing oncoming climaxes that promised to be so much that Efrosin quaked in fear and longing for it.

His balls drew up with a shocking wrench in his gut, and he held on tight, tangling his fingers into Dmitri's dark hair, kissing him again, running the tip of his tongue along the roof of Dmitri's mouth. And then, faster than he wanted, it was over.

Efrosin arched, his toes flexed, and as his cock rubbed alongside Dmitri's, slick with their sweat and over-eager seed, he felt something hard and heavy drag up through him, as if from an internal depth he never knew existed. It settled in his gut, burning and weighing there, before he screamed.

Afraid and ecstatic, he clawed at Dmitri's back and shoulders as he pulsed, his cock spurting and his eyes locked in shock on Dmitri's own. It was like nothing he'd ever felt before, and he shook, wondering if his heart would stop from immense wonder.

Dmitri kissed him again, a sharp moan in his throat, more like a desperate plea, before thrusting his prick against Efrosin's stomach, now sloppy with Efrosin's spendings. He jerked, shaking on top of Efrosin as bursts of wet heat shot over Efrosin's stomach and chest.

"Oh," Efrosin cried, still shivering and watching in delight as Dmitri's face contorted in pleasure. "Was that…is that…?" Efrosin was breathless. He felt addled, confused and utterly deconstructed.

Dmitri pulled back to look at the mess between their bodies and, with a groan, unloaded a last, surprising shot of seed onto Efrosin's stomach. Dmitri's pupils were blown wide and he stared open-mouthed and panting at Efrosin.

"That was ravishing then? No wonder it is so highly recommended by romance novels and plays."

Dmitri nodded, wordless and still shuddering.

Efrosin's mouth seemed to have found words, even if his mind was yet lost in orbit. He shifted beneath Dmitri, a subtle shivery tingle filling him up again like a tide or eddy, and then pulling away, leaving him breathless and limp. "It was frightening, but really quite wonderful. Is the end always like that? I was afraid I'd come apart. I almost could not bear it."

Dmitri's mouth twisted into a smile, and he laughed softly, ducking his head to lick and kiss at Efrosin's sweaty neck. He pushed Efrosin's hands, which floated in the air beside them, down to the mattress. "Did you not know?" he asked, clearly amused, his dark eyes sparkling.

"I...no. I've seen it before and watched other men crumble and cry out under its power, but..." Efrosin trailed off, blood rushing down to his still-sensitive prick, stiffening it again, at the memory of what he'd just felt, what they'd done.

"Watched?" Dmitri asked. "Is it not a private thing elsewhere in the kingdom? My parents gave the idea that taking one's pleasure in another's body, or even one's own, wasn't something done in front of spectators."

Efrosin pulled one hand free of Dmitri's restraining grasp and flapped it in the air, waving the words away. "No, it's private. Though I have heard rumors of brothels where...but no, it is private." Here Efrosin felt a shocking thing—heat that rose over his chest, up into his cheeks, and burned his ears. Was this shame? He'd never felt anything quite like it before. "However, men and women do not often check their rafters whilst seeking release."

Dmitri's brows lowered and he shifted his body, the sticky mess between them smearing. "Do you not know that's wrong?" His voice seemed to hold no censure, however.

"I was curious. But my prick never did those things." Efrosin re-membered how funny it had seemed, the urgent rutting, the cries and wails, the silly faces as the end drew near, and the mess. He'd been unable to refrain from busting out in chortles on more than one occasion and he'd had to dodge flying slippers and boots as he bobbed down the hallways of the castle, ringing with laughter at what he'd seen.

Now, feeling Dmitri's weight holding him down, and still vibrating with the resounding pleasure they'd taken together, it did not seem so funny. Efrosin did not know what to make of that. He felt almost afraid, but when he looked up into Dmitri's face, seeing no anger or malice there, and felt Dmitri's cock lengthening between their bodies again, he felt in his bones that he was safe.

"You've never…?" Here Dmitri flung his fist back and forth in a crude gesture to illustrate self-pleasure.

Efrosin shook his head. He'd always been vaguely curious as to why his cock didn't seem to function as others' did, and so Efrosin had asked Geoffry about it once. The old dear, sputtering and looking red in the face, had answered, "It's a rather grave undertaking at heart, sire. A primal urge. Quite deep. Perhaps your affliction doesn't allow you to reach down to such base impulses."

All it had taken was one kiss from Dmitri, Efrosin realized, and his dormant, earthly desires had risen in him fast and ruthlessly hard. He'd been quite…what was the word he'd heard the knights use? He'd been quite the trollop.

Dmitri stroked a finger over Efrosin's lips. "That was the first time you've ever spent?"

"It was."

"You looked so beautiful."

"As did you. Have you felt it before?"

Dmitri laughed, a warm chuckle that spread through Efrosin until he was laughing, too. "More times than I could count. But never with another. It's different with you."

Efrosin laughed harder, as if the chuckle he'd caught from Dmitri had reminded him of his nature. His body started to rise, his feet and head and hands floating up where Dmitri did not hold them down. Dmitri's hand slid between them and grasped their cocks together, squeezing. Efrosin gurgled in a combination of renewed lust and amusement.

"You begged me to bugger you," Dmitri said, his voice thick with want again.

"Oh please do. The knights who take each other that way cry out so loudly. Given how often they do it, and how they squirm and beg for more, it must be ever so wonderful. Do you think I will squirm? Shall I beg?"

Dmitri bit his lip, his eyes going even darker with lust, and then he shifted off Efrosin to lean over the side of the bed, rummaging for something under it. As he did, Efrosin rose up with a stomach-lurching swiftness, but Dmitri grabbed him by the ankle and pulled him back to the bed, holding a jar in his other hand.

"Of course, I should warn you," Dmitri said, as he reached for edge of the blanket their rutting had wadded up against the side of the bed. "I've never buggered anyone before."

He held Efrosin down with one palm flat on Efrosin's chest as he used the other hand to shove one end of the blanket between the mattress and the wall, and then, moving away, he pulled the blanket taut over Efrosin's upper body to hold him in place. He tucked the other side under the mattress, and then leaned back, double-checking his handiwork.

Efrosin's arms and legs floated up, but his body was trapped against the soft, worn mattress. The blanket was not of a fine material, and it rubbed Efrosin's hard nipples roughly, making him want to rub against it and simultaneously move away. He squirmed to test its limits, surprised when the binding held.

He felt contained and vulnerable, with his hard cock and twitching balls bare below the blanket. Dmitri's eyes were fixed there, his tongue running over his lips as he knelt between Efrosin's floating legs and seemed to study Efrosin's prick and exposed anus.

"Have you never put your fingers there?" Dmitri asked, and Efrosin shuddered at the thick, muddy sound in his voice.

"Yes," Efrosin said. "It hurt. And I couldn't stop laughing. It was too funny. I stopped at two."

"You know enough from watching, I assume, to understand what I must do?"

Efrosin nodded, though at the moment his mind was blank, and he could recall nothing other than the fact that he was bound naked to a bed, cock and balls alive in a way he'd never known, and his asshole flexing in a distracting, tingling way under Dmitri's gaze.

Dmitri opened the bottle and spread the slick contents over the fingers of his right hand, and then over his cock, before pouring some into his palm. Efrosin bucked, his heart thudding, his legs quivering in the air next to Dmitri's shoulders, and then Dmitri leaned forward, two fingers pushing tentatively at Efrosin's asshole. He rubbed and pushed until Efrosin felt his pucker give way and take one finger in.

It was a sharp sensation, a burning stretch, and then Efrosin felt his body adjust, a softening and welcoming that took place deep within Efrosin's soul, and he moaned. Dmitri's second finger worked in, and Efrosin reached out with his hands, fingers wriggling in the air, as he rotated his hips and pushed down, forcing Dmitri's fingers farther inside.

Efrosin bit his lip, and Dmitri's mouth parted, his eyes wide and hot, his firm chest heaving with lust. "Is this all right?" Dmitri asked.

A lust for more welled within Efrosin, and he whimpered and begged with his body. He squirmed down on Dmitri's twisting fingers, heart pounding, his cock rigid with urgency. Dmitri's eyes sparkled. "I know what you need," he whispered, and Efrosin felt flooded with relief when Dmitri edged a third finger into him, drawing his asshole breath-takingly tight.

"Dmitri," he whimpered.

As Dmitri fucked him with his fingers, Efrosin rolled his head back and forth, surprised by the sudden weight of it against the soft pillow, but then the thought was gone. He cried out and kicked his feet in the air, overcome by a sensation he'd not known to expect. Then it came again. Efrosin gasped, his sight blurred, and sweat broke out over his skin as he writhed in the throes of ecstasy.

Dmitri had hooked his fingers and touched something, something that was the very meaning of deep, the very opposite of airy, and Efrosin rode Dmitri's fingers wantonly, pushing his ass at him, begging to feel it once more. He kicked at the air, his body tensing and clenching around Dmitri's solid, working fingers as the fantastic feeling exploded through him, shocking him with depths of pleasure.

With a groan, Dmitri muttered, "Can't wait. You need it. You need it so much."

Efrosin's eyes squeezed shut. His heart pounded, his legs floated and shook, and he tangled his hands into his own hair, tugging hard to keep from falling so heavily into sensation and lust that he'd never crawl out. Then he felt the horrible sensation of Dmitri's fingers pulling free, and just as he cried out, bereft, there came a pressure and stretch—so thick, so big—that nearly blew off the top of his head.

He pushed down to accept Dmitri's prick, arching his neck as he cried out. He felt the burn and stretch at his asshole, and then the pain seemed to drill into him, touching him somewhere inexplicably deep, like an undiscovered mine inside him was bleeding jewels.

Efrosin threw his legs around Dmitri's back, jerking and crying out as the thick head of Dmitri's cock pushed past his ring of muscle with a pop that jolted him to the core. Then there was a thick, slow, deep slide in, and Efrosin pounded Dmitri's back with his heels and squirmed, his body spasming and releasing as he took Dmitri's length.

Efrosin had never felt so unfathomable, and yet when he opened his eyes, his breath caught on a whimper. Dmitri was there, his cheeks flushed, and tender understanding on his face.

"There, there," Dmitri whispered, bent over, holding Efrosin's arms down. "It's almost in. Bear down, my Efrosin. Take me."

Efrosin felt a hot prickle at the back of his neck, and then a sweeping, consuming, burning chill that made him quake all over with mad, mad lust. He threw his hips up to meet Dmitri, slamming Dmitri's cock in to the root, clawing at Dmitri's back to better grasp his solidity.

"Oh God," Dmitri groaned, his eyes screwed tight as he lunged forward, hands gripping the pillow underneath Efrosin's head. He muttered, "I've never…" And he froze, his face flushed with effort, flexed into Efrosin's body, stretching him open.

Efrosin squeezed his ass around Dmitri and he bit his own lip, digging his heels into Dmitri's back. Dmitri's cock felt heavy, a thick weight where it stretched Efrosin's inner walls and brushed against him deep inside where he had never been touched before. The thought alone made him whimper again. He shifted beneath Dmitri's weight, digging his prick into the scratchy trail of dark hair beneath Dmitri's navel.

"Good God," Dmitri cried, his body straining over Efrosin, holding so perfectly still.

When Efrosin brought his arms around Dmitri's neck, they stared into each other's eyes. Their breath mingled as their bodies pulsed and ached where they joined, and Efrosin didn't feel like laughing. Not even a little bit.

DMITRI KNEW IF he moved he'd spurt his seed. He'd never been inside another man before. Never known the sweet, delicious tightness and heat. Never felt the fast thud of another's pulse around his cock, nor watched another's eyes open wide with feverish need as he pushed into their ass and held there, trembling.

It was that need most of all that had him hanging on the edge. His very bones seemed compelled to answer its call, and yet to move would surely make him spend. It was a desperate paradox that left him sweating and moaning.

That it was Efrosin—a man more beautiful than any Dmitri had ever seen, a prince troubled with an astounding lightness of body that made Dmitri feel as though his cock was thrust into a surprisingly solid ghost—only served to drive him closer to the edge. Somehow, despite the heavy scent of their previous coupling, Dmitri thought he could still smell the sharp odor of clouds in Efrosin's hair and taste it on his skin.

He leaned forward, sucking on Efrosin's earlobe, groaning as Efrosin squirmed under him, eyes rolled back in his head, pulling against Dmitri with his hands, urging him on with his body. As moments passed and Efrosin's body screamed for more, Dmitri felt himself slip until he was clinging to the edge.

Efrosin moaned low in his throat and met Dmitri's eyes, begging, "Please! More!"

Unable to deny such outright need from Efrosin, Dmitri rolled his hips, fucking deeply with a powerful thrust. Grimacing, he plummeted over into ecstasy. He twisted in Efrosin's embrace as he yelled and shook, shooting his seed deep into Efrosin's body.

Efrosin jerked. "Oh my God! Oh it is so much!" His voice was laced with confusion and want.

Dmitri didn't pull out, driven by his need to see Efrosin through to the end. Everything about Efrosin's wide eyes and open, red mouth told Dmitri that their coupling must go on, and his own desire rose again to meet that requirement. Dmitri had been so alone, and now he was tangled with another, moving as one, commingled fluids and breath making him quiver. He wasn't ready for it to be over either. He hunched and thrust, driving his too-sensitive and still-hard cock into Efrosin's tight, hot, slick hole, now made sloppy by Dmitri's seed. Both of them crowed and clawed, hunger once again consuming them.

Efrosin felt heavier in Dmitri's arms, and Dmitri leaned forward to kiss his crooning mouth, shocked to see a depth in Efrosin's eyes that hadn't been there before. As he plunged into Efrosin's body, swiveling his hips, hitting every angle, he knew that he'd rubbed the sweet spot inside when Efrosin's legs kicked out on reflex, and his fingers clenched on Dmitri's shoulders, nails digging in.

Then there was the sound—the noise of sheer wonder and terror combined—that tore out of Efrosin at those times, and Dmitri almost slowed his rapid assault on Efrosin's hole, thinking that it must be rather scary for him to feel these things when he'd never even known the pleasure of his own hand.

But he did not. He couldn't. His hips did not slow, his pounding did not ease, and Efrosin's screams of, "Yes! Yes! Please!" overrode the trepidation that Dmitri saw in his eyes. Understanding Efrosin's need for more was greater than any need for comfort. Consumed, he slammed into Efrosin, seeking their climax.

Efrosin didn't last long, not once Dmitri found the right angle, and he rammed the thick head of his cock over the place within again and again until Efrosin struggled in his arms, desperately trying to get his hand between their bodies. Before he could, Efrosin stiffened, crowed with a startled bliss, and his ass spasmed and clenched around Dmitri.

Efrosin's seed splashed against Dmitri's stomach and, looking between them, Dmitri saw another great glob of it land across the top of the blanket that was still anchoring Efrosin down. Dmitri kissed Efrosin's mouth, swallowing the sound of his cries, and pulled back to gaze into his blue, surprised eyes, crinkled at the edges with such ready joy. Dmitri gave up to that sweetness, cocking his hips and thrusting hard. He yelled in delight as his cock convulsed inside Efrosin, filling his hole with seed again, and he shook all over as the ecstasy raked over him, leaving him feeling exposed, like earth freshly tilled.

Dmitri tore the blanket away before collapsing on top of Efrosin, who reached up with one shaking hand to stroke Dmitri's hair as they rested, skin to skin, trembling, and still joined below.

Dmitri knew that what he felt was impossible, but having been alone for so long, he found he couldn't help himself. In his heart, where it had no business and did not belong, Efrosin had planted a seed as surely as Dmitri had loaded Efrosin with his own. It was a seed of friendship, affection and—worst of all—love. Dmitri knew then, kissing Efrosin's red, bitten lips, and feeling his body clench and tremble around him, that this seed would be his undoing.

After Dmitri wiped their spendings from Efrosin's stomach and between his legs, he realized Efrosin began to rise up again, a steady increase in his flotation until he was difficult for Dmitri to hold down. It was as if Efrosin's body longed for the sky.

"That was so beautiful," Efrosin said, eyes shining and his lips ruby red from their kisses. There were stains on his neck and jaw too, from where Dmitri had bitten and sucked, and he looked like a debauched angel, especially with his arms and legs levitating effortlessly. The only thing holding him against the bed now was Dmitri's strong arms around his waist.

"When they find me, you must come home with me," Efrosin said. "You could be my consort, my lover, my pretty peacock of perpetual penile pleasure." And he laughed, a tinkling sound more like what Dmitri had heard from up in the tree, and not the deep rumbling one that had filled them both when Dmitri had been buried deep inside him. "You must come. I don't think I can live without you."

Dmitri thought he sounded anything but sincere, but understood Efrosin probably couldn't sound sincere about something as serious as death if he tried. "I can't."

"Of course you can. You have nothing but a hovel here. I can give you a castle, and servants, and anything your heart desires. You'll come stay with me, sleep in my bed, drag me down from the ceiling to have your wicked way with me, make me heavy with your seed and then drop off to a snoring sleep as I watch you from above like a guardian angel. No one would ever dare bother you. You'd have a place by my side and my father would have to accept you. Wouldn't that be lovely? How can you say no?"

"Because I can't. I can't leave my land—my father's land."

"For heaven's sake, whyever not?"

Dmitri touched Efrosin's handsome face, his thumb tracing the light line of his golden stubble, and told his story.

Chapter Four

ONCE UPON A time, there was an old woodcutter who took a pretty, young wife to live with him deep in the forest. Always eager to fulfill the needs of good-hearted people, the earth fairies saw to it that the woodcutter and his wife had all that they could ever want with their small but fruitful garden, a lake for fishing and woods for trapping game.

In the midst of so much plenty, the differences between them, given his old age and her youthful bloom, seemed unimportant, and they were quite happy there, alone amid the trees on their several acres of land.

Eventually, the young wife let the old woodcutter know that she was with child. Both of them were quite filled to the brim with joy. The earth fairies seemed to share their happiness, for the garden was never so prolific as it was that summer. As autumn approached, the wife's belly swelled with the melons from the furrows, and not wanting any time apart from his lovely bride, the woodcutter gave up his trade, happily settling into domestic bliss in the last years of his life.

But the birth did not go well.

The child was too well rooted in the mother, and when his head finally came forth, he could only be persuaded from her body with a giant tug from the woodcutter. The wife screamed, and the babe came free of her like a plant ripped from the earth. But then the blood began, and the fever, and the woodcutter despaired.

To his great astonishment, five fairies, all grown as tall as men, with skin the color of sun-baked mud and eyes dark as dirt, filed into the cabin to tend to his wife. The woodcutter was not sure if they were male or female, or perhaps a bit of both. He watched the fairies argue amongst themselves in a language he didn't know, fear keeping his tongue silent. No magic, nor medicine, nor herb given seemed to help his wife.

Then, in words he could understand, the fairies told the woodcutter what he must do next. Reluctant, but desperate to save his wife, he saddled his old horse and left her and the infant in the care of the fae, going, as the fairies had insisted, in search of a very old midwife.

"She lives on the boundary between the known world and the mountains," one fairy had said. "Tell her we send for her. Bound as we are to our land, we cannot leave. Call her Mother. Be polite and plead with her. Do whatever you must. Ignore her cruelty. If you love your wife, do as we say."

Not even half a day into his journey, the woodcutter rounded a bend and found an old, bent woman waiting in the middle of the road. She leaned on a staff and a blackbird perched on her shoulder. The woodcutter eagerly approached. "Perhaps you can help me, good lady. I desperately seek a woman who lives at the end of the world. Might you know of her?"

The old woman's eyes glinted, and the bird on her shoulder let out a loud caw. "A midwife, perhaps? For a wife sick with childbed fever?"

The woodcutter couldn't believe his ears. "Yes. The fae of the earth have sent me to find one called Mother."

The woman licked her dirty lips. "I am the Mother you seek. But this child should not live."

"He is but a babe, my only son. Please, you must help my Dmitri and my wife."

The old woman smiled, revealing teeth as black as coal. "Dmitri, you say? Lover of the earth. 'Tis a lucky name, and I'm feeling merciful. I will only punish those at fault on this day. Lead the way, fool."

Upon returning to the cabin, the midwife took in the squalling child held against his mother's fevered tit. The five fae fell to their knees before her, beseeching. She tsked sharply, and they cowered. Then the old woman uttered something that made the fae blanch in terror, crying out as one before bursting into flame.

The woodcutter ran for a bucket of water, but the fire burned itself out with a whoosh, leaving only traces of fine ash where the fairies had been. He stood before his wife and child, arms outstretched to shield them from the woman. "I beg you, do not harm them."

The crone cackled. "Do not fret. I will cure her. But first give me the child. No harm will come to him," the witch said. For yes, she was a witch, of course she was.

Terrified, the woodcutter passed his small son into the witch's dirty hands. She whispered in his ear and cackled to herself before turning to the man. "This one will be bound to the land. Never will he leave until death claims him."

The woodcutter wordlessly accepted the price, clutching his wife's hot fingers. They had all that they wanted, and so long as his wife and the babe lived, they had no need for more.

The witch kissed the boy's head before putting him back to his mother's breast. She touched the woodcutter's wife upon each eyelid and spoke in unintelligible words. Then she turned her back and walked from the house, never to be seen or heard from again.

From that time forward, the woodcutter's child was bound by his father's bargain. The father and mother saw it as a price well worth paying, but the son saw it as a curse, and resented it every day of his life.

EFROSIN'S EYES SHONE and he clapped at the telling. Despite that it was his own tale of woe, Dmitri wondered at the sense of accomplishment it gave him to receive an ovation from a prince. Surely Efrosin had heard better stories than his during the parties hosted by the king at the castle, and yet Efrosin's enthusiasm was undampened by any snobbery.

Efrosin said breathlessly, "What a wonderful story. Where are your parents now?" He snuggled into Dmitri's arms, Dmitri's weight keeping him safe from floating.

"They died five years ago. A traveling salesman brought the pox." It was strange to speak of it, being so alone as he was through the years. The grief flared hollowly in his chest.

"Oh how exciting! And what did you do with their bodies?"

Dmitri frowned. "I buried them."

Efrosin's lips twitched. "Grave digging. That sounds quite—oh wait a moment. I am sure Geoffry covered this in his teachings. Laughing about death offends people, you see…so, let me think. Oh yes, I am to look sad—" Here Efrosin's face contorted in a terrible attempt at misery. "And I am to say, 'My greatest sympathy for your loss, dear citizen'." Efrosin grinned. "There. Do you feel much better now?"

Dmitri narrowed his eyes and said, "No. I shall never feel 'much better' about digging a grave for my parents' bodies."

Efrosin seemed to ponder this. "I suppose not. Tell me, have you ever tried to leave your land?"

"Not until my parents died. While they were alive, they needed me here. But once they were naught but a memory, I resolved to leave this place and journey to the worlds I've only read about in my books. Yet I could not due to my father's promise. I am truly bound." The heaviness in his chest made it difficult to draw breath.

For a moment, Efrosin appeared genuinely troubled, but the graveness of his expression soon flickered into a smile. "Then let's talk about something else. What of the lake near your cabin, and the river that feeds it? Does it flow from the castle? If so, should no one come for me, when I wish to take my leave I could happily swim home. I quite like to swim. In fact, it is fair to say that I love swimming more than life."

"Of course you'll want to be going." Dmitri sighed. He touched Efrosin's neck, feeling Efrosin's pulse against his fingertips. He hated that this would be the end of it, though of course it must be.

Efrosin peered at him curiously and asked with a tone of pure wonder, as though the idea of what he was asking was somehow thrilling, "Do you get awfully lonely then?"

"Lonely? When I'm alone, confined here to this parcel of land, for all of my days? Whyever would I be lonely?" Dmitri could not keep the bitterness from his tongue. He was tempted to bend down and kiss Efrosin's mouth to replace it with the taste of clouds again.

"And no servants at all? However do you eat?"

"I hunt and fish, and grow a bit of food. Sometimes, if I'm lucky, someone will happen by and trade for some seeds or fresh fruit."

"Ah, I see. Well," Efrosin, said airily, and looking as though it was a contest and he intended to win. "I grow lonely too."

"You? A prince at a castle bustling with servants, knights and diplomats? You've already said that you are always surrounded by people."

"True. I am. But none of them like me. I don't have any friends," he said gaily. "Who wants to play with a child who floats away? The boys could not play ball with me, or go riding or hunting. They tried to strap me to a horse once, but it was for naught. He couldn't feel my weight on his back and ran wild. Oh what a terrifying thrill that was. I laughed so hard I threw up."

Dmitri had to stifle a chortle at the picture that brought to mind even as he felt an answering pang at Efrosin's lack of friendship. He would be the finest friend Efrosin ever had if only given the chance.

"Do you ride?" Efrosin asked.

"I had a horse…but she died a few years before my father passed away. We never had need of another." Before Efrosin could ask what had come of the old horse's body, Dmitri continued on, "But we were speaking of you, not me. Surely there were girls at least?"

"Girls? Oh certainly, but who wants to braid my hair and put in ribbons when I float to the ceiling half the time? And they hated that I was prettier than they."

Given that Dmitri had at first believed Efrosin to be an entangled angel, there was no room for bringing Efrosin's ego down a peg. He truly did possess an otherworldly beauty. "Well, you certainly don't seem sad about it."

"That's the curse, you see. I couldn't feel sad if I tried. It's quite…well, sad really."

"I actually meant maidens and courtesans to please you."

"Oh, pleasing me. I've told you, until you kissed me, I could not be pleased. And even if they tried, they weigh so little it would require that they tie me down, and it grows so tiresome being tied down. Unable to move or go wherever you wish. The constant rope burn. Can you even imagine?"

"Yes, my prince. I understand not being able to go wherever you wish," Dmitri said, smiling at the bright outrage that glowed alongside an odd glee in Efrosin's expression. "Though, I admit, you have me beaten with the rope burn. I do not have that particular trouble. I suppose I should be grateful for small mercies."

Despite it all, Efrosin's eyes sparkled with joy, and he wriggled beneath Dmitri. "Oh I won! I truly won. I am sadder than you!"

Dmitri didn't have the heart to tell him that he hadn't actually won, and that Dmitri was quite sure burying his parents in a plot by the house—digging the graves with his own two hands before returning his parents to their beloved land—surely trumped some rope burn, and not having friends to play with, or girls to braid his hair. Yet he found himself absently rubbing Efrosin's wrist where the rope had chafed the soft skin.

"Dmitri," Efrosin said, and then sucked in a breath as his floating hands dropped down to the mattress. "That is so odd," he exclaimed, but then he blinked and went on. "About your story, I think I missed a part, for I truly don't understand one thing. Why did the witch curse you?"

"Don't witches just like to do that kind of thing?" Dmitri asked, elbows framing Efrosin's face, and his hands buried in Efrosin's fine hair. He twisted a longer piece of it around his finger. "If she had a reason, it is lost to me."

"It is rather amusing, I'm sure," Efrosin agreed. "Why, if I could curse people, I'd have so much fun. It's probably a very good thing that I cannot, though I do derive a great deal of mirth from merely imagining it."

"I can see," Dmitri said drily, though Efrosin had such a beautiful smile that it gave Dmitri a thrill to see it so artlessly there upon his face. "And your own affliction?"

"Oh yes, I am roundly cursed," Efrosin said. "As you yourself saw. I cannot walk, or crawl, or set my foot alight upon the ground without the effort of others."

"Have you tried pockets full of stones?"

"Of course. What do you take me for? A fool? Even if I am, my father is the king of this land, and he has physicians of the highest intellect at his command."

"The stones didn't work?"

"For a few moments, yes, long enough to walk perhaps ten steps, but then they become as part of me, and no longer hold me fast. They tried everything—diamonds in the soles of my shoes, gold in the hems of my clothing. All the heaviest gems were tried—zircon, sapphire, garnet, topaz, peridot—and not a one would weigh me down. Tying me often does the trick, but I must be fastened to something quite big. Bigger than me, and too heavy for me to carry."

"Hmm. You are surprisingly strong. I can attest to that." Dmitri caressed Efrosin's firm chest.

Efrosin grinned. "Yes. I prefer to be tied to someone, or many someones, because then they can ferry me about, which is a great deal more entertaining than being tied to a tree or a stone or a bed." His eyes lit up. "Though being tied here to your bed would be very fun indeed."

Dmitri couldn't disagree, and he felt his prick react to the hint. He kissed the side of Efrosin's face, right where his lower lip met his cheek, and sighed. "Do you believe the rescue party will be here soon?"

"I hope not." Efrosin laughed. "I hope they do not find me for days and days."

Dmitri couldn't help feeling much the same. There were many things his body craved to do with Efrosin, many needs he was driven to meet. Efrosin was by far the most interesting person Dmitri had met in all his years, though granted, Dmitri had met only the odd trader or traveler. Even if Efrosin was strange, lighthearted and altogether too airy for his own good, he was a revelation.

"The physicians your father employed—what did they deduce your ailment to be?"

Efrosin laughed. "A curse, silly. My friend, perhaps you are the fool and not me." Joy flickered across his face. "Oh! Are you indeed my friend? Perhaps we have found our first true friend in each other."

Dmitri found himself smiling broadly, his chest suffused with warmth. "Yes. I should like to call you my friend."

"Then I decree it so. How wonderful!" His forehead creased momentarily. "What were we talking about? Oh yes, I'm cursed, you ninny."

"Yes, but a curse is merely physics, is it not? For every curse, there must be an equal and opposite cure. Have you tried eating dirt? Perhaps a bit of good earth in your diet—"

"Enough," Efrosin said, putting up his hand. "Discussion of my predicament is so tiring. Have you tried a cure? What, pray tell, is the equal and opposite cure of your curse? Flight? Height?"

"Death," Dmitri said. "It is the only release from the bonds of this world."

Efrosin's eyes went wide. "Oh. Well then, let's not talk of that. I rather like you alive and touching me."

Dmitri ran his hands down Efrosin's body, and then beneath him to grip his buttocks, squeezing them as he pressed down with his hips, seeking evidence of Efrosin's renewed arousal. Efrosin's breath caught. "Ah, yes please. Do that again." Dmitri did as he was asked, and Efrosin crooned, his prick growing hard between them.

"Efrosin," Dmitri whispered. "Surely we should leave a signal, some sort of sign for the knights who are seeking you. I fear that they may ride on by."

"God willing," Efrosin said, his eyelashes fluttering on his cheeks. "Please, Dmitri, if you cannot go with me, then let me stay—at least until you bore me, which will likely happen soon. I am quite easily bored."

Dmitri felt he should be offended, but he was not. The idea that Efrosin would not wish to leave as soon as possible invigorated him, and he was deeply grateful for this short reprieve from loneliness. The last person he'd met had been an old trader, little more than skin and bones. He'd offered Dmitri some dried fruit, desperate for any meat. Dmitri had given him far more than he should have for the paltry berries, but the man's need had been great.

"And what should I do if I did not want you here?" Dmitri asked. "Toss you to the winds and hope they blew you home?"

Efrosin chuckled. "It would be much kinder of you to drop me in the river and let me swim for it. The river would never let me drown."

"I would never let you drown either, nor float away—"

"Nor leave this bed?" Efrosin asked, pulling Dmitri down for a kiss.

Dmitri had to admit that Efrosin's suggestion was tempting, especially as Efrosin whispered in his ear about the filthy, perverted things he'd seen the knights do, and suggested Dmitri try them out on him. To properly explore each one could take days, weeks, months, years.

Dmitri knew that he was a fool, but the seed Efrosin had planted in his heart cracked open, and the smallest of fragile shoots bloomed.

Chapter Five

"**T**HIS ALE IS quite pleasing." Efrosin licked his lips before taking another bite of rabbit stew. "I've never tasted anything this good in the tavern near the castle. Of course my father forbade them to serve me ale, so I suppose it stands to reason. But now I'm of age—it's my birthday, did I mention?—and shall drink ale to my heart's content."

After another round of lovemaking, this time with their mouths to give Efrosin's tender ass a rest, they sat at the rough wooden table in their trousers. Well, Dmitri sat; Efrosin was tied to the bench, and his buttocks floated several inches above it, but at least he was able to reach the stew without spilling much.

Dmitri chuckled. "And what else does your heart desire on your special day?"

"Only one thing. To dive into a bracing body of water. That's what I want next, Dmitri." He felt his rump touch the board of the bench for a moment, and then he rose up again. So very curious.

Dmitri crunched on a biscuit—from a batch that wasn't light and flaky at all—but Efrosin got distracted by the delicious stew and strong ale before he could complain. "If you want to clean up, the water from the bowl is good enough for me, but I shall happily get out the tub and warm the water over the fire for you."

"A tub? As if that could replace the marvelousness of an open lake, surrounded by earth and sky. I should think the water in a tub would not even have the weight to hold me down."

"Have you never bathed in a tub before?" Dmitri asked.

In fact, Efrosin had not, at least not in his memory. For as long as he could recall, he'd spent more time in the river than out of it, and never needed to wash himself in a tub.

Besides, Efrosin wasn't interested in cleaning up. He wanted to swim, and he wanted to swim immediately, and he said as much.

"It's late in the day and far too cold to swim, Efrosin. Besides, it's not yet summer. The blossoms haven't even begun to fall from the branches of the Springsimmon."

"Oh the curse of the Springsimmon. Swim too soon and you'll die. I swim as soon as they can break the ice on the river and have done every year since I was a child." Dmitri looked pinched about the mouth in a way that Efrosin didn't quite like, and so he kissed the expression away.

Breaking off the kiss just as Dmitri moaned and leaned into it, Efrosin looked up from under his lashes and pressed his upper teeth into his lower lip. "I have heard that I am unbearably beautiful when wet. Not to mention I have it on the highest authority that I'm much easier to converse with when submerged; I have a bit of weight then. It is when I am most truly happy."

Dmitri softened. "I only want to keep you safe. But if you feel you must…"

"Yes, you must take me to the lake, or I will die of unhappiness." He unknotted the rope binding him to the table with a dramatic flourish and snatched up his white silk top before floating to the ceiling.

Efrosin knew that was an exaggeration while simultaneously feeling quite sure that it was absolutely true—should Dmitri fail to take him to the water, he would somehow dry up instantly and turn into dust. He'd been so happy only moments before, full of a physical, humming satisfaction, but now he felt a high-flying anxiety that would only dissipate once his body was enveloped in a watery embrace.

"But getting you there." Dmitri pulled on his shirt, regarding Efrosin with wide-eyed worry.

Efrosin flapped his hand to dismiss those charmingly realistic concerns as he slipped his arms into the silk. "You can strap me to your chest and carry me to the lake. You have rope and lengths of fabric. The knights do it all the time—especially Sir Carlisle. You are as strong and brave as a knight, are you not?"

He kicked off the ceiling and somersaulted through the air before noticing Dmitri's dark expression at the mention of Sir Carlisle. He wondered at the wild joy that stirred in him as he fanned the sparks of Dmitri's jealousy. "Though you don't have a beard like Sir Carlisle, so perhaps that makes all the difference."

Dmitri growled, snatched Efrosin by the ankle and dragged him down. He bound Efrosin to his chest with several long, rough ropes, and carried him out into the forest. The sun still shone beyond the canopy of the trees, and Efrosin gazed up happily as Dmitri bore him away, arms tight around him.

The trees were so thick and grew so close to the water's edge that Efrosin barely had time to gasp before they were there. Ringed by trees, the lake sparkled in the late-day sun, a crystal blue that Efrosin thought he could get lost in forever. It was so much bigger than the river he was used to—he could barely make out the other side.

"Quick. Untie me." His palms itched, body twitching with the need to dive into the cool depths.

Dmitri obliged immediately, releasing the bonds and pushing Efrosin down gently to the water. Efrosin dove under and pulled off his silky clothing. He blew out, chuckling in his throat as bubbles gently tickled his face on their effervescent journey up. Following them, he broke through the shimmering surface, gasping for air, and shook the water from his eyes. He tossed his sodden garments to shore and grinned at Dmitri, who watched from the bank, a small smile playing at his lips.

After diving up, down and all around, exploring the depths of the lake, the water soothing on his naked skin, Efrosin flipped onto his back. He gazed up at the lovely sky—the very one that had almost swallowed him forever mere hours ago. How things had changed since then. How wondrous and strange.

Now the light faded around them, a rosy glow in the west indicating that the sun was on its way to bed. Efrosin twisted in the water, facing Dmitri again, admiring him where he sat amidst the new green grass shooting up all over the muddy bank. With his shirt tossed aside, exposing his hard stomach and handsome chest, and with his brown, steady eyes never leaving Efrosin for even a moment, Dmitri began to talk. "You know my story, so now I'll ask you. Why are you cursed? Let me guess—your father forgot to invite a powerful witch to your christening?"

Efrosin lifted an eyebrow and clucked his tongue. "Not every curse begins with a christening, my dear Dmitri." He pushed a bit harder with his legs to stay afloat.

"Of course not. Mine didn't. But yours did."

"Why, then you know the story already."

"Perhaps. There is much lacking in the gossip of old women trading their wares. So did a missed invitation cause the trouble?"

"Oh rather the contrary," Efrosin said, splashing lightly. "It could be argued that I'm cursed because Papa invited a powerful witch to my christening. Perhaps if she hadn't been invited, then she'd have just stayed away and minded her own affairs."

"Doubtful," Dmitri said, shrugging and leaning back against the embankment, his eyes straying up to the sky, clearly taking measure of the light. "Cursing is what witches like best. So...your father invited a powerful witch to your christening and then what?"

"Well, he invited two powerful witches, which is why I'm still here at all. Oh bother. Where to begin?" Efrosin chewed on his lower lip as he paddled languidly. "There is much to tell, but night is falling and I would dearly love it if you'd bugger me again before bedtime. Let me make small bones of this giant beast."

"As you wish," Dmitri chuckled.

"My mother, Queen Inna, died giving birth to me. After a suitable amount of time—one year to be precise—my father invited everyone of any importance to my combined birthday party and christening."

"Always ominous," Dmitri said.

"Indeed. My father invited Mother's eldest sister, Ereshkigal, the witch of the earth. She arrived and offered herself to my father as his new wife. She had loved him madly for years, you see, and never forgiven my mother for marrying him. My father laughed at her. As did I, though I was just a baby, and let's face it, I laugh at everything. She was insulted, of course, and gave me the delightful christening gift of this lovely curse in order to punish my father and to spite me for simply existing."

"But there was another powerful witch there?"

"Yes, my mother's younger sister, Uriti, the witch of fire. She wove a spell that tempered my curse with my mother's gift."

"Your mother's gift? I don't understand."

"My mother was the witch of strong waters. The only place I have any weight is in water from the river bearing her name." Efrosin indicated the lake of fresh, clear water he was swimming in. "The Inna River—and all of its lakes, streams, pools and ponds—is my favorite place to be. I would live in these waters if I could. All in all, it's not so bad of a curse. It could be much worse."

"Not so bad? If you say so."

"I met you because of the curse, didn't I? Admit it, there is something delightful in that." Efrosin reached toward him and waggled his fingers, calling, "Come. Come in with me."

Dmitri shifted. "It is too early in the season to swim. Perhaps you're unaffected thanks to your affliction."

"Don't tell me you're truly afraid to swim before the Springsimmon blossoms fall. Do you always follow the rules?" Efrosin asked, sighing. "They make life so boring."

"Always follow the rules? I should say not. I took you home, didn't I? I kissed you and touched you, I bit your neck and pushed my prick into you, when any sensible person would have refused and found a way to summon the search parties instead. So no, clearly it is not required that I follow the rules. I have catered to your every need."

Efrosin chuckled. Rather than looking pleased or proud, Dmitri appeared a bit uncomfortable and puzzled over his choice to lie with Efrosin instead of follow his common sense. "Damn the Springsimmon then," Efrosin said, and splashed the water in a large arc that missed Dmitri only because he managed to roll quickly away. "Get in the water."

"No," Dmitri said, laughing. He dug in the sack he'd taken with them and tossed a bar of brown soap at Efrosin. It plopped into the water and popped up to the surface again. "Wash yourself. I want to get you back inside where you're safe." Dmitri's eyes glowed more brightly than the sun sinking closer to the trees. "And I want to lick and kiss your hole before I hold you down to fuck you again."

Efrosin licked his lips, remembering Dmitri's thick prick ramming into his ass, and the sudden descent of an ecstasy so arresting that he'd bitten down hard on the curve of Dmitri's shoulder. He now felt a sharp jolt in his gut at the sight of the reddish bruise left by his teeth and the purple blooms of love bites he'd sucked into Dmitri's chest and neck. He shivered.

"Tell me you don't want that too," Dmitri said, voice low. "You need it. We both do."

By all rights, Efrosin should be sated—his body still hummed pleasantly from their exertions, and his hole felt a bit sore and abused. Yet he already wanted it again. But he wanted it his way.

"It's true," Efrosin agreed, and smiled at Dmitri's triumphant expression. "But we have time. The night is almost upon us and they won't search for me in the dark. We'll have hours in your bed."

Dmitri cocked his head. "You sound almost...reasonable. It's odd. Nor are you laughing yourself sick at every moment."

"It's the water. It changes me." He lifted his hands in the air, presenting himself for a moment, before ducking beneath the surface again, coming up grinning. "Do you like it?"

Dmitri seemed to consider the question seriously. "I do. But I liked you before too." His brow furrowed. "It's the water?"

"It must be." Efrosin stretched out his hand. "Come on."

"But it's freezing."

"It's not so cold." Efrosin turned on his brightest smile, summoning his more common enthusiasm from where he could feel it waiting in his lungs, like a balloon ready to rise. "Do dive in. It's thrilling!"

"I've no doubt. I'm sure it will thrill me until my skin is quite blue."

"Charming! Then you'll look like a water pixie." Efrosin tipped his head back, observing the sky turning the color of the knight's bruises after a tournament. It was dusk and anything was possible. "I have always wondered what it must be like to cavort with pixies. To be whisked away to their parties, dancing and twirling the night away, while godly men and women sleep unknowingly in their beds."

"Shh." Dmitri glanced around. "Don't speak of the blue folk. They're dangerous and should be respected."

Efrosin smiled, swallowed back a laugh—so much easier to do in the water—and took the advantage Dmitri had unwittingly offered. "If you get in, I won't mention the pixies again."

"And if I don't?"

Efrosin felt a surge of wicked delight. "Then I shall summon them."

As he opened his mouth to do just that, Dmitri put out his hand to stop him. "Please, Efrosin. Don't. My mother always warned me to stay far away from the earth fairies and water pixies. They are a menace."

Efrosin cleared his throat and projected his voice. "Blue pixies of—" He got nothing more out before he was swamped by a huge wave of water. Sputtering and wiping the excess from his face, he laughed and splashed back, amazed. Dmitri had leapt into the lake, breeches and all.

Together they were gleeful and happy, as the light faded around them and a rousing swirl of belching frogs lifted up their nightly song. The world was nothing but laughter and water, and slick skin against skin. Not to mention wet cloth that rubbed roughly against Efrosin's cock as he and Dmitri wrestled in the lake. They shoved and dunked each other, and Efrosin shocked Dmitri at one point by getting his footing in a shallow area, lifting Dmitri up out of the water and tossing him several feet despite the difference in their size.

"The water gifts you with inhuman strength too?" Dmitri chortled, splashing Efrosin's face and laughing when Efrosin choked, diving toward Dmitri and dunking him under.

"No," Efrosin said. "I'm simply much more than you think."

"I think you're everything," Dmitri exclaimed, which earned him a kiss, and then a push back into the water.

As the night closed around them, they tussled and raced, until finally Efrosin held Dmitri's slick shoulder with one arm, chest to chest, his other hand twined with one of Dmitri's. His feet pressed into Dmitri's solid form, kicking at him playfully until suddenly Dmitri pulled his hand free from their clutch, reached between Efrosin's kicking legs and took hold of Efrosin's bollocks.

Efrosin went completely still, a sweet wonder engulfing him as Dmitri squeezed gently. Dmitri rolled them in his hand before gripping them a bit harder and Efrosin gasped. The water lapped at their skin, and the song of nightingales broke the quiet descending darkness as Efrosin let his legs relax in the water. Holding onto Dmitri's neck and breathing his breath, he stared into Dmitri's dark, warm eyes. *This is intimacy. This is trust. This is real.*

Efrosin had learned the rules of these games from the best tutors his father could buy, but it was only now, his most sensitive part held firmly in Dmitri's grasp, that he understood the reason for them. And with a moan he realized that the deep place inside him, the one he'd only just unearthed in Dmitri's bed, was ever so much darker, deeper and full of secrets than he'd ever been able to imagine before.

"I don't want you to leave," Dmitri said, his voice rough.

Efrosin understood. Should the search parties find him, he would go. As wonderful as it was to dream of staying, he was a prince, and Dmitri was a woodsman cursed to remain on his land. They were not two of a kind, no matter how their bodies sang for each other now. The day would come—likely tomorrow—when Efrosin would be discovered, and he'd be carried away on horseback, strapped helplessly to Sir Carlisle's chest. Efrosin felt as though he'd swallowed a rock.

Dmitri massaged Efrosin's bollocks enough to knock them together inside the sac. Efrosin groaned as violent jolts of sensation shot through him, tightening his nipples and making his asshole clench desperately. Dmitri didn't seem to expect Efrosin to say anything, which was good, because all that Efrosin could do was feel—the vulnerability of his tender sac in Dmitri's calloused palm, the sweet pulse of his cock as the water swirled around it, and the pounding of his heart in his chest.

And just like that the newly found, heavy place inside him broke open and spilled out until he wasn't light like air and he wasn't wet like water. Instead he was dense like sun-warmed earth mixed into mud. He had never felt so thick, waiting with his lips resting against the stubble on Dmitri's chin, aching to be molded into shape.

Dmitri released Efrosin's sac and grabbed his cock instead, pulling it in a fast, eager rhythm. Efrosin moved, grabbing handfuls of Dmitri's dark hair, finally kissing his lips. He licked into his open mouth, tasting water and spit, seeking the traces of his own seed that he'd shot so eagerly onto Dmitri's tongue in the cabin. And when he found it, he moaned, sang out in happiness and began to beg—for what he didn't know, just something more and something now.

Dmitri shook in Efrosin's arms and seemed to read his mind. "Yes, yes. I'll give it to you." They thrust against each other, legs tangling, until they slipped beneath the water, still kissing, and then pushed up and out again, coughing, gasping for breath and still unwilling to release the other's mouth.

The water and Dmitri's saliva mixed on Efrosin's tongue, a sweet elixir that he swallowed greedily as he struggled to keep afloat, until finally he pulled Dmitri by the hand toward the shallows by the bank. As they got close, he let go and flung himself onto all fours. Efrosin crawled forward as far as he dared, his hands and knees sinking into the mossy, murky bottom of the lake.

The water was up to his elbows and thighs, rooting him in wetness like a flower in the ground. Efrosin lifted his bare ass up in the air, arching like a dog in heat, begging to be mounted. The head of his hard cock breached the water, and he felt the constant soft movement around it, and the occasional brush of a fish. He dug his fingers farther into the sediment. His hole felt bruised and tender from their earlier endeavors, but he didn't care. Dmitri had unearthed the hot, desperate depths of him, and Efrosin couldn't get enough.

He panted, looking over his shoulder as Dmitri swam the short distance to him before shakily kneeling behind him in the shallow water. The very last of the sunlight illuminated him from behind, water dripping from his hair, nose and chin, his breeches plastered to him and streaked dark where Efrosin's feet had rubbed lake-bottom mud onto them in their tussle.

Dmitri's voice was rough. "Yes. God yes. You're so very beautiful, Efrosin. I will taste you and give you what you need." He didn't hesitate, grabbing Efrosin's buttocks and squeezing before spreading him apart. "It seems to wink at me," Dmitri marveled. "Let me kiss it, lick it."

"Please," Efrosin whimpered.

Efrosin shuddered and moaned, arching his ass toward Dmitri's mouth. He could feel the heat of Dmitri's breath on his hole, and his throat went dry. He bent his head to let his forehead drop into water. The wet, slopping sounds of the waves lapping at the shore came to his ears as he waited, pulse pounding for whatever was about to come.

He never had much patience out of the water, but now, fingers digging into soft, wet earth and Dmitri's taste on his tongue, he felt that every moment was worth waiting for, though he quaked with desire and shivered eagerly.

The first touch of Dmitri's mouth on Efrosin's hole sent him scrambling and splashing in ecstatic shock, and Dmitri grabbed hold of his hips to haul him close. "It tickles!" Efrosin gasped, shoving his ass back for more. He squirmed, laughing deep in his belly as Dmitri swirled his tongue all around Efrosin's asshole.

"It tickles, Dmitri."

As soon as he said the name, he felt a sensation almost like a blanket covering him. Then the tickle was no longer funny at all, but so deliriously good that Efrosin forgot he was in the water, collapsing down farther and farther, shoving his ass higher up, grinding it against Dmitri's mouth, teeth and chin. He suddenly found himself coughing and choking, having dropped his face into the lake in his ecstasy.

Dmitri held his hips tightly and didn't stop until he finally groaned and flung himself on top of Efrosin, rubbing his cock between Efrosin's buttocks. He wrapped his arms around Efrosin and clung tight, all of his weight bearing down on Efrosin's knees and hands, which sunk deeper into the muck.

"Please," Efrosin begged, and he realized he'd said it so many times now, it was a litany, a chant, and it had lost all meaning until he added, "Fuck me."

Dmitri pulled back enough to get his hand between them, and Efosin yelled at the thick intrusion as Dmitri pushed his cock head against Efrosin's tender asshole, and then Efrosin's skin prickled with encompassing pleasure as Dmitri breached the muscle, sliding inside— steady, heavy, and filling him with weight.

Dmitri's long, strong fingers gripped Efrosin's cock, and together they rocked and moaned in the mud at the edge of the lake, the water splashing against their thighs. When Efrosin's wrists gave out and he fell down to his elbows, it splashed them in the face as they hunched and writhed together.

Dmitri's teeth raked over Efrosin's shoulder then latched onto the back of his neck, worrying there as he rammed his cock into Efrosin. Then, like an escaped prayer, Efrosin cried out, his body tensing as he reached into the surprisingly deep well of feeling inside him, grabbing fistfuls of wet dirt as he did.

Time stopped, shot through with rapture, until Efrosin burst out of the depths and back up to the edges of his skin, bringing it all with him.

Wild cries and convulsions rattled him as he shot his seed into the water that had always been home.

Gasping and exhausted, Efrosin could barely keep his face above the surface while Dmitri moved inside him with slamming, long strokes. He reached back to grab Dmitri's hip and clutch him close when Dmitri cried out against his back, and hot, heavy bursts of his pleasure filled Efrosin's ass.

"Don't go," Dmitri whispered.

Efrosin opened his mouth to say the things he knew he'd say at any other time. Easy things. Hurtful things. The kinds of things that had tripped off his tongue since he'd uttered his first words.

But there in the shallows as the stars twinkled into sight, the heavy warmth of Dmitri's body covering his, and with Dmitri's spendings weighing inside him, he stayed silent instead.

Chapter Six

AFTER THEY'D TRYSTED, they had both been covered in so much mud that they'd had to dive back into the deeper parts of the lake with Dmitri's soap to scrub themselves clean. Then Dmitri had strapped Efrosin to his chest again—this time naked as night was black, unwilling to risk him getting caught on a breeze as he put his clothes on.

He'd carried him back through the thick forest, walking slowly in the dark so as not to trip over downed limbs or undergrowth. All the while, Efrosin tormented him by pressing kisses onto the crook of his neck, licking the shell of his ear and sucking maddeningly on his earlobe. By the time they reached the cabin, both of their pricks were aching, and Dmitri had wasted no time tying Efrosin to the bed and buggering him again until, exhausted, they'd finally slept.

At dawn, Dmitri listened to the sounds of the cabin creaking, and the crackle of the dying embers in the fireplace. He watched Efrosin sleep in the trappings of the covers Dmitri had rigged to keep him against the mattress, additionally secured by the weight of Dmitri's leg tossed over Efrosin's body.

Efrosin's eyelashes lay against his cheek, and his mouth was slightly open, red-lipped from such quantities of kissing and biting, as well as the exertion of sucking Dmitri's prick. A pleasant expression danced on Efrosin's face, as though he was dreaming about something vaguely amusing. Dmitri touched his finger to the corner of Efrosin's up-turned mouth and decided that, knowing Efrosin, he probably was.

Dmitri remembered Efrosin's words the night before. "Is it always this way, Dmitri?" Efrosin had asked. "I'm so happy. I don't think I've ever been quite this happy. I've been delighted and cheerful and eager and silly and many other things, but this is a different thing altogether. I feel quite full with it."

Looking at Efrosin, so effortlessly handsome in his sleep, Dmitri felt full with it too. But then he frowned as the heaviness of reality settled over him. This couldn't last for long, and that it might in fact end this very day filled him with a sense of wounded despair. Yet what was best for Efrosin had to come before his own petty needs and wants.

Sighing, Dmitri carefully rose and pulled on his warm breeches, dried by the fire the night before. As he slipped on his rough shirt, so much less fine than Efrosin's soft clothes, he glanced at the bed. Efrosin snuffled softly but didn't wake. Dmitri looked closer, and he blinked a bit in surprise. Efrosin's head, hands and legs were touching the mattress. They did not float as they had the morning before, and as Dmitri watched, one of Efrosin's feet slipped from the bed and dangled close to the ground instead of drifting into the air.

As Dmitri stared, Efrosin's foot began to slowly rise, as though regaining its levity, and soon it was floating again. Dmitri frowned, then shrugged as he took up the sharp blade he kept for shaving as he usually did in the mornings. But then, remembering Efrosin's numerous mentions of Sir Carlisle's beard, he left it.

Dmitri tugged his boots into place and quickly shoved his hunting knife, some rope and a biscuit into his bag, deciding to check the traps. He'd never made it the day before, and he did not like to think of an injured animal left suffering in his traps for lack of a human hand to bring it the comfort of death.

Dmitri hovered by the bed, his hand outstretched to shake Efrosin awake, but at the last moment he refrained, not wanting to disturb Efrosin's rest after their long night of intense lovemaking. He needed to rest, possibly to heal, after the rough coupling they'd done in the small hours of the morning. Dmitri's heart felt pricked as he observed the tousled golden hair against Efrosin's forehead, and the thud of Efrosin's pulse in his neck. Even it looked light and cheerful, beating away there like the flutter of a bird's wings.

He pressed a kiss to Efrosin's lips and soothed him back to deep sleep with a soft "Shhh," and then went on his way.

He hadn't gone very far into the woods when a black bird swooped onto his path, cawing. Dmitri stepped back, a little frightened by the way the bird snapped its wings and blocked his way. It was then that he felt her, the great, terrible weight of presence behind him. He turned slowly away from the bird, reluctant to take his eyes from it lest it attack, but needing to see what creature had appeared at his back all the same.

The old woman was small and not small all at once. Her hair was coated with mud, and tiny seedlings grew from her head—evergreens and maples, tiny oaks and baby lindens. Her hands and feet were thick with dirt, almost as if she'd used them to claw out of the earth, and her dress looked made of black moss, with ants and small beetles crawling over it. Her face was startling to look upon, so dirty and streaked with grime, but her eyes glittered provocatively, and her lips curled in a withering smile. Dmitri stared.

"Don't you have a kiss for your mother?" she asked, leaning toward him with her mud-smeared lips puckered.

He pulled back instinctively to get away from the fetid smell of her breath and person. "You're not my mother. You're the witch who cursed me as a babe."

She cackled. "I'm everyone's mother, and no one's mother, boy." Her fingers curled into claws and she lurched at him, grabbing a fistful of his shirt. "If not for me, you'd all be dead—especially you—and yet do any of you want to kiss the old woman, fill her with your sweet young prick?" She spat on the ground.

Dmitri's throat felt dry as he swallowed convulsively. The woman—no, the witch—ran one finger down the side of his cheek and trailed it over his lips. "All red and swollen, I see," she said. "With the telltale signs of a man's stubble against your chin." Her finger was bone dry as it touched the tender skin of his jaw, raw from Efrosin's evening beard. "Cavorting with a missing prince perhaps?"

Dmitri's tongue felt heavy, as if weighted by magic, and he could only stare at the woman as she nodded slowly and licked her lips with a tongue that was dark as the most fertile soil. "Oh yes, the entire kingdom is looking for him. It seems he floated away." She tsked slowly. "Such a shame. His father fears he's dead."

Dmitri felt stabbed through with guilt. He hated the thought that anyone might feel the same grief that he endured after his parents' death. He should have tried harder to get Efrosin back home or to draw attention to his whereabouts. But Efrosin had such need—desires echoed in Dmitri's own heart.

"The king's mourning is full of rage. He holds the prince's minder responsible, even as the man scours the land for his missing charge. The king will execute the man's wife and children at dawn should the prince not be returned. The king is an unreasonable man—so cruel, so selfish. I understand him. I'm cruel and selfish too."

Dmitri shuddered. "I must get Efrosin back to the castle. He said he could swim..."

Her eyes flashed and her long nails dug into Dmitri's chest. "Oh yes, he can swim. But don't fret, his saviors are on their way. My friend here," she indicated the bird, "told the young prince's manservant where they could find him. How long will it be, darling, before they arrive?"

The bird cawed.

"Ah, within the hour," the witch said.

Dmitri's emotions swelled inside him, a jumble of relief that Efrosin would be safe, despair at losing him, and violent terror of the witch and her bird. He opened his mouth to speak but could not. The witch raised her other hand and held it to Dmitri's heart. His eyes bulged and he began to shake; his heart felt as if it was slowing down and growing rigid in his chest.

He could not break his gaze from the witch's face. He tried to force his legs to move, to run, but he was held fast to the ground as though he'd been turned to stone. The witch kissed him, shoving her tongue into his mouth, and he gagged at the taste of mud and rotting compost.

She grimaced when she pulled back and said, "Disgusting. You're corrupted by love." Then suddenly Dmitri's knees buckled and he was on the ground at her feet. She pointed at him. "Stay."

He found that he could not move even if he wanted to. He could not even blink.

"Let me tell you a story, little one," the old woman said, her teeth shining in the morning light like beads of black onyx. "It's a very important story, you see. It contains your life and death. So pay attention."

And then the witch told Dmitri her tale—and his.

ONCE UPON A time, there was a strong-running river called Inna, named for the beautiful witch of the waters. She was one of four beautiful sisters, each a sorceress, and each holding dominion over an element.

The first born was Ereshkigal, witch of earth. She was dark and thick of body, with skin that was milky-white and eyes that were the color of fresh dung. She was born old, older than time, and strong. Many common humans believed her to be a steady sort, earthy and rich with generosity. But she shifted violently beneath the surface, full of hot, liquid yearning that boiled and bubbled, passionate and wanting.

The second born was Aira, witch of the wind. She was beautiful with her white hair, soft as clouds, and her blue eyes as vast as the sky. But she was a flighty, reckless thing, never staying any place for long, darting from lover to lover, changeable as the wind can be, incapable of attachment or loyalty.

The third born was Uriti, witch of fire. She too was beautiful, with red and blue-streaked hair, bright cheeks and flaming eyes. But she was hot tempered and hard to control, often leaping from bed to bed, burning a path of intense but short-lived passion through the world, destroying many a marriage and home as she went.

The fourth born was Inna, witch of waters. She was beautiful with light hair and eyes that sparkled like the sun dancing on waves. Her manner was easy and accommodating, flowing from one activity to the next, easily bypassing obstacles and laughing beautifully along the way. Her embrace was complete, and many a man drowned in love for her.

Then King Leo rode into their lives.

He arrived in the valley where the known world converges on the unknown on horseback, bathed in blood from battle, adorned in armor, shining like the sun. The sisters waited there for him, having all four felt the pull of destiny; all together in the same place for the first time in their lives.

Leo was strong of arm and stronger of mind, unyielding in his intentions. He announced his desire to wed one of them, and commanded each to give their best argument why she, and only she, should be his wife.

Aira laughed and departed at once, preferring the joy of airy freedom. Uriti raged briefly at his impudence, scorched his armor and then disappeared as well, eager to get back to the bed she had been burning with lust when she'd received the summons.

Inna, for her part, merely waited to see what would happen next, good-naturedly dancing about, her hair flowing out behind her, and her feet tripping easily over the rocks and fallen trees.

As for Ereshkigal, she fell in love with him upon first sight.

The truth of Ereshkigal is that she is not steady. She is cruel, changeable and punishing. Rivers of lava from an erupting volcano are her temper tantrums. The violent lurching of the ground splitting apart, and coming together, destroying everything that has been built on top of the earth are her rages. Winters of starvation after crops fail are her most even-handed punishment. Ereshkigal merely laughs and shrugs as mothers and children waste away, crying out in hunger, and begging, "Why?"

The answer, dear child, to that time-old question is this—she despises you for raking the skin of her beloved earth with the tines of your plows, for scarring her, for taking the fruits of her land to multiply and grow your own kind, and not one of you making love to her, stuffing your prick into her old, worn carcass with glee and joy, nor caring if she herself is barren and lonely, not noticing that no one loves her gently, or takes her roughly, or fills her with sweet progeny of her own.

Selfish, all of you, wanting only what you can have. Wheat and fruit for yourselves, and grass for your horses, scorning the old lady who is too proud to beg for the sweet taste of love. Scorned and laughed at, despised and rejected by men and women alike. Men like Leo, who spit on Ereshkigal despite her love for him.

"Get thee away from me, wretched old cow with the teeth of rotting corpses," Leo cried, shoving Ereshkigal aside and setting his eyes on Inna. "Why would I want an old woman like you when I can plow that sweetness there?"

Ereshkigal boiled, bubbled and raged. For Ereshkigal was the one who was fertile, the one who should be plowed and sown. That was what she was made for, could the fool not see? She was earth, she was mother, she was giving and cruel and harsh and generous. She was young and old. She was the beginning and the end.

Inna was beautiful but not meant to grow life in her belly, not meant to push that life out and live to do it again. But the king saw only her easy beauty, lusted for her, and wanted her for his own. Inna, for her part, felt the tug of destiny, if not the consuming fire of love, and turned her back on her powers to marry the king, abandoning witchhood to be the wife of King Leo. Death is what comes of a witch subverting her power for the love of a vain, violent king.

Ereshkigal saw it all. She saw the future and she knew her revenge would come. Her sister would die, and then Ereshkigal would destroy the king's happiness by cursing his murdering infant son. She made him repellent to the earth, certain that the sky and the stars would claim him 'ere long.

But even a witch like Ereshkigal cannot control it all. Her sister, Uriti, saved the child with his mother's gift of water, and within that wet embrace the curse does not hold dominion. Even now the thought makes Ereshkigal shriek with rage.

And then there is you, born Dmitri, the little farmer, born straight from the dirt of the earth—and fathered by the fairies. Oh yes, my boy. You think that fool woodcutter, old as he was, got your mother with child? Don't be stupid. His prick could barely piss much less crow with proud, life-giving seed.

Once upon a time, there was a lonely woodcutter's wife. Beautiful and young, married to a man who was good, indeed he was, but he was old and unable to rouse lust in one as ripe as she. The old man traveled often, carting his wood from house to house, selling it for pennies, while his wife was left alone to tend their garden and cabin.

One such day, the mud-baked earth fairies, those bound to the earth and tasked with making the land fertile, heard the keens of her loneliness and distress. They felt your mother's wish for a child, and could not bear to see her need go unfulfilled. They are empathetic creatures, earth fairies, obnoxiously eager to encourage life at all turns.

It can't be helped. Just as they are bound to the land, they are compelled to meet the needs of humans. So the fairies grew tall with their urge to comfort her, and when they were quite human height, they knocked on her cabin door. For hours they took turns with her.

Have no fear, boy. It was not rape. She sobbed only with pleasure and grateful joy at the unflagging thrusts of their robust pricks, just as you trembled with gratitude while you plowed the cursed prince you're harboring in your bed because you could not refuse his need.

And when the fae left your mother shivering in wanton delight, covered in their mud and filled with their spendings, they returned, right-sized, to her garden. It burst into full bloom and bulged with early ripened crops.

She was planted full of you, Dmitri, her little farmer. Full of earth and life, making you part mud, and far too much fairy. I sensed the wrong done, the earth fairies planting where they ought only to tend, but they have minds of their own, don't they? Do they obey Ereshkigal? No, they do not. But I had no need to curse you, boy. Your fairy half binds you to this land, alone for all your days.

Until you plucked the prince from the sky, seducing him into your arms, weighing him down, undermining my curse. You have seen the evidence yourself. Your presence gives him weight, your very name on his lips drags his toe against my sacred ground. Why do you think he was so taken with you? You fulfill his every need. Oh don't bother with your sob story of how you never meant to thwart me, that you didn't know, that you never dared. It is your destiny; you could not have prevented it if you tried.

Together, you and he are earth and air and water, and your passion is fire—a balance that offsets my curse. But I cannot allow it. Are you listening, child? This is where it gets interesting.

There behind you is a lake, or shall I say there was a lake? For within the hour it will be empty, disappeared through a tiny hole—just about the size of your big toe—flowing into an underground channel out and away to the ocean, hundreds of miles from this land. As it goes, so will every river, pond, lake, well and stream in the Kingdom Goldenthal, now and forever more. No rain will fill them, no snows will melt and make them replete again.

The people will thirst. They will suffer and die. It shan't take long—don't worry. It's an ugly death, but a fast one all the same. It takes longer for my bird here to peck one to death, and longer yet to starve. I could be less merciful, you see.

Why, you want to know? Because Leo's son, my sister's brat, will not have both love and water. My curse will not be undermined by your freakish existence. It is a correction I make to a wrong done—you should not exist, and your lover should not go unpunished for the sins of his father. I was merciful when you were a babe, allowing you to live, bound to the earth that is a part of you and your fairy fathers.

There will be no more mercy from Ereshkigal. My misery will belong to all.

How is it possible to dry up every last drop of water, you ask? A curse, of course. And just as you say, for every curse, there is a cure, if only one can find it. But I won't make you hunt. I'll tell you now how you may save your prince's happiness and the people's wretched lives.

Are you listening carefully? That small hole I punched in the earth under the lake is enchanted and can only be filled by the big toe of a man. This man must voluntarily give his life to plug the hole, and it will not stay sealed should his toe ever be removed. Clever, isn't it? For Ereshkigal has always been clever. One life sacrificed shall save so many.

And think, Dmitri, you will be free. Just as the fae who sired you are no longer bound to this earth now that they are but ashes on the wind, you'll be free. Did I mention the man who gallantly plugs this hole must be half-fairy, half-human and in love with a prince who lacks gravity? Do you know of any such person?

I think you might.

Chapter Seven

G EOFFRY TIED HIS naked charge securely to the bench next to the wooden table in the small cabin where they'd found him and began to clean Efrosin. The lad was covered in the remnants of intercourse, and any thought Geoffry might have had of Efrosin being unwillingly seduced was countered by his delighted recounting of far too many details of the events.

"It truly is the best feeling, is it not, Geoffry? I feel I've sorely missed out before now, and it's quite unfair to be deprived of so many years of pleasure."

"You are not so very old, sire," Geoffry said, his face flaming bright red as he wiped at the dried evidence of Efrosin's enjoyment. "There are many years yet to experience this joy." He cleared his throat. "Sire, it is imperative that you dress. We must soon be on our way. There is a dire situation that can only be—"

Efrosin didn't appear to be listening. "His name is Dmitri, did I tell you? Oh you must meet him, Geoffry. He is so very funny."

"You think everyone is funny."

"But he truly is. He buried his parents! In graves he dug himself!"

Geoffry blinked, untied Efrosin from the bench and watched him bob directly up to the low ceiling. "Truly, we must go. As I told you earlier, I'm lucky to be alive. Your father nearly hanged me the first day, and my children—"

Efrosin clapped as his eyes lit up. Kicking off the ceiling, he grabbed hold of Geoffry's lapels, dangling there in front of him, his feet drifting heavenward. "Oh yes, bravo. Tell me, Geoffry, how did you do it? How did you survive such peril? It must have been so thrilling."

"I promised your father, should he spare my life, that I would bring you to him before sunrise tomorrow. He holds my dear ones in my stead, so I must get you back to the castle, sire."

Efrosin prattled on as if Geoffry hadn't spoken. "I'm glad, by the way, that you live. I had writ you off for dead. Even Dmitri will be surprised because I told him you had surely been put to death for losing me. You must meet him. His eyes are like chocolate, and his lips are sweeter than Papa's best wine, and he smells of the earth and tastes like dirt. Did you know that dirt tastes ever so delightful? Well, it does when it's Dmitri."

Geoffry cleared his throat, blushing as he said, "Surely there is someone who will taste just as fine at home."

"I think not. Of every man I know, Dmitri is the only one I want. Well, except perhaps Sir Carlisle, but he does not dabble in men. Which is a shame, because his thighs and arms are so very strong, and—"

"Sire," Geoffry stopped him before he could go on. Sir Carlisle and the other knights of Efrosin's escort waited just outside the door, all of them embarrassed enough by the state in which they'd found his highness—tied to a bed with a rosy, hard prick, wet at the tip from longing, and clearly thoroughly debauched.

Geoffry put aside the uncomfortable memory and went back to attempting to engage Efrosin's cooperation. "Please put on your clothing."

Efrosin ignored him. "No, no, even though Sir Carlisle has many fine qualities, there is no one but Dmitri for me." He sighed, allowing Geoffry to help him with a shirt. "Can you not simply send a message? Surely the knights can ride on ahead, tell my father that I live, and I can stay with Dmitri. I told you, I'm not ready to leave him yet."

"Your father will not believe us, Prince Efrosin. He's out of his mind with suspicion and grief. He'll think I am lying to buy my children time. And you will find someone more…suitable. At court. Where your father awaits you with a heavy heart, mourning you for dead."

"Oh poor Papa," Efrosin said airily, and Geoffry sighed. Some things never changed. He gathered more water on the rough cloth he'd found and scrubbed at the clumps of spendings in Efrosin's golden chest hair. Then again some things did.

"Wait—what was that you said about your children?" Efrosin asked.

Geoffry blinked in surprise. "We must return by dawn, or the king will see my offspring dead for my crime of losing you."

Efrosin frowned. "But that is quite unfair, is it not?"

"It is, sire. So we must be going. We will return with hours to spare, but still, let us make haste."

"Indeed. We must just find my Dmitri and we may be off."

"The gentleman will not be going with us?" Geoffry asked.

"Of course not."

Geoffry was pleased that Efrosin now saw the folly of that association. "That is well."

"Dmitri is cursed to remain here on his land," Efrosin said. "Which is why I must say goodbye and let him know that I'll return to him anon."

Geoffry helped his prince get his stained pants on and quietly signaled for the knights. He hated to go against Efrosin's wishes, but he had no choice.

"Wait! What are you doing?" Efrosin asked, pushing against Sir Carlisle's shoulders as he was effortlessly plucked from the air and restrained.

"We don't have time," Geoffry said. "I'm sorry, but you must leave without saying goodbye."

Efrosin squirmed and kicked. "You said we have hours to spare."

Geoffry was appalled by the young man's lack of manners when he actually attempted to bite Sir Carlisle in his attempt to get free. Once they had wrapped him tightly, and Sir Carlisle exited the hovel, Efrosin stilled and grew quiet, likely due to his fear of the endless sky.

Geoffry felt unsettled as they climbed upon their horses with Sir Carlisle holding Efrosin tight to his chest while he mounted his great stallion. Geoffry could not take his eyes from Efrosin's pale face as they rode away, walking the horses in the close quarters of the thick, cloying forest. "Are you quite all right, sire? You look," and here Geoffry frowned, "sad."

"I find I am not at all right, actually," Efrosin answered, staring back the way they came. "Something is lodged inside my chest. I find it rather hard to breathe. I believe this horrible feeling would stop if I went back. I must be with Dmitri."

"You must continue home."

"But this feeling. This horrible, awful feeling, Geoffry." Efrosin's expression was stricken. "Is it gravity? It feels quite heavy and hard."

"No, sire, I believe this feeling is what we call 'love'. But knowing you as I do, I believe it will pass."

"No. Love is what I felt when I was happy in Dmitri's arms last night. This is something horrible and I don't think I can bear it much longer."

Sir Carlisle shifted Efrosin against his chest, a bewildered expression on his face as Efrosin's eyes took on an odd glow, and he began to chant in a whisper, "Dmitri, Dmitri, Dmitri, Dmitri," over and over with a backing note of determination in his voice that made Geoffry shiver.

Sir Carlisle grunted and hefted Efrosin a bit. "He grows heavy," he said. "What sort of magic is this? I have carried him since he was but a child, and he has never weighed an ounce."

Efrosin began to shout Dmitri's name, and as he did Sir Carlisle struggled with his sudden weight. Geoffry cried out as Efrosin's fingers worked quickly to untie his restraints, and when Sir Carlisle tried to grip him tighter, Efrosin threw a wild and direct punch, landing it squarely on Sir Carlisle's nose. Blood spurted, shouts erupted, and before Geoffry's stunned eyes, Efrosin jumped from the stallion's back and lighted upon the earth.

"Dmitri! Dmitri!" Efrosin's body rose lightly in the pause between the words, his feet barely touching the ground, but he did not float away. As the brave knights sat frozen and shocked upon their horses, Efrosin raced into the forest, stumbling over branches but never quite falling down, screaming his lover's name.

Geoffry's heart raced madly. His Efrosin, his prince, was cured! Joy rivaled with frustration at Efrosin's selfishness, and despair for the impending loss of Geoffry's family should Efrosin not return home by sunrise. He called out, "We must retrieve him!"

Their horses raced down the path into the deep of the woods, following the sound of Efrosin's voice on the wind.

EFROSIN'S THROAT FELT torn. His voice was fading fast. The force with which he had to yell Dmitri's name in order to stay on the ground was more than he could sustain for long. He didn't know what magic allowed for this miracle, but he'd felt the changes in him from the moment he met Dmitri and the first time he'd uttered his name.

"Dmitri! Dmitri!" If his voice gave way entirely, he would be lost. With that in mind, he headed toward the lake.

Just let the knights try to drag him from the water. He could outswim them all. He was not leaving until he had seen Dmitri, pledged his love and given his promise to return. If Dmitri should return from wherever he had wandered and find the cabin empty, he would fear Efrosin had been caught on a breeze and floated away.

The thought of Dmitri frightened for his sake made Efrosin's skin feel tight and prickly, as if it did not quite fit right. He supposed the sensation was what Geoffry had told him was "empathy" or perhaps "guilt", but either way he didn't like it, and he would risk anything to stop Dmitri from feeling such pain.

Besides, he told himself, the castle was but a few leagues' ride away, and they had until sunrise to stay his father's hand. There was time yet.

As the lake came into view Efrosin's breath caught in his throat, and he lifted off the ground in his stunned silence. The water was low—

quite low—little more than neck-deep in places where he and Dmitri had been in well over their heads only the night before. He floated another foot higher as he spied a person in the middle of the lake, standing stock still, the water coming up almost to the man's chin.

"Dmitri," he breathed. His toe grazed land. "Dmitri!"

Dmitri did not turn, his shoulders set squarely to the southern mountains. Efrosin chanted Dmitri's name, his toes barely touching the ground, and he dove into the shallow water without bothering to take off his clothes. He felt the sweet relief of the lake's embrace only dimly in his panic, for there was something wrong. He didn't know just what, but a strong physical pull in his gut, groin and chest told him to swim to Dmitri. Now.

As Efrosin approached, Dmitri's lips were set in a grim line, his eyes closed. When Efrosin called his name, he did not respond. Efrosin's stomach twisted painfully, like the stomach cramps he had after eating bad oysters as a child, and he felt he might be sick though he didn't know quite why. Efrosin finally reached Dmitri and gripped his arms tightly, shaking him, expecting him to move easily through the water and slide wetly into his arms.

Instead, Dmitri held fast. Efrosin shook him, "Dmitri! Are you caught?"

"Efrosin…" Dmitri's eyes opened and his voice was soft. "Am I dead already? Are you my angel even still?"

"Dead? I should think not. I've found you now. Have no fear. I'll save you, Dmitri. Just hold on. We must act quickly. The water is rising fast—where did it disappear to?"

Dmitri stared at him tenderly. "How did you get here? Did you fly?"

"Are you ill? Answer me, Dmitri. Tell me where to pull!"

Dmitri's eyes sharpened then. He shook his head. "Leave me. It's too late."

Fear gripped Efrosin far beyond his prior imagining. He dove beneath the surface and, following the line of Dmitri's body down, he finally located the problem—the big toe of Dmitri's left foot was caught in a tight hole. Efrosin pulled hard at Dmitri's leg, but the toe was stuck fast, and Dmitri did naught to help.

Lungs burning, Efrosin burst through to the surface and saw even in that short amount of time the lake had risen to cover Dmitri's chin. From the corner of his eye he saw the knights and Geoffry dismount from their horses near the shore. They called for him, but he remained focused.

"You must help me, Dmitri. Pull as I tug. We must get you free. The water is rising."

"Efrosin," Dmitri said, reaching out to him, pulling him close. "Don't fight it. Only know that I did this for you and for the people of our land."

"Whatever are you talking about?" Efrosin's throat was so tight he could barely speak.

"I don't have time to explain it." Even now the water was slipping into his mouth, and Dmitri had to tip his head back to keep it from filling his throat completely. "There's only one thing you have to know—my toe must never leave the hole at the bottom of the lake or the water will drain from the kingdom. No matter what happens, never dislodge it. Do I have your promise?"

Efrosin shook his head violently. "I will never leave you here."

"It's my dying wish." He coughed, choking on the relentless water. "You can't take my toe from its place in the bottom of the lake. Promise me now before I die."

Efrosin blinked rapidly and then gave a short, fast nod. He turned and yelled to the knights swimming toward them. "I need a knife! Bring me a knife!"

"It's too late," Dmitri said, gasping for breath. "I'll be free now. I know you can't mourn me, but do think of me from time to time." He spluttered and coughed desperately.

The water closed over his mouth, and then over his nose and eyes. Efrosin cried out in agony, tugging at Dmitri's shoulders as he stared down at his lover's brown eyes gazing up at him from beneath the clear water.

Then the bubbles of Dmitri's final breath released, and Efrosin dove beneath the water, pressing his lips to Dmitri's and breathing into his mouth. But Dmitri did not take the breath, and there beneath the water his body spasmed and jerked, his eyes going wide before he stilled completely.

Efrosin broke the surface, shouting again for a knife, and when the knights reached him he grabbed the blade from Sir Carlisle's hand and swam down to Dmitri's foot, slicing in rough, jagged swipes at his toe. The bone was hard to sever, but Efrosin's panic gave him strength. Blood clouded the water, rising and twisting around him as he worked, but he didn't give up until Dmitri's body was released.

All but for his toe, which Efrosin left as promised in the greedy hole at the bottom of the lake.

AT THE WATER'S edge, Efrosin knelt in the shallows and watched Geoffry work on Dmitri. A sound clawed its way from Efrosin's throat, piercing the air around them. He couldn't stop touching Dmitri, his fingers clinging to the wet fabric of his breeches.

Geoffry pounded on Dmitri's chest, slapped his face, lifted him up and thumped on his back. Still Dmitri's eyes that had been rich with life like the most fertile loam remained unseeing. Time seemed to stop. The knights stood watch, unmoving. The leaves on the trees were still; the very clouds in the sky were frozen. The only motion was Geoffry as he worked, and the treacherous lake as it deepened around Efrosin's thighs.

"I shall choke," Efrosin cried. "I am crushed beneath this weight. You must save him, Geoffry. You must!"

Geoffry worked tirelessly, but for naught. Finally, Efrosin felt his heart sink to the lowest depths of hell as Geoffry looked up at him with tired, sad eyes. "Sire, he is gone."

Efrosin could not breathe, could not feel his heart beat where it had plummeted so deep into despair. He threw himself up out of the water, onto Dmitri's body, gripping his neck tightly. "No!"

To the shock of everyone, Efrosin burst into sobs. What's more, he did not float at all. Like a cloud erupting with heavy rain, he found his gravity weeping against his dead lover's neck. He flowed with hot, wild tears that rushed from him in a mad torrent that could not be staved. They ran down his face, one after another, onto Dmitri's unmoving chest.

The world seemed to release its bated breath. The outcome had been determined. Dmitri, half fairy of the land, was dead. The wind tossed the leaves in the trees, and the clouds skittered across the sky. The knights fell to their knees in prayer, and Geoffry ran his fingers over Efrosin's hair, clucking a sound meant to soothe.

Efrosin pressed his lips against Dmitri's motionless mouth, sobbing into him, and as his tears fell into Dmitri's still-open eyes, he choked out, "Heaven can't be better than me, Dmitri. Please. I need you. Don't go."

I need you.

Don't go.

DMITRI HAD NEVER known such freedom. His soul was boundless, infinite. The light was bright and comforting as he traveled toward it effortlessly, and he was reminded of Efrosin rising up toward the sky. The thought hurt and he grabbed his chest, glancing down to find he was rising above the earth.

Kneeling knights and a weary man circled his body, and upon his lifeless form was Efrosin—delightful, joyful, beautiful Efrosin—sobbing without restraint, his tears raining down on Dmitri's empty face.

He looked down into his own eyes, wet now with Efrosin's tears, and shivered. He wondered at Efrosin's grief. Did he...was this for him? He had not imagined Efrosin capable.

I need you.

Don't go.

It reached him like a prayer, a magic enchantment. Yet now that he was released from the mortal coil, his fairy blood no longer tugged at him to meet Efrosin's need. Now it was only Dmitri's own heart and soul that yearned to quench that desire, comfort that grief and fill Efrosin with an answering adoration. He glanced up one last time at the warm, golden light awaiting him. He turned away...

Heavy.

His lungs burned, a terrible pressure in his chest. Coughing, Dmitri jerked up, knocking Efrosin from him. He expelled lake water from his lungs until he vomited it in a massive stream. Hands beat against his back and shoulders, and he gasped for air, finally dragging in a long, clean breath. He became aware of a fiery sensation in his left foot, a throbbing agony he couldn't explain.

Efrosin still sobbed next to him. Dmitri tried to tell him he was back, and Efrosin could stop crying now, but nothing came out save a croak. Efrosin's hands were greedy on him, gripping his wet shirt, twisting into his short hair, and his mouth was everywhere, kissing his lake-water lips, eyelids, nose, neck, mouth, cheeks and every inch in between.

"Never go, you can't go," Efrosin cried, his voice ragged and wild.

Dmitri grabbed Efrosin close and held his shaking body, realizing he was shaking himself. He kissed him gently. "I'm here. Don't cry now, my Efrosin."

"But I must. I truly must."

Dmitri held Efrosin tight as the tears continued to flow, marveling at the number and intensity of them. It was as if Efrosin cried for all the wounds and pains of his life for which he'd never cried before. Dmitri stroked his back, murmuring, telling him not to fear—he'd live as long as Efrosin commanded him to live. This only set off fresh sobs.

Dmitri gritted his teeth as one of the knights bound Dmitri's foot tightly with cloth. The knight spoke to Geoffry. "His short-lived demise seems to have slowed the flow of blood. Still, he must have the wound attended to by the healer."

Geoffry nodded. "Of course." To Dmitri he said, "The sooner we go, the sooner you may be treated and my children's lives saved."

Dmitri frowned. "Your children?"

Efrosin's tears did not stop flowing as Geoffry explained their predicament, and Dmitri held Efrosin close before forcing himself to his feet, wincing at the terrible pain in his foot. "Of course, we must go immediately."

Two of the knights helped Efrosin to his feet, and since walking was a feat of gravity that Efrosin did not yet entirely grasp, Sir Carlisle aided him in his steps. The other knights helped Dmitri hobble to the horses, and when they reached them Efrosin clutched Dmitri's hand.

"Dmitri, will you be all right here alone while you await my return with a healer? Should I leave one of the knights with you?" Efrosin sniffled loudly.

Dmitri swiped his thumb across Efrosin's wet cheek. "There's no need to wait. It was just as I told you. Death released my bonds. I am free." He'd tell Efrosin about his fairy heritage when lives didn't hang in the balance.

"Truly?"

"Truly."

Efrosin face brightened, and then his expression turned determined. "Bring the horses," he ordered the knights. "We must leave quickly."

Geoffry bowed his head in gratitude. "Yes, thank you. Let us make haste."

"Dmitri and I shall ride together."

"He is weak. You shall ride with me, sire." Sir Carlisle led over his horse.

Efrosin snatched away the reins. "I think not." With a grunt, he attempted to heave himself into the saddle as the horse neighed.

"Not a stallion, sire," Geoffry said. "Please, you may take my horse. She's steady and polite, not meant for hard riding like a knight's steed."

Efrosin, to Dmitri's surprise, didn't argue, and took the few troubled steps, assisted by Sir Carlisle, to the horse Geoffry proffered. He again tried to haul himself onto the saddle.

Sir Carlisle said, "You must first learn to befriend gravity, sire."

"There is no time like the present," Efrosin said in an odd mix of new gravitas, pragmatism and his usual cheerful lack of sense.

Sir Carlisle helped Efrosin get his leg over the animal's broad back. "Careful. Not too far or you'll fall off the other side."

"This gravity everyone loves so well is rather useless," Efrosin grumbled, his still-wet lashes sparkling in the midday sun.

"Useless?" Dmitri asked, gritting his teeth as Sir Carlisle helped him settle behind Efrosin atop the mare. "My Efrosin, you are not floating away into the clouds. Given my wish to keep you safe, I find that rather useful indeed."

Off they rode, travelling in a single line through the dense forest. Dmitri kept his arms tight around Efrosin and gazed about avidly, paying no attention to the throbbing from his foot, so eager was he for a glimpse of new lands. Suddenly there was an odd clacking sound in the distance.

His pulse raced as the woods thinned and they approached the growing din. There before him, a road wound into the distance—a road with many carts rumbling and horses clopping. He swallowed hard, thinking of his many books and the faraway lands he'd only read about. Tears prickled his eyes.

"Dmitri?" Efrosin asked. He glanced over his shoulder. "Are you well?"

The boundaries of Dmitri's world became as limitless as the sky itself. "Oh Efrosin. What a grand adventure this shall be."

Dmitri bent and kissed Efrosin's parted lips. It tasted of clouds. Of freedom.

Epilogue

A LONG, LONG time ago, the sun set on a kingdom that was changed from the one it rose upon. For the Light Prince was light no more, and his beloved was unbound.

After shocking the prince's father with evidence not only of Efrosin's life but of his sudden onset of gravity, Efrosin and Dmitri were tended to by healers, and Geoffry's children set free with nary a hair on their wee heads harmed.

And once it was confirmed that, yes, the prince's weighted condition would not be reversed, and yes, his consort would survive the loss of his toe, Efrosin and Dmitri celebrated their love and freedom with weeks of joyous trysting in every private corner of the castle.

Once they had both learned to walk—for one was unaccustomed to bearing weight, and the other unaccustomed to a left foot that bore no big toe—they travelled together to distant lands, exploring the world Dmitri had previously only dreamt of seeing. As they journeyed, their affection for one another grew deep roots of love until they were inseparable—always where there was one, there was the other.

While they were afar, Ereshkigal the witch called a meeting with the aging king. "Come with me," she said, reaching out to Leo with her mossy fingers, grinning with her black teeth. "Your power is waning. But I can return you to full strength. Come, and you may have all you've ever desired. We have always belonged to each other."

Leo, lusting for more power than was rightfully his, followed her and abandoned his kingdom. Efrosin and Dmitri hastened back from their travels at the news, and the young prince depended greatly on the steady, generous heart of his lover to help him during the kingdom's time of need.

The prince sent his best knights to seek Ereshkigal's lair or any sign of his father, to no avail. The witch and king seemed to have vanished deep into the very earth. When many months had come and gone, his father was declared dead and the Light Prince was made king. Geoffry, who had loved and cared for the prince over many years, was appointed his closest advisor, and the new king ruled with fairness and grace.

Not long after their return and Efrosin's coronation, a wedding was celebrated unlike any the kingdom had ever seen. Both grooms dressed in resplendent white and silver, and upon the bank of the river they repeated their vows before God and the world—before diving in for a swim.

Which leaves but one story to tell of another joyous day when the sun set again on a world made new.

Once upon a time, there was a kingdom at the edge of what was and what could never be. At the center of this kingdom was a castle, and within this castle was a king. Inside this king was a terribly happy heart.

For on that day, the king and his prince stood hand-in-hand in the birthing chamber watching over the delivery of their child. Neither particularly cared if it was a girl or a boy, only that it be born healthy— and preferably free of magical entanglements.

The maid who had offered her services to be mother of the heir squirmed on the massive oak bed and cried out, her swollen, naked body sweating. Efrosin turned his head away, burying his face in Dmitri's neck, whispering, "Let me know when I may look again. Dear God, the poor woman. We must reward her well."

Nine moons before, their lovingly obtained spendings had been mixed in a vial, and a midwife had deposited the contents deep within the maid, close to the mouth of her eager womb. The child had taken the very first month, so sure was it of its desire to be brought into the world.

When a cry filled the air, Dmitri felt something stir in his chest, an already-love that took his breath away. Beside him, his husband's eyes gleamed with tears as he smiled, weighted with the heaviness of emotion and the enormity of responsibility.

The sun burst into the room as the shutters were thrown wide. Efrosin and Dmitri stood framed in the window of the high turret room, holding their naked child between them.

"Kneel to your future Queen!"

The infant's wails were soon drowned out by the cheers of the people rising high into the sky. Dmitri smiled wide, for only he and their child heard over the roar of the crowd below the laughter bubbling up from Efrosin's chest, echoing the joy in his own heart.

And they all lived happily ever after.

THE END

FLIGHT

Leta Blake

There's no greater mystery in the kingdom than where Prince Mateo's sisters disappear to each night. The king is determined to discover where they go and issues a challenge to all the nobles to help him learn their secret. Hoping to protect them, Mateo hides beneath a magic cloak and follows his sisters to an enchanted world of fairies and lusty delights.

Ópalo has waited years to finally meet his human lover. Fairies are bound by fate, and Ópalo is eager to embrace his, and plans a future with Mateo. But while Mateo soon succumbs to the pleasures of the flesh, he refuses to surrender his heart so easily. As their worlds collide, Ópalo has to risk everything to win his man forever.

Prologue

"ONCE UPON A time, in a castle by a great, foamy sea, there lived a kind-hearted king and his beautiful queen." Mateo knelt on the dirt floor of the castle's dovecote, surrounded by the children of servants. The doves cooed and swooped, and a few of the older boys ducked their heads, but the youngest were far too rapt to take much notice.

"In sets of two and three, the queen gave birth to eleven girls, each more beautiful than the last, and finally to one handsome, healthy boy."

"Does that mean you think Princess Luz is the prettiest, sir?" a tall, dark boy interrupted.

"*Silencio.* I'm telling a story. Are you looking to get me into trouble with my sisters?"

Mateo was accustomed to being accosted by the children during his walk from the castle to the dovecote. He was known for spinning a good yarn, and he'd long made himself available to the young ones of the kingdom in a way he generally refrained from with the adults. Unlike unscrupulous courtiers, the children never asked for favors greater than an apple or another tale.

In some ways, he thought of himself as more like them than not. He was young and didn't yet suffer from the heavy weight of many courtly responsibilities. Just last month his sister Blanca had gone so far as to pinch his cheeks before the knights. It had been humiliating, if rather expected. A knot of frustration grew in the pit of his stomach. He and Luz had come of age several weeks past, so no matter how young at heart he might be, his family should treat him accordingly.

"More, sir?" a quiet, shy one asked, her eyes bright with hope.

Mateo had planned to spend the morning working with his doves, and he hoped to send the children away sooner rather than later, but how could he refuse such a face?

"Of course, naturally, all the king's children were vibrant, intelligent and sometimes mischievous creatures."

The children all laughed and tittered at his description of himself and his sisters, but Mateo spoke the truth. While he thought his own appearance was pleasant enough, what with his dark, curly hair, warm brown eyes, fit form and an eye for fashion—his sisters were in truth remarkably beautiful and much sought after despite their wayward tendencies.

"Laugh all you like, but the king loved them all with every beat of his heart." Mateo tried in vain to keep his mind from the fact that his father's heart was old and failing now. "And as the prince and princesses grew, the king and queen agreed theirs was a charmed life."

Mateo glanced up at the doves that seemed to be listening along. One of them cooed, and Mateo sighed. No good story came without sadness—not even his own.

"The king and queen also knew that like all beautiful things, it was too good to last." The children's gazes fell to the ground, for the whole kingdom had suffered the loss. "One dark day their fears came true. Fever ravaged the court. But the kingdom was lucky. Only one was lost. The queen fought bravely, but in the end she left the kind-hearted king and their handsome children behind."

There were other, far more pleasing and fantastical stories Mateo could tell about lands of fae, and nights of dancing, stories passed on to him and his sisters from their old nurse, but he often found himself telling this sad, all-too-true story instead. In some way it gave him comfort.

"After the queen's passing, the king became even more attached to his outrageously handsome son," here Mateo stopped and feigned arrogance, "and his eleven astoundingly gorgeous daughters."

The young ones laughed again, and Mateo continued. "He hated to let his children out of his sight, chafing even when they ventured into the village or the seaside. He worried terribly any time the princesses and prince left the castle itself, pleading with them to stay at his side. Despite the many suitors requesting their hands, the king always refused, much preferring to keep his children near him than to suffer the loss of their company."

Mateo smiled a little bitterly at this. The only people who had ever talked to his father about asking for his hand once he came of age had not been to his liking. The first had been an older, widowed king who, having found through the years that his taste ran in such a manner, hoped to start a new life with a young, handsome prince of the same persuasion. The second was a princess that Mateo believed was actually much more interested in his sister Adelita, but everyone knew Adelita's tastes did not run that way, given how she flirted with the knights.

Mateo's wants and needs had been little considered by either con-tender for his hand, so when his father refused on his behalf without even consulting him, Mateo had felt only relief. As a child, he'd dreamed of one day meeting a man who cared for him and for whom he felt admiration and love in return. But time passed, and stifled as he and his sisters were by their father's affection, Mateo no longer looked to love and marriage as a path to freedom and happiness. Rather he saw any such commitment as a smothering restriction at worst and a recipe for crushing grief at best.

Mateo sought instead a man for whom he might feel a mild affection or an enchanting affinity, and with whom he might slake the natural desire burning in his loins. For now, he was content to indulge in heated fantasies featuring one or two of the most attractive of the knights. The king and his people did not care if he married a man or a woman, so long as the marriage benefitted the kingdom.

His sisters were another matter. They had become so restless that the oldest set of triplets especially argued for their father to let them go to a husband—or a wife, in the case of Herminia. Or even to go beyond the castle's walls. Mateo could not blame them, for he yearned to spread his own wings. Yet of late, all such complaints had halted utterly. Mateo frowned, thinking of his sisters' mysterious behavior.

As if summoned by his thoughts, a voice, worn and ragged, cried out, "Mateo!" The children all stared, likely wondering who would dare to address their prince by his first name.

"Lámina," Mateo said softly, rising from his crouch to better see his old nurse above the heads of the children. She was barely as tall as the oldest of the bunch, her fuzzy hair looking thinner than ever, and her skirts muddy from her dash across the wet yard. She was panting, eyes wide, and held her hand over her heart. He feared she might collapse. "What's the matter?"

"Sir, your father." Lámina paused to catch her breath.

Mateo's heart wrenched. His father had so many spells of late. Had he collapsed? Was he all right?

Lámina alleviated his greatest fears. "He's quite angry. You should go to him immediately."

Mateo left the telling of the story, the doves and the children behind, knowing even as he raced toward the castle and into his father's court just what the crisis would be.

"YOU *WILL* TELL me where you've been going. You cannot deceive me with sweet looks and lies." The king's face was red and his second chin wobbled with righteous anger. His long red robes glowed in the sunlight streaming in from the windows overhead, and his finger shook as he pointed it at each offender one by one.

Mateo skirted around the edges of the room, moving through the dark recesses beneath the columns, pushing past courtiers, who watched and listened avidly. When Mateo finally stepped into the open area before his father's dais, he saw his eleven sisters standing in a line before the throne, dressed hastily in unkempt clothes, their hair still tied into braids for sleeping. On the floor before them, their slippers rested soles up, revealing holes worn all the way through each pair. Mateo walked past, pausing only to try to catch Luz's eye for some kind of explanation. Finally, he stood next to his father and put a hand on his unsteady shoulder. Despite his father's health and advanced years, Mateo suspected pure rage caused the tremors.

"These slippers were given to you new yesterday morning. And this is not the first time, my daughters. Every morning for two weeks you say that you go nowhere, that you do nothing, and yet look! Explain these holes. They do not come from 'nowhere' and 'nothing'." He smacked his palm against the arm of his throne.

Mateo squeezed his shoulder. "Calm, Papá."

"Papá, we have slept in our beds every night," said Adelita, the eldest and their father's favorite. She appeared a bit ragged around the edges—though somehow still vibrant—as she bowed her dark head and lowered her eyes. "We swear it."

"Yes Papá, we swear it," Blanca echoed. She was born fourteen minutes after Adelita, and her usually white cheeks were as flushed as hot-pink roses. Her eyes glowed with the obvious lie.

"Catalina," the king addressed the third of the eldest triplets, born ten minutes after Blanca. "You have always been a steadying influence on your siblings, a mother to the younger ones and a friend to the older. But now it seems you're an accomplice. You bring me shame. Redeem yourself and answer your father with the truth."

"Papá," Catalina said softly, her hands trembling along with her voice. "Please, Papá."

"Answer."

"Every night. We, all of us. We go."

The king leaned forward in anticipation of his most dependable daughter uttering the answer to his very simple question. Mateo waited too, certain that Catalina—who had never been able to tell a lie—would confess their sins. He watched his sisters squirm under their father's gaze.

"We go to sleep. In our beds. Where we remain until morning, Papá," Catalina said, lifting her chin to meet his gaze with a defiant eye.

Down the line the king went, questioning them all as Mateo silently watched. The second set of triplets—Delfina, Elisa and Felipa—and the quadruplets—Gracia, Herminia, Imelda, Josefina—and finally his twin sister Luz all insisted they'd spent the night in their beds.

"Every evening for the last two weeks you lock us in and put guards at the doors, Papá," Luz said, tension crackling in the air. She met Mateo's eye and added with a bit more shame on her face, "How could we go anywhere?"

"Yes, Father," Imelda said. She folded her arms over her chest and growled. "We don't know what happens to our shoes. Perhaps the fairies borrow them to dance."

A titter went through the court, and Mateo glanced toward Lámina, who had staggered in looking sweaty and on the verge of death. Lámina's fairy stories had been their nightly fare as they grew up and had no doubt inspired Imelda's comment.

"Please, Papá dear, may we be excused?" Herminia asked sweetly, obviously hoping to soften her sister's impertinence.

"What more do you want from us?" Imelda said. The other sisters shot her a warning look. "We've told you all we know."

"What more do I want?" The king's voice was so loud the doors rattled at the back of the room and every person within flinched, covering their ears with their hands. "The truth."

The king turned to Mateo then, his rheumy eyes burning with hot rage. "Mateo, you and Luz have always been thick as thieves. Do you have nothing to add to this conversation?"

"No, Father," Mateo answered, his eyes focused on his twin sister's face. If only he did. The king had only been the best father, gentle, kind, loving—if overly possessive and too protective by half—and it saddened Mateo to see his sisters deceiving him thus.

The king rose. "So be it. Let it be known!"

Each ear in the room turned to the king, awaiting his proclamation. Mateo saw the hopeful brightness in each eye, and noted which courtiers stepped forth from the dark shadows in anticipation of whatever drama was about to unfold before them.

"No matter how they come about the information, whatsoever man or woman can tell me where my daughters go at night, and what they do to leave their shoes in such a state, will be rewarded with a residence befitting royalty, horses and household servants."

The crowd murmured, eager voices rising until the king silenced them with a glare and continued.

"And a chance as heir to my throne with the choice of any of my children to take as wife or husband."

In the stunned hush, Mateo watched his sisters' faces, seeing panic flash through them as they understood the implication of their father's decree. Then he realized with a twist of his gut that his own fate had also been offered up to whatever rogue might manage to solve the puzzle.

"The prince too, sire?" a voice called out.

"Indeed," the king answered.

Heat surged through Mateo—anger mixed with adamant rejection of his predicament. It wasn't fair!

The king looked about, clearly anticipating that someone would come forward with information now that a general pardon had been given and such an extravagant reward offered. Mateo half expected one of his sisters to finally betray the others, perhaps by bargaining for the rights to her own hand. But their claim to innocence held fast. No sister stepped forward.

Mateo's eyes fell on Sir Franco, a knight whose strong shoulders and arms had featured prominently in Mateo's midnight fantasies. He held his breath, hoping Franco might take up the challenge, even though the man's tastes ran invariably toward women. But alas, Sir Franco turned to move deeper into the shadows. Mateo didn't know if he was relieved or disappointed.

The king gritted his teeth. "Leave me. All of you. Girls, retire to your room and remain there." To Mateo's surprise, none of his sisters moaned or wept about their confinement, but instead scampered off as though they could think of no better place than their chambers to spend the rest of their days.

Alone on the dais after his father exited as well, Mateo was immediately set upon by the courtiers, all with questions about his sisters—did he know where they went, did he have any ideas? Mateo knew that it was only a matter of time before one or more of them took up the gauntlet and tried for his father's proffered reward.

When the distinct sound of the court messengers trumpeting the king's proclamation to the village reached him, Mateo finally broke free from the insipid courtiers—none of them Sir Franco, which he decided was not disappointing. He was a grown man now and didn't need a knight to fight his battles for him. He had to convince his sisters to reveal their secret or find a manner to discover it himself. With steps fueled by determination, Mateo returned to the dovecote to feed his birds and create a plan.

Chapter One

A FTER THE KING'S proclamation, more than two hundred people from all walks of life—soldiers, tailors, princes, countesses and thieves—had come forward to try for the prize. None were turned away. As arguments broke out, a proper list was made and a procedure established.

With the caveat that any impropriety would be severely punished—and none would dare lay a finger on the princesses and enrage the king further—each fortune seeker was allowed three nights in the sisters' chambers. Then if they could provide no answer as to the girls' activities, the king moved on to the next in the long line of chancers.

So far, three men and two women had entered the sisters' chambers confident of their ability to penetrate their veil of secrets, only to fall asleep, night after night. They woke in the mornings to find the princesses, all pink cheeks and smiles, tucked in their beds—and their slippers worn through.

Of course Mateo had confronted his sisters himself, starting with Luz, but that conversation had gotten him nowhere.

"Don't you see what you're costing Papá with your games? There are murmurs in the court that if he cannot control even his own daughters, how can he rule? Own the truth, Luz. What can be the worst of it?"

Luz had merely tossed her dark head, lifted her shoulders in an elegant shrug, and walked away as if he were nothing more than an annoying bee buzzing about her head. He'd seen that gesture from his other sisters his entire life, but it was the first time from his twin. She hadn't even bothered to look remorseful.

It had gone no better with the older ones. They'd laughed at him outright, cooed, clucked and spoken to him as if he was still a child. He'd been lucky to escape their clutches with only a few flowers braided into his hair. *That* had certainly pleased the giggling servant children he'd passed on the way to the dovecote. At least Pura, his favorite dove, had plucked the blossoms from his hair and absconded with them to her nest, using her beak to twist prettiness out of his humiliation.

After the fifth fortune seeker had failed, on a day when the king was discouraged, angry and thundering with threats of taking a harsher course with his daughters, the same widowed king who'd once made the unsuccessful bid for Mateo's hand stepped up to take his chance.

"I, Rey Hernando, do hereby declare my intent to discover what mischief the princesses commit. I ask as the prize for my certain triumph only the hand of Prince Mateo. For I have riches, lands and servants already—all of which I am only too happy to share with your son, good king. I require only his companionship, kindness and his sweet love to warm my bed."

Hearing the murmur of the courtiers, and knowing full well the pictures King Hernando's words brought to their minds, Mateo's skin prickled with hot embarrassment. He had no choice but to smile politely upon the stooped man's grizzled face. He'd expected to be Hernando's choice, of course, but having it announced so baldly to the court was humiliating. The very idea of being beneath someone so old—or, depending on King Hernando's inclination, on top for that matter— made his stomach roil.

When King Hernando smiled at him, licking his mustached mouth with a red, wet tongue, Mateo wished for the first time since the whole business began that his sisters would continue to outwit them all—if only for three more nights.

King Hernando arrogantly outlined his plan for success. He'd brought with him a giant bell and six men. These men would stand outside the sisters' chambers, taking turns banging upon the bell every few minutes, ensuring that King Hernando would stay awake the entire night. At Mateo's father's request, the men demonstrated the power of the bell.

An hour later, Mateo's head still rang with the noise. He had to admit that King Hernando stood the best chance of anyone so far of discovering his sisters' secret.

Unfortunately, he was no closer to discovering it himself.

"WHY DO THEY rebel in such ways, Lámina?" Mateo asked as he followed her through her herb garden, watching her bend low to pull a weed, then stoop to snap off a branch of rosemary.

She made a noise that offered little information about her opinion.

"It's not as if they are bad girls. Well, Catalina is a good girl. They are all good girls," Mateo said.

When Lámina cleared her throat, Mateo laughed and amended, "Except for Adelita and Blanca and Delfina and Herminia and Imelda and Josefina. They're a bit of trouble sometimes."

"And you are no trouble at all," she countered.

"I don't make problems as they do."

Lámina shrugged. "Trouble is many things. Sometimes trouble is refusing the hands of old men and princesses when it is your duty to accept." She glanced up at him, shielding her eyes from the sun. Her smile was crooked and revealed brown teeth. "Old Lámina sees how it is with you."

Certainly, he'd come to seek her advice, but he'd given away nothing of his plan—or lack thereof—yet. "It's rather like being sold," Mateo said, kicking at a clod of dirt.

"Is it now?" she murmured, returning her focus to her plants.

"Indeed. Only, instead of being sent along to the highest bidder, I am a prize to be won by the first to outwit eleven mischievous girls."

"I believe they are women, *mi pájaro.*"

Mateo sighed. Of course they were women. They were women who should have, by all accounts, been married with families of their own. If they had all been settled, their antics would not be Papá's problem. Mateo doubted—if they were properly matched—they'd even have time for mischief amidst their wifely duties.

"They should be married," Lámina said, her voice raspy and quiet. "As should you. You are a man grown and proud."

Mateo's head snapped up. It was not the first time Lámina had expressed such a sentiment about his sisters, but it was the first she'd mentioned anything at all about his uncoupled state.

"Leaving me aside, I agree."

"Why leaving you aside? Is there someone particular you would choose? Sir Franco? Old Lámina sees how you look at him."

Mateo shrugged. "No. He doesn't share my interest. Regardless, I have no desire to be handed over to a stranger as a prize, expected to find affection where there is none."

"There's something you are not telling me."

Mateo ran a hand through his hair and looked away from Lámina's deep-set eyes. He thought of his father standing beside his mother's grave. He recalled the way his father's shoulders still shook with sobs whenever he remembered their joy and her death. "Truth be told, I don't wish to marry at all. Marriage for love only ends in grief. And marriage for any other reason is far too unpalatable."

"And what of lusts? Of urges?"

Mateo shrugged. "They can be satisfied without love or marriage, surely. I've heard as much admitted among the knights."

Lámina clucked her tongue. "Oh no, you don't cause trouble at all, *mi pájaro*. Blaming your sisters when you bring the greatest trouble of all."

Mateo looked up to the sky, squinting into the sun. "Is a full commitment of heart and soul really necessary for happiness, Lámina? Must I give my heart to another person when trusting in someone leaves me exposed to such pain that I could be wrecked for all eternity? I don't wish to end my life like father, sad and clinging too hard to his children."

Lámina's fuzzy brows lifted, white caterpillars smugly inching toward her hairline. "You will see for yourself, Mateo. Love is not something you avoid or throw to the dogs. Love is always the victor when it seeks you out. And you are marked by love."

Mateo sighed. He should have known better than to allow himself to go so far off course in this conversation. Lámina was a romantic old fool, overly fond of fairy stories and too full of love for him and his sisters to believe in anything but her own rose-colored dreams for them. But the problem was not his future and whether love would play a part, but rather if he would find himself forced into a marriage to King Hernandez, or some other equally unwanted chancer.

"Lámina, my sisters are the issue here. And yes, I suppose if I'm honest there is little to wonder about in their rebellion. Luz is of age now, and the others grow restless. They've all put our own lives aside for Papá's happiness. That cannot last forever."

"I dare say it has already come to an end."

"I know you have talked with father about his plans for the girls in the past." He reached down and rubbed a piece of sage between his fingertips.

"For you and for your sisters, yes."

Mateo's head snapped up. "What sorts of plans for me?"

"Only whether there are any princes in neighboring kingdoms who share your inclination toward other men." Lámina stared at the rosemary, her eyes distant as she considered.

"And are there?"

"Indeed, *mi pájaro*. There are a few. But your father never found one he favored for you. Nor any prospects that he deemed proper for your sisters."

Now it seemed his father had grown less particular in his choices for his children. Or perhaps it was only desperation and a loss of control over his wayward daughters that had left him willing to compromise them all without regard for affection, politics or bloodlines.

"If King Hernando has anything to do with it—" Mateo broke off, unwilling to contemplate that any further. It must not happen. He must find a way to discover his sisters' secret himself.

Lámina raised an eyebrow as she considered him, as if he'd spoken his thoughts aloud.

"I intend to put an end to this contest for our hands, Lámina. But I need help."

Lámina's old eyes were a strange gray-green that seemed to shift like the water of a deep lake. She studied him and he let her. For the entire length of an evening birdsong she studied him. "Come," she said.

Mateo realized he'd been holding his breath. He let it out slowly and followed where Lámina led, just as he had since he was able to walk. Lámina's cottage was small, messy and overflowing with dried herbs. No place in the kingdom smelled as pungent and aromatic. Mateo took a deep breath as he stepped inside.

"I have something for you," she said, motioning to him with her crooked, bird-claw fingers toward the dark shadows at the back of the cottage. "Something I've been waiting to give you for quite some time."

The cloak was of a dark but indeterminate color. It could have easily been blue, black or green in hue, but in the shadows Mateo could not say. The material was finer than anything Lámina could possibly afford, and Mateo opened his mouth to ask how she came by it. More importantly he meant to reassure her that he had no need for such a gift. He had many cloaks to his name, and would never want her to part with such a handsome object.

But Lámina stood on her tiptoes to press a finger against his lips. Mateo towered over her and not for the first time, he wondered at her smallness. Although he was as tall as the knights of the court, her arm was stretched to its full length just to keep her long nail pressed against his mouth, and only children were so tiny.

"Hush now," she whispered. She took her finger away and lowered herself down to her flat feet. "You have always been my favorite. I want nothing more than to see you happy, loved, cherished, adored. You will need a young man who can match you pleasure for pleasure, thrust for thrust. I know you, my Mateo. I know what you seek."

Mateo felt the roots of his hair grow hot at the accuracy of her words.

"That's why you came to me. You know old Lámina will help you get it." Her eyes glinted in amusement. "Unless I am wrong? And you do seek to marry the old man with sour breath and a shriveled prick?"

Mateo could only laugh and shake his head.

"I thought not. This cloak is no ordinary cloak. It's woven with magic. Shh, don't ask how or why or where. I'll never tell. It is my secret and promise. The wearer of the cloak is invisible."

Mateo looked at the cloak in his hand. He was skeptical but could think of no point in his life when, aside from fairy tales and stories, Lámina had ever told him or his sisters an untrue thing.

"Try it on. Walk about. See that no one will take notice of you so long as you wear it."

Mateo shook the cloak out and swung it around his shoulders. He felt unchanged, but when he turned to look in the mirror hanging on the opposite wall, he gasped. He was invisible as Lámina promised, from head to toes.

"How you use it is up to you," Lámina said, moving to her table, mounded with flowers in all stages of drying. She began to tie up the ends of the rosemary she'd brought in. "You could give it to King Hernando to aid him in his mission should your feelings toward him soften. Or, you could use it yourself to hide in your sisters' rooms, to watch how they rid themselves of old Hernando's unwanted presence and follow where they go."

Mateo took the cloak off. Yes, he was visible in the mirror again. He started to laugh, a giddy bubble bursting in his chest. "This is amazing, Lámina. Amazing!"

"It is," she agreed. "Oh, but I forgot one important thing."

"Yes?" Mateo asked, whipping the cloak over his shoulder again and watching his reflection wink out in the mirror.

"Old Lámina said you would be invisible, and that is true. Invisible to all but one."

Mateo slipped the coat off again, distracted. "All but one," he repeated slowly.

"Yes. The one who sees you despite the cloak's magic is…how shall I say?"

"Dangerous?" Mateo asked.

Lámina's eyes flickered as though she was holding something back. "Is special. *¿Comprendes?*"

"*Sí. Un amigo.*"

"Not just any friend, Mateo. Your best friend."

Mateo frowned. "Luz is my best friend." Being seen by Luz would defeat the purpose of the cloak, at least as far as his half-formed plan went.

"Not Luz," Old Lámina said, waving the idea away. "A different kind of friend than she could ever be."

"Then who?"

"Time will tell. Or perhaps time will not tell. In all the worlds seen and unseen, only one such person exists for you, Mateo. Do you get Old Lámina's meaning?"

Mateo held the cloak up, staring at its darkness, wondering what man might be the answer to the riddle the cloak contained. "I believe I do. The cloak not only renders me invisible, but reveals my truest friend."

"*Sí*, I believe you understand old Lámina now." She toddled over and patted his arm, gazing up at him with her deep, sea-like eyes.

Mateo's throat felt dry as he whispered, "Do you know his name?"

"Shh," Lámina's smile was as tender as when he was a child and he cried out in the night, terrified of the dark. "Let us make a bargain. You solve the problem of your sisters, and if you still don't know the name of your friend, Old Lámina will whisper it to you."

Mateo's heart pounded as he considered her words. "I accept, Lámina," he whispered. Then he stepped close, put his arms around her and kissed the top of her head. "*Gracias.*"

LÁMINA HAD NOT been lying—of course she had not. Mateo wandered the castle, the grounds and the stables, and no one noticed him at all. It was the most freedom Mateo had ever experienced. The cloak's magic worked perfectly on people, but with animals not as well. The horses seemed oblivious to him, but, Whitey, his sisters' Bichon Frise, little fluffball that he was, barked and barked and barked in Mateo's general direction until Herminia and Elisa scolded the poor animal harshly and cast him out of their presence.

Mateo smirked as the dog trotted along beside him through the castle, yipping and nipping at his heels. The guards were befuddled, but they thankfully blocked the dog's way. In the dovecote, Mateo stood in the middle, waiting to see if the birds noticed him. He smiled softly when Pura swooped low, landed on his shoulder and cooed.

"All right," he said, pulling a loose thread from the end of the cloak and letting the dove take it from his fingers for her nest. Then Mateo pitched his voice to sound as authoritative as the men in his father's council who pounded their fists on the table as they demanded something or someone be shown the power behind the king.

"Tonight, I put an end to it. I will discover the truth of where they go once and for all."

The dove seemed impressed by his performance, and Mateo lifted his chin in half-amused pride.

Chapter Two

KING HERNANDO PRESSED a gold ducat into the guard's palm. "Thank you for your good service. My men shall take over from here."

Mateo stood to the side, secure beneath the cloak and close enough that he would not miss his opportunity to follow King Hernando into his sisters' chambers. His father brandished the sole key to the door, which he now kept with him at all times. He even slept with it tied around his waist beneath his nightshirt. Such was his obsession with discovering the girls' secret, and so strong was his suspicion that an accomplice yet lurked in the court.

"I do wish Prince Mateo had joined us for dinner," Hernando said. "It would have been encouraging to see his face before this endeavor. I find his sweet brown eyes so fortifying, and his clean-shaven cheek a pleasure to touch."

Mateo shuddered, remembering the man's fingers on his face that morning at breakfast, claiming Mateo had a smear of jam on his cheek had been all the excuse necessary. The caress had been more than enough to solidify Mateo's resolve that the man's fingers never touch another inch of him again.

"My children's lack of manners and gratitude wounds me daily," his father said, looking grieved indeed. "Had they more of either we would not be in this situation. Their mother would be ashamed."

Mateo swallowed back his urge to dispute that. It was at times like this he had to admit to himself that, as the youngest, he and Luz had not really known their mother. She existed for them only in stories. Perhaps his mother *would* be ashamed of them. Thinking of his sisters and their unbecoming defiance, perhaps she should be.

"I assume Mateo's dark, curly hair comes from your late queen," Hernando said, as if he'd not heard the tone of sadness in Mateo's father's voice.

"His hair, his mouth, all that is good of him."

The king unlocked the door and stepped inside the rooms. Mateo could hear him demanding the girls line up, and he called each of their names beginning with Adelita and ending with Luz, confirming they were all present.

Mateo plugged his ears as Hernando's men set up the giant bell, already dreading the noise of it. Silent, silent, do not breathe, do not make a sound, he reminded himself as he took position behind Hernando.

When Hernando was called upon to enter, Mateo slipped through the door with him and into the darkest corner of the antechamber. He adjusted the dark cloak over his shoulders and watched as his father swept past with Whitey growling softly in his arms. Mateo was sickened to see his father's face so sad and drawn. Yes, it was time to put an end to his sisters' escapades. Even if Mateo himself chafed at his father's control, he wouldn't see him so heartbroken.

As the lock turned in the tumbler, Mateo stepped into the light from the large candelabras on the walls. He waited. Then he waited longer. Finally, the bell clanged, rattling him to the core, and he used the distraction of the noise to edge open the inner door leading to his sisters' bed chamber. In the open doorway he paused, half-expecting that the cloak's magic would not work, despite having tested it all day.

Through the door from the inner anteroom, he could see his sisters in their bedchamber, all wearing thick nightgowns and braided hair. They rested in their beds, facing King Hernando, who sat across from them in a straight-back chair at the writing desk. Most of them paid the king no attention as he prattled on about his own genius and his plan for the bell.

After several minutes, the bell rang again, drowning out his words, and Herminia frowned and stabbed a needle back and forth through fabric, drawing more blood than thread with each jab. Gracia and Josefina both read books, and several of the others talked quietly.

Mateo sank down to the floor of the antechamber as quietly as he could, his legs already growing tired of the aimless standing. When the bell stopped reverberating through the rooms, Hernando had moved on to the various changes he planned to make to his largest estate in order for Mateo to be more comfortable there.

"I believe the boy likes doves, does he not?"

"He does," Luz agreed, and Adelita shot her a dark look. "What, now? Are we to lie to him about what our brother likes?"

Adelita just glared at her and grabbed a brush from her vanity, starting to work out a knot in her hair.

"I intend to build a magnificent dovecote for him, bigger and better than any he's ever seen," King Hernando said. "It renders me nearly delirious to think of how he might smile when he sees it. Think how many doves he can raise! Do you think that would please him?"

"Do you think that will make him any happier to taste your prick?"

Mateo barely stifled his gasp, horrified by Imelda's comment. He waited for his sisters' reprimands to fly, but none did. They instead stared at King Hernando as if they wanted his answer. The man turned bright-red and gulped his wine down, coughing.

Catalina climbed from her bed, a contrite expression on her face, and poured the King another draught. "There," she said softly. "That should help."

"Doves…" King Hernando started again, sounding a bit dreamy suddenly, as if he'd spent hours in his cups. "They are delightful, honest things. And so smart. Like your brother. He is no doubt as pure as a dove."

"No doubt," Imelda supplied. "For no man has dared try his ass. Is that what you dream of, King Hernando? Our brother's sweet, round ass?"

King Hernando looked scandalized. "Is this how you do it, then," he pondered, his words slurring as he took another long swig of wine. "Do you show yourselves so crass that...that..." He blinked, looking somehow stupider than he had only moments before. "Oh." He concluded, and then doubled over, passed out in the chair.

"Good Lord, he is a monster," Imelda said, tossing aside her sheets and stretching high. "We are saving our brother a great deal with this one."

"A monster?" Josefina asked. "For wishing to build Mateo something wonderful to make things easier for him? I rather thought he was kinder than I expected. Though not the right man for Mateo, naturally."

Each of his sisters climbed out of bed and pulled on fresh pairs of pale-pink slippers, delivered that evening to the castle from the shoemaker in the town.

"Luz," Adelita instructed. "Go check the antechamber. Ensure no one else lingers inside."

Mateo scrambled back, sitting very still under the portrait of their mother hanging to the right of the bedchamber door, and bit the inside of his cheek. The bell rang yet again, making him feel quite secure that none had heard his clumsy movement.

Luz carefully tried the main door. Then, sniffing at the air, she froze in place. She turned around slowly, scanning her eyes over the dark corners of the antechamber. Mateo's heart hammered as her eyes fell on him, but then skimmed away.

"Mateo?" Luz shoved a long, curly strand of black hair off her forehead, revealing her shining brow. Her frown was accompanied by her usual sharp commentary as she moved aside the curtains and tapestries on the opposite wall. "Too much cologne, Mateo. Sir Franco won't be seduced merely from the scent of cloves and musk wafting across the court. I am certain you must actually speak to him to make your intentions known, little brother."

Little brother. As if nine minutes made such a difference. Mateo held perfectly still, hoping that Luz wouldn't walk into him in her search.

"Mateo?" she sounded confused, but then straightened her back. "My imagination is playing tricks on me." Luz returned to the bedchamber.

Mateo waited a moment before creeping on his hands and knees back into the doorway to watch. His sisters were now in various states of dress and undress. Luz was the only one who made no move to change from her nightgown. The others had put on fancy dresses or were in the process of donning one.

Mateo generally didn't pay attention to his sisters' attire, but he could tell by the material that they were all quite fine, the frills and shine of them fit for a ball. He wondered if he were to throw off his cloak and barge in now whether they would all claim that they were only dressing for bed. He could imagine the tale Delfina would spin about why she was preparing to sleep in a diamond necklace and drop-pearl earrings.

"There was no one?" Gracia asked Luz. She tightened Adelita's corset a bit before helping her step into a dress of blue-and-white sky.

"Mateo?" Luz said uncertainly.

The sisters' heads all snapped up and searched the doorway where Mateo stood. Seeing no one, they went back to their powders and ribbons and perfumes.

"Is he gone?" Felipa asked.

"Yes." Though Luz didn't sound convinced. "I'm not sure he was ever there at all. I only caught the scent of him."

"Ah, yes. Mateo's cologne." Gracia laughed softly. "Who does he imagine it will impress?"

"Maybe Mateo has softened toward him," Herminia said, nodding toward the drugged and snoring king. "Perhaps our baby brother came to wish his future husband luck." Her hands sifted through the jewelry box on the desk in front of her and finally came up with a sparkling comb encrusted with diamonds. She shoved it into the bun at the nape of her neck, and preened in the mirror.

Mateo barely held back a small gasp. Herminia had never shown interest in jewelry before. She preferred men's clothes and had convinced the caballeros to teach her to spar. Even when attending court functions or balls, she preferred to wear plain, functional gowns and never applied paint to her lips or cheeks.

"I'm glad old King Hernando drank the wine so quickly. I could not bear it if he'd begun to tell us his dreams of poor Mateo's wedding night," Josefina said as she twisted her hair up in a complicated manner.

Luz looked over her shoulder toward the open door, and Mateo felt her gaze burn into his chest. For a moment he wondered if she could see him after all.

"Mateo," Elisa snorted. "He is in the palm of Papá's hand."

"He cannot be trusted," Adelita added, applying a dab of pink paint to her mouth.

"Don't say that," Luz said sharply, and Mateo noted how all the sisters looked her way before busying themselves again, focusing anywhere but on Luz. "Mateo is better than you credit him."

"Oh come, Luz!" Gracia interjected. "You know as well as I do that his temper would override all else. He would consider it his duty to defend our honor."

"Indeed," Adelita said. "He might not be as protective as Papá, but he's still too gallant for his own good, especially when it comes to proving himself entirely grown. And wouldn't this just be his chance?"

Luz frowned. "But given his leanings, it seems possible that he really might be the one."

"In time," Adelita said, cutting her off. "The joy of so many can't be put at risk in order to test a theory. We will continue as we have until we know for certain."

"But what of Mateo's joy?" Luz crossed her arms over her chest in defiance. "Doesn't he deserve to be as happy as the rest of us?"

Adelita threw up her hands. "Darling, we don't even know if he's the one."

"He must be. It is quite obvious."

Adelita groaned. "They are all expecting another sister. Admittedly, it's been since he was a babe in arms, but last I saw the parts in question he was decidedly not a sister."

"Yes, the last waits for a bride," Elisa chimed in.

"But!"

"Mateo can't be trusted, Luz," Gracia said. "He'll report us to Papá as surely as the sun rises and sets."

"There now," Blanca said, rising from her ornate vanity to put her arm around Luz's shoulders. "Let's not argue." She glanced at Gracia and Adelita. "Or pick on our little brother, whom we all adore. Are you not going with us, Luz? You know you must attend!"

"There's no question about that. Of course I'm going."

"Why are you not dressed?"

"It doesn't matter what I wear," Luz said softly, red creeping up her neck.

A frisson passed between the sisters, each of them seeming to burn a little brighter.

"No, I suppose it does not," Blanca agreed. She pressed her hand against her bosom and her eyes gleamed with something akin to fever.

"Mateo really does wear too much cologne," Elisa said, her nose wrinkling. "Someone should tell him. I'm quite sure Princess Sara will not find it at all nice to hold a handkerchief to her face so that she may breathe while she courts him."

"Perhaps he wears it to ward off the princesses," Adelita said.

"Princess Sara is to be the next to try, then?" Felipa asked. "It's unfortunate that she won't succeed. And while Mateo would not enjoy her as a wife, I've always liked her rather well. She's a delightful correspondent."

"Prince Leon has been added to the list," Gracia broke in. "I think he's a good match for Mateo. Handsome, funny and properly inclined from what his older sister writes."

"If King Hernando is too old, Prince Leon is too young. Just a boy. He hasn't even grown a beard." Adelita waved off the idea.

"Do you think there is no hope that Mateo may find something appealing in Sara?" Herminia asked, a gentle note to her voice. "She's a good huntress. She brought down three deer on the last visit she made. Do you remember?"

A collective groan went through the room. Mateo wondered how long his sisters had been so interested in his marriage prospects. He'd not even known they cared.

"Please, spare us waxing on about the lovely Sara," Adelita said. "As for Mateo, we all know he longs for stronger things than any princess can give him." She held up her hand to stop Herminia from speaking. "Three slain deer from a feminine hand will not suffice."

"Unless she hides more than a shocking skill with the bow behind those muddy riding skirts, he'll never be interested in her," Imelda added, her black eyes snapping in amusement.

Herminia didn't reply, her face going dreamy.

"Ah, look at her. She thinks of the green fields beneath Cacatúa's skirts," Imelda said with only a touch of a sneer.

Cacatúa?

Herminia grabbed a folded fan and threw it at Imelda. "Shall I tease you about the way you nearly toss up your own skirts at the sight of Gallo?"

Toss her skirts up? For a rooster? Mateo's heart raced. Was he hearing all of this correctly? Had Imelda been compromised, and willingly? And Herminia too, with a woman called, of all oddities, Cacatúa? Such names befit travelling performers, not courtiers, and where would his sisters meet such folk?

Mateo stared at each of his eleven sisters, trying to see if any stain appeared on their faces or bodies that would tell him if they'd been ruined already. The bell rang again, an aching sound that shook the furniture in the room. King Hernando slumped so that his hands touched the rug.

Then, as the irritating reverberation from the bell passed, his sisters' clock struck the hour. The comparatively gentle sound swelled in the room and seemed to stretch into a pulse that beat with anticipation. Everything slowed, the air itself moving in visible currents. Mateo's heart pounded in his chest, his throat and mouth dry while his sisters transformed in front of him. They grew brighter, as if someone had lit hundreds of candles behind their eyes. Each of them became nearly too beautiful to look at, and Mateo lifted a hand to shield his eyes from their light.

"The window," Luz said, her skin glowing as though she was made of shifting sunlight. "It's time."

The casement grew and flexed, and to Mateo's amazement, the glass seemed to crinkle and then vanish as a set of three steps appeared before it. Adelita guided Catalina first, and the other sisters lined up behind her, with Luz taking the rear. To his disbelief, Catalina and Adelita walked up the stairs together and stepped out the window holding hands. Miraculously, they did not fall to the cobblestones below, but instead appeared to briefly walk on air before they disappeared.

Mateo stuffed his fist into his mouth to keep from crying out. Luz turned back, her eyes searching the space around where he was standing. Shaking her head, she faced her sisters. "Hurry, the window will close soon. We don't want to miss it."

"You are quite eager, Luz," Imelda said. "Wearing only a shift to make it easier for him. Urging us to make haste. What would Father think? Or Mateo?"

"As if propriety matters now," Luz shot back, stepping behind Imelda up the three stairs. "Just hurry, will you?"

Mateo rushed up behind Luz. At the top of the stairs he hesitated, his stomach in his throat, staring at the stones below. They were near the top of the castle, far above the trees in the courtyard. He watched his sisters walking on air. Luz waited until all the others had disappeared before stepping out herself.

It took all the trust in Mateo's soul to step out of the window. When he did, he found he did not fall, and the air was as solid as earth beneath him. The stars grew so bright that he could not see. The wind rushed around him and he shielded his face with his hand.

For a moment Mateo was overwhelmed with the urge to retreat to the safety of the castle. Then he strode onward, into the abyss.

Chapter Three

THEY WERE IN a wood—but no ordinary wood. The trees were tall and shaped like maples and oaks, but were heavy with silver leaves. Mateo reached out to touch, and the metal felt cool and bright, like pure moonlight against his fingers. He tugged on the shining leaf until it broke free. He quickly stashed it in his pocket as his sisters turned at the snap.

"Did you hear that?" Catalina asked.

"It was a deer," Adelita said. "Come, we're all here now and we mustn't keep them waiting."

The ten eldest started off into the woods in their usual way. Adelita, Blanca and Catalina in the lead as the others followed arm-in-arm with their birth-mates, whispering in excited tones. Luz alone lingered, searching the forest behind her and sniffing at the air. Finally Luz gave up and followed her sisters. Mateo kept her in his sights.

The way was not short. As they walked, the silver forest gradually gave way to another wood of burnished gold. The golden glow cast from these leaves lighted his sisters' dark hair with fire, and drew out the warmth of sun from their skin so that they more resembled fantastical paintings on the castle's gallery wall.

Mateo didn't dare risk breaking another leaf from a branch, but many lay scattered on the ground glinting in the moonlight. He quickly bent to pick one up, putting it into his pocket next to the silver leaf he'd taken earlier.

The golden forest shifted into diamond-laden trees, and Mateo blinked in the dazzle. The light from the moon glittered wildly against hundreds of facets in every leaf, blinding in its opulence and beauty. Mateo didn't resist. He reached out and tore one of the leaves from the tree. Luz glanced behind her at the noise, but the other sisters were oblivious, moving ever more swiftly, their skin dancing with rainbows of refracted light.

They no longer looked human, but like multicolored birds who might take flight. Mateo glanced down at his own skin beneath the cloak and saw that he too appeared as a changeling. It was a delirious illusion brought on by the unearthly light from the trees—his sisters were still women, and he still a man.

Just when Mateo began to doubt they would ever stop walking, the diamond forest opened onto a dark, wide lake. It was bigger than any lake he'd ever seen, with no end on the horizon. The moon on the waves left the impression of a glowing, heaving bosom, or the rolling flesh of man mid-coitus. Mateo felt stirring in his groin as he watched the waves move in relentless rhythm.

There had been no male in the court he could trust to bed, not even once he came of age. Despite the courtiers vying for his favor, offering with simpering smiles to bend over for him if only to gain power, not a one of them had been daring enough to give him what he'd needed. But the dark, undulating lake brought to mind all the lust-fueled dreams that had long left him in a sweat, shaking with desire.

He tore his gaze away from its seductive depths—and found in the water before them a row of strange men standing tall in wide, flat-bottomed boats that were half-filled with flowers.

Adelita approached the first boat. The man who helped her in was of the most extraordinary appearance. His clothing was of an unusual style, colored in the most vibrant hues. In fact, Mateo realized, his garments appeared to be made entirely of feathers. And though Mateo could hardly believe it, the man's hair was the yellow of a sunflower, and just as that flower follows the sun, his eyes followed Adelita walking toward him. He took her hand, kissed it with a redder mouth than Mateo had ever seen and guided her to sit.

Blanca approached the second boat. The man who helped her inside had hair the colors of pink roses and sky twirled together. His nose was rather beakish, lending an avian air to his face. He brought Blanca's hand to his lips and helped her settle before passing a bright-pink rose to her, then starting out across the lake.

Like balloons floating barely above the ground, his sisters drifted to the boats and climbed in, exclaiming over the flowers. It was only when Herminia approached that Mateo realized not all of the men were...men. Herminia's boat was commanded by a woman with dark hair twisted into the shape of a birdcage. The woman's dress was of white and black feathers, with blue-green trim. Herminia did not simply take her hand to climb in, but kissed it passionately.

Imelda was next and Mateo did not hold back his gasp as she allowed the man with red-and-purple hair to pull her into a close embrace, nearly tipping over in their enthusiasm. He could not believe his eyes when the man reached below to cup Imelda's sex, and she did not cry out or bat his hand away, but leaned into the touch. Mateo turned his eyes resolutely away as their lips met.

He was relieved when Luz merely allowed the man with clover-and-sky hair to kiss her fingers before she sat down opposite him, smoothing her nightgown. In the face of all the unbelievable things Mateo had experienced so far that night, his sister wearing her nightgown outside her chambers was certainly the least shocking, and yet he noted the impropriety with dawning comprehension as he watched his twin sail away.

One boat remained.

The man in this boat was as startling to look upon as the rest. He was smaller than the rest of the creatures, his hair short and quite pink, sticking up in all directions as though he'd just woken from sleep, or perhaps never used a comb. He wore a riot of colored feathers woven into a shirt and breeches made of the softest brown leather Mateo had ever seen. Mateo's own fine woolen trousers and exquisite silk-trimmed tunic seemed almost shabby in comparison to the wild wonder before him.

The man's lips were the same pink as his hair, and his eyes were blue, fierce—as though they contained a soul stronger than his form. Mateo's blood coursed. He was as captured by the look of this man as he'd been captivated by the sensual lure of the water. Mateo swallowed hard, hesitating. Did he dare get in? He must to follow his sisters.

Mateo stepped forward and the creature smiled. Frozen in place, Mateo checked that he still wore the cloak. Lámina's voice echoed in his mind. The one who sees you despite the cloak's magic is a friend.

"Ópalo!" the man rowing Luz called as distance grew between his boat and the shore. "Next time, perhaps."

Ópalo, for that must be his name, did not look away, keeping his eyes on Mateo's own. "One moment more." He quirked his lips into a small, amused smile and rested his oar against the side of the boat.

Mateo took a step forward and Ópalo's eyes lit up. He lifted his chin slightly, almost imperceptibly, with a motion that indicated Mateo should come. Mateo lifted his hand in a small wave, and Ópalo nodded his head and smiled. It was a toothy, pretty thing that made Mateo catch his breath and take a step back.

Surely not.

"Come!" Luz's man called again.

"Patience, Azulejo!" Ópalo answered.

"We must not be late to the dancing."

"You must not. I can be as late as I wish."

"Stay then, and yearn for your bride to come. It changes nothing," Azulejo said before bending himself to the oars, speeding Luz away at an alarming rate.

Seeing Luz's white nightgown and dark, shining head disappear across the lake broke Mateo from his shocked state, and he quickly clambered into the boat with Ópalo. He ignored the offered hand as he stepped aboard, causing the boat to rock dangerously, nearly toppling them both out. Mateo's stomach lurched, and there was a spray of cold water against his face as Ópalo steadied the boat with his oar, digging it into the bottom of the lake. Mateo sat down quickly.

"Pardon me!"

Ópalo grinned, his blue eyes—blue as a summer sky—twinkling, and his lips spread again into that beautiful smile. "No need to be so formal."

Mateo wasn't sure what to make of the casual tone, but there was nothing customary about the situation. He'd traveled with his sisters into a magical realm while hidden beneath a cloak that rendered him invisible, and which had apparently determined in some unfathomable way that this man, of all men, was to be Mateo's friend. He knew he should find more comfort in that, but he felt quite the opposite. It was hard to concentrate over the ceaseless thrumming in his veins.

Ópalo went on. "I'm so glad you came. I've waited for you. You have no idea how long."

Up close, Mateo could see that Ópalo seemed made of the shifting light from the diamond forest, his skin a mottle of beautiful colors that glowed breathtakingly in the moonlight. His eyebrows and eyelashes were pink, like the hair on his head, except that none of it was hair. Instead he had feathers, longer and thicker on his head, but short and fine around his eyes. His eyelashes appeared to be the daintiest feathers that Mateo had ever seen. And Mateo, out of either the arrogance of royalty or the shock of the moment, reached out a hand to feel them, only pulling back from touching the beautiful oddness at the last moment.

"I apologize."

Ópalo shook his head, and then reached out to grab Mateo's hand with a strong grip. He leaned forward, offering his eyebrows and hair up to Mateo's touch.

Mateo pulled back without making contact, a belated terror pumping through him. "Who? What?"

"Shh," Ópalo said softly. "They can hear. Sound carries over the water. You're hiding for a reason?"

Mateo swallowed, nodded his head, and realized he was shaking.

"There will be time to talk at the dance. Everyone will be busy and it's quite loud. Lean back. Relax. We'll go now." Ópalo's voice was warm and sweet.

Mateo sat straight as an arrow until the rhythm of the waves and Ópalo's quiet regard lulled him. The water lapped against the side of the boat, the oars splishing and splashing as the boat glided smoothly on and on. The moonlight rippled against the undulating lake as far as Mateo could see. Perhaps it was not a lake at all, but an endless sea.

His limbs loosened, and Mateo discovered he was very tired. It was late, and he'd walked quite far. He leaned his head back against a cushion and looked at the night sky, seeing no constellation with which he was familiar. He brought his gaze back to Ópalo, who still studied him with intent admiration.

"Why do you watch me?" Mateo asked quietly.

"Haven't you ever been hungry?"

"Yes. Of course."

"When you're hungry and food is set before you, what do you do?"

The thrumming that had at last dissipated under the steady pull of the boat over the water roared through Mateo again. Could the cloak be wrong? Perhaps these people consumed humans and Ópalo was not a friend at all. Perhaps they were taking him and his sisters to be a feast for trolls in fairyland. For that's where they were, Mateo had no doubt. His sisters were in fairy thrall and now so was he, drowsing on a fairy lake, under the gaze of a fairy man with luscious lips and sparkling sky-colored eyes.

"Are you going to eat us?"

Ópalo's laughter was a joyous, riotous twitter of early morning birds in spring, and Mateo heard it echo across the lake. So much for being quiet. "Of course not, *mi pájaro*."

Mateo narrowed his eyes. My bird? Lámina sometimes called him that. It was quite the liberty, but no doubt things worked differently here, and Lámina had said that this man was meant to be his friend. Mateo cocked his head, took in Ópalo's handsome face, long neck and strong hands on the oars. Yes, perhaps somehow…more than a friend. "Then what?"

Ópalo murmured, "I only mean that I can feast my eyes on you."

Mateo didn't say anything for a long time after that. There were too many questions crowding his mind. Finally, Mateo indicated his cloak. "How…?"

How did you know of the cloak? Why is it you who can see me when others cannot? How did you know I hid from my sisters? Who exactly are you and who are the others with my sisters? How, pray tell, has this come to pass?

Yet Mateo couldn't form the words.

"Lámina must have explained the cloak to you," Ópalo said.

Mateo sat up, jostling the boat. "You know Lámina?"

"She was once our old friend. She's the fairy who preferred to live with humans."

"Lámina?"

Ópalo chuckled softly. "Yes, that's her name." He went back to Mateo's previous question. "As for how—well, oh, surely you know?"

"We'll become friends."

Ópalo's cheeks flushed and the feathers on his head seemed to bristle. He rowed more quickly as he grew flustered. "Yes. Friends. So first, I hope you come to trust me."

Mateo's head churned faster than the oars dipping into the lake. "Trust you." He rubbed a hand over his eyes and peered around. "Truly this is all astounding. And Lámina is a fairy?"

"She was," Ópalo said. "When she left our world, she became something other. Closer to human, farther from fairy." As he said the words, the truth of them seemed so clear.

The details of the stories Lámina told them their whole childhood flooded Mateo's mind—a lake, fairies with feathers for hair, twelve lovers destined for twelve fae.

"FOR THE FAE lack your strength, children."

They were crowded onto and around Lámina's bed, all twelve of them. There was barely air to breathe, they all huddled so close. Even the eldest triplets had elbowed their way to good spots on the mattress next to Lámina's outstretched legs.

It was a special night, for Mateo and Luz no longer required the care of a nurse, and Lámina was to be given a cottage near a wide plot of land. There she could grow herbs and help Mateo with the dovecote being built for him. This was to be one of the last nights she would spend with the children in the castle.

Mateo felt tears burn his eyes at the thought of her leaving. But he was twelve, and it was nearly as embarrassing to have an old nurse tending to him as it was painful to let her go.

"Old Lámina tells you the truth! Fae cannot live as magical creatures in the human realm. Unlike you, who can pass back and forth with nary a change to your strong human blood. Every hour that a fairy spends in the human realm saps him of his essence, until eventually he may never return to fairyland."

"That's why they kidnap us," Imelda had said, her dark head rising above Mateo's own. "To marry us and have stronger children, ones who can pass between the worlds?"

Lámina shrugged and reached out to grip Mateo's chin, looking him over closely. "I suppose they'd take the lot of you as mates and happily spend their love on you, it's true. And your children could pass between the worlds more easily than those of fae blood alone. Though it's not just your children they want, but your human hearts as well. Listen to old Lámina. Human love strengthens and stabilizes their world. The royal family has always made alliances with humans, and always will."

"Why? Is their world falling apart?" Mateo asked, imagining a world like the old dovecotes he'd seen while riding with his father, in need of strong beams to replace the old, cracking wood, and a coat of good plaster to hold the structure steady.

"It is at that," Lámina said. "But aren't they all, though?"

"Is it a structural problem?" Mateo went on. "Has a support beam gone bad?"

His sisters groaned and jostled about on the bed.

"*Sí*, it is just as you describe, Mateo."

"Can't they have a carpenter look at it?" he asked. "Love doesn't seem like it would do much to fix a structural problem."

"Worlds are not like dovecotes," Lámina whispered, and all the sisters leaned close as they always did when she spoke quietly. No one wanted to miss a word, for Lámina's secrets were always worth hearing. "Giving and accepting love is the real strength. Remember that when the time comes. Remember that, *mi pájaro*."

Mateo nodded up at her, mouthing the words "I promise" so that she smiled at him, showing her brown, stained teeth.

"And if the human doesn't love them?" Luz asked eagerly, if a bit bloodthirstily. "If the human heart isn't so easily theirs to enjoy? Will they perhaps eat it? A sort of heart-shaped cake?"

"Yes, Lámina," Imelda said, her dark eyes glinting. "Would they murder us with their sharp fairy claws and teeth?"

Lámina's smile was slow and kind, almost like she pitied Luz and Imelda for asking. "Listen to old Lámina. You love the fae. You always love them and they always love you. It is how it is. It is how it shall be."

Mateo felt the truth of her statement deep in his bones, and he settled in close to her, wanting to tell Lámina he loved her, but knowing his sisters would mock him for the babyish sentiment.

"Tell us the story of the fairy king and his twelve children," Adelita requested. "I haven't heard that one in years."

"Because you have been 'too grown up' for old Lámina's stories for years. Or so you've said as you scoff at your siblings for their bedtime tales." She scolded, but her voice was full of affection.

Adelita settled in closer, smiling at Lámina sweetly. Lámina reached for Luz and pulled her up to tuck under her other arm, freeing up a bit of space on the mattress for Gracia to slide into.

Beneath her warm chin, snug against her soft nightdress, Mateo's hand resting on her wrinkled, dry arm, Mateo vowed he would never be too grown up for Lámina's stories.

"In a kingdom very close and yet very far, there lives a fairy king and his twelve fairy children. Merry, smart and talented, they each await a chance at human companionship in hopes of strengthening their kingdom…"

Chapter Four

THE OARS HAD not ended their rhythmic splashing, and Ópalo still gazed at Mateo with the same steady expression as Mateo reeled in the memory.

"You've been expecting us."

Ópalo nodded.

"I apologize if I'm slow to understand, but I thought they were only stories."

"I find your confusion charming."

Mateo had no words for that, and instead latched on to a story from the memory. "Your father is the king of this realm?" Mateo confirmed.

"Was the king, yes. He died."

"*Lo lamento.*"

Ópalo smiled again, his eyes crinkling at the edges, his pink, feathered lashes brushing against his flushed cheeks. "You are very polite, *mi pájaro.* Truly, you are charming."

Mateo's stomach fluttered in response to the flattery.

"My eldest brother has inherited the throne of this land, and my siblings and I assist him as necessary." Here Ópalo motioned with his head to the other boats to illustrate his relationship to the fae escorting Mateo's sisters.

At least if his sisters had been compromised then it had been with royalty. Fairy royalty of course, but perhaps that was not so very terrible?

"When your sisters arrived without you day after day, I nearly despaired." Ópalo nodded to the east. "Look, morning breaks."

Mateo turned away from Ópalo and yes, the sun's rays broke over the horizon. The light cast the lake into a fiery sparkle, as though each wave was opal. His heart jolted and Mateo gasped. "It's morning! Papá! He'll see that we're gone!"

"Shh, quiet," Ópalo said, lifting one of his fine hands to silence Mateo. "Your father will still be sleeping. He'll sleep for days of our time. There's no need to rush. However, the portal is always open from our side. Whenever you wish to return simply say the word and I'll take you back to the shore."

"Always open on this side, but not on the other?"

"Your sisters tell us the portal only opens at night on your side, once a day for a short time."

"How short?"

"I don't know. It stays open for as long as it should, and not a moment longer. Magic doesn't often follow rules."

"But how? The portal leads to my sisters' chambers. This was by design?"

"I believe Lámina chose. I know little of her magic, except that it finally brought you to me. And that she made sure the portal was always open on this side, so you and your sisters can leave freely."

Mateo stared at the sunlight shifting on Ópalo's skin, washing away the rainbow opalescence of the night, and leaving him a pale, beautiful bird of a man. His feathers shone in the light, his eyes brighter than before, and his lips looked plump as pillows in the clear morning sun. There was no reason to believe him, and yet there was no reason to doubt him either.

Ópalo grinned. "You're very handsome. Dark as you are, with such red lips."

Mateo's face grew hot, his blood rushing pleasurably.

Ópalo didn't stop there. "And you're every bit more human than I could have hoped."

Everything about Ópalo was like gazing on something too good to be true, like the sweetest, most lovely cake the castle baker had ever constructed. Mateo felt sure that eating such a thing would leave him aching for more and less. It was tempting, but ultimately superficial. Mateo's pulse quickened, but he hardened himself. Friendship was one thing, but if this fairy intended to feast on love from Mateo's human heart, he was going to have to work harder than that.

"Nothing but sugar. Your words are too sweet and lack sustenance."

Ópalo's eyes laughed at him. "I see that friendship will not be granted without good cause, no matter what your cloak has declared."

"You see correctly. And you'll find I am not always so polite."

"You're quite forgiven. Look at the sunrise. Watch how it comes up over the bridge."

The bridge? Were they finally getting somewhere then?

Mateo turned and saw the boat carrying Luz slip beneath an arched stone bridge. On the other side was a castle—the largest, most ornate castle that Mateo had ever seen. As they rowed closer the light hit the great structure and Mateo gasped. Each cupola, each arch, every window and door casing—of which there were hundreds—and each buttress big and small were all built of birdhouses. White birdhouses, gold birdhouses, tangled together and stacked one upon another, a feat of design and engineering, lifting the castle into the blue sky.

As the shadow of the bridge passed over them, a trumpet sounded, and there was a great noise, the flutter of thousands of wings as a swirl of birds flew out of the houses of the castle and swept through the sky before careening back again, swooping low and screeching.

Mateo stared in wonder, shielding his head when some dropped exceedingly low and close.

"They won't hurt you," called Ópalo over the noise. "It's only our cousins welcoming your sisters home. And you, of course."

"Home?" Mateo turned to Ópalo. "How can this be their home when they've spent all their years in our father's realm?"

"Time is different here, *mi pájaro.*"

The repetition of the odd endearment was a prickling reminder of how far out of his depth he was in this strange land. He felt dizzy and a little sweaty. The calling of the birds was too loud in his mind, and the amazing tower before him dwarfed all of his previous ideas of what was possible. "My bird? You dare to address a prince in this way? Not once but many times?"

"I do, yes."

"Do you care nothing for the possible consequences of such an affront?"

Ópalo's mouth twitched. "No. I do not."

Mateo narrowed his eyes. Being trapped as he was on a boat in the middle of the vast lake, he said only, "Such liberties! Speaking to me as a friend when you don't even know my name." Mateo drew up, attempting to look more regal, as he did when he practiced for court functions in the mirror. Ópalo seemed amused, which left Mateo rather certain he'd failed.

"Of course I know your name, Mateo. And you may call me Ópalo. Again, there's no need for formality here."

Confusion and curiosity warred within him. Mateo's eyes snapped to Ópalo's face.

"Luz speaks of you often." Ópalo volunteered in answer to Mateo's unspoken question. "She misses you terribly when she's here."

"You make it sound as if she doesn't see me every day."

"For Luz, many days pass between the few hours you spend together."

"Time is not what it seems, children," Lámina said, her eyes hooded as if she was revealing a secret. "In fairyland, a single night can last for days."

"When Lámina didn't send a bride through for me, I was relieved at first."

A bride? Mateo stared. Of course, how had he not realized? Twelve lovers for twelve fae. He shook his head. What had Lámina done—and what had his sisters wrought?

Ópalo continued on as though unaware his words had set Mateo reeling. "Though I've lain with females and males, I always hoped to take a man as my love." Ópalo looked around, as though measuring who might be listening. Luz and her fairy man were quite a distance away, and it would be impossible to hear much of anything over the call of the swooping birds.

"When I listened to Luz speak of you, your kindness, your handsome face and the dedication you've shown to your doves, I couldn't help but hope that you might be *la hermana* intended for me."

Mateo's jaw flexed, his stomach flipping as images pierced his mind—debauched, delicious images of being this fairy's lover. Heat flooded through him, arousing—and terrifying. He gritted his teeth and clenched his fists. "I am no 'sister'."

Ópalo's mouth twitched and his eyes glittered with humor. "No, I can see you are not."

"I'm a prince."

"For which I am very glad."

"And when I return to give my father the news of my sisters' misadventures, I'll win the right to choose my own fate."

Mateo recalled the stories Lámina told and her certain voice. *"You love the fae. You always love them and they always love you. It is how it is. It is how it shall be."* As a child, he'd been certain too, never believing any of it could be real. But no more. This was no children's tale, and such love must be earned.

The power he sensed from Ópalo was enticing. Mateo couldn't deny the deep pull of it, and though on the surface the fairy seemed slight, there was something brutal and confident in his face. Mateo questioned his ability to resist Ópalo should it come down to it.

"My human heart is my own." Mateo put his chin up. Then a splat of bird shit landed on his sleeve.

Ópalo chuckled, reaching into a hidden pocket in his feathered shirt to bring out a handkerchief. "Favored already. I'm not surprised." He wiped at the dropping with the soft cloth and tossed it overboard. "A treat for the fish."

Reassured that Ópalo had not disputed his declaration as to the state of his heart, Mateo turned his attention to the doves as they swept by them again and again.

"Can they see me?"

"Indeed. All the cousins can. If anything will give you away before you're ready, it will be them. They mean no harm. They simply don't understand you're meant to be invisible."

A dove swooped low and cooed. Ópalo smiled in response and answered it.

"Yes. He's here for me." Ópalo gestured at Mateo. "A youngest son for a youngest son."

Mateo opened his mouth to dispute this, but held his peace, because just as the birds had swept down suddenly upon them, they swirled away, some returning to their homes in the castle walls, others flying out over the lake.

"Earlier I spoke of hunger," Ópalo said. "Take my advice, *mi pájaro*. While you're here you may drink whatever you like, but you must eat nothing."

"Why?"

Ópalo seemed to dim slightly, and he looked away for the first time, gazing off to where the sun rose higher. The light played on his face. "So your human heart may remain your own for as long as you choose, unlike your sisters'." Ópalo's voice held a note of melancholy.

Mateo blanched at the idea that his sisters' hearts had already been given—and perhaps not of their choosing? "Are my sisters in danger?"

"Only if love is danger."

Mateo was about to demand a more thorough response when he saw that Adelita and Blanca's boats had arrived. They stepped onto a well-built wooden dock with their fairy men. Each of his sisters waited for her turn to disembark. As the boats crowded close together, Luz looked toward Ópalo with a curious, worried expression that lifted when Ópalo smiled at her.

"Ópalo!"

That was Adelita's voice. She stood by the edge of the dock and called to him. "I'm sorry you again waited in vain. We have no more sisters, as I've said before."

"I live in hope," Ópalo called to her.

Adelita seemed bemused by this optimism. "Hope will not create a sister where there is none!" She waved as her fairy man escorted her away.

"His name is Canario," Ópalo said softly for Mateo's benefit. "An eldest brother for an eldest sister, and so on down the line. And now there is you for me." Ópalo smiled.

"I am not a 'sister'," Mateo muttered again, wanting to make that very clear for some reason he couldn't put his finger on. He swallowed, confused as to why the words "and I am not for you" got stuck in his throat and refused to come out. Surely the cloak could not compel him to commit to something his heart did not feel?

"You are not a sister," Ópalo agreed. "But you should still take my hand when we disembark, lest you taste the cold of the lake."

Mateo swallowed his pride and did just that. When he released Ópalo's hand and stood before the great castle swarming with birds, having rowed miles across a lake so vast he'd never seen its like, Mateo stared in awe at the world around him. It was a jumble of beauty such as he'd never seen.

"Ópalo," he breathed, uncertain and amazed. The name tasted like sweetness on his tongue. "It's just as she said it would be, just like her stories described."

Ópalo's eyes softened. "Come. You're safe with me. I promise."

As they entered the castle, Mateo allowed Ópalo to retake his hand.

Chapter Five

Four Months Earlier…

TOES IN THE water, Ópalo sat by the edge of the lake, watching their bird cousins twist and dive in the air as his siblings decried their lot in life.

"The brides do not come." Canario moaned. "We wait and we wait, and yet they never come. Azulejo and Ópalo are of age now. What else could be holding Lámina back from sending them?"

"Perhaps the youngest bride hasn't joined them in adulthood?" Zafiro rubbed at his thick eyebrows so vigorously that the small feathers stood up from his face in red and orange ruffles.

Canario waved that off. "You know that's not possible. She's yet another twin, or so father said."

"She's the only reason Ópalo was even called into being," Tulipan said.

Ópalo never knew how he was supposed to feel about the fact that he'd been conceived solely to be the mate to a human child in order to complete his father's plan to strengthen their land.

"Yes, after the incident. And perhaps that is the problem. We wait because we have not yet had word from Lámina of the readiness of Ópalo's bride. All of us wanting and waiting, and for what? But he's not a true brother, only a half. Fate recognizes these things," Halcón said.

"I'm sitting right here," Ópalo noted, but his siblings ignored him.

"We should move forward without consideration for his…problem."

"I'm as much a member of this family as the rest of you."

The others, especially his sister Cacatúa, rallied to him, agreeing wholeheartedly that he was not only their full brother in heart and spirit, but perhaps the best among them. "Your heart is full of love, and you are the most beautiful of us all," Cacatúa murmured in his ear as she caressed his feathers. "Halcón is only jealous. Ignore him, baby bird, just as you always do."

Ópalo didn't like the coddling any more than he liked the insult from Halcón, but he tolerated it. There was no escaping that he was youngest, and that they had all, except for Azulejo, cuddled, fed and dressed him when he'd been a tiny fairy. Given his mother had died in birthing him, his siblings had all cared for him more than most.

After everyone but Halcón had made some sort of amends to Ópalo for what had been said, Canario paced along the edge of the water. "Perhaps Halcón is right." He held up a hand to forestall Cacatúa's complaint. "No, not about Ópalo. But maybe it's time to abandon waiting for Lámina's word and act for ourselves," Canario said, the leader as always.

Cacatúa clucked her tongue softly, sounding for all the world like her namesake, and she said, "But that's not proper, Canario. That is not the bargain that Lámina made with our father."

Since infancy they had been instructed to wait for Lámina to send the brides. When the brides passed through the threshold, the cousins would know, and they would alert the princes and princess to take the boats to the far side of the lake to await their lovers. Once in their presence, the brides, human as they were, would succumb to the siblings' natural fairy thrall. And once they'd consumed the food of fairyland, they would surrender to their natural passions. That was as it had always been, and as it would always be. Lámina's role was to make sure the brides came.

"Waiting has gotten us nowhere. Didn't Father also tell us that sometimes one must take matters into one's own hands?" Canario said with the particular flint in his tone that said the decision had been made and no amount of arguing would change his mind.

As Ópalo watched the cousins fly toward the portal that night, messages for the human brides tied to their feet, anxiety curled in his gut and he wished to call them back. He didn't want a bride. He never had and never would. He'd lain with many of fae blood, but did not wish to lie with a woman again, preferring to spend his pleasure on the men of the court. The idea of being tied to a human bride didn't please him at all. Perhaps a human woman would be somehow different, but Ópalo feared she would not. Deep inside, he wondered if his doubts had played any part in the delay of the brides' arrival.

Yet he didn't want to hold back his siblings any longer. They had all waited for such a long time. Ópalo had no idea what his brothers and sister had written to their prospective lovers, but his note was short and sweet.

Dear bride, come at once. Let us see what our future may bring.

ÓPALO HELD ONTO Mateo's fingers. He felt the strength in them, the pulsing warmth of blood bringing a heat to the surface of the skin. Fae were not so hot-fleshed as humans, though they were often just as hot-tempered—if not more so—and unfortunately lacking the scruples so many humans were rumored to hold dear.

As they followed the others into the castle, Ópalo kept an eye on Mateo's face, noting his expressions of awe and wonder, and the ripple of fear beneath it all. A protective affection rose within him, reminding him of his brothers' comforting arms around Mateo's sisters' shoulders the night they first arrived.

When Mateo had arrived at the edge of the lake—lush lips, golden skin, dark hair and brown, soft eyes wide with both fright and bravery— Ópalo had remembered his father once placing a precious red-skinned apple into his hand and saying, "This is from the human world."

Ópalo had kept it for days, delirious with its beauty and the potential of its crisp flesh. During that time, he'd learned much about the mysterious fruit. It promised to be delicious and meaty, yes, but it was also easily bruised. When he'd finally taken a bite, he'd nearly cried from the joy of it.

Mateo reminded him of that apple. Ópalo wanted to admire him for years, taking in every facet of his beauty, his textures and scents. He wanted to caress the tiny curls he could see just behind Mateo's ear, run his finger over the fringe of his eyelashes, and touch the small dimple in his chin. Then, only after an ecstasy of waiting, would he finally take a bite and consume him entirely—taking his love into Ópalo's body. Turning him into his strength. His heart.

As they'd rowed and talked, Ópalo had fallen in love. Yes, love. Because Ópalo was as ready for it as the night sky is ready for the stars to pierce it. Wide open and eager for light. It felt like flying, running, jumping, swimming and laughter all rolled into one vibrant emotion. Ópalo already adored Mateo's intoxicating mix of insecure arrogance and brave, kind heart.

And if Mateo wanted his heart to be his own, then Ópalo would keep it safe for him. Ópalo decided as soon as the words left Mateo's mouth that he would never use fairy magic to influence or secure Mateo's affections. Feeding Mateo a fairy cake would be easy enough. Ópalo had witnessed his siblings' successes in that regard, but there was little choice in that kind of love. If Mateo was to give Ópalo his heart, it would be of his own volition, even if it meant that Mateo, like the apple, might be damaged and bruised. Lost.

He imagined his siblings would find this foolish, but none of them had faced a human lover like Mateo. His sisters were all quite different from him—eager to be brides and to fall in love. Surely, though, he would not wait long for Mateo's affection. Patience would be rewarded soon, he was quite certain. How could Mateo resist the pull between them? He must surely feel it when Ópalo felt overwhelmed by it.

Ópalo squeezed Mateo's fingers as they stepped into the ballroom, the fairy glass tossing rainbows everywhere in pools of color, the tables laden with only the most beautiful spreads of cakes, meats and wines. "It's lovely, isn't it?"

"Yes." Mateo spoke quietly so his sisters wouldn't hear.

The musicians struck an opening chord, bird cousins flew in to begin their symphony and the sisters were led to the tables. Each took up a cake in her fingers, and with varying expressions of eager expectation they took small, dainty bites. They accepted the wine Ópalo's brothers and sister offered and washed the rest of the cakes down.

"Are you hungry?" Ópalo asked.

"You told me not to eat."

"So I did, but that wasn't my question. Are you hungry?"

Mateo seemed to consider and then answered, "No."

Ópalo squeezed Mateo's hand. "This is important. You won't feel hunger, no matter how long you stay with us, but you will be tempted to eat anyway. Out of habit or curiosity for the food. Do not indulge, I beg of you."

"Why?"

While Mateo seemed impressed by the ballroom, the birds and the castle itself, Ópalo could see that his patience was wearing thin, and his nerves were fraying from the effort it took not to do something to gain control of his sisters.

"Fairy food, when consumed by humans, is a promise that can never be broken. They're bound to fairyland and their lovers forever, and must return to us at least once an earthly moon, or suffer greatly." Ópalo hesitated, but the rest needed to be shared as well. "There is an aphrodisiac effect as well."

He realized his error in revealing this information when Mateo began to unhook his cloak. Ópalo admired the flash in Mateo's eyes, the flush that rose to his face and his willingness to toss aside his own safety to save his sisters from that which they'd already succumbed to long ago. But things would only get very ugly if Mateo challenged Ópalo's siblings. He put a finger against Mateo's soft lips. "Shh, shh now, *mi pájaro*. It's too late. They've been here many times before and consumed much."

He held Mateo by the shoulders, feeling the strength of his body. Eventually, the fight went out of Mateo with a long exhalation. Ópalo's chest constricted at the look of sad defeat on his face.

"Please don't take it so hard, Mateo," Ópalo said, grabbing a cup of wine from a passing servant. He pressed it into Mateo's hand. "Drink. This will calm you."

Mateo stared at the cup, but took a hesitant sip when Ópalo urged him again.

"*Mi pájaro*, they are consorts of my brothers and sister, the most respected fae in our realm. There is nothing to be upset about."

"Nothing? They are under a thrall. They didn't choose this."

"But they did. Your sisters knew the consequences of eating the cakes. They do so willingly, eagerly even. They longed for the freedom."

"Freedom?"

"From your father's control. From their own inhibitions. They came here with eyes open. I admit my siblings encouraged them, but your sisters' wildest dreams have come true. They are so very happy."

Mateo nodded, but looked a bit numb as he took several deep swallows of wine before speaking. "Are they here to stay then? Are we all here to stay?"

Ópalo wished he didn't sound unhappy with the thought. Was the idea of being here so very terrible? "They can come and go as they please, but they'll always return. That's the promise they made when they ate our food. The promise they gave joyfully." Ópalo smiled reassuringly. "Look, the dancing has started."

Ópalo wished he could view the scene through Mateo's eyes. He'd only heard stories of the human realm, first from his father, and later from Mateo's sisters, but he knew enough to understand that Mateo had never seen anything like what he was witnessing now.

The ballroom was large, the biggest space in the castle by far, and made entirely of fairy-glass and platinum bars to hold the panes. The sun shone down into the room, setting the colors alight with a life of their own, pooling against the tile floor in some places, spinning and whirling in others. The birds and fae alike had thrown themselves into the dance—twisting, swinging, lifting and twirling, whether in midair or on the dance floor. They used their heels to drum the rhythm of the songs, whooping in delight as the festive mood escalated.

Luz and Adelita swirled by on the arms of Azulejo and Canario. The blue and white of Adelita's dress along with the yellow of Canario's feather hair combined reminded Ópalo of a summer day. Luz's billowing nightgown, mixed with Azulejo's blueness, was a cloud dancing with the sky. Glancing at Mateo, Ópalo saw that his eyes glittered with amazement. Pride in his world and the wild beauty it offered burst through Ópalo.

The feathers of birds and fae molted with each climax of song, confetti of floating color echoing the vibrant cacophony of music, birdsong, delighted cries of fae and the human laughter of Mateo's sisters. A river of sound poured over them, smoothing away all roughness.

Soon, the atmosphere of the room became a wild torrent of joy, and Ópalo sensed Mateo softening to it, becoming caught up in the jubilant chaos. As he drank the wine, his expression lost the harsh edge of worry and took on the exaltation of awe. Mateo's eyes at first followed his sisters, but eventually left them to their fervent fairy-magic dancing as he began to watch the birds and the fae, gasping occasionally at some spectacular display. It wasn't long before Ópalo saw Mateo had relaxed. His head moved to the music and his limbs, which he'd held tightly since he'd roused from his relaxation in the boat, went loose and easy, swinging along to the beat. Ópalo's heart lifted in his chest, taking flight with emotion. If only Mateo would relax enough to understand their destiny together!

Cacatúa swung by in the strong arms of Herminia, faces flushed, eyes glowing and their lips wet and open from the kisses they'd already shared. Next Josefina and Narciso twirled past, oblivious to everything but the desire pulsing between them, and then Gracia spun by Zafiro's side, teasing him with her eyes, drawing him closer and pressing wantonly against him. Mateo's sisters were lost deeply in fairy magic, their bodies and mind spinning with lust and passion. Ópalo could see his own siblings were focused entirely on their conquests, eager to bed them, but dragging the torment of the sensual dancing on just for fun.

"They won't notice if we join in," Ópalo said, eager to feel Mateo's body against his own. He took Mateo's empty second cup from him and handed it off to a servant. "All the fae and your sisters are so lost in the revelry now, delirium has set in. Nothing we do will seem amiss."

Mateo's breath visibly quickened, and he kept his eyes focused on the crowded dance floor. He didn't answer, but licked his lips as his pupils dilated, tugging the cloak closer around his shoulders. Ópalo stared at his beautiful brown eyes, drawn into their bright warmth. He noticed the dark hair curled around the edge of the pink shell of Mateo's ears, and his chest ached with a need to possess Mateo as his own.

Shaking himself free of the spell of Mateo's beauty, Ópalo turned to Mateo and bowed. He offered his hand and said formally, "May I have this dance, good prince?"

A shock of lust and rightness set Ópalo's mind aflame as he placed his hand firmly in the small of Mateo's back and guided him into the steps. He looked up, meeting Mateo's eyes, which had taken on the same glow as his sisters' after they consumed fairy cakes. Delirium seemed to consume him as well, brought on perhaps by exhaustion, two cups of wine, too many new wonders and more than a little shock. Mateo soon moved against Ópalo without any measure of shyness, his arousal evident.

It was as Ópalo had told his siblings, though they hadn't listened to him. The thrall of fairy cakes wasn't necessary. A fairy's nature—sensual, sexual, free—would inspire lust, and the usual desired outcome would arrive easily enough. There was no need for aphrodisiacs, and once they'd brought each other pleasure, Mateo would love him soon, surely.

"I want you," Mateo whispered, amazement in his tone and his eyes dark with desire. "I've felt this before for men, but this is stronger. Tell me, is this how I'm meant to feel?"

"Yes." Ópalo pressed his cock against him, gratified when Mateo shifted his thigh into Ópalo's hardness.

"Is this what my sisters feel?"

"They feel it more. The cakes escalate their passion until it's unbearable not to act on their urges. Your sisters tell me that the immensity of sensation while under their influence is quite glorious."

Mateo bent low, his face dropping close to Ópalo's, his eyes focused on Ópalo's mouth. He whispered, "I'm envious then. Although I can't imagine feeling more than this."

The tempo picked up, and Ópalo led Mateo into the dance with focus and fervor, moving against him so that their arousal was unflagging. He directed Mateo easily, finding him shockingly pliant in his arms, eager to follow and be led. Ópalo burned with the images that came to his mind—Mateo in Ópalo's nest, Mateo yielding and eager, Mateo following Ópalo over the edge into a trembling climax. His heart overflowed with love at these thoughts. Ópalo drove them both harder, moving them across the floor, not caring if they bumped into other fae in their exertions. All in the room were lost in the dance. No one paid attention to jostling from an invisible dancer and his fairy.

Mateo was out of breath and a thin trickle of sweat ran down his stubbled cheek. Ópalo dragged Mateo's head down as he lunged forward, rubbing his own fairy-smooth skin against the grain of hair. It scratched enticingly and he shuddered, repeating the gesture. He wanted nothing more than to feel the scrape of Mateo's odd, human hair against his skin again and again. He wondered if he tasted as delicious and different as he felt?

Mateo groaned, and Ópalo was surprised by the tentative hand in his feathers, pulling his head closer with a delicious tug. His brows and scalp ruffled in anticipation.

"Perhaps a cake would serve me in good stead," Mateo said, his voice pitched lower than before, urgent.

"I don't believe you require one."

Mateo appeared feverish, and Ópalo's gut clenched in rough desire.

Mateo practically growled as Ópalo gripped Mateo's chin. When he didn't jerk away, Ópalo dove up for a kiss. The softness of Mateo's lips and the wet warmth of his tongue tasted even better than the apple of Ópalo's youth. Human and fairy saliva mixed in the eager crush of their mouths, tasting bright and sweet at once. The heat between them grew in urgency. He shoved against Mateo, pushing him out of the whirling dance and across the ballroom until Mateo's back hit the wall.

Dancing fae swirled past them, birds swooped and called, and on either side, down the stretch of the wall, couples moved together, kissing, arching, thrusting, skirts and pants shifted aside. Grunts, moans and cries added to the rush of sound in the room.

Mateo's eyes went dark and hot, his hips moving against Ópalo's with what seemed to be mindless desperation. "Where do we go, how do you take me?"

The promise of those words!

"Here," Ópalo said, his heart slamming happily against his chest. Lust swelled, his feathers bristling on his head, his cock throbbing. Kissing Mateo again, he pressed against him, trying to get more pressure. Mateo grabbed him closer, lifting him up to his tiptoes to kiss at a better angle and thrust his hips against Ópalo's own.

Ópalo pushed against his strong chest, struggling free of his arms.

"I'm sorry," Mateo started breathlessly, but Ópalo stopped his apology short by shoving his hand into Mateo's trousers to grip his hard, thick cock.

Mateo's mouth dropped open, round, soft and glistening red. Ópalo couldn't resist sucking on those lips as he moved his hand in rapid strokes. Mateo whimpered, gripping Ópalo's hips to drag him close, clutching at Ópalo's ass as he submitted to his kiss and hand.

Mateo's prick was hot, blood rushing under the skin, heady, intoxicating and powerful. Ópalo stared into Mateo's wild eyes as he sucked Mateo's lips, licked the inside of his limp mouth and jerked his hand up and down the shaft of Mateo's cock, the sound of the dancers' heels pounding on the tiles behind them keeping the time. His heart danced with them.

Mateo moaned and shifted his feet. He released Ópalo's ass and clutched his feathers, gripping until the quills strained against Ópalo's scalp. Mateo's kiss became urgent, his lips moving roughly against Ópalo's, his tongue pressing into Ópalo's mouth. The sounds of Mateo's cresting passion swelled in the space around them and stirred every cell of Ópalo's being to thrilling joy.

Ópalo felt the surge, knew the moment was upon them, and with nimble, fast fingers, used his free hand to fully undo Mateo's trousers. He pulled out of Mateo's embrace, hearing the disappointed cry of denied release even as he felt the hard tile under his knees. He yanked Mateo's trousers down around his hips, freeing his cock and sac, taking a moment to admire the thick strength of Mateo's prick. He looked up to Mateo's face, struck by joyous lust at the sight of his dazed expression and wet lips.

Ópalo opened his mouth and in a quick move—perfected on many fae since he'd come of age—engulfed Mateo's cock, sucking him into his mouth before opening his throat to take him deeper. It throbbed against Ópalo's tongue with the rhythm of Mateo's human heart. Affection rose urgently through him and he stared up at Mateo, hoping Mateo felt the same connection.

"¡Dios mío!" Mateo moaned. His hands moved to Ópalo's feathers, gripping them hard enough for tears to sting Ópalo's eyes, but Mateo didn't move, simply gasping and staring down at Ópalo with a wild expression. Ópalo pulled off, licked the head and dove down again.

Mateo released Ópalo's feathers and pounded his fists back against the wall, shaking helplessly as his climax hit. Spurt after spurt of salty human seed filled Ópalo's mouth and he swallowed it eagerly. He coaxed more from Mateo's shuddering flesh by sucking hard on the head of his prick, working the shaft roughly with his hand until Mateo squirmed and pulled desperately at Ópalo's feathers.

Ópalo stood, his own cock aching, but he helped Mateo straighten his clothes before buttressing his shoulder under Mateo's arm. Mateo slumped, panting, red-faced and beautifully human against the wall. It was intoxicating to see.

The dance went on behind them as Mateo shook and shuddered, limp in Ópalo's arms. Ópalo gripped Mateo's chin and brought his head down for kisses, wet and deep, full of all of his eager hopes, as he used his other hand to work open his own breeches. Releasing his prick, he shoved Mateo down to his knees.

Eyes dilated, body still trembling, Mateo didn't protest and Ópalo rubbed his thumb over Mateo's lower lip in anticipation. He jerked his hand rapidly over his cock, thinking of the future, feeling his heart beating for Mateo already, and shifting his adoring gaze between Mateo's liquid brown eyes and the sweet, red opening of his mouth. Lust ricocheted up and down his spine, making his feathers stand on end, and his heart beat bird-fast. Mateo thrust his tongue out between his lips, a flat, slippery surface that Ópalo couldn't resist.

He grabbed a handful of Mateo's hair and slid the head of his aching cock over Mateo's tongue, feeling the twitter of end-song in his blood and balls, rushing through his pelvis. Mateo's eyes snapped with a playful seductiveness as he flicked his tongue at the slit in Ópalo's cock head. Ópalo fought the urge to force Mateo's lips wider to shove into his waiting throat. Later, later.

Instead he threw his head back and sang his pleasure and bright, new love as Mateo licked his sweet seed from where it leaked. As his feathers bristled, the song rushed harder through him. The music around them grew louder and louder, the sound of laughter, dancing, shouting and others achieving end-song seemed to swirl with Ópalo's own urgency. Mateo's lovely mouth was wide open, his eyes glazed with lust and his tongue out.

Ópalo crowed as he came, loud and raucous. Pink feathers exploded in his peripheral vision and his white, creamy seed burst onto Mateo's tongue. Mateo's eyes went wider and he squirmed. Ópalo held his hair tighter, decorating Mateo's cheeks, forehead and eyebrows with the slick of his release, delighted to see the evidence of his pleasure on his lover's face. Panting, shuddering, full of a sweet love and longing he'd been promised but never believed, he dropped to his knees. He wrapped his arm around Mateo's neck and licked the sweet fairy spendings from Mateo's stunned face.

"You're shaking," Ópalo said when they had both caught their breath.

"Am I?"

"Are you all right?"

"Oh, yes. I'm quite close to excellent, in fact."

Ópalo stroked a hand down Mateo's sweaty, spit-slick cheek, wiping away the dampness. Happiness whirled inside him as wild and beautiful as the dancing around him. "Come, let us dance. It's far from over."

Mateo nodded dumbly and stood when Ópalo did, following him out to the dance floor. Mateo's knees looked wobbly and his steps less refined, but before long the swing of the music and fairy madness overtook him again until they were kissing, rubbing, flying.

Chapter Six

THE DANCING WAS nothing like a ball at Mateo's court.

In the churning throng of barely restrained passion and primal desire, Mateo had been overcome by the lust in the air. If it had not seemed entirely fitting in the halls of the fae, his behavior would have embarrassed him beyond all ability to recover from it. As it was, he looked only at Ópalo as the music began to wind down—his blue eyes, his red lips, his feather-hair and his skin that in candlelight seemed to be made of a softer version of the stone for which he was named. Ópalo had done well for a distraction from the inappropriate behavior of Mateo's sisters.

Very well indeed.

Mateo had never imagined behaving so indecently—to taste and be tasted in public. Even though none had noticed, lost as they were to their own delirious lust, it still made him flush to remember how he'd been wanton as a whore.

Now with the dance over and his sisters flung over the shoulders of their fairy men and taken off to chambers within the castle of birdhouses, Mateo felt heat rise in his neck and face as he stared down at Ópalo's intense blue eyes.

"Come, *mi pájaro*," Ópalo murmured. "You could do with some air."

Mateo allowed Ópalo to lead him from the ballroom out onto a veranda overlooking the lake and bridge under which they'd rowed earlier in the day. It seemed a lifetime ago—and only moments, all at the same time.

The air off the water was refreshing on Mateo's hot cheeks, and he leaned against the cool stone of the baluster, careful to keep his cloak in place. The moon was low in the sky. Somehow an entire day had passed as he'd watched the fae and their cousins swoop in revelry, and he had no idea how to gauge how much time had gone by at home.

His gut twisted at the thought, but then Ópalo was next to him, pointing out the birdhouse villages beyond the castle. Mateo's mind returned to the wonders around him, and all that he'd seen and done.

He thought of Ópalo's light, firm hand on his waist, commanding him through the dance, even as he'd gazed up from several inches down. Ópalo was small, but nothing about him was anything less than fierce. Even his kindness had an edge of strength that could not be denied.

"Are you well?" Ópalo asked, his voice like Pura's low-pitched, comforting coo.

"I am bedazzled," Mateo answered truthfully. "What I have seen today!" He gazed into Ópalo's eyes. "What I have learned and felt. I don't have words for it."

Lámina would probably have words for it, story upon story, tale upon tale, but none of them had prepared him for the fever-pitch delirium of the fae world. The sensuality would never have been appropriate for children's ears, and yet Mateo wished that Lámina had given some sort of hint. "I am bewildered."

Ópalo's lips quirked at the confession, and Mateo wondered if he should be embarrassed, but he wasn't. There was no loss of regard in Ópalo's amusement.

"What do we do now? How long does this last?"

"If you were to return now, perhaps an hour would have gone by in your world. Your sisters usually stay for three days and return in time for breakfast with your father."

Three days. Mateo felt a strange tug in his chest, like the lilting song of a morning bird, hopeful and new with optimism at the sight of the rising sun. "Three days here, in exchange for the time lost in a single night?"

"You sound so disbelieving. Is your world so lacking in magic that you can hardly imagine this is true?"

Mateo blinked at him. "Our world lacks any magic at all."

Ópalo seemed horrified by that thought. "None at all?"

"Not in the least."

"Your sisters had never mentioned that. Though I suppose I ought to have guessed, as delighted as they are by the smallest bit of magic. I always thought a little of our world must seep through to yours, and find myself saddened that it hasn't."

"Stories," Mateo said. "It comes through in stories."

Ópalo smiled. "Well, now you have three days to see the truth of those stories for yourself."

"And what are we to do during these three days? Something more than dance, surely. Though, given the state of my sisters' shoes when they return, I might be supposing too much."

Ópalo laughed. "There is plenty of dancing, yes, but Luz likes to row the lake and walk the gardens, talking to Azulejo about the books he reads her at night. Cielo and Blanca enjoy painting and archery. Adelita and Canario spend much time studying the maps, discussing politics and provinces. Diamante and Elisa play chess for hours, though I suspect it's merely an intellectual prelude to a different kind of game. Catalina and Halcón often swim, splash and fight. They are an odd couple, less suited than I might have thought, and yet they rut constantly."

"Stop." Mateo raised his hand. "I cannot hear this. My heart will never recover from such images."

"Then I shouldn't mention Gallo and Imelda. There's no dark corner that hasn't been graced by their amorous embrace. Tulipan and Felipa ride out every morning and rarely return until night. They're enthralled with one another and seek only to be out of sight of other fae or human. Would you like to know of the others?"

Mateo knew he should care. But he found he didn't. "No. But tell me, what shall we do?"

"You intend to stay then? You don't wish me to row you back at once?"

Mateo gazed about, taking in the beautiful, strange world around him once more. How could he leave now? It seemed that he had only just stumbled onto a most marvelous discovery. "Yes. I will return with my sisters."

Ópalo's teeth, pressed into the pink pad of his lower lip, gleamed in the light of the moon. "I can't tell you how happy this makes me. As for how we spend your time here, I'll leave those choices to you, *mi pájaro*, until we discover what activities we enjoy."

Ópalo leaned against him, the heat of his body drawing Mateo closer until their mouths were mere inches apart. "You've walked a great distance, seen too many new things and danced with great energy. It's time to rest."

Mateo licked his lips. He didn't wish to rest. His body felt alive, as though perhaps he had tasted fairy food. He thrummed and ached and wanted. A sweep of giddy emotion washed over him with an impulse to stand up on the edge of the balustrade and fling himself over to see if he, like Ópalo's vibrant cousins, could fly.

"My home...it seems far away. From this. Your world." Mateo gazed out at the water. Everything seemed so exciting, alive and marvelous.

The birdhouse villages shimmered on the horizon in colors Mateo had never imagined, and the fae themselves were shimmering, feathered beauties such as he'd never known possible. He thought of the village surrounding his father's castle, the dark, drab buildings, the grim stonework and the dirty villagers in their dingy clothes. Compared to Ópalo and his family, Mateo's father's and sisters' own garb seemed dull.

"What do you know of my world?" Mateo asked.

"Very little. Perhaps nothing in the scheme of things. I know that apples taste nice, but not as nice as your mouth."

Mateo laughed. "Nor as nice as yours."

"Indeed?"

"Indeed." Mateo took several more deep breaths and turned his back on the view, focusing on Ópalo's handsome face—the blue of his eyes, the marvel of his pink feathery eyebrows.

"You're certain of the passage of time?" Mateo had never known that blue eyes could be so warm, and he licked his lips, dropping his gaze to Ópalo's mouth.

"Quite sure."

"And staying does me no harm?" Mateo murmured.

"No harm at all. You're safe here. Relax and enjoy yourself."

"Tempting."

Ópalo indicated some side doors leading into the castle. "Come with me then?"

Mateo nodded, unable to find any reason to voice an objection, and let Ópalo lead him.

LIKE THE REST of the world into which Mateo had followed his sisters, Ópalo's chambers were strange and bizarrely beautiful. The ceiling was a domed mass of straw, sticks, and pieces of bright-colored threads woven into the fuzz of worn fabrics—an inverted nest. The internal walls were made of warm-colored materials and covered with brightly colored swaths of fabric, all frayed about the edges as though birds had pulled at the seams to extract threads for nests elsewhere—and Mateo believed they had, for the external wall was truncated with the top half open to the air.

A warm breeze wafted through the room, carrying the scent of the flowers he'd spotted on the veranda below, and the stars and moon were clearly visible in the night sky. To Mateo, who had lived through long, cold winters, the room was overwhelming in its beauty.

The chamber was sparsely decorated otherwise, with a wooden desk in the corner revealing a mess of what appeared to be plans or designs of some kind, an ornate armoire with the doors left open, revealing a spill of rich fabric and feathers within, and nothing else.

"Sleep will refresh you."

Ópalo motioned toward the pallet on the floor. Circular in shape, like the ceiling, it was more a nest than a bed, made of piles of colorful patterned blankets shot through with gold and silver threads, and plump cushions of such obvious softness that Mateo yearned to lie down on them, resting his weary body and propping up his sore feet. But sleep was something he didn't yet want.

He allowed himself to be maneuvered closer to the nest, his fingers shaking as he undressed himself, his eyes tracking Ópalo to the armoire.

"For you." Ópalo lifted a warm, brown nightshirt. "It may be small, but I'll have clothes made for you tomorrow, and this should do."

"No need. I prefer to sleep naked." If Mateo was in fairyland, then he intended to march bravely into debauchery. Too late to turn back now. "And as it stands, I don't want to sleep," Mateo said.

Ópalo's lips curved into a smile and he whispered, "Then we don't have to."

The nest was soft and warm. The pillows and blankets were smooth against Mateo's naked skin, and he felt safe lying on his back in its hollow while he watched Ópalo's clothes fall to the floor.

Mateo gripped his own cock, blood rushing hard as Ópalo threw his shirt aside, revealing a pale, sculpted chest and stomach with nipples so red they already looked kissed and bitten. Mateo moaned softly and licked his lips, eager to make them redder and harder, to tease them with his teeth and tongue.

As Ópalo's breeches dropped, Mateo's stomach curled with sharp desire and he gasped, jerking his cock slowly. He'd licked the head of Ópalo's prick, but he'd never imagined such beauty, such odd, fierce, strong beauty—solid and long, standing up in an eager hardness from a mat of pink feathers. And his balls! They looked so human and vulnerable within the wrinkled, tight walnut bulge of soft skin surrounded by the soft feathers above.

Mateo bit into his bottom lip, remembering the taste of the sweetness shot from them. He reached out to Ópalo, wanting him to kneel over Mateo's face so he could mouth his sac, grab that delicious-looking ass and thoroughly debauch himself in ways he'd only dreamed of before. While true friendship—or more—seemed impossible to fathom at the moment, there was no reason Mateo could think of now, resting comfortably as he was in Ópalo's nest, to hold back from his lusts. He'd yearned for a man's touch for years, and Ópalo had the skill and clear desire to share his own knowledge on the matter.

Yet Ópalo turned to the desk and opened one of its many drawers, withdrawing a bottle. Moonlight poured in, sparkling on the glass, lighting a path on the floor and dancing over Ópalo's skin.

"We'll need this," Ópalo said as he climbed into the nest.

Ópalo crawled toward him and Mateo reached to grab. Ópalo looked so light, as though his bones were hollow, and yet when he moved, it was with such strength that it took Mateo's breath away. Their kiss was not tentative, not even tender, but rough and full of want and promise. Mateo moaned for more of it, and as their hips surged together, pricks colliding again and again, they kissed and sucked, bit and whimpered, rolled, wrestled and struggled.

It was only when Mateo was pinned on his back, his right leg hitched up by one of Ópalo's arms, and Ópalo's slicked fingers pushed their way into his asshole that he realized in the midst of their passionate writhing and kissing, they'd been fighting for position—and he'd lost. Thank God he'd lost, for it was the sweetest defeat. He moaned as Ópalo's fingers breached him.

"Take me!"

"Shh," Ópalo soothed him, then nipped Mateo's earlobe. "Oh, I will take you."

Ópalo thrust his fingers in and out, and Mateo squirmed down, wanting more. It was all he'd wanted since he was old enough to know, all that no one had ever had the daring to take—being held down, being thrust into with fingers or cock, whatever they wished, calmed and stroked and mastered as he shook and begged for more. This, this had always been his dream—the secret things he'd longed for in the dark of his chambers.

"You're unused to this treatment, *mi pájaro*," Ópalo murmured. "You're so tight on my fingers."

"Please, please," Mateo begged, panting, his eyes stinging with sweat that dripped from his forehead, blurring his vision so that the ceiling became nothing but glinting color and light.

Ópalo's weight was firm against the back of Mateo's raised thigh. His fingers twisted inside Mateo until he found something. Mateo clenched his fists in the blankets under him, arched and made a sound he'd never made before—high pitched, unrestrained. And then Ópalo did it again. Mateo's balls drew up, his cock lifted and he almost shot his seed, but Ópalo shifted down to bite Mateo's lip hard, and instead of coming he cried out in surprise.

"Shush, now," Ópalo whispered, licking softly at the sore place he'd made on Mateo's lip. "Steady yourself. You're so handsome like this! All red lipped, hot skinned, and inside! You are so hot inside!"

Ópalo worked his fingers roughly over the place that made Mateo see flames behind his eyelids and set his asshole, prick and balls raging with need. The kisses Ópalo fed him now were gentle, full of nips and licks, but quite tender compared to Ópalo's treatment of his hole.

"Do you intend to drive me insane?"

"I intend to ready you."

"I believe you've done well enough of that," Mateo gasped.

"Do you? Perhaps you're right, *mi pájaro*."

When Ópalo slid his fingers out, Mateo almost grabbed Ópalo's hand to push them back inside, but Ópalo soothed him some more, and showed him the bottle.

"Let me slick myself," Ópalo whispered, and Mateo watched as the clear fluid in the bottle poured into Ópalo's palm. "Don't be afraid."

Glistening and ready, Ópalo's cock suddenly looked incredibly large, but Mateo was determined. "Do it. Now."

Ópalo's eyes were hot as blue fire as he grabbed Mateo's legs behind the knees, pushed them up with a strong grip and lined himself up.

"Hold your legs open," Ópalo ordered, and Mateo obeyed, focusing on Ópalo's swollen lips, his burning eyes and his prick pushing for entrance at Mateo's hole.

The sharp burn that shot through his pelvis took his breath away. He squeezed his eyes shut as memories he'd nursed for years filled his mind—the smooth thrusts of the buggers he'd witnessed in the stables during his fourteenth year. He remembered the cries of pleasure, the body-shaking, howling end that had taken the impaled groom by storm and the milky seed that shot from his hard cock like cannon fodder.

This was not like this. This was pain. Where had the bliss from Ópalo's fingers run to? Now he felt as though his ass was being cleaved in half. He almost kicked Ópalo away. But Ópalo, in his surprising strength, took hold of his chin and forced Mateo to look up at him. "Do not take your eyes from my face."

Mateo stared at Ópalo, taking in his fierce commanding soul pouring into Mateo through his eyes. Mateo relaxed under his hand. As he did, Ópalo withdrew and then pushed inside again.

"That's it, *mi pájaro, sí. Sí.* So lovely, *muy guapo,* so tight and slick. That's it. Sweet, sweet bird. Sweet bird."

Ópalo moved against him, his stomach rubbing seductively against Mateo's cock, feathers tickling softly. Mateo relaxed more and more, and Ópalo's eyes grew hotter, and then it was good, deliciously good, and Mateo reached between their bodies to grip his own prick.

"That's right. Touch yourself. Bring yourself pleasure. ¡*Sí!* Oh, Mateo! How good you feel around me!"

Mateo panted under Ópalo's rapid thrusts. He tried to keep his eyes on Ópalo's face, but couldn't for long, falling into a place where only the pleasure existed—his cock, his ass, Ópalo's prick slamming into him, the cries that sounded like desperate birdsong circling around them.

Then the world contracted, as though the room squeezed him tight. Ópalo pulled his cock out of Mateo's hole, jammed it back inside with much less care than the first time and collapsed onto Mateo, his hard, pale body fucking into him. Mateo's world exploded into pleasure, convulsing limbs, jerking pricks, spurts of wet seed, open mouths mashed together and too much ecstasy to comprehend.

It was more powerful than any climax Mateo had known. All consuming and stuffed full with shuddering joy. And as he managed to open his eyes, panting and sweating from his exertions, he found himself holding Ópalo's shaking body tight against him while small, twittering cries of pleasure ripped from Ópalo's throat and pink feathers puffed from Ópalo's head and floated down around them. Mateo kissed Ópalo's temple, grinning at the tickle of feathers against his skin as they settled.

"And I haven't even tasted your heart yet," Ópalo whispered against Mateo's sweaty shoulder.

"God help me if you do," Mateo whispered.

His soul felt weak in the aftermath of pleasure. He was certain if Ópalo asked for his heart now and pressed a fairy cake to his lips, he'd eat it. The thought scared him, but not enough to move out of Ópalo's embrace or to regret a moment of what they'd done together. If anything, the rush of fear made him want to drown it out with more of Ópalo's skin, feathers, mouth and cock. Mateo squeezed around Ópalo's prick, still hard inside of him, and reveled in the madness.

Chapter Seven

Ó PALO SHIVERED AGAINST Mateo, remembering his own first experience of lying with another fairy. He'd been insatiable, wanting more of the fairy's cock, more of his kisses, more of everything, until he'd burned out bright and exhausted after a few days of near-constant pleasure. Ópalo hadn't felt that way since that first time, enjoying encounters well enough when he sought them out, but he'd always known he was meant for more. He was meant for Mateo.

Looking at Mateo's shining, sweaty form, still trembling around Ópalo's cock, he felt that same endless virility all over again. Mateo's hole spasmed against Ópalo's shaft, sending a surge through him, and Ópalo was tempted to roll his hips, thrust and start the pleasure all over again. He could ride Mateo's squirming, bucking body all night.

But he also sensed Mateo was inexperienced and he didn't wish to hurt him. Humans healed more slowly than fairies, his brothers had warned him after their own peerless first nights with Mateo's sisters.

"Was I too rough?" Ópalo asked softly, gently pulling his cock free and pressing his fingers to Mateo's hole.

"Put it back," Mateo commanded.

Ópalo snorted softly, lifting his head to smile at Mateo. "Eager for more?"

"Yes. Please, Ópalo. I want you back in me."

Ópalo mouthed at Mateo's shoulder, scraping his teeth against Mateo's hot skin. "I think not. After that, I must declare you are well and truly used, *mi pájaro*. You need rest."

"No, I'm fine. Ópalo, I'm ready. Truly. Let us do it again."

Ópalo smiled and touched Mateo's lips gently, feeling the dull thud of blood under their red, swollen skin. He obliged Mateo's begging by lining up his cock and pushing it back into Mateo's tight ass. "Better?" he asked.

"Mmm," Mateo answered, his eyelashes fluttering against his flushed cheeks.

Ópalo thrust gently, his own spendings smoothing the way. "One more time," he whispered, taking hold of Mateo's cock and pumping it gently.

It didn't take long. Mateo was relaxed and wanton, whining and moaning for more and harder, while Ópalo was gentle and slow, keeping his thrusts long and even. Mateo writhed against him, trying to speed his tempo, but Ópalo was determined not to break his human lover— certainly not on the first night.

"I need it," Mateo whimpered.

"I know you do. I'm giving it to you."

Mateo tossed his head, clenched around Ópalo's cock, grabbed handfuls of blankets and keened.

Ópalo grinned, keeping his thrusts steady and his hand moving on Mateo's straining cock. "There," he said, proudly. "There."

Mateo's face in ecstasy was beautiful—red cheeks, mouth blooming with cries, eyes wide and hot, staring into Ópalo's own. Then there was the tension in his muscles, wiry and strong. The animal beauty of his cock straining and finally pulsing once more with hard, strong kicks from his balls through his shaft. His pleasure wrenched him through a series of spasms that Ópalo captured in the clenching around his cock.

"¡Dios mío!" Mateo whimpered, dark curls sweaty against his face, his body heaving.

Ópalo pulled out of Mateo's ass, bent low to kiss it once as it spasmed and twitched closed, and then knelt over Mateo's form, moving his hand quickly along his own prick until he threw his head back and wrenched out drops of seed, singing to the rafters as he climaxed.

"Oh sweet fuck," Mateo cursed, watching him.

"Yes," Ópalo agreed, collapsing on top of Mateo, kissing his neck, his stubbly face and then his mouth.

They clung to each other, both trembling, until Mateo whispered, "I think I'm tired now."

Mateo fell asleep almost immediately, rolling away and curling onto his side, a sleep-smile on his lips, his face boyish in the moonlight. Ópalo turned his attention to the spendings smeared over both of them. He scratched at the drying clumps of it in his lower feathers before reaching out to run his fingers over the fresh seed on Mateo's hard stomach. He brought the white fluid to his lips. It tasted salty, different. Human.

Ópalo was tired too. Tired and a bit sore from the intensity of his end-songs. But sleep seemed an impossibility. He ran his eyes over Mateo's long limbs, sprinkled with dark hair—such an odd, soft and yet scratchy thing hair could be, so unlike feathers, and yet so lovely. Ópalo lingered at the matted tangle of tight curls around the base of Mateo's cock and admired the soft shape of it.

Bristles of hair also led from Mateo's cock up to his belly button, and Ópalo took another swipe of Mateo's seed from his stomach, licking it clean. Ópalo grinned, a thrill shooting through him. Mateo had arrived finally and was now naked and sated in his bed.

Oh Mateo. Mateo of the brown, wide eyes that seemed to grow ever darker as his lust grew, and then clenched close in a spasm of bliss as he came. Mateo, who made him feel as though his soul was flying. Ópalo felt as though he could rhapsodize over Mateo's handsome form forever, and yet—something was not quite as Ópalo had expected it to be. As happy as he was, he did not feel complete, not the way his siblings had described it to him after the arrival of their mates.

Ópalo fell back to the bed, examining the emptiness that dwelled somewhere beneath his rib cage. It was an ache he had a long acquaintance with.

"BUT IT DOESN'T feel right, Father," Ópalo said, sitting on his father's knee, watching the rest of his siblings learn the latest dances from the lovely Baila.

Every day his father oversaw the dancing. Aside from the guidance he gave to Canario with regard to the maps and some especially important alliances with fae from other kingdoms, dance was the only part of their education their father oversaw.

"Dance is a fairy's birthright," his father used to say. "To dance is to be fae. So you must learn to dance well, my darlings."

Soon Ópalo would join his siblings in the exhilarating lessons. He couldn't wait. The swinging movements that seemed to echo the flight of their cousins were intoxicating to watch and Ópalo wanted desperately to be part of it.

At his age, he was withheld from the great ballroom during the high dances, but one day he would be old enough and would join in. So he practiced daily with his siblings in their rooms, Azulejo being his most common partner. But sometimes Cacatúa swept him up and together they twirled about for hours.

"What doesn't feel right, *mi pájaro?*" his father asked, tugging on Ópalo's pink feathers affectionately.

"This hole in my heart." Ópalo put his small hand over his chest. "It doesn't hurt badly, Father, but only just. It cries out all the time for something to fill it."

"Ah." His father patted his head and frowned softly. "Unfortunately my boy, you must become accustomed to it. I'm afraid that ache in your heart won't be soothed for quite some time."

Baila spun Halcón around until he nearly tripped. Ópalo clapped when Halcón righted himself and began an even more difficult step, completing it with ease. Halcón sneered at Ópalo, rebuffing his childish enthusiasm as he always did, but his sneer slipped when their father lifted a hand in his direction.

"Never mind him, Ópalo. He misses his mother."

Ópalo never understood what that perennial excuse for Halcón's dislike had to do with him, but he was accustomed to it, and the world would not seem right without Halcón's glares and sneers.

"Do you have it too, Father?"

"What? Oh, the hole? I do. Mine never went away. Not with their mother, and not with yours. I'm afraid a human heart is the only remedy, and there was never a human heart meant for me. My father's alliance with the humans was broken." His father tapped Ópalo's nose with the end of a long gray feather. It had fallen from his father's head at the beginning of the lesson when Baila had used Father as a partner to demonstrate a step. Since then, they had taken turns tickling each other with it. "But that is where you are lucky, Ópalo. You have a human heart and a human bride waiting for you. I have seen to it. And when she arrives, the ache will be gone. All you must do is grow up and be patient. Do you think you can do that?"

"I can try, Father."

Baila and Cacatúa were taking their turn now, and Ópalo watched them spin. The blur of their skirts was dizzying, and when they both set their heels down in time, striking a pose together, Ópalo smiled and clapped with giddy joy.

Father patted him. "That's my good little bird."

ÓPALO SIGHED, TURNING back to study Mateo's dark lashes resting on his golden cheek. Patient, his father had said, was all Ópalo had to be. Ópalo was unusually good at cultivating patience. His work called for it, and dealing with all of his brothers and his sister required it. Then there was the matter of waiting for Mateo to come. So long he'd waited. Not as many years as Canario or any of the older siblings, but long enough that he was eager now for the ache to end.

But now it seemed he must wait even longer, because Mateo did not yet return his devotion. The choice to warn him against the fairy food seemed foolish in the light of Mateo's beautiful body and the pleasure they'd shared—and especially when measured against the continued ache in Ópalo's chest.

Perhaps his siblings had been right to take the shorter approach, bypassing whatever a human might require before falling in love under the power of fairy magic. Because now that Mateo was here, Ópalo didn't know just how patient he could continue to be.

Exhaustion began to overwhelm his excitement, and he curled up next to Mateo, taking in the scent of his skin and the warmth of his breath. Ópalo started to drift off, his hand wrapped around Mateo's forearm, brushing softly against the hair his fingers found there. He reminded himself that he had three days, after all. Surely Mateo would love him by then? And if he did not, then perhaps when he returned….

Ópalo jolted awake. His next thought so terrible that his heart pounded in his chest, and his skin went clammy with fearful sweat.

What if Mateo leaves with his sisters and never returns?

Ópalo rose from the bed and paced, watching the moon traverse the sky, wondering at his own stupidity in not taking the easy way.

Chapter Eight

MORNING OPENED WITH a symphony of birdsong and Mateo stretched luxuriously, reveling in the heavy relaxation in his limbs. His lower back felt loose and warm, and he knew if he opened his eyes, he wouldn't find himself in his room at the castle. Instead he was naked in the nest of a fairy with whom he'd shamelessly shared carnal delights. He kept his eyes closed, prolonging the moment before he faced a world in which fairies truly existed and his sisters were as good as married.

When Mateo was ready, he found the room a brighter version of what he'd seen the night before. The light from the morning sun sparkled in the golden threads throughout the ceiling nest above and reflected off a mirror hanging next to the armoire. He heard the cry of a bird just before one soared into the room, tore a long length from a red piece of fabric hanging on the wall opposite, and flew out again.

Slowly, he turned onto his side to face the naked, curled form of the fairy next to him. As he met Ópalo's intent gaze, a wave of heat flooded Mateo's belly and chest, rose up his neck and warmed his cheeks. It wasn't shame or even embarrassment at what they'd done, but it was a shyness that took him by surprise, a bashful sort of joy he'd never felt before.

"Hello," Ópalo said softly. "Did you sleep well?"

"I did. And you?"

"You snore," Ópalo said by way of answering. A grin dimpled his cheeks. "Has anyone ever told you?"

"No, I didn't know."

"It's a funny-sounding snore, with a whistle at the end."

"My apologies. It must have kept you awake."

Ópalo's eyes softened and he tilted his head against the pillow. "No, it was my pleasure to listen to your hideous night noises." He laughed and propped his head on his hand.

Mateo sat up, pink feathers sticking to his skin. The bed was littered with them. He remembered puffs of molted color when Ópalo had reached climax, and Mateo plucked one off his thigh and studied it. The stem was a deeper pink than the barbs, almost red, and the downy part at the bottom was so light it was nearly white.

"I enjoyed last night," Mateo said, keeping his gaze on the feather.

"As did I."

"And at home, it's still the middle of the night?"

"Yes, in your world they'll sleep for days yet."

Mateo twirled the feather. "I must decide what I intend to do."

Ópalo bolted up beside him. "About?"

"About my sisters and their marriages." He looked to Ópalo, raked his eyes over Ópalo's mouth, his long neck and his firm chest. He dragged his gaze back up before he lost his train of thought contemplating Ópalo's hard cock. At the edge of his peripheral vision, he could see how the rosy head of it pressed against Ópalo's stomach. Mateo swallowed hard. "About you."

"Do you want to decide before or after breakfast?" Ópalo asked.

Mateo frowned. "You told me not to eat."

"My breakfast," he clarified. "I'm famished."

Mateo watched Ópalo rise from the bed, his cock swinging in mid-air, proud and erect.

"Do you mind?" Ópalo asked. "I'll call for them to bring me something, and then I'll happily listen as you decide what to do about your sisters and their marriages. What you decide to do about me."

Mateo nodded dumbly, unable to speak around the lust rising through him. His own cock lengthened and strained for Ópalo's attention. He rubbed a hand over his face, trying to concentrate. He'd been thinking about the situation with his sisters, about the fae and the prospects for marriage.

Ópalo let out a loud call, and birds echoed it from outside. He grabbed a red sheet from the pile of fabric spilling from the armoire and wrapped it around his waist, accentuating his pale skin, bright nipples, red mouth and pink hair. Mateo swallowed hard. He'd never known he could be so moved by these particular details of a man's body. He'd been aroused by Sir Franco's forearms and broad chest, and there had been others fair of face and strong of shoulder, but red nipples had never entered his mind as being the apparent aphrodisiac that they were.

It's because he's fae. It's the power I sense from him, some kind of fairy thrall and nothing more.

And yet, he found he didn't care.

Ópalo seated himself at the edge of the nest, smiling. "Go on then?"

Mateo's cock was insistent now, fairy thrall or no, he wanted to rub his hard length all along Ópalo's neck, down his chest, over his trail of feathers and then squeeze it up next to Ópalo's cock. "I'm afraid I can't think."

Ópalo shrugged one shoulder and said, "Would you like me to suck you while we wait for my food?"

Mateo said nothing. He was so desperately aroused that falling back on the bed and spreading his legs was all that he could manage.

ÓPALO WAS ACCUSTOMED to keeping his silence while other people worked through issues and made plans he might not agree with. He never would have survived his childhood with eleven older siblings had he not. Yet with Mateo he found it harder than usual not to interject.

Perched side by side on the edge of the nest, they faced the window. Ópalo listened as Mateo ruminated. He spread nectar over his morning boiled eggs, a combination that made Mateo cock his head curiously.

Ópalo almost offered up a bite, but then remembered with regret that Mateo would not be eating during his time here.

"I should reveal myself to my sisters," Mateo said thoughtfully, running long, handsome fingers through his soft curls.

Ópalo popped several berries into his mouth, enjoying the combination of flavors. "What will they think when they see you?"

"I'm sure they'll at first believe me here to thwart their happiness."

"Isn't that why you came?"

"Hardly. I came because I wanted to discover their secret and put a stop to whatever it was they were doing that's causing my father so much distress. He has an old heart, you see. He can't be expected to live much longer under the strain they've put him under."

"So your aim was to thwart their happiness for a noble cause."

Mateo frowned and leaned forward to put his elbows on his knees, gripping his hair in both hands. "I had no idea what I would find. It isn't as though I could have known fairyland was real, that fae exist and that my sisters have given themselves over willingly to them."

"As have you."

Mateo scoffed. "My body perhaps. My heart is still my own."

Ópalo hid his flinch and busied himself with adding more nectar to his eggs. The hole in his own heart throbbed at Mateo's careless reminder. *He doesn't know what it means for you. Don't think him callous.* Ópalo took a steadying drink of water and met Mateo's eyes again, listening.

"Their hearts have been given away utterly. I can see that for myself. It explains everything. Their behavior toward our father, the cold reaction to my pleas that they stop before they kill him. The fae have their hearts now. Their souls."

"You seem under the misapprehension that my siblings are somehow controlling your sisters. They choose for themselves, *mi pájaro*. Out of love for your father they return to your world. They could easily have chosen to stay."

Mateo stared at Ópalo, seeming to measure the veracity of his statements. "Why haven't they been honest with him then?"

Ópalo shrugged and popped egg into his mouth. "I imagine it's out of fear that the truth will kill him, or he'll somehow stop them from coming. He could block off the portal, or destroy it entirely. It's a risk they've been unwilling to take."

"They should have been honest. At least with me."

"Luz was considering it and I was hopeful she would since I'd begun to dream you might be the bride."

"I'm no one's bride."

"I've been waiting for you." Ópalo didn't point out that Mateo had shared his bed quite willingly and that save for Ópalo's inopportune fall into love and subsequent decision to forego the fairy cakes during their row on the lake, Mateo would be his bride—happily so.

"Yet she didn't tell me. She left me to discover it all for myself. I would have expected my twin to take me into her confidence and allow me to enter this world more prepared."

"Prepared with what?" Ópalo lifted his brow and made the mocking motion of shooting a bow. "An army perhaps?"

Mateo shifted guiltily. "It isn't as though we are a martial people. Father and I, had we understood the full extent of their dedication to their lovers, would have come to a reasonable conclusion, I'm certain. We wouldn't have hurt you."

"We fae are peaceful unless provoked. Then we are quite dangerous. We have magic, our cousins' claws and beaks, and an arsenal of fairy weapons on our side. Perhaps your sisters wanted to forestall any possibility of outright conflict. Because if my siblings felt their brides were threatened, rest assured, they would hurt you."

As I will hurt anyone or anything that tries to bring harm to you, mi pájaro.

Mateo's jaw worked and his gaze turned to the open wall. The sky was incredibly blue and the clouds were white spires in the air. The cousins darted about playing games of chase.

Mateo sighed. "It's complicated. I can see that now."

"Perhaps your sisters simply hadn't had time to figure out an elegant resolution to the problem."

Mateo laughed, but it wasn't a pretty sound like the sweet giggles and chuckles Ópalo had elicited from him earlier in the nest. "Hardly. I rather believe that in the end they found a great deal of amusement in fooling everyone, in proving they were smarter than all those silly suitors. Smarter than all of us."

"Suitors?"

"Didn't they tell you? I suppose they wouldn't for fear you might not allow them to go back. My father is even now running a contest, one might call it. Whosoever can tell him where my sisters go at night and what they do there will win the hand of any of my father's children and the riches to go with it."

"Any of his children?"

"That's right. Even me. My sisters' shenanigans have put my future and my happiness on the gaming table. I think you begin to understand why I feel they owed me an explanation."

Ópalo could indeed. "Were there any contestants for your hand?"

Mateo's brow arched and his red lips quirked. "Why? Would you like to compete?"

Ópalo swallowed another bite of egg rather than replying. The idea of going up against a human for Mateo made his heart pound with a bloodthirsty thrill he'd never experienced. His feathers twisted on his head, and he felt a cold sensation sweep over him. He'd win if it came to physical combat. He was small, but he was fierce, and he wasn't going to let Mateo just walk away with some hot-blooded brute of a human.

"You'd be going up against a princess who hopelessly loves my sister Adelita and an old widowed king who wants to build me the biggest dovecote I've ever seen in exchange for me being sweet about sucking his prick."

Ópalo's feathers settled again. The odds of winning should it come to confronting these opponents had gone from certain to dead certain, and he no longer felt the urge to shred his napkin. "Do you want either of them?"

Mateo's laughter was genuine this time. "I say not. I gather you understand the princess lacks a certain something I'd sorely miss, and the king...well, I think I made myself clear of my opinion of him in my original description of his Highness."

"Then I see no reason to compete. I'm incontestable."

Mateo snorted. "Overconfident, I'd say."

"Would you?"

"Indeed. If I had to choose between you and one of them, I'd choose you of course," Mateo said, but his tone was not exactly encouraging. "Still I'd rather not be forced to choose at all. I don't intend to marry. I'll win my own hand from my father and do as I see fit with my life."

Ópalo's chest felt tight. He couldn't stop his mind from turning back to what they'd shared in the nest—pleasure, sweat, laughter, cries of ecstasy—and wondering how Mateo could make it sound as though choosing Ópalo would be such a disappointment.

Ópalo cleared his throat. "So you will reveal your sisters' secret to your father?"

Mateo nodded. "I will. I'm not quite sure when or how just yet. But I'll reveal it to him once I've determined whether or not arrangements for their marriages to your siblings are something I can condone." Then his face softened. "And when I'm quite sure that the portal won't be damaged or destroyed. Because I don't believe I'm done playing with you just yet."

Ópalo licked his spoon clean of nectar, keeping his eyes averted. He'd always been so sure of himself, and Mateo's casual disregard for the hole in Ópalo's heart and the call of their fate was an unexpected bludgeon to his confidence. Yet Mateo didn't seem to mean any harm by it. He spoke like it was perfectly natural and as if Ópalo couldn't possibly feel any more strongly for him that he felt for Ópalo.

Humans were so oddly protective of their hearts when not under the sway of fairy magic. He wondered if their world made it so, or if it was a defect in Mateo alone. Perhaps this reluctance in him was what had held the brides back for so long. Perhaps this was why Lámina had not sent them before.

"I am not done with you either," Ópalo said, putting his napkin and spoon aside. "The cousins have no doubt delivered the message to the tailor with your measurements by now and fresh clothes should arrive within the hour. We should spend that time in my nest, don't you think? I believe there is a position you'll enjoy."

Mateo's cheeks flamed, and yet he crawled back into Ópalo's nest before Ópalo even stood to drop his feathered robe to the floor.

Chapter Nine

L UZ'S DARK HAIR splayed out in the green grass where she lay next to the blue-feathered fairy Mateo had seen her with the night before. She wore a grand dress constructed of purple and green feathers. Though Mateo rarely paid much attention to the fashion of the *damas de corte* or his sisters, he recognized that it was unlike any gown she owned back home.

As Mateo approached with Ópalo's hand at the small of his back, his stomach tightened. Certainly it was time to confront his sisters, starting with Luz, and let them know of his presence in fairyland. But would she be able to look at him and know that he'd spent the night and morning in Ópalo's nest, held down and mounted?

For all the teasing Luz and his other sisters had given him over the years, his experience with Ópalo was too private and still far too raw to be the subject of his twin's amusement. He could feel the control he'd been seeking over his older sisters—yes, nine minutes made a difference—flying from him like the birds that scattered from the edge of the lake at his approach.

Luz twirled a flower in her fingers and laughed at something the fairy next to her said before taking note of the birds' flight and turning her head. Mateo barely had time to work his mouth into the form of a greeting when Luz was up and barreling toward him, charging into him with a grin and a hug so fierce he took several steps back, accidentally knocking Ópalo to the ground.

"Little brother!" she cried, kissing his cheek and clutching at the bright-green jacket Ópalo's tailors had constructed for him so quickly that fairy magic must have been involved. "I knew it was you following us in the forest!"

Mateo blinked rapidly. He'd been so certain of his own stealth. "You knew? How?"

"Your cologne, silly. But never mind now. Tell me, how did you do it?"

Out of the corner of his eye, Mateo saw his sister's fairy help Ópalo up, and felt certain that he'd failed to be gallant in some important way. But Ópalo was grinning as he knocked the dirt from the seat of his breeches and didn't seem offended by Mateo's distraction from offering him a gentlemanly hand.

"How did you follow us without being seen? You, who could never win at hide-and-seek, managed to fool Adelita and all the rest!"

"Lámina gave me a magic cloak. It makes me invisible."

It was absurd when he said it aloud, but Luz accepted it easily enough. Why shouldn't she? They were in fairyland, keeping company with fae. What was so amazing about a magic cloak in comparison to that?

"An invisible cloak! How wonderful." She laughed. "Oh Mateo. I'm so glad you're here. Is it not marvelous? Is it not beautiful?" Luz gripped his arms and shook him slightly. "Aren't you happy I didn't make a scene in the forest and reveal you to Adelita then? Though what would she have done, really? Made you wait there for our return? Hardly. You're happy to be the final bride! I knew it!"

"You didn't know anything," Mateo said, sounding ridiculous to his ears. Now was not the time to be childish. Still, there was comfort in the ritual of their teasing. Amidst the madness of nests, bird cousins and fae that seduced humans beyond caring, it was nice to know that Luz was still going to take credit for all of his accomplishments, and he was still going to dispute it.

"Don't I though?" Luz reached up and rumpled his hair. "You look well-tumbled if I do say so myself. Is it not wonderful? Is it not all the poets said it would be and more?"

Mateo's cheeks went hot, but he narrowed his eyes at her. His feelings on the matter of his couplings with Ópalo were jumbled and he didn't intend to share any of his confusion with Luz. A few months ago, when their relationship had still been open and honest, he would have gone to her eagerly, hopeful she could help him put his thoughts to right. Now after all her deceit and knowing full well the extent of her own commitment to the fae, how could he trust her with the intimacy of his pleasure and Ópalo's strange and poorly concealed expectations?

"I would say by the state of him and my brother's expression that well-tumbled is an understatement. Well done, brother," the blue-green fairy said with a wicked twinkle in his eye. "You were always a patient one and an overachiever in the arts of dance and defense. It should not surprise me you'd perform well in the nest too."

Given what the fairy had no doubt done to his sister—and with the aid of fairy aphrodisiacs no less—Mateo bristled at this easy discussion of his private intimacies.

"I don't believe this is a topic we need to discuss," Ópalo began.

But Mateo drew himself up, pushed Luz aside and stepped close enough to the other fairy to be intimidating. He felt the tug of Luz's hand on his arm and Ópalo's fingers close around his other wrist.

"I don't believe I know your name."

"Azulejo. I am at your service." The fairy's eyes darted to Ópalo, apology evident there, but to Mateo's mind directed at the wrong person.

Mateo studied Azulejo's face, not backing down. Finally, with a slow, even tone, he bit out, "So you're the man who took my sister's heart."

"Is that such a bad thing?"

"Yes, when you didn't even allow her to freely choose, and instead fed her enchanted cakes."

"Mateo," Luz said sharply. "I made my choice. Quite freely."

He ignored her, jerking free of Ópalo's hold and stepping close enough to Azulejo to see the blue feathers of his eyebrows ruffle.

"You didn't offer him cakes?" Azulejo asked Ópalo, not tearing his eyes from Mateo's face. "Are you really such a fool?"

"Azulejo," Ópalo warned.

"Never mind. Apparently you are. I wish I could claim surprise, but you always did go your own way. It makes Halcón crazy, but oh well, brother, I suppose it must make life interesting."

"Don't act as though I'm not here," Mateo said. "It is me you should be addressing. Look me in the eye or else."

"Do you threaten me?" Azulejo asked, amusement tinting his vibrant voice. "You intend to take us all on, then? We're vicious fighters, I should warn you. All claws and sharp beaks."

Mateo felt a wave of uncertainty swell inside his chest. No fae had beaks that he had seen, but Ópalo had spoken of their magic and their arsenal.

"Azul!" Ópalo's voice now held a razor's note.

Mateo did not look away from Azulejo's smug face.

Azulejo broke first, bowing deeply, the feathers at the crown of his head brushing against Mateo's chest as he swooped down and then back up again. "As you wish, little brother." He lifted a feathered brow at Mateo. "Our strength shouldn't be underestimated, but I forgive you. You've had quite a shock."

Mateo flared his nostrils, and Ópalo chose that moment to wriggle between them, his pink feathers tickling the underside of Mateo's chin.

"Azulejo is closest to my age, enjoys singing, dancing, writing poetry and making a mess out of the statesman duties our elder brothers assign him," Ópalo spoke in a rush, his voice quivering with tension. "You'll like him if you only give him a chance."

"And control your temper, baby brother," Luz said.

Mateo snorted. "Nine minutes!"

"Nine minutes means nothing at all," she said. "But before long, you'll meet the others, and Azulejo is a darling compared to Halcón, who will sooner rip your throat out and deal with Ópalo's displeasure after than bear any disrespect!"

Ópalo actually moved against Mateo in a way that could only be described as protective at the mention of Halcón's name. Mateo gently pushed him aside, squaring his shoulders. He didn't need protection. Or at least he didn't want to appear as if he needed any. Not in front of Luz, at any rate. She'd only tease him mercifully later when he was least expecting it.

Assuming I don't murder her and all my sisters for getting us into this predicament to begin with. Why could they not have been happy at home?

Mateo remembered the hours in Ópalo's nest and knew the answer to that, whether he liked it or not. How could being locked up in their father's castle compare to this paradise?

"*Tu novio* is feisty, brother," Azulejo said with a smile that still put Mateo's teeth on edge. "I like him. So much more your style than any delicate *mujer*. It truly explains much. So…" Azulejo said, stepping back from Mateo, breaking the tension. "What took you so long? My brother has waited for months."

Mateo said nothing, noting how Luz wrapped her arm through Azulejo's and smiled up like he was the sun and she was a flower who would follow him across the sky. He'd never seen Luz look at any man that way.

If Ópalo had been different, if he'd fed me, would I be like her? Lost to him and desperately in love?

Even now he was under the influence of a more subtle fairy thrall, and while he didn't wish to break it for the time being, he wasn't fool enough to believe it was real.

"A man must make his own way," Ópalo said, his chin up and his eyes bright. "There's no shame in taking the long route."

"You always had more patience than any of the rest of us, Ópalo." Azulejo laughed before plopping down on the grass again, patting the spot next to Luz after she followed him down. "Place your shameless selves here and enjoy the day with us. Tonight's dance will begin soon enough, and then the long gratifying night. We'll require rest to fully enjoy pleasure."

"Please sit, Mateo," Luz said. Her voice reflected an uncertainty that relieved Mateo's mind. At least she seemed to realize now that something was different with him than it was with her and the others.

After a few awkward moments of silence upon the grass, the twitter of birds the only noise and Luz's concerned glances the only eye contact, Ópalo and Azulejo began to discuss plans for the night's festivities.

Luz scooted closer to Mateo and ducked her head to catch his eye. "Why are you angry, Mateo?"

"Can you truly not guess the answer to that? For weeks, no, months you've lied to me, to Father, and brought his health near to breaking. Not to mention nearly traded my hand to that beastly King Hernando!"

"We never would have allowed that."

"Why? Because you're all so very smart and your schemes entirely foolproof? What if Hernando had not taken your drugged wine?"

"But he did."

Mateo glared at her.

"What? Mateo, come now. He did take the wine. They always do."

"Just as you took the food offered you here and now you are trapped. But you don't even see it, believing yourself in love when all you are is enchanted."

Luz shook her head. "Trapped? Here? I know what I feel. I know the joy it brings me, the freedom. We are all so very happy." She sounded even more confident as she went on. "Look at Imelda! Who in our world would ever want her crass mouth? Here Gallo laughs heartily at all of her wicked jokes."

"Your happiness isn't real, Luz. Don't you see?"

"We weren't forced, Mateo. We ate willingly."

"You knew the price before the first bite? That you must return to fairyland forever or suffer? That you would then feel...that the fairy thrall would cause you..." He motioned with his hand trying to indicate the aphrodisiac effect. "You knew all of that and still chose?"

"Yes." Luz spoke truly, her gaze unwavering. "We knew. We were ready to become the women we are meant to be. As soon as we crossed the portal we knew our fate was at hand. Do you not...can you not feel it?" She frowned. "It is as Lámina foretold. Surely for you as well?

"I don't know. I wish I did."

Luz went on in a rush. "But Lámina knew, Mateo. Lámina sent us. She sent you as well." Her eyes lit up. "Oh! Here!" she reached into a nearby basket and pulled forth a small iced fairy cake, intricately decorated. "If you eat just a little, you'll see and you'll be happy too."

Mateo stared at the shiny cake. It would surely taste of every sugary, heavenly thing that had ever passed between his lips. His fingers itched to take it from her, and he licked his mouth in anticipation.

Suddenly the cake was dashed from her hand onto the grass.

"No," Ópalo said, leaning over from where he sat next to Azulejo. "I promised he would not be influenced. He is uncertain still, while you and your sisters never hesitated." His pale face was set, as though it pained him to say the words, but he didn't waver. "Mateo alone will decide if he ever eats of fairyland."

Azulejo let out a low whistle of disapproval, and previously unseen birds took flight from the field around them, cawing what sounded to Mateo's ears a message of censure.

"Oh," Luz replied, surprise looking pretty on her, as nearly every emotion did. "I see."

I could snatch it up even now and eat it.

The thought was similar to his urge to climb upon the balustrade the night before—against every fiber of his being, but somehow exciting. He resisted.

"Then you haven't decided what you plan to do, Mateo? About us? About father?"

Mateo pulled his eyes away from the discarded fairy cake. "It seems there's nothing for it but to convince Father to allow you to marry your fairy lovers."

"Oh thank you!" Luz cried, throwing her arms around him. He held her and smelled her hair. He realized that the new scent he'd noticed on her recently was not a new perfume, but fairyland itself.

He whispered in her ear, "For who else will have you now?"

Luz pulled back, dark eyes hot with anger. She seemed about ready to slap his face, which Mateo almost welcomed. He still felt she and the others deserved a good shouting at, but he turned to Azulejo and asked with every appearance of making a genuine effort, "So, you dance every night?"

"Only the nights our brides are present," Azulejo said.

Mateo was ready to protest the description of his sisters—and especially himself—as brides, when Ópalo took hold of his hand. His fingers were smooth and cool.

"Now that's settled," Ópalo said softly. "Why don't you come with me to visit our dove cousins, Mateo? There'll be time for making friends with Azul later."

"Oh yes, Mateo, you should go," Luz said. "You've never seen the like. Ópalo showed me their dovecote several visits ago and even then I longed for you to see it."

Mateo agreed, since further discussion of their situation was only going to bring up sticking points such as his sisters' enchanted state, their deceit and lies, the danger to their father's health and Mateo's unresolved anger about the situation.

Luz kissed his cheek and whispered in his ear, "Please Mateo, give it time. You could be so happy here with us if you would only let yourself."

Mateo imagined that was true. The pleasure he engaged in with Ópalo was not without joy. But he had no intention of surrendering his heart, just as he'd no intention of surrendering his hand to Hernando.

"We'll see you at dinner," Ópalo said, nodding to Luz and Azulejo.

"Enjoy your first day as a married fairy," Azulejo said, winking. "Or should I say as the fairy thrall of a reluctant human, since you didn't feed him properly."

Ópalo rolled his eyes and wordlessly slipped his arm around Mateo's back, guiding him away from Luz and Azulejo.

Chapter Ten

"WHERE IS THIS dovecote?" Mateo asked, the vibrant flowers and verdant grass around him both familiar and yet fresh to his eyes.

"You can see it from here." Ópalo pointed toward a wide tower of birdhouses Mateo could just glimpse on the horizon, soaring up to the bright white clouds.

As they walked, Ópalo began to talk. "Azulejo is a good fairy, Mateo. He's kind, joyful, funny and loving. He's stood up for me many times, even in the face of some heavy opposition from our older brothers."

"Not your sister?"

"I've always been Cacatúa's pet. But my brothers, well, they are a story for another day. Let me assure you Luz is in good hands. I understand you're uncertain of what has transpired, but you must admit she seems well."

Mateo couldn't deny it.

"Give some leeway to the fact that our world doesn't share the same morality as yours. We're open, high-flying children of the sun and the sky, the cousins of birds. We don't dress out of modesty, but out of a joy in the colors with which we can decorate ourselves. Our knowledge of goodness is pleasure, peace, laughter, joy. Here, what Azulejo and your sister have shared is celebrated and honored, no matter the enchantments their love was first built upon."

Mateo's head reeled. It was all too much to take in. He began to wish he'd never left Ópalo's nest. Sleeping off his night of indulgence would have been a better thing for him surely than tramping through an unfamiliar landscape and challenging his sister's lover. Perhaps he should simply give his sisters a blessing. Their lovers were royalty after all, and happiness shone brightly on Luz's face, marred only by his own apparent buffoonery in the face of what he didn't understand.

They walked in silence until they closed in on the towering structure of elaborate, stacked birdhouses. Doves swooped and called as they approached and Ópalo waved as if to old friends. "This dovecote was constructed over the course of a hundred years and we still add to it today as our population of doves grows."

"This is…they are magnificent," Mateo said. "I have a dovecote at home and I've considered investing in a much larger one, but I've never imagined, much less seen, such an amazing structure."

"The view from the top is the most lovely in our land."

"We are to climb?"

Ópalo looked up at the tower of birdhouses and frowned. After a long moment he turned his gaze back to Mateo and laughed. "I suppose not, *mi pájaro*. Big, strong human that you are, you might pull it down on top of us. Wouldn't that be a waste of a hundred years' labor!" This last was spoken with a playful trill that Mateo felt in his gut, and he wanted to jerk Ópalo close and kiss him.

Ópalo smiled, raising a hand for a large dove to light upon. "We take the homes of our cousins quite seriously. You should see where the crows live. If you stand at the highest point of the castle at dawn, you can see it to the east with the sun reflecting off all its stolen, shiny baubles."

The dove on Ópalo's wrist cooed and ducked her head to better examine Mateo.

"She reminds me of Pura," Mateo said, looking at the bird's beautiful gray feathers. "My favorite dove at home."

"She likes you. She thinks you're handsome. And kind."

"She can tell that much by looking?"

Ópalo's brows lifted as he considered the dove's expression. "You'd be rather surprised what the cousins can see."

"I always trust my doves' opinions of people," Mateo admitted. "Pura knew that King Hernando was a prig. She flicked her wings at the sight of him and tried to take a piece out of his finger, though he thought she was after his crust of bread." He chuckled, remembering. Mateo's father had not found it so funny.

"King Hernando?"

"The old, unattractive man who smells of cabbage and who is at this moment snoring on the floor of my sisters' chambers, no doubt absorbed in dreams of winning my hand and gaining my mouth on his prick."

Ópalo's feathers seemed to bristle on the crown of his head and the dove clicked before she took flight from them. They stared after her together. "You've been close enough to the man to smell him?"

Mateo couldn't miss the thread of anxiety behind Ópalo's demeanor. "Unfortunately."

Ópalo took his chin. "Has he ever touched you?" Ópalo's eyes were not laughing.

Mateo chuckled softly. "Are you jealous? He touched my cheek, devised a reason to rub his thumb over my lip and took my hand on more than one occasion."

Ópalo made an animal noise, growling low. "Never again," Ópalo said softly, his eyes lingering on Mateo's mouth. "You're with me now."

"Oh, am I?" Mateo laughed.

Ópalo's lips twisted down at the edges, as though Mateo had questioned something essential to his understanding of the world. "Of course you are."

Doves flew down from the tower above and landed in the dirt beside them. Mateo felt their eyes on him, and he suddenly remembered a man on trial in his father's court, standing before the tribunal of men who would decide his destiny. *Will they tear me apart if I reject him?*

"I daresay I'm not. I barely know you."

"You know enough."

"While it's true that what I do know I'm enamored of, I fear these feelings are based in something not entirely real."

Ópalo looked queasy. The birds clicked and made barking noises of agitation.

Mateo swallowed against the odd sense that he was telling a lie, even though every word he said was true.

"This is real. And I believe you will choose it. You will choose me." Ópalo's hands shook, but he seemed convinced of his own words.

The shimmer of Ópalo's eyes pulled at Mateo. He felt rather convinced himself, which was deliriously ridiculous and deliciously reassuring all at once. Still, he couldn't keep his mind from supplying an argument. "For all your talk of choice, telling me not to eat the fairy cakes so I can be completely free to come and go as I like, where is your own choice in all of this?"

"What do you mean?"

"Only that you've waited for your 'bride' your whole life, and now that I've arrived, you've accepted me without a second thought. How can you be so certain I'm the man for you? You might not even like me once you've known me more than a day or two."

Ópalo stared at Mateo as though he'd just grown a second head. His pink feathers bristled and shifted, puffing slightly as though his inner irritation was pushing up through to the surface. "It's the way it is. How it always will be, Mateo. Didn't Lámina explain it to you?"

You love the fae. You always love them and they always love you. It is how it is. It is how it shall be.

Mateo had to admit he already felt a strong compulsion to be near Ópalo, but was that love? Or the natural consequence of the shared pleasure they'd taken together? Pleasure that Mateo, without a doubt, strongly desired to share again. It was possible he wanted that more than anything else in his life, but should their passion wear away, would he even like Ópalo? His gut told him yes, and his heart seemed to agree. Yet his head was unwilling to commit.

Ópalo lifted his hands as though to present himself. "I am Ópalo, the youngest of the twelve fae. I am the fairy meant for you." He seemed confident but also vaguely horrified, as if he also felt that his own existence and reason for being were on trial between them, and Mateo's judgment would justify or extinguish him.

Mateo had no idea what to say. Ópalo was handsome, fascinating and terribly confusing, but he could not say he felt they were designed for each other. They'd only just met.

"I'm apparently the human made for you, but if you're asking for my hand or some sort of commitment in the form of eating a fairy cake, I'm not giving it."

Ópalo swallowed hard, turned away and walked toward the tower. Some doves pecked at the ground and others followed him, flying into the air and making urgent noises that seemed designed to send Ópalo back.

Mateo crossed his arms over his chest, observing Ópalo's feathers glaring bright in the sunshine as he moved with avian grace.

Ópalo slowed, stopped and sighed. He turned back and headed for Mateo, his blue eyes glowing as he approached.

"It's not easy for me," Ópalo said, a sad smile on his lips. "I've waited for you forever. After that apple my father gave me as a child, I dreamed of the sweet taste often. My whole life I was told that my bride would be even better than apples. No matter that I never wanted a bride. When you appeared, it seemed better than I could have hoped. Once we lay together...even more beautiful than I had ever imagined. But it's not the same for you, is it?"

Ópalo seemed to soften. He studied Mateo for a long moment before continuing. "Some men come to fairyland and leave claiming it was all a dream," he said, his arms coming up to wrap around Mateo's neck. "But you'll know the truth. As for me, I chose you the moment I saw you standing so lost at the edge of the shore. My heart was gone in that instant. But I won't require you feel the same. I will win you over, *mi pájaro*. You don't know me, but I am very patient. We have two more days to learn about each other—if you return."

"When I return. I'm no one's bride or groom, and I never will be," Mateo said, "but I'm unwilling to deny myself the pleasure of your company and body. If you're still willing to give it without the promises you crave."

"I'll take you as long as you'll let me have you," Ópalo admitted, though it seemed to cost him something to say it. Mateo felt a little tug in his gut and he wished he could smooth the tension out of Ópalo's feathers and rub it free from his neck, which looked stiff as though he was forcing himself not to slump with disappointment.

"When you return," Ópalo began, his expression lightening as he said the words, "we'll have three more days to learn each other. And then three more, and so on. We'll have much time."

Relaxing, Mateo wrapped his arms around Ópalo's back. He might not yet know what to do about his sisters, or his own strange situation. But he had time to let this settle, to enjoy his embraces with Ópalo. To kiss and be kissed. To be taken.

Raindrops, unexpected as everything else that had happened, began to splat into the dirt all around them, streaking in fat lines down the massive dovecote. Ópalo tilted his head up to the darkening sky, revealing his long, slender throat and the Adam's apple that Mateo had sucked on that morning. A drop of rain hit it.

"An afternoon shower. Nothing more, but we'll be soaked through," Ópalo said, reaching up to wipe the drops from Mateo's face. "Should we run for it?"

Mateo shook his head and leaned forward, drawn by Ópalo's fluttering pulse, eager to lick the rainwater from his skin. The doves lifted their wings to flap playfully in the cool water as the rain started to fall in earnest. By the time Mateo and Ópalo did run back to the castle covered in mud, the storm was over and they laughed.

Chapter Eleven

I N THE CASTLE baths—long winding halls of connected heated pools open to the warm sun and cool rain—Ópalo was relieved to leave behind the serious discussions that made his chest squeeze with tight, helpless panic. Patience was an easy virtue to speak of, but a difficult one to practice when all he truly desired was for Mateo to present his heart for Ópalo to take, as Ópalo had already presented his own.

The water was wonderfully warm after the freezing rain, and the breeze from the open walls brought tingling gooseflesh as they splashed and sputtered, wrestled and dunked each other. Eventually, their play dissolved into kisses and another foray into sucking and rutting that left Ópalo feeling well used.

Relaxed and sated, Ópalo sat up out of the water on the ledge that wound along beside the baths with Mateo standing between his thighs, gazing up at him with wet lashes and dark, smiling eyes.

"Was that satisfactory?" Mateo asked shyly, but with a gleam that made it clear he knew the answer.

Ópalo didn't know how he could doubt it. He'd made a loud enough racket to rouse his cousins to cries of ecstatic empathy. "I think you could do with some practice," he answered.

He carefully combed his fingers through Mateo's wet curls, mesmerized by the difference between them and the feathers that sprouted from his own head. "Perhaps tomorrow you could swallow my cock again and I could determine if you've improved at all."

If there was to be waiting and choosing later, then he could play at that too.

Mateo wrapped his arms around Ópalo's waist, turning his head into Ópalo's fingers with an expression of a bird being scratched at just the right spot. "As you wish. I am at your command."

If only that were true. Ópalo shook away the uncomfortable memory of Mateo's unnerving reluctance to understand their relationship. He focused again on Mateo's hair, which was the color of black honey shining in the fading afternoon light.

"It's like thread. Soft thread, the softest thread imaginable," Ópalo murmured. "But it's slippery and slick when wet." He shuddered, feeling the quills of his feathers lift and shake water free from his own head. "Does it hurt when these strands come out?" he asked, noting a few fallen hairs on Mateo's strong shoulders.

Mateo laughed. "I don't even feel it."

"What if you lost many at once?"

"If someone pulled a handful out, you mean? Yes, that would hurt." He laughed again. It was a sound that Ópalo found strange and yet wanted to get used to. It was so different from the laughter of fae—more the gurgling of a brook than a twittering bird.

Ópalo climbed down into the warm shallow water in front of Mateo, carefully studying the growth of beard on his face. It was amazing, astounding and something he'd never seen on a fairy before. "It grows here as well. Scratchy and rough, not soft as on your head. More like the hair around your prick, but shorter."

"I usually shave every day, otherwise it would grow rather long," Mateo said, getting down into the water, his own fingers coming up to graze Ópalo's cheek. "Yours is quite smooth. No bristly feathers grow in there, I see."

Ópalo sat in the bath and continued to explore the roughness of Mateo's face. "Do you need to…shave now? Will it hurt you to leave it as it is?"

"A beard is out of fashion where I'm from, but if it pleases you it does me no harm to grow it a bit." Mateo's shoulders lifted and fell, and Ópalo couldn't resist kissing them, licking along the line of the right one, up his neck to his ear. Unable to restrain himself when Mateo gripped him closer, he dug his fingers into Mateo's ribs, licked the shell of his ear and wormed his tongue into the hole.

Mateo laughed loudly, convulsed and shoved Ópalo away, crying out, "Ticklish!" Water splashed around them, and Ópalo went under, the bubbles of his breath surfacing noisily as he broke through, shaking the wet off.

"Just as my sisters' dog shakes himself." Mateo chuckled. "Only with more feathers."

Ópalo let Mateo pull him close again, promising not to stick his tongue into his ear again—at least not until they were both recovered and ready to play again. Then, perhaps he'd be horrible and tie Mateo to his nest and tickle him until he begged for mercy. Mateo, flushed as he was from laughing, seemed like he might enjoy that.

"Tell me about growing up in your world," he said. Because if Mateo needed them to know each other, then know each other they would. Ópalo pulled himself back onto the ledge, the water sluicing down his back, and reached for a towel to wrap around his shoulders. He pulled his knees up to his chest to keep warm and watched Mateo spin in lazy circles in the water, his profile glowing in the setting sun.

"I was happy," Mateo said. "Until I was not. Then I grew mostly happy again." He flashed a grin. "That wasn't a fair answer. It's hard to quantify a whole life in a few sentences."

"You were happy before your mother died, and then you were not happy for a long time, and then you eventually grew happy again."

"Exactly. I suppose you know how that feels having lived through your father's death."

Ópalo shrugged and then was ashamed. He wished he could say that he did understand and they could bond over their shared losses. "My father and I started out close. I was his last born child to his favorite mistress. In the end, by the time he passed away...well, it's a long story of disappointments and misunderstandings."

"I'm sorry to hear that." Mateo looked as if he blamed himself for bringing up something so awkward, but then he pushed the matter further. "What came between you?"

"You."

Mateo blinked in confusion. "Me? But I never even met your father."

"No, of course not. You asked earlier, how it was I could be so sure you're the one for me. The truth is, I wasn't always certain of you, *mi pájaro*. At times growing up, I was quite sure the bride Father and Lámina had arranged for me was little better than a prison."

Mateo's dark eyes sparked with interest, and he drew closer, standing between Ópalo's legs. "So you understand my doubts?"

"I was told to expect *una novia*, yet I had no wish to lay with a woman. As you can imagine, I was furious with my father. But when I confronted him, he told me to be patient, to have faith in Lámina. I cursed him and shunned his presence from that point on. Then he passed away. When I saw you, Mateo, I understood. I should have trusted my father more. The damage it cost our relationship is something I can never take back. Father died while I was still angry with him."

"I'm sorry."

Ópalo decided to get the unpleasant task over with and simply tell him the rest. "As for my mother, she died when I was born. I never knew her. I heard she was a lovely woman. My siblings liked her well enough, though she was not their own mother. Cacatúa took care of me, and all the others helped of course, but it mostly fell to Cacatúa and Canario."

"You didn't have a nurse?"

"No. Fairy children are different from humans, I'm told. Our infancy is short lived and we grow into adulthood much more quickly than our human counterparts. I've been of age for several years now, but you have only just reached full maturity, have you not? That's one reason the wait for you to come seemed so very long to my older siblings."

Mateo seemed to ponder this. "So if my sisters and your brothers were to bring forth children…?"

"They would likely grow up a bit faster than they would in your world, but their humanness would slow their maturity a bit. At least, that is what we've been told. It's been a long time since our kind took brides from your world."

"Has something changed then?"

Ópalo sighed. "Our world needs the stability of human love to hold it. We need the strength of human hearts. After a certain number of years, as the humanness leaves our blood, we are born hungry for it. And often one brave fairy will take up the task of providing brides."

"Lámina."

"Indeed. She was your nurse, was she not?"

"She was. A good one at that."

"I'm glad to hear it."

"She told the best stories." He pushed back slightly and indicated the room with his hand. "It seems they were not so fantastical after all." He grinned. "As a child, did you hear fairy stories?"

Ópalo laughed. "Of course! We never had a nurse, but we had a tutor, and my father was adept at weaving tales. As were my older brothers and sister."

Mateo swam close again, and rested his cheek against Ópalo's thigh, saying drowsily, "My sisters were always far too interested in their own pursuits to spend much time on me and Luz. But as Father says, Luz and I were thick as thieves. We had our secrets we kept from the others. It made us feel important. Father always encouraged our little club. He believed that Luz and I were special, though Adelita has always been his favorite."

"You're close to your father, then?" Ópalo ran his hand through Mateo's wet curls again, letting them twist around each of his fingers.

"Very close." Mateo turned into Ópalo's strokes. "He's always held a bit tightly to us all. He was so full of grief when my mother died. It's part of why…well, I've never felt that love was all that useful. Not when it leaves a person so lost when it goes away."

Ópalo's fingers stilled. "Must it go away?"

Mateo sighed and swam off, splashing idly at a dry patch along the edge of the bath. "Now you sound like Papá when I've confessed my thoughts to him on the subject." His voice took a bitter turn. "Of course, he's now in the midst of bargaining my hand away, so I have no idea where 'love' is on the agenda for him any longer."

"He's getting older."

"Yes, and he fears he's losing us. Well, losing my sisters, and he's desperate to know where they go and what they do. Desperate to take control again, even if that means marrying us off to someone we don't love and who likely will not love us."

Ópalo cleared his throat. "This king who wants you…he doesn't love you?"

"Oh, he loves me. If what he feels can be called anything at all, I suppose it can be called that." Mateo's mouth twisted in an unpleasant way. "It's hot and passionate, and he wants me to smile all the time. There's no doubt he desires my joy, but I feel nothing for him. I never could."

"Just as you feel nothing for me." Ópalo felt the hole in his heart throb with barren hope as he spoke his fear.

Mateo's head came up. "No. It isn't the same. I…well, I can't give you what you most desire, but I feel…more for you somehow. An affinity. Passion. I definitely feel passion."

Ópalo swallowed, almost afraid to feel relieved, but still taking heart in Mateo's words. "Yes, humans are different creatures. Love is not something that comes so easily to them. At least, not without enchantment."

Mateo frowned and pushed a wet lock out of his eyes. "Let's leave this behind before you grow any sadder. Tell me more about your childhood. Did you and Azulejo have a special bond?"

"Azulejo was my best friend growing up, but even so he and I are quite different. He's insouciant and I'm a bit more serious. At times we complement each other, and at other times we drive each other mad."

"And your other siblings?"

"I have never meshed well with Halcón. He's always doubted my paternity for unknown reasons, and there are few good feelings between us. But the rest of my siblings and I get along most of the time."

Mateo hesitated before asking, "And your father? It seems quite sad how things ended between you."

Ópalo pulled the towel around his shoulders tighter. It had been a very long time since he'd allowed himself to use the word sad when it came to his life. Still, it did bring an ache to his throat remembering how much he wished he could see his father's eyes shining at him one last time.

"I do wish I could tell him how sorry I am for wasting our last years together. I've wished that for a long time, even before I saw you by the lakeside."

Mateo's expression softened. "I understand."

"But every life has such difficult disappointments, do they not?"

Mateo's eyes flared with recognition and he nodded. "Indeed."

"Perhaps so, but it isn't an aspect I like to dwell upon."

"Of course."

"I'd rather talk about how good I am at building things," Ópalo said, sitting up taller and thrusting away the painful thoughts. "I'm a wonderful carpenter and celebrated for my work, even if my brothers and sister say I would be better off spending that time socializing with the court or learning more about politics, treaties and vast-but-boring holdings."

"What do you build?" Mateo asked, hefting himself up onto the ledge too. His dark, hairy legs rubbed against Ópalo's in an exciting and new way that made Ópalo's breath catch. Memories of their rutting crashed through his mind—the rough texture of Mateo's legs rubbing against his hips as he thrust into Mateo's clenching heat. He flushed, bit down on his lower lip and looked down at Mateo's prick. Was it still too soon?

"Hello, have I lost you?" Mateo asked, waving a hand in front of Ópalo's face, his cheeks bright with color and his eyes turning rather hot.

"Tables, chairs, birdcages, desks, bookcases, boxes with secret compartments, almost anything you could want that is made by hands skilled with wood."

Mateo's lips quirked up. "Your hands are quite skilled with my wood," he whispered, sounding ashamed of his own joke, but laughing too.

"I could show you other things I'm skilled at. I'm told my tongue has no rival when properly employed," Ópalo murmured, unfolding himself and pushing Mateo onto his back. The hard stone of the ledge under his knees was distracting, but that was forgotten as soon as he thrust Mateo's legs apart, staring down at his thick, hard cock and the tight sac beneath it. He spit on his fingers and rubbed them over the exposed head of Mateo's prick, pleased when Mateo's eyelids fluttered and he bit down on his lush lower lip. "Lift your legs. I think you'll like this, *mi pájaro.*"

Mateo's choked, shocked, high-pitched shout of surprise only encouraged Ópalo when he lunged forward, pushing Mateo's legs up higher, and worked his face between the cheeks of Mateo's ass. As he trilled his tongue over Mateo's tight asshole, feeling the muscle flex and clench against the tip of his tongue, Mateo cried out and kicked, his foot connecting with Ópalo's shoulder hard enough to bruise. Surprised, Ópalo moved back.

Mateo reached down to grab Ópalo by the feathers and urged Ópalo's mouth back into the musky, hot space, whimpering, "Please. More."

Ópalo obliged. He'd practiced this on many fae, bringing several of them to sweaty, desperate, tear-stained climax. He licked into Mateo's hole, thrusting his tongue inside. Mateo lifted his legs higher, spreading them and opening himself as wide as possible, moaning and gasping.

When Ópalo was sure Mateo was moments away from coming, Mateo suddenly clenched his fingers in Ópalo's hair. Mateo dragged him up, kissing him before rolling him over and impaling himself on Ópalo's prick. He cried out as he rode Ópalo fast and furious, his long neck tossed back, wet hair throwing water droplets everywhere. His ass gripped Ópalo as Mateo gave over completely to his lust.

Ópalo couldn't get his hands everywhere fast enough. He ran his palms over Mateo's hairy thighs, loving the rough scratch, and up over Mateo's tight abdomen to his chest. He tweaked Mateo's sweet, tight nipples and lurched up to lick and bite them, making Mateo squirm, moan and pull too hard on Ópalo's feathers.

Without warning, Mateo pulled off, pushed Ópalo's legs up and ducked down to mash his own mouth against Ópalo's hole. Ópalo squawked—for there was no other word for the shocked sound that came from his mouth. He arched and writhed as Mateo shamelessly worked in his tongue, such a quick study. Then Mateo pulled back to slide the thick head of his cock around in the spit he'd left on Ópalo's hole.

"Yes, *mi pájaro*, anything. Take anything."

Mateo pressed in a little and then, as if unable to hold back, he pushed harder. He was barely inside when his face crumpled and he cried out. The wet heat of Mateo's climax spurted into Ópalo's hole and dripped down as Mateo collapsed on top of him, panting.

Ópalo pulled Mateo up to kiss his slick lips, savoring the musky taste. He took his own prick in hand and with a few quick jerks found the edge he needed and flew over it—fluttering, twittering, singing out as his end-song throbbed in his throat and was swallowed by Mateo's open mouth.

Moments passed—drained, trembling moments. Mateo slipped off him, a grin on his face as he dropped back into the water of the baths. He helped Ópalo down again too, rubbing away the slick spendings from their skin.

"Tables and chairs and bookcases?" Mateo murmured.

"Yes. Would you like to see?"

Mateo grabbed him and kissed his neck, startling a laugh from Ópalo that bounced off the high ceiling of the baths. Birds echoed his joyous sound, swooping just outside on the breeze. "I'd love to see."

Ópalo grinned helplessly. "I didn't realize carpentry would stoke your fires so high. Silly me, hoping to win you over with doves when the thought of hewed wood makes you ardent."

"The thought of you and wood seems to endlessly intrigue me," Mateo said, and he laughed at his innuendo again.

"I think you should see my workshop, then."

"Indeed, I think I should."

ÓPALO COULDN'T HELP but run his hands over his work as he talked about it. He was proud of the smoothness of the wood, the precise fit of the joints and the sturdiness of his creations. He never used fairy magic in his work, preferring the end result that his own steady hands could make. He pointed that out to Mateo.

"Perhaps it's my low origins," he explained. "My mother was a servant, you see. Of course, my brothers sometimes joke that it's my poor breeding leading me to want some sort of occupation beyond the responsibilities of royalty."

He'd never enjoyed being idle, and while he'd had several lovers since he came of age, Ópalo couldn't entertain himself solely with sex, dancing and politics as his siblings did.

"My sisters are the same about my doves," Mateo said, studying an intricate birdhouse Ópalo in which had taken a great deal of pride. The design was spectacular and when he'd gilded it, he had no doubt that a special cousin would honor him by choosing it for a home. "They tease me about getting my hands dirty, but it's still a gentleman's hobby."

Ópalo smiled softly, showing Mateo how the latch worked on a small box. "Here," he whispered and sprung the compartment. Mateo sucked in air and appeared delighted as he examined the small drawer revealed at Ópalo's touch.

"It's…why, I never would have known to look for it, much less found the compartment itself. It's truly handsome work."

"Thank you. I designed it myself. It took some time to find the right way to disguise the mechanism. I'm quite proud of it, I must admit. Canario requested one almost just like this for his last birthday gift."

"What does he keep in the compartment?" Mateo asked.

Ópalo lifted a brow. "Only Canario would know that, I'm afraid."

Moving on, Mateo knelt to examine some bookcases and Ópalo knelt too, leaning a hand on Mateo's sturdy thigh as if to balance, but truly in order to feel the heat of him under his palm.

"I have a question," Mateo asked, not looking away from the freshly sanded cases. "Why were you born late? The others…they all came as my sisters did in sets of two and three, did they not? What made you different?"

Ópalo reluctantly pulled his hand away from Mateo's warm leg and stood up, a knot of discomfort in his stomach. "I was born to replace a lost twin. Azulejo's twin originally meant for you."

"You aren't my original fairy soul mate?"

There was a twist to Mateo's words, a humor, but Ópalo frowned at the thought. He hated the idea of Mateo having been originally intended for anyone else.

Mateo's smile faded and he stood too. "That frightens you, doesn't it? Why? Do you worry perhaps we aren't star-destined to be betrothed, or that you might have been excluded from Lámina's machinations?"

"It doesn't bear considering. She wouldn't have sent you otherwise."

Mateo crossed his arms over his chest, cocked his head and narrowed his eyes as he examined Ópalo closely. "Lámina gave me the cloak because I asked for her help. I wanted to find out where my sisters were going at night but didn't know how to trick them into showing me. That's the only reason I'm here. She didn't send me."

Ópalo shook his head. He didn't believe that. He couldn't.

"How do you know Lámina?"

"I have only known her through tales told by my father of the fairy who gave up her life here to bring us brides. Even Cacatúa. Father knew from before her birth she would crave a strong woman and not a man. Wives for us all. Except I didn't want a wife." Ópalo watched Mateo's eyes, how they shifted down and the small crease between the brows grew more prominent. "You wouldn't have wanted a wife either. Azulejo's twin was a girl."

"You're saying Azulejo's twin was killed? Because of what I want?"

Ópalo gasped. "Of course not. She caught fever and died, just as her mother did. Don't be absurd." Yet the seed had been planted. The thought was there. No. His father had been obsessed with the completion of his plan—twelve fae for twelve humans—but he was not a cruel man.

"So you were born then."

"Yes. Born to be your bridegroom."

Mateo sighed and rubbed the bridge of his nose. "Did my sisters ask any of these questions?"

"The fairy cakes," Ópalo said simply. No other explanation was needed, but he added, "Questions fly from the mind. Pleasure and contentment is sought. They didn't think to ask. They're happy. As they should be." *As you ought to be.*

"Luz seems happy. That I've seen with my own eyes. My other sisters are the same?"

"See for yourself. Dinner is soon. We should prepare ourselves and attend. Of course, you shouldn't eat anything, unless you wish to obligate yourself to return."

"Would you like that?" Mateo asked, running a hand through his hair and looking confused, frustrated. Lost.

"It would make it easier." The admission was necessary. "But no. I've met your inquisitive side and though it troubles me, I suppose I couldn't do without it now. If you ever choose to eat, it will fill me with joy. But as it is, I'll take you as you are."

Ópalo was relieved when Mateo seemed satisfied with that, but still Mateo didn't smile as he had earlier.

"I dread seeing them," Mateo said suddenly, and Ópalo understood.

He was proud to finally introduce his "bride", but knew his siblings would have plenty to say about it. If not now, then when Mateo returned. The very thought of rowing Mateo back across the lake and watching him walk away took any appetite Ópalo had worked up during their pleasure.

"They've all been where you are now. They'll be happy you're here."

Mateo snorted. "I doubt it."

Ópalo didn't ask why. He knew. The youngest—least and last—was always considered a likely candidate for tattling and ruining the older siblings' fun, as well as often accused of destroying their most prized possessions. Ópalo only hoped he might end up being prized enough by Mateo that none of them need worry at all.

Chapter Twelve

THE TABLE WAS full of splendid-looking foods, and his sisters sat around it with their lovers at their sides. Mateo walked a step behind Ópalo, keeping his chin up, determined to meet the gaze of everyone present with firm confidence.

"Mateo," Adelita gasped. She sat at the right hand of a yellow-feathered fairy who must be the eldest, Canario.

The other sisters turned to stare at him, color leaving their faces. They all went still, except for Luz who took a sip of wine and leaned back in her chair, cheeks radiant and eyes shining. "Hi, little brother."

The sisters' lovers placed protective arms about their shoulders, challenges in their eyes. The woman with her arm around Herminia sported a terrifying glare of red-fringed feathers. Mateo followed Ópalo wordlessly to the two empty chairs near the foot of the table and sat down at his left.

His sisters remained frozen, eyes wide. Luz took another sip of wine and lifted her glass in the air. "A toast to our brother, the surprise bride." She laughed gaily.

Mateo said nothing. Ópalo's hand on his arm was cool and it calmed his desire to rush in with a display of temper. Instead, he just looked each of his sisters in the eye, staying quiet as Ópalo waved a pretty servant over to remove Mateo's plate and fill his wine glass.

"Mateo will not be supping with us." Ópalo looked pointedly at Canario. "Shall we make introductions, brother?"

His sisters slowly relaxed as their lovers introduced themselves to Mateo and it became clear that he was not going to attempt to take off anyone's head or stir up an ugly cock fight at the dinner table.

"This was your doing, I suppose," Adelita finally said, her voice tight as she glared at Luz.

"Mateo thinks for himself. He discovered where we were going. I simply didn't mention that I thought he was following us. I'm shocked you didn't realize it, Adelita, reeking as he did of cologne. I'm glad you bathed him, Ópalo. He's more endurable now."

"What will you do?" Catalina asked Mateo, her hands twisting together and ignoring her sisters. "When we return, will you turn us over to Papá?"

"Or will you join us in this double life?" asked Blanca, her pale eyes glowing with fire and hope.

Mateo looked at Ópalo's pink feathers and flashing eyes, admiring the fairy power that poured from him. "I'm not a bride, as you have deemed yourselves to be. I've entered into no betrothals and made no promises."

The fae at the table began to vibrate, their feathers puffing and bristling.

"Regardless, I'm not one to deny love where it's bloomed, or to insist promises made in steady affection be tossed aside due to the unexpected nature of the suitors. And I have reasons of my own to agree to your engagements and to want to return to this place myself."

"So you'll keep our secret."

"I didn't say that. You all must know that it cannot be kept. There are men and women in competition for your hands seeking to crack open this mystery. They are going to lengths both extreme and ridiculous. It can't hold."

Adelita and Blanca looked at each other, and then nodded. Mateo met each of his sisters' eyes and said, "We require a plan."

"Then you're an ally." Adelita spoke for all of them as usual.

"Have I ever been against you?"

"Yes," Gracia declared. "There was the time you wanted our little Whitey banished for chasing your doves."

"In anything that mattered?"

"Whitey matters."

"*¡Dios mío!* Gracia, I'm talking about your marriages and a way to legitimize them in Papá's eyes and you wish to argue about your dog?"

Adelita laughed softly and agreed. She lifted a glass of wine to Mateo and took a sip, her cheeks glowing and her eyes growing hot. The temptation to steal a bite of the fairy food beckoned to him, but he fought it off.

"I dare say, little brother, with you on our side, we may have found a way to have what we all want. Papá will never deny you, his very favorite child."

Mateo couldn't stop himself from scoffing. "Has the fairy wine muddled your head? You know full well that you have always been Papá's favorite, Adelita."

"Don't be dim, Mateo. You are his only son and you only look at something and he provides it for you. That damn dovecote for one!"

"Oh please, yes, let's have this fight," Luz said, her words rich with the effects of the wine. "Everyone here wishes to know who's Papá's true favorite."

A scattered response of "Adelita" and "Mateo" came from the other sisters.

"Perhaps your father has two favorites," Canario said, resting his hand on the back of Adelita's chair. "That cannot be so unusual."

"Who was your father's favorite, Canario?" Elisa asked, her fork poised to stab into another piece of cake.

"I was, of course."

No one disputed him.

"It is decided then," he went on, clapping his hands together with authority. "Mateo will speak to your father and soon we will all be wed. This is cause for celebration! But first, finish your meals." Canario's yellow feathers fluffed beautifully in the candlelight. "There is dancing to be had!"

Ópalo, who had been looking vaguely worried ever since Mateo had denied being betrothed to him, suddenly smiled and leaned forward, clearing his throat to get everyone's attention. He nodded toward Mateo. "He is really a lovely bride, isn't he?"

As Mateo swallowed down his irritation at being called a bride, his sisters choked and laughed, and Imelda went so far as to voice her agreement with jeers and entirely inappropriate hand gestures. Mateo wondered how she had turned out so very crass, but noticed Gallo truly didn't seem to mind, and even shared her penchant for crudity.

"I see you've stopped shaving, brother," Blanca said once she caught her breath.

"Such a manly bride," Luz said, laughing. "He is divine, Ópalo, truly."

"I agree," Ópalo said, giving Mateo a long look that left nothing to the imagination.

Mateo felt warm and stopped himself from biting into his lower lip. The last thing he wanted was to give away to his sisters how thoroughly aroused Ópalo left him. Adelita was finally treating him like someone with something to offer and while they no doubt knew exactly how he was spending his time with Ópalo, he didn't wish to give them anything more to tease him about.

Not until he'd convinced his father to legitimize his sisters' commitments to their fae, anyway. Then they'd all owe him an immense debt of gratitude that no amount of teasing could overcome.

AFTER ANOTHER NIGHT of dancing and his third day in fairyland spent alternately trysting and exploring the various halls and rooms of the castle—and then trysting in them too—Mateo was exhausted. He didn't think he had the energy for another evening of revelry, but Ópalo insisted they not miss out.

"Have you noticed you're not aching?" Ópalo asked, swiping a finger against Mateo's well-used asshole when Mateo bent over to pull up his new trousers. They were made of pink feathers mixed with dove down. Mateo suspected the pink was Ópalo's, though he didn't ask.

"Let me guess, your fairy seed magically heals me."

Ópalo laughed, his cheeks turning red. "No, of course not. It's the healing water of the baths." His feathers fluffed in amusement.

Mateo blinked. "Because magical healing water is much more reasonable than magical healing seed?"

"Of course!"

Mateo laughed and kissed him.

Looking pleased, Ópalo said, "And it's not just the baths. All the water of my land is healing. It helps prevent disease, which leads to our longer lives. It heals wounds. Even the most deadly if the water is applied soon enough and in sufficient quantity."

Mateo chuckled. "Then how does one of your kind ever die? Why are you not immortal?"

"There are a few sicknesses the water is powerless against, and there are some wounds too mortal for it to cure. And in the end, we all must pass on to the next world. In humans, it's less effective against aging and illness, but it heals most wounds quite easily, and can slow down the aging process so you become suitable mates and companions for us."

Mateo pondered this as he continued dressing. While most of the day had been spent pursuing pleasure, he'd spent an hour that morning with his sisters discussing how to break the news of fairyland and the sisters' engagements to their father.

Although Mateo could see in Adelita's imperious gaze that she thought herself in charge, he didn't entirely approve of her plan. It was simply to continue as they were, allowing chancers to attempt to discover their secret until they were forced to reveal themselves.

"He is old, Mateo," she'd said. "There may be no need to tell him at all."

"You would rather he die despairing of his daughters than to brave the truth with him?"

"What if he isn't pleased?" Catalina whispered, her eyes brimming with tears.

"How could he be more displeased than he is now? At least he'll have answers."

They'd agreed to go with Adelita's plan for several more nights, but Mateo wasn't sure he had it in him. If he had to endure the longing stares of King Hernando for even one more day, he wasn't sure he wouldn't blurt out the truth over dinner, and his father deserved privacy for this revelation.

"Mateo," Ópalo asked from the doorway. "Are you ready?"

Mateo adjusted his new clothes, enjoying the play of the feathers in the light. His light beard made him look less baby faced. Older and somehow stronger. He thought he was rather handsome, if he did say so himself.

"Does the water work outside of your world?" Mateo asked thoughtfully, thinking of his father's gray hair.

Ópalo crossed to him, ran a hand down Mateo's chest and gazed up at him earnestly. "Yes, but it can't reverse time. You're thinking of your father, aren't you?"

"Yes." Mateo fingered Ópalo's soft feathers. "May I take some with me when I go?"

"Of course."

Nuzzling Ópalo, Mateo scraped his cheek along Ópalo's neck, earning him a gasp and a kiss. "Let's go," Mateo said. "Before we stay."

The dancing was no less fervent and inspired the third night. Mateo had never imagined he would allow himself to be fucked up against a wall in a crowded ballroom, but everyone was lust drunk, and no human or fairy could spare a moment to look at him, so caught up in their own dancing and desperate lovemaking that he'd become invisible even without the cloak.

The night had worked something wild on him, and he was more aflame with desire than he'd ever known possible. The cacophony of music, birdsong and cries of ecstasy served only to keep him flushed and aroused until he followed Ópalo away from the dance.

On his elbows and knees, Mateo gripped the soft fabrics of Ópalo's nest in his fists, grunting with each rapid thrust of Ópalo's cock. He'd started this encounter with the intention to tumble Ópalo to the bed, open him up and get his own cock into Ópalo's small body, since perhaps that was as it should be. That Mateo should prove his manhood. But between his lust and Ópalo's talents it had not gone to plan.

Ópalo was a distracting and persuasive lover. Not with his words, but with his tongue and his fingers. The next thing Mateo knew, he was rubbing his face in the pillows while Ópalo buggered him, sharp chin digging into Mateo's spine and his arms wrapped around Mateo's middle, holding on tight as they moved together.

Mateo had to admit that in his heart of hearts, this was how he longed it to be—his secret, deepest desires made real. On his knees, submitting to his lover, being filled with cock. Being completed.

It was only the third day Mateo had known what it was to be taken in this way, and he was getting to be good at it, he could tell. Mateo worked his hole to milk Ópalo of more pleasure as he gripped on Ópalo's slow pull out.

"That's it. That's so good, *mi pájaro*. Delicious. Tight."

Filthy, slick noises squelched between them, and Mateo smelled the musk of their earlier sex all over the pillows he rubbed against his face. He breathed deeply, fire burning in his veins.

"Squeeze me. Yes, tighter," Ópalo gasped. "So good, my bird."

The intense drag of Ópalo's cock and Ópalo's mutterings spiraled through Mateo, leaving him racked with need. He let go of the sheets, wormed a hand down to grab his own hard cock, and moaned. Unbearably sensitive, his prick was so hot and hard and throbbed with such desperate urgency that his hand didn't feel like enough. He gripped it ruthlessly, pressing the tip of his thumbnail just under the head so that the pain dulled his frantic need. He whined and bucked into Ópalo's strokes.

"Shh," Ópalo hushed him, pulling Mateo's hand away and replacing it with his own. "Let me have you."

Mateo buried his head in the nest again, letting his hips go, rutting forward into Ópalo's hand and then back onto his prick, moaning and sweating, tossing aside everything but his insistent craving for release.

"Harder! Harder!" he cried.

Ópalo gave him what he needed. His hand jerked fast and urgently, his hips snapped forward with loud, smacking thrusts, and Mateo's mind was ablaze. His balls curled with heat before he convulsed, waves of pleasure shattering over him. He smelled his own spendings first, before the shock of the climax hit him fully. His stunned cry burned his throat, until the full height and depth of his pleasure shuddered through him and he was sure he'd never recover from the grandeur of it.

Still shuddering, he dropped into the nest, rubbing his cock against the soft, seed-spattered blankets. Mateo trembled through another wave of pleasure, his limbs jerking and twitching while Ópalo moved slowly still inside him.

"That was beautiful," Ópalo whispered, pushing sweaty hair from the side of Mateo's face and never letting up his strokes.

Mateo was too tired to squeeze any longer and he felt Ópalo move more easily in and out. He let himself relax into the rhythm, taking the thrusts limply, whimpering when Ópalo slammed over the place inside that seemed to blind his eyes with sunlight even in the dark of night. Gradually Ópalo increased the pace, clearly seeking his own climax. Mateo spread his legs, opening himself as much as possible, wanting more of Ópalo's thrusts, eager to feel his prick pulse inside him and fill him up.

"You..." Ópalo hitched Mateo's hips up, and he followed the motion, clambering to his hands and knees gamely, despite his exhaustion. "There. Just there, *mi pájaro*. Take it, take me. Yes."

Then Ópalo was throbbing, singing, pulsing, shuddering all over as he reached his pleasure and Mateo felt the hot, slick seed pushing out around Ópalo's still thrusting cock to slip down over his balls in a wet, warm rush.

After, they lay in a heap together, sweaty and naked. "Tomorrow you leave," Ópalo said. "You'll be gone for three days, and my heart will ache, I'll miss you so."

Mateo kissed Ópalo's feathers, tucking Ópalo's head under his chin. He didn't know how to respond. He knew that the coupling they engaged in was intense and so powerful that he didn't want to even imagine going back to a life without it. But perhaps pleasure with another was always like this?

He'd never lain with any of the courtiers. Would it be the same with them? No, he didn't think it could be. He could think of no one, other than Sir Franco, he might want to lie with—and even the knight seemed boring and staid in comparison to Ópalo with his brilliant pink feathers, beautiful carpentry and fanciful birdhouses. His fairyland.

Still, Mateo couldn't say if his heart was fully aligned with Ópalo's just yet. He still barely knew him. He was definitely dazzled, of that he had no doubt.

One thing was for certain. Being with Ópalo had cemented that he would never be strong-armed into marriage to King Hernando or anyone else who didn't inspire as much lust and desire as Mateo felt even now tangled in Ópalo's bed, with damp, pink feathers sticking to their arms and legs, a tide of exhaustion washing over him.

It simply could not be.

Chapter Thirteen

MATEO SAT SULKING—THERE was no other word for it—upon his high-backed chair next to his father's throne as the ministers talked endlessly of finances and alliances. He twisted his head from side to side and rolled his shoulders, restless and eager for the council meeting to be over so he could speak to his father alone.

He was even more eager for night to fall so he could return to Ópalo. It was astonishing that time could drag in such a way that the mere hours he'd spent away from fairyland felt twice as long as the days he'd spent wrapped up in its birdsong.

His eyes were drawn to the gray stone ceiling, a marvel of human innovation when the castle had been constructed, or so his tutors had instructed him. But it was nothing compared to the open wonder of Ópalo's castle. He shivered, remembering the baths, a serpent of warm delight winding through to many secret alcoves, giving privacy to consummate one's affection in wet bliss. There was always time for bliss in fairyland.

"Now we must return to the pressing matter of the princesses."

Mateo sat up straighter at that, his mind dragging away from the memory of Ópalo fluttering his feathery eyelashes against the head of Mateo's cock, leading Mateo to beg for his tongue, his lips, his mouth, anything—just more.

"Indeed," his father said, rubbing a hand over his eyes wearily. "Hernando failed last night, but he intends to try again."

"God save us all," someone muttered and the king nodded.

"That infernal bell. Perhaps tonight he will be successful, lest we lose two more nights of rest to this madness." His father sighed miserably. "Let us not discuss it further now. What is there to say?"

The courtiers left the room at his father's hand wave of dismissal and Mateo couldn't fail to notice how slowly his father moved as he stepped down from the dais.

"I missed you at breakfast, Papá," Mateo said, walking beside his father as they started down the long corridor leading to his father's chambers. Mateo found all of the rooms rather grim and dark now. It had always been home, but now that he saw it with freshly scrubbed eyes, it was hardly a cheerful place. "I was left alone with only my sisters to ward off the ugly advances of King Hernando."

His father groaned. Mateo half expected a lecture on the suitability of Hernando and Mateo not turning into an ingrate like his sisters. Instead his father rubbed a tired hand over his face again and muttered, "He truly is an imbecile. I regret throwing you into this, Mateo. You should not pay the price for your sisters' lies."

Mateo sensed an opportunity. "Then we can call off the whole endeavor?"

"Alas, no. We must finish what we've begun. I'm sorry, Mateo, but my honor is too compromised as it is. I can't afford to appear weak or indecisive. With any luck, the man will fail again. If he doesn't? Well, he is taken with you and will likely allow you other lovers. It is a workable arrangement."

Mateo's gorge rose. "I don't find it workable at all, Papá."

"No, I suppose not." He sounded so weary and his skin was so gray that Mateo feared he might collapse at any moment. He guided him to the bed. "Sit. Rest. It's been a long night."

Mateo settled his father and pondered what to say. He smoothed his hand over his freshly shaven cheek. He'd begun to enjoy being unshaven. It had felt strangely freeing. Sitting beside his father, he took his hand. In the darkness of his father's chamber, Ópalo seemed unreal, as if he was only a dream. Mateo almost wished the waters of fairyland hadn't worked so well—at least then he'd still feel the effect of their times together.

He sighed, thinking of his sisters and their lovers, of Ópalo and all they were hiding from their father. He was an accomplice to it now. But his father was so weakened. Could his old heart bear the truth? What of Mateo's own heart? Parting from Ópalo had been harder than he imagined.

THE SUN AT the side of the lake shimmered against the diamond woods, sending rainbow light everywhere. It danced over Ópalo's skin, coloring him as brightly as the birds he claimed as cousins.

"I'll return tonight," Mateo said, touching Ópalo's smooth cheek.

Out of the corner of his eye, he could see his sisters bidding good-bye to their lovers in varying degrees of amorous abandon. He rubbed his thumb over Ópalo's cheekbone, and slipped his hand back to grip the base of his feathered head.

"You'll return in three days," Ópalo corrected, and Mateo nodded. Ópalo handed him a small wooden box. "A gift."

"I have nothing for you."

"Bring me something when you return. An apple perhaps?"

"Of course." Mateo smiled, looking over the beautiful craftsmanship before spying the mechanism. He touched it, springing open the hidden compartment to find a small stoppered bottle. "What's this?"

"The healing waters you requested. Not only might it help your father, but it's my insurance that you, and your sisters, will stay well enough to return to me. Only a few drops do wonders."

Mateo bent forward and kissed Ópalo, his lips firm and soft against his own. He pulled away enough to press his forehead on Ópalo's, gazing down into his eyes. "Why is it so hard for me to go? For me it will only be a few hours before I return."

"I wish I could claim it was love that held you, but my heart tells me otherwise." Ópalo pressed a hand against his chest.

Mateo kissed him again and forced himself from the boat onto the sparkling crushed-diamond shore. He looked back only once to see Ópalo standing forlorn in his boat, watching Mateo leave.

He followed his sisters through the forest of diamonds, then gold and finally silver. They had donned the clothes they'd arrived in, and after all the walking and the dancing of the first and last nights, his sisters' slippers were in near tatters. His own boots were little worse for wear, though. He carried the cloak in his arms, the need for invisibility past.

Eventually the path through the forest of silver led them to a shimmering circle of light hanging mid-air. Mateo watched as one by one his sisters stepped through. He was the last—and the sensation was almost like falling. A rush of wind, a shriek of noise and then he stood in the air outside his sisters' window casement, the stars a shining map of magic stretched out above his head.

Luz reached out the window, grabbed his hand and jerked him inside. "Don't stand there gawking, baby brother. If the portal were to close with you not quite through, well, I suppose at best you'd fall to the courtyard below and break your legs, and at worst your neck."

King Hernando was still slumped upon the floor, snoring and drooling.

"Ópalo is a much better looking husband, Mateo," Imelda said. "Surely you would rather have him than that old dog."

Mateo felt sudden heavy exhaustion drop onto him. He hadn't even realized he was tired, but now he could barely stand. All of his sisters seemed to slump at the same moment.

"It's closed," Adelita murmured.

Looking at his sisters' faces, Mateo could see the fairy thrall had broken. Their eyes were tired and duller somehow, although he supposed it was how they'd always looked. Mateo took Adelita by the arm, her smooth skin cool under his hot palm. "Tell me you still love him."

Adelita's smile was small but genuine. "I love him, Mateo."

"And you, Blanca?"

"Yes, it's true. I love him."

Down the line of them Mateo went, and each sister confirmed that even now she loved the fairy she'd left behind with all her heart. He sighed, and they all jumped and shouted when the loud clang of King Hernando's bell filled the room. Hands to their ears, his sisters glared at the drooling, drugged sleeper on their floor.

Mateo nudged King Hernando with his boot. He moaned Mateo's name softly, much to the sisters' snickering amusement. Mateo rubbed a hand over his hair, exhausted and overwhelmed in an entirely different way than he had been his first night in fairyland. "I bid you all good night. We'll talk more on the morrow."

Luz followed Mateo to the antechamber, closing the room to their sleeping quarters behind her softly. "Mateo, wait."

"Yes?"

"What of you? How do you feel now that the portal has closed?"

Mateo studied her black eyes, shining up at him and so full of worried love. "I...." He paused, searching himself for emotion, and didn't know if he was surprised to find his affinity for Ópalo didn't seem much lessened. The difficulty of having left him behind was gone, but he still desired to return to him that night and, if given the choice, he'd be happy to find Ópalo in his bed when he reached his chambers. "I feel tired," Mateo finally said.

"But about Ópalo?"

"It's a complicated emotion." Only it was not complicated at all. He liked Ópalo, enjoyed his company, thoroughly loved the intimacies they indulged in and felt a warm affection he had not felt for anyone else before. But it still did not match with Ópalo's expectations, or mirror Ópalo's feelings for him.

Luz's brow furrowed and Mateo smoothed it with his fingers. "Shh, Luz. I need some rest. Come now, help me leave." He kissed her forehead and swung the cloak over his shoulders. He slipped out the main door, Luz's voice ringing right behind him as he skimmed past the guards, who all lurched into position to block the sisters from attempting an exit.

"I'm hungry," Luz said. "Please call for a small loaf of bread."

Mateo then turned the corner of the hallway leading to his room, but he didn't remove the cloak until he was safely inside his quarters with his back against the door, his chest heaving with strange emotions that he was simply too tired to attempt to understand.

EVEN NOW HE was confused by his feelings for Ópalo, and though he should be concentrating on what to do about his sisters' engagements and on how to reveal the truth to his father, he had to admit that whenever he let his thoughts stray away from sex with Ópalo and more toward Ópalo himself, the unwanted stirring of his heart confounded and concerned him.

"What troubles you, Mateo? Aside from your heartless sisters, I mean?"

Mateo smiled and kissed his father's knuckles before answering the question. "Father, when did you know you loved our mother?"

A soft smile spread over his father's face and though his eyes remained closed, Mateo thought he was seeing something wonderful. "Ah, your mother. Well, I was slow to believe, you see. My old nurse told me when I was about your age that I should marry your mother, but I insisted I was far too well positioned to marry a princess from a lower station than mine." He laughed a little. "The arrogance of youth! But then it seemed another would have her hand, and I realized my feelings were such that I was going to kill the man if she accepted him. Oh how my old nurse laughed at me then!"

"Was she like Lámina?"

"My nurse? Heavens no. She was no mad fairy like old Lámina."

Mateo startled so that his father opened his eyes. "You know?"

"What, my boy?"

"That Lámina is a fairy?"

His father chuckled. "Of course I'm aware of her yarns. Old Lámina came to us years ago, a mad little lady, spinning a tale of fairyland. She told us she'd given up her youth, her life and her kingdom to come be the nurse to our children. Your mother found her delightful, and I could never refuse your mother, so I agreed. I've often laughed at her story, but she has always been dedicated and wise when it comes to the twelve of you."

Mateo whispered. "Have you spoken to Lámina about where she thinks our sisters go at night?"

His father pulled his hand from Mateo and waved it beside his own head. "She thinks they go to fairyland. I cannot tell if she is laughing at me or if her mind has truly gone."

Mateo nodded slowly. "I see."

"Leave me now. I need sleep so that I can help King Hernando tonight with his new plan." He groaned again. "How he slept through that infernal bell when it kept the rest of the castle awake, I'll never know."

Mateo brushed his father's hair back from his face, watching his tired eyes close. He kept up the gentle caress, remembering how Lámina had stroked his forehead in just this way as a child until he'd drifted off into dreams. His father's hair was fine under his fingers, white and steel-gray mixed. Truly, what was he waiting for? His father deserved to know.

"Father, I know how he slept through it."

"Good, good," his father's voice sounded half asleep. "Perhaps you can help him stay awake tonight."

Mateo stood, reached into his pocket and pulled out the silver leaf, the gold leaf and the diamond leaf. When he had them in his hand, he said, "Look, Father."

But the moment had passed.

Mateo watched as his father began to snore softly. The leaves glittered in his hand, and he set them on his father's bedside table. He flicked his eyes over the room he'd always loved so dearly—the soft couches and tables, the wardrobe that still held his mother's carefully preserved dresses. It was just as it had always been, but he wanted to throw the windows open, let in the light.

He strode to the closest window and unlatched the shutter. He gazed down at the tossing sea that churned on the soft sand shore. It was gray and white, tired and old, like his father. How had his view of his world been so changed in the span of one human night? His eyes strayed to the small house near the herb gardens. Leaving the shutters unlatched and the leaves he'd gathered in the fairy forest on the table, he left his father to rest.

Lámina smiled at his approach, her teeth the same stained brown they had always been. The herb garden was still lush, but somehow less green and verdant after the dazzling world of the fae. "You return!"

Mateo held the cloak out to her.

"No, no, it is a gift for you." She waved it off, but eventually took it from him when he didn't drop his arms. She put it aside on a bench and took hold of his hands, examining him closely.

"So, my favorite boy, you went. Old Lámina sees that clearly. But you didn't eat?" She clucked her tongue. "The doves had told me the youngest fairy was unpredictable and yet moral. I should have guessed. What is his name?"

"Ópalo," Mateo said.

"Yes, now I recall. Ópalo. We fae do enjoy colorful names." She took his arm and they strolled toward the house together, the scent of mint rising around them as they walked. "If this young prince, Ópalo, told you not to partake, he is a brave one indeed. Few fae would risk a human's own judgment. They are too desperate to feed on the love of a human heart. But this is better than I hoped. He will be perfect for you, Mateo."

"Will he?"

"Why he would not be?"

"Because he's a fairy and lives in another land? Because if I do not wish Hernando to be thrust upon me, why would I prefer another admittedly more attractive man who seems to love me even more blindly?"

Lámina smiled. "Because you do."

Mateo rolled his eyes and followed Lámina into her house. The strong, familiar odors were welcoming, and he took a deep breath. The house seemed dark, as all the buildings did to him now. "Do you really prefer the windows closed?" he asked, going to one to open it, surprised to see the latch had rusted, it was so rarely used.

"I like the cold, damp, ugly human world. It sings to me," Lámina said.

Mateo took in her tiny form and tried to decide if she was joking. He thought she was not, and he didn't understand. "Why would you trade there for here?"

"There it is all pleasure, all fun and dancing, delicious things to eat and so little work. I prefer a hard grind to life and the grim specter of men dying young. It adds a certain spice to life that I missed there." She smiled. "I am odd that way, so they say." Lámina tutted at him. "Do not pretend you don't understand me, *mi pájaro*." The endearment sounded wrong coming from Lámina now. Somehow Ópalo had claimed it during the time Mateo had been in his arms.

Lámina studied him. "It is why you hesitate when your sisters flew so willingly away. There is part of you that likes the hardness of this life too."

"My mother was here," he said.

Lámina nodded. "Your lover is there. So you will straddle, as I knew you would. The moment I saw your wrinkled, red face screaming on your mother's tit, I knew you. Still, you will love the fae and the fae will love you. That is how it is. That is how it will always be."

Mateo sat down at her table. He picked up various bunches of herbs and smelled them, until Lámina snatched one from his hand, sniffed at it, chewed a leaf and nodded. "There, give that to your father. It will calm him enough to survive the shock."

Mateo stared at her. "How did you know?"

"Old Lámina knows you, and now she knows of the brave Ópalo. You won't gallivant in secret. You won't keep it from your father. You won't keep it from anyone."

"But what if I never love him?"

Lámina waved the question away. "What if the sun does not rise? What if birds do not fly? What if you never return to the man who makes your blood sing? What if, Mateo?"

"What if?" he repeated.

"Yes, what if?"

The sun was lower in the sky when he left Lámina's house, and he felt a burst of excitement and relief. Shortly he could be with Ópalo again. He thought of Ópalo's fingers in him, the twist of his wrist, the pleasure of him rubbing against the place inside that made Mateo sweat and plead.

Then he glanced down at the bunch of herbs in his hand. His heart pounded for a different reason now. His father—he must tell his father, but—perhaps not tonight? He could have three more days of undisturbed bliss with Ópalo.

"Prince Mateo!"

King Hernando stood on a stone balcony jutting off the side of the chambers he had taken over for the duration of his stay. "Prince Mateo, do come to my rooms. I have a splendid surprise for you!"

Mateo waved at him, but pretended not to understand.

No—he must tell his father tonight. It was time to put an end to this horrible challenge for his or his sisters' hands, and to give his father the truth he deserved. At least with Lámina's odd honesty through the years, perhaps his father wouldn't find the existence of fairyland to have been wholly without warning?

Besides, even one more day of Hernando and his wooing was entirely too much.

He reached the main castle entrance and had only just bent down to pet Whitey, who leapt and barked for attention, when Luz came running toward him, her skirts nearly making her trip in haste.

"Mateo, Mateo, it's Papá!"

Her hands were like ice when she grabbed hold of his and tugged. Her face was so white, her black eyes stood out like dark stars. "Hurry, the physician sent me to find you!"

"Fetch Lámina," Mateo barked to one of the guards standing watch. "What's happened?" Mateo asked as he and Luz ran together toward their father's chambers. "When I left him a few hours ago, he was sleeping soundly."

"He rose and collapsed in the kitchen while sneaking an early bit of dinner. The younger cooks were in a panic but at least the chef kept a cool head. The doctor was fetched at once and Sir Franco carried him to his rooms."

Outside their father's door, Luz grabbed him tightly. "Wait. Wait, Mateo. They found these by him." She held out the leaves. "Has he collapsed from nerves? Did you tell him?"

"No. Not yet."

She swallowed hard, her eyes on the leaves glittering in her hand. "We should never have lied to him. We've weakened his heart with even more grief. Perhaps he could have borne the truth better after all."

"Shh, don't talk as though he's gone."

Luz's throat worked and tears filled her eyes, spilling down her cheeks. "I wanted him to meet Azulejo, Mateo. I wanted him to see our new home, and to give his blessing. I wanted that so much and now, what if he's left us?"

"He hasn't."

Mateo hugged her tightly, kissed the top of her head and then let her go. Luz's mention of Azulejo had reminded him of something very important. He pushed Luz away and raced back down the hallway.

"Mateo, where are you going?" Luz chased after him. "Papá needs us!"

Mateo ignored her, running to his chambers to fetch the box Ópalo had given him. He triggered the mechanism while Luz watched from his elbow and lifted the stoppered bottle out. "Fairy water," he murmured and her eyes went wide in understanding.

"I have some too," she said. "In my room. Azulejo gave it to me."

"Get it," Mateo said. "Ask the others if they have any as well."

Moments later, they pushed into their father's room. The courtiers moved aside until Mateo was close enough to see and then moved back in behind him. The physician rubbed ointment into his father's chest and the priests said prayers by his head. Mateo was relieved to see his father's chest rise and fall though it was far too shallow for his liking.

"Papá." Adelita's voice was tight from the doorway, and the sea of courtiers parted again to let her through. She took hold of their father's hand and knelt by his side, kissing his knuckles fervently. "He will be well soon?" she asked the physician who simply shook his head.

"Yes." Lámina's voice came over the crowd, and then she was there too, tiny but fierce, with a pot of foul-smelling herbs mashed into a paste. "He will be well."

The physician threw up his hands and rolled his eyes to the ceiling, but moved aside to allow Lámina room to work.

Mateo and Luz shoved their bottles into Lámina's hands. She looked at them and nodded, holding the king's nose pinched between two fingers and then pouring the contents of Luz's bottle and most of the contents of Mateo's down their father's throat.

He coughed and sputtered, but his breathing improved immediately.

Soon the other sisters crowded in, clutching their own bottles of fairy water—all of which were waved away by Lámina. When the room grew too crowded, the physician banished all but family, Lámina and Sir Franco, who stood crammed into a corner, strong arms crossed and a deep, handsome crease of worry between his eyes.

"Thank you," Mateo said softly, drawing close to him.

"I am always honored to serve my king," Sir Franco said, not taking his gaze from Mateo's father.

"I understand, but my gratitude remains. Though he grows old, he isn't light. I imagine he was quite a load to heft despite his poor health."

"I've carried heavier, my prince."

Mateo had seen the knights practice, had arranged his schedule in order to witness their sweaty exertions at times, and he knew Sir Franco spoke the truth. Still, he wanted to ensure that Sir Franco understood his actions would not be unrewarded. "There will be favor shown for your help, good sir."

Franco pulled his eyes away from the king and studied Mateo. "You look quite changed, sir. Are you well?"

Mateo's heart skipped a beat. Could Franco tell somehow? Did Mateo truly appear different? "Aside from worry for my father, Sir Franco, I am well, yes."

"Of course." But Sir Franco uncharacteristically went on, indicating Mateo's face with a sweep of strong, long fingers. "You seem matured, somehow. It suits you."

Luz tugged on his shirt sleeve and Mateo took his leave of Sir Franco, following her across the crowded room to a private corner.

"Mateo, how can you be flirting at a time such as this?" Luz whispered, her wet eyes going from where Lámina still worked on their father to Mateo. "What of Ópalo? Would you throw him over so easily for Sir Franco's boring face? There's not a feather or a spark of magic to be had in that man."

Mateo didn't know where to begin with such accusations. "I was not flirting," he said softly. The words felt trivial in the face of their father's pale, shirtless form still being worked over so urgently by Lámina's rough, old hands. "I feel nothing for him."

"Good."

"But if I did, it would be none of your business, my sister. Nor Ópalo's for that matter. I owe him nothing."

Luz glared at him.

"What?" Mateo demanded.

"Shh!" Adelita looked at them both over her shoulder. "If you are to act like children, get out," she said, nails in her tone.

Luz wiped at her eyes and spun on her heel, leaving the room. Mateo was torn between following to comfort her and staying to watch over his father. In the end, he stayed, and Luz crept back into the room a few minutes later with red-rimmed eyes and shaking hands.

"I just hope the fairy water is enough," she whispered. "I thought it would work faster than this."

"He's old. The magic doesn't know what to heal first," Mateo whispered, hoping that what he said was true. "But it will heal him. Eventually."

As the physician despaired, they watched their father fight for his life under the skilled hands of Lámina. Mateo cradled Luz close, tucking her head under his chin. There they all stayed, in clumps of two and three, huddled together.

Chapter Fourteen

Ó PALO STOOD IN his boat waiting alongside his brothers and sister. It had been a long three days, during which he'd made several birdhouses of increasingly elaborate design to give Mateo upon his return.

"They're late." Canario's voice was tight and Ópalo felt more than saw all eleven heads of siblings look to him. "Hours late."

He closed his eyes and listened to the soft splish-splash of the water lapping at the side of the boat. The flowers he'd chosen were all roses, red to bring out Mateo's dark beauty, and pink to serve his own cheeks in good stead as they moved across the lake. He had spent long hours that day thinking of the slow, drawn-out torture that rowing would be. He'd even wondered if they might pause somewhere in the middle and carefully take their pleasure in the bottom of the boat, throwing the flowers overboard for more room, stowing the oars and then rocking together under the moonlight, feeling the gentle roll of the lake beneath them.

"They don't come," Halcón said, his tone vicious.

Ópalo felt it as a slash.

"You should have bade him eat." Cacatúa, who had always stood up for him, seemed ready to cast her lot with the others. Her red feathers crackled with fear.

Ópalo bowed his head. He couldn't deny that the brides were late. He couldn't even claim that he was not wondering at himself—why had he not placed just a little fairy crumb between Mateo's lips as he slept? Yet he still believed with a burning, baseless certainty that Mateo would come.

"Did he promise to return?" Tulipan asked.

Of course Mateo had not promised. He'd said that he wanted to. He'd been reluctant to go, and they'd held hands, they'd kissed, they'd fucked prettily one last time. But no, Mateo had not promised to return.

"Perhaps there's a problem," Azulejo began.

"Yes, the problem is that Ópalo was a fool," Halcón growled.

There was a flash of light and color in the forest of diamonds, and Ópalo's knees went weak. A dove appeared, reflecting rainbows from the trees, and flew directly to Ópalo, lighting upon his outstretched arm. She lifted her foot daintily and cooed.

"Pura," Ópalo whispered.

"What an odd cousin," Cacatúa exclaimed. "She doesn't speak in any language I can understand."

"She comes from their world," Ópalo said. "She brings a message from Mateo."

A leather strap held the tiny tube, and Ópalo's fingers shook so badly that it was hard to work it free. Finally, he tapped out and unrolled the small piece of paper, squinting to read the few words printed there.

Our father has fallen ill. We cannot come this night. We send our regrets.

"Thank you," Ópalo whispered to Pura dully.

She rubbed her head against his cheek and then flew again, a white-and-gray streak heading back the way she came.

Canario climbed from his boat, shored it up and splashed through the shallows until he reached Ópalo. He snatched up the note and read it before shoving it into the small pocket at the breast of his shirt.

"They do not come tonight," he called to the rest of them. "Their father is ill."

A murmur and twitter went through the others, and Ópalo swallowed hard, looking at his feet, waiting for what he knew would come next. The suspicion had already been raised and now would come the doubts and recrimination. He was familiar with how his siblings' minds worked.

"How can we trust a note from him?" Halcón spoke the question haunting all of their thoughts.

"Luz trusts him," Azulejo piped up, giving Ópalo an encouraging look. "I trust my bride. Do you not trust yours, Halcón? Catalina is fond of Mateo, is she not?"

"Yes, but Catalina is an innocent. I am not so easily fooled." Halcón sneered in Ópalo's general direction. "His lover has betrayed our brides and is keeping them from returning to us."

"Let's not jump to conclusions!" Cacatúa sighed heavily. "The bird was sent to us. That is an act of good faith, I'd say."

"If their father is ill, we must be patient," Canario said, squeezing Ópalo's shoulder, but even his eyes were shadowed with doubt. "There's nothing for it but to wait until three days hence. Then we'll see if our brides return."

But three days later, their brides did not arrive. Neither did Pura.

"I told you," Halcón thundered. "His lover is keeping them from us. He's probably spirited them away to realms far from the portal, or married them off to hot-blooded humans!"

"What of Lámina? She would send a dove through to tell us if that had happened, would she not?" Cacatúa said uncertainly, looking between Canario and Ópalo as if uncertain who would be best fit to offer her reassurance that her lover was safe and would return to her.

"He's likely killed Lámina," Halcón declared, his claws extended and his feathers rustling with rage.

Ópalo gritted his teeth. "Mateo is no murderer. Their father was ill. They sent a bird last week to tell us. If they do not come today, then it is because their father is worse."

"He gave you no vow." Halcón spit into the water in disgust. "You fool! If you've cost us everything, you misbegotten bastard, I'll show you what pain is." He lunged from his boat, sending it rocking into the waves as he dove for Ópalo's throat.

Canario stepped between them before Halcón could grip anything more than Ópalo's shirt. Canario shoved Halcón away and brought his own claws out in warning. Halcón made as if to attack Ópalo again, but held back when Canario raised his feathers and moved into a fighting stance.

"Our brother is safe until we know more," Canario said. "Do you understand?"

Halcón sneered but nodded, stomping into the waves to capture his boat.

The next three days passed in a precarious and hostile truce during which Ópalo avoided Halcón entirely, and his other siblings as much as possible. He was wretched. His throat was tight and the hole in his heart a freshly carved wound. His mind a tumble of terrible doubt. Had Mateo decided not to return? Was he keeping his sisters from coming back as well? Had he truly been so good at deception?

The evening they were to row out again to wait for their brides, Canario, Cacatúa and Azulejo cornered him in his workshop. He sat at his table staring at the shavings on the floor, unable to work or do more than contemplate in abject misery how the curls of dark wood reminded him of Mateo's hair.

His siblings each pulled up a chair and sat down all around him, their feathers bristling in their obvious discomfort.

Canario began. "Azulejo tells us that you may have more information about this situation than you've shared with us."

"Luz mentioned something odd to me," Azulejo said, looking guilty, but also considerably duller than usual, the anxiety for his bride having cost him feathers and gleam. "There was a man, a human, who wanted Mateo for himself, was there not?"

Ópalo sat up straighter. "Yes. There was."

Suddenly, his mind was on an entirely different tack than it had been before. Had the man, King Hernando, he believed the name was, discovered Mateo and the others upon their return? Had he presented the information to their father and claimed Mateo for himself, compelling him to honor his father's wishes?

"But Mateo would never agree to marry him," Ópalo said aloud, his heart hammering in his chest and his fingers curling into his palm, claws growing and digging in sharply.

Canario tilted his head curiously. "Marry him?"

"Yes," Ópalo said, hastily explaining the contest attached to their brides' hands.

"You didn't consider this information worth sharing, Ópalo?" Canario asked.

Even Cacatúa looked terrified. "How could you withhold this from us? We should never have allowed them to return!"

"That is the reason they didn't tell you themselves," Ópalo countered, thumping the table. "They wanted the right to come and go. They're strong-minded women and their love would not withstand being imprisoned here." He saw that his point was nearly made when Cacatúa bent her head and Canario sighed, but Azulejo continued to appear stricken. "You want their hearts, Azul, and if you kill their love by forcing them to stay, their hearts are lost to you."

Canario stroked his eyebrows thoughtfully, smoothing the feathers back and forth. "Did you state that anyone can win one of their hands?"

Ópalo nodded.

"Anyone at all?"

"Yes, assuming the message Mateo sent spoke the truth, and they have not been found out already." Ópalo's eyes caught fire and he sat up even straighter. "I could cross the boundary, tell their father everything and win Mateo for myself."

"At the hazard of your health," Cacatúa reminded him. "Crossing over is dangerous."

Azulejo frowned. "Yes, if you stay too long, you'll become human like them."

"I don't care. Someone must go and retrieve our brides. Everyone agrees that this predicament is likely my fault for failing to feed Mateo cakes and securing his return. Still, I believe he will come when his father is well, that they all will. He knows if his sisters don't return at least once a human moon, they'll suffer greatly. And he loves his sisters.

Perhaps Halcón would not believe me, but he truly does."

Cacatúa nodded and took his hand. "I believe you. I saw how he was with Luz and Adelita. He'd not want to watch them suffer. I believe you're probably right, that he does intend to return with them."

Ópalo smiled at her and let her brush her finger through his feathers. "Regardless, if they don't come tonight, I will go to them. You have my word that your brides will return to you."

"And what of you?" Azulejo asked, his blue eyes narrowing.

"I don't know what the human world holds for me or how easy my task will be. But you'll have your brides before their suffering starts, or I'll die trying."

Canario kissed his head and Cacatúa threw her arms around his waist. Ópalo let them hold onto him while Azulejo covered his face with his hands and gave in to soft, sad birdsong.

MATEO MONITORED HIS father's intake of broth, listening to Adelita read from a book from the other side of their father's bed. Mateo was immensely grateful that King Hernando's bell and advances had taken leave of the castle since the contest had been abandoned. He shivered with disgust at the memory of Hernando's wet and inappropriately lingering parting kiss, and swiped at his lips again.

His father grew stronger, and Mateo hoped to tell him the truth soon enough. Hoped his father would accept his sister's fairy grooms. Hoped…for what? His own fairy groom? Aside from his worry for his father, Mateo had been able to think of nothing but Ópalo. He hadn't thought it possible to care for someone so quickly. To miss someone so deeply.

He needed to send Pura through the portal with another note for Ópalo, a note to reassure him that Mateo and his sisters would return. For of course they would. The longing to see Ópalo again—to hold him and touch him and feel the tickle of his feathers on Mateo's skin—was consuming. The men Mateo had once found appealing, like Sir Franco, now seemed drab and ordinary. Ópalo was so much more. It wasn't just his touch Mateo missed, but the lilt of his laughter, the gleam of his smile. His...everything.

A maid burst in. "Someone has jumped from your sisters' bedroom, my lord! We need the physician!"

"Jumped?" Adelita cried, dropping her book and grabbing her father's hand, wide eyes finding Mateo's. "One of our sisters?"

"A boy. With feathers for hair, or so they are saying in the kitchens. A demon! Or an angel! No one is quite sure."

Adelita gasped, her face going pale. "Feathers for hair?"

"Indeed, my lady."

The king was still frail, but his cool head prevailed. "Adelita, find the physician. Mateo, seek out Lámina. There is probably no hope for the poor boy, but we must do all we can for him. Hurry, children."

Mateo and Adelita didn't need to be told twice.

Chapter Fifteen

MATEO DIDN'T THINK he'd ever seen so much blood. It was everywhere and coming from various wounds faster than the physician or Lámina could wipe it away. Mateo felt violently ill at the sight of pink feathers soaked black with blood and his lover's broken body smashed on the cobblestone street. Luz's arms around his waist were no comfort.

They'd both run as fast as they could, Mateo stopping only to save Adelita from her skirts twice. The courtyard was crowded with peasants and the courtiers alike, but no one drew too near to the broken body lying twisted on the cobblestones. Birds circled overhead, their cries harsh like screams in the air. Then Mateo saw the feathers that drifted slowly down through the air, landing in the puddles of blood.

Pink.

"No, no," he said under his breath. "No!"

He fell to his knees by Ópalo's head. He put his hands on him, touching him, whispering, "Ópalo, don't. Please don't. Come now. You're all right."

"Mateo," Luz said. "We need the water."

"In my room," he said. "Get the others too."

The rest was a blur of terror. A white-and-red wash of horror consumed him. He saw his sisters crowd around, could hear their voices, and then there was water—not a lot, but maybe enough. Adelita poured what was left of hers over Ópalo's face and Gracia over his chest. One by one they emptied the bottles until Mateo felt the smooth wood of the small wooden box pressed into his hand.

"I don't know how to open it," Luz said softly in his ear.

Mateo thumbed the mechanism and the door sprang open. There wasn't much left in the bottle—less than a third. He'd given most of it to his father. Mateo unstopped the bottle and poured it between Ópalo's bloody lips.

He waited.

There was no change. Mateo's heart hammered so loudly in his ears that he could barely hear the voices of the peasants surrounding them. His sisters sounded as though they were underwater, calling to him from very far downstream. He could only stare at Ópalo's barely moving chest, desperate to hear his birdsong voice.

Then the physician was there shaking his head. "Nothing we can do."

Mateo couldn't process the words in the face of so much blood and the rattle that had started in Ópalo's throat.

Until Lámina shoved the man away, squawking in a sharp tone and moving quickly. Her eyes met Mateo's with a wild urgency and she slapped his cheek hard.

"He needs your help, *mi pájaro!*"

Mateo sucked in a harsh breath and nodded. "What do I do? How can I help him?"

"Give him your heart!"

"What?"

Lámina stared at him, a flash of something horrible in her eyes. She frowned. "You'd sooner see him dead?"

Mateo swallowed hard, looked down at Ópalo's face, swollen almost beyond recognition, and his fingers twitching in spasms that threatened to inch up his arms and take over his whole body. Death throes. The thought of losing him was unbearable. "Yes, yes. Anything!"

Lámina grabbed Mateo's right hand and forced it against Ópalo's chest, then drew up his left to press against his own. "Tell him."

"Ópalo," he said, kneeling low and whispering in his ear. "You can have it. Anything you need. Please don't die…" Mateo licked his lips, trying to find the words. A coldness was starting in his chest, a deep chill that sank into him with a finality that terrified him. *"Mi…mi pájaro,* I'll give you my heart. It's yours. I'll give you anything at all, if you'll only live."

Ópalo's eyes fluttered open, blue and wide, and his mouth twitched into a broken smile. Then he was gone again.

Mateo was pushed aside so several knights could move Ópalo onto a tarp. Putting one foot in front of the other, Mateo followed them to Lámina's cottage, aware of his sisters clotting around him, shifting in and out to kiss and touch him. It soothed through the cloud of numbness and sharp, heightened reality that he didn't quite understand.

When they reached the door to Lámina's cottage, she shooed the curious peasants and courtiers away. She then grabbed Mateo's chin and gazed up into his eyes. "Do you feel it?"

Mateo stared at her, shaking his head in confusion, his mouth hanging open and his mind awash in terror. "Feel what?"

"His heart, your heart. Do they beat as one?"

Mateo tried to focus on his heartbeat. He looked down at his chest and found it covered with blood, his own hands a mess of red as well. "I feel nothing, Lámina. My heart…feels dead."

A gleam shone in her eyes. "Good." She slammed the door in his face.

WHAT SEEMED LIKE hours passed. Mateo stood there with his sisters, unable to talk, unable to do anything but stare at Lámina's door waiting to know if Ópalo would live. If Lámina could save him. If his heart had been enough.

Finally, when Luz couldn't take it anymore, she pounded on the door and demanded Lámina let them in. "I'll summon the guards to kick the door down, Lámina! Don't think I won't!"

The door opened with a creak moments later, and Luz and Adelita pushed Mateo in first. Their hands felt like ice on his overly hot skin. The interior of the cottage was dark, but the scent of the herbs filled Mateo's lungs and brought him back to himself for the first time since he'd seen the waft of pink feathers in the air around Ópalo's body.

"You wanted in," Lámina croaked by the table where Ópalo was laid out. She stood over him, painting his wounds with a paste the color of algae from the sea. "Come see him. You've already given your heart to him. Don't be stingy with it now, or old Lámina will have something terrible to say about that."

Mateo shuffled toward the table as if his feet were moved by someone else's volition. Ópalo looked as if he was near death. Mateo's heart clenched and he felt gorge rise in his throat.

"The fairy water you and your sisters gave him has healed a few of his wounds, but there wasn't enough. He needs to be doused with it, or dunked even, soaked with the stuff in order to recover fully."

Ópalo's eyes were closed, but his eyebrows and head had been wiped free of blood for the most part. Except he looked different.

"Lámina," Mateo whispered, surprised to find his voice worked after the silence that had seemed to reign over him before. "His feathers are white."

"Indeed," she agreed. "He's changing, becoming human. It's part of the problem. The change is fighting the water's healing. He must go back tomorrow night when the portal opens, lest he change entirely."

Mateo touched the soft feathers, noting that blood still crusted near the quills.

Lámina went on, "Unless that was your plan? For him to join you here in this world?"

"No. No, that was never our plan! No," Mateo whispered. "Why would he come here?"

Lámina lowered her bushy brows at him. "Why? Do not play that game with me, Mateo. You think one note is enough to keep fairies from their brides? Any fool would have known to send a note every night. You're lucky it was just him and not the lot of them lying broken in the courtyard."

"He must have come through the portal and found the window closed to him," Mateo said softly, remembering the lurch of his own heart when he'd found himself walking on air, and the swift jerk of Luz's hand on his wrist pulling him inside.

A collective gasp rose from all eleven of his sisters, crowded around them in the small cottage. They blanched in horror and cried out the names of their lovers as they shoved and pushed their way back out the door, deserting him with Lámina and Ópalo.

"They've gone to open the shutters," Lámina said. "Lest their own lovers come through and meet the same fate."

Mateo nodded. Of course they had. If Ópalo had come through, the others might decide to join him, and then they'd have more dying fae on their hands. Not this one, shuddering soul who seemed so frail, but must be so strong to have survived the fall for even a second.

"He will live?"

Lámina sighed. "Whether as human or fae depends on the timing, but yes, he will live. He will not be undamaged, though. Especially if he becomes human as I did. We simply do not heal as well as the fae." She studied him. "Your heart. How does it feel now?"

Mateo concentrated on his heartbeat, his throat tight, tears prickling his eyes. There was an ache that seemed all consuming, a gnawing sensation that filled him entirely until he almost couldn't speak the word. "Hurt."

Lámina collapsed into a chair next to the table, set the bowl on the floor beside her and muttered. "Excellent. Now we wait."

ÓPALO OPENED HIS eyes into a kind of darkness he'd never known. He slowly rolled his head to the side, a horrific pain following the motion.

He held in the gasp, uncertain of his safety or surroundings. He appeared to be in some sort of hovel, or a cottage, resting on a waist-high hard surface. Everywhere there were bundles of gray dried vegetation hanging on the walls, and an empty straw-backed rocking chair that was still moving.

Carefully, he rolled his head the other way and blinked when he saw Mateo sitting with his dark-circled eyes closed, his head leaning back against a wall. There was blood all over his shirt.

Mateo is hurt! The thought jolted him to the core and he sat upright, a wrenching, horrible agony ripping through him. He heard a scream and recognized it was his only after Mateo's eyes flew open. He leapt to his feet, coaxing Ópalo back down again.

"Stop, stop! You have broken bones and myriad other injuries," Mateo said, his voice soft and soothing as a dove's.

"But you're wounded," Ópalo said, his tongue even ached to form words.

"I'm healthy as an ox. It's you who are hurt. Now lie still again."

"The blood." He motioned weakly to Mateo's shirt.

"Your blood, *mi pájaro.*"

Ópalo's eyes flickered. "Why did you call me that?"

"Don't you feel it?" Mateo asked. "I gave you my heart."

Ópalo frowned and shook his head. "Why? You don't love me."

An old woman with white caterpillar-like eyebrows leaned over the bed. "Hush now. You'll hurt yourself more and you've only just begun to heal. His heart was necessary or you'd have bled out on the pavement. The fools had so little fairy water after giving it all to their father. It's a wonder you survived the fall at all."

"Fall?"

"Careless fairy, popping through a portal without ensuring the other end was a welcoming place to land. It could have just as easily been under the ocean, or in a pit of vipers, but did you think of that? Oh no, you did not."

Ópalo licked his lips, tasting blood on his tongue. "Their room.

They said it led to their room."

"Oh, just a few steps shy is all," Lámina said and clicked her tongue. "So I could be sure any visitors from the other side were welcomed guests and not intruders."

Ópalo's body began to shake and his eyes rolled up, and he heard Lámina smack Mateo's arm. "Kiss him. It will help. Have you not heard of the power of love's kiss?"

Mateo dutifully pressed his lips against Ópalo's. Ópalo felt his heart convulse in his chest, a painful flipping feeling that took his breath away. Was this what it felt like to have Mateo's heart? He didn't think so. He felt drained of all that was best in life, tired and on the verge of death.

"There," Lámina said when Mateo pulled away. "Do you feel better?"

Ópalo only murmured, worried his answer would only frighten Mateo and possibly anger Lámina. He was as hollow as ever—hollow and broken. Mateo may have intended to give his heart, but he hadn't. Love, Ópalo understood, couldn't be forced or willed into existence—not in this world. Not without fairy charms. Surely Lámina must have once known that, but perhaps she had forgotten? The fairy waters had done their work to bring him this far from the brink.

"The portal," Ópalo whispered.

"Closed on this end until tomorrow night," Lámina said. "Now tell us, are we to expect more visits from heroic brothers searching for their delayed brides?"

Ópalo whimpered.

Lámina tutted softly. "Let us hope so. It is your best chance."

Unless it is too late. Ópalo could feel the swelling alterations within, making him more human moment by moment. He took a steadying breath and whispered, "How long until the change is complete?"

Lámina bared her crooked teeth in a smile. "It took me three horrible hours, but your injuries are slowing your transformation. Old Lámina is surprised, I must say. Only your feathers have already gone white. At this rate, in several days time they are likely to fall out and you'll grow nice, fuzzy hair like me."

Mateo made an odd sound, and Ópalo glanced his way. "Don't worry, *mi pájaro*. I will get back to fairyland in time. My feathers won't desert me. I promise."

It was an empty vow, but one he made all the same, relieved to see Mateo's expression soften a little.

"Only heal, Ópalo. That is all I ask of you."

"Let the boy sleep then." Lámina waved a strongly scented bottle under his nose.

Then the stars were swimming in Ópalo's head, making rainbows out of blackness.

Chapter Sixteen

MATEO APPROACHED HIS father's room hesitantly. His hair was still wet from the bath he'd taken to wash himself clean of Ópalo's blood. He was almost too tired to be nervous, save for a lingering fear that what he was to reveal would damage his father's health all the more.

He found his father alone, propped in a comfortable chair by his window, pondering something in his hands.

"Papá," Mateo said softly, pulling up a wood chair. He rested his hands on his knees and sighed.

His father held the leaves of gold, silver and diamond, shifting them back and forth, contemplating them with a serious expression. "I have been expecting you, Mateo," he said. "I believe you have the unfortunate task of telling me the truth, do you not?"

"I do, Papá."

"I imagine you and Adelita tossed a coin for this difficult task and you lost."

"No Papá. Adelita and I are in rare agreement on this front. We both thought I should be the one to talk to you."

"The young man with feathers, the jumper the maid saw. He did not jump, did he?"

"No, Papá."

"These leaves, they are rather remarkable. Are there truly forests of them?"

"Indeed. How did you know?"

"Before you were born, long ago, your mother and I would listen to

Lámina telling stories to your older sisters. There was one, a particular favorite of hers, about twelve royal fae who fell in love with twelve royal humans. In one version, forests of silver, gold and diamond played a part."

"As it stands, all twelve of the humans have given their hearts to the fae. My sisters wish to wed their fairy lovers, and having met them all, I give my blessing."

"I see." His father frowned out the window. "If I give mine as well, what then?"

"Nothing will change, Papá. They love you and will return to you all the days of your life. Perhaps, as children come along, their visits might slow, but surely the joy of grandchildren will lessen that blow."

The king nodded slowly as if considering. "They are happy?"

"Quite. And very much in love. They will be well taken care of forever there, and treated with respect. They will be the highest of royalty and given much honor. I believe they will be happy."

"I'd like to meet these fae when I am well enough."

"I am quite certain they'd like to meet you too." Mateo smiled, though deep down he wasn't sure it was true. Canario and the rest would be polite, he was certain, but he knew his father's blessing meant less to the fae than to his sisters.

"The young man who fell. He is your lover, I suppose?"

Mateo swallowed and nodded. "Yes. If he lives, he will be my lover."

"If he lives?"

"My sisters return to fairyland tonight to bring back more of the healing waters that saved your life and his. We didn't have much left for him, so he's fading, I'm afraid. If he makes it until morning, then he can be saved. However, the laws of fairy are such that time spent in the human world will alter him, turn him into a human, like Lámina. If he's not returned before that takes place, he'll be trapped here with us forever."

His father's rheumy eyes grew sharp and he studied Mateo. "This isn't what you wish, is it?"

"Not for him…and not for me," Mateo conceded. He didn't want to feel responsible for Ópalo's life in that way. When he'd imagined them together, it had always been in fairyland, away from his world. Their affection and intimacies had seemed a step above all that was common and grim, and it pained him to think of losing that. Less selfishly, he knew Ópalo loved his family and would want to return to his home. Mateo, at least, would be allowed to straddle the worlds, but Ópalo would be forced to give up his should the worst occur.

"Can you not take him back tonight?"

"The journey is too far. Lámina says he will die for certain if he attempts it."

"Then I pray your sisters return in time."

"Thank you." Mateo waited a few minutes, looking out the window with his father at the vast, churning sea. "Are you angry, Papá?"

"No. I am hurt your sisters did not trust me. Sad that I went to such lengths to discover the truth, only to be shut out of their lives and decisions time and again. I am ashamed that not a single one of my children thought I could be trusted with this information. I have only ever wanted what is best for all of you."

"I know, Papá. But your heart is so frail."

"My heart is not so worthless that I could not have been told of my daughters' joy or survived the surprise of discovering the unknown. As I grow old, I find I'm always on the verge of the greatest unknown there is, death. It gives me hope that there is more than I've been led to believe. Strangely, I find comfort in this new knowledge, not fear."

Mateo rubbed his face. "Papá, then why the contest?"

"When you are an old man and everything is slipping from you, you will understand desperation. Now that I know my children are happy, I can rest. I admit I went too far. And I admit…all these years I've kept you and your sisters close to me. I've stifled you. It is no great wonder my children kept this truth from me."

"Ah, Papá, I wish they had told you sooner. I only just found out myself."

His father tried to pass him the leaves, but Mateo stayed his hand. "We needn't worry about the treasury, at least," he told his father, smiling. "My sisters can simply collect a few of these every visit and the kingdom will be wealthy for years to come."

"What of your young man, Mateo? Are you afraid for him?"

"I am, but I must admit my heart doesn't feel quite right. I care for him, and I feel I will grow to love him, but I don't understand why I feel as I do. I gave him my heart when he was dying, Lámina said it would cure him and help him live. I believe it did, but something still feels amiss. I want to know him more, and yet if he dies, I might lose that chance. If he lives I'm afraid of feeling pain like this ever again. My fear for him is great enough as it is. If I grow even fonder, his loss would be devastating."

"I understand, my dear boy, but as one who has loved greatly and lost, there is no reason to pass up joy for fear of grief. If nothing else, look what fear of grief has brought us in this debacle."

Mateo took his father's hand and kissed his knuckles. "You are wise and I will endeavor to take your words to heart, hard though it might be."

"Your heart isn't hard, my son, just cautious. That's not an unwise thing to be. Your young man waits for you, does he not? You should return to him, keep him comfortable and calm until your sisters can return. Perhaps they will bring enough water to ease the suffering of my people as well."

"We can keep some on hand, Papá. It cures all but the most dire of human ills, and for fairies it can cure almost everything except for old age and death itself."

"I see there are many blessings that will come of these unions. The greatest of which, if what you say is true, will be that I can keep your sisters near in a way that marriage to others would never allow."

"It is true, Papá, for time is quite different here than it is in fairy-land."

"Tell me another day, Mateo. Your young, wounded man should not be alone while he awaits his fate."

Mateo nodded and hurried back to Ópalo with his father's blessing, one of the knots of anxiety in his gut finally unraveled.

ÓPALO TRIED TO get comfortable in the soft bed prepared for him in the study only one door down from Mateo's own room. The physician had wrapped Ópalo tightly in blankets, hoping to hold his mending bones in place, but the trip from Lámina's cottage to the comparative luxury of the castle had been excruciating anyway. Ópalo was limp with exhaustion and pain.

Ópalo was startled by Mateo holding out a shiny red apple.

"I know you cannot eat it whole quite yet, but I can feed it to you, if you'd like, in small slivers."

Ópalo smiled, or tried to. The fairy waters and his own magic were working wonders on his injuries, but the change within him, altering him quite slowly, particle by particle into a human, was a confounding countermeasure.

Mateo sat down next to him in a beautifully carved wooden chair, heavier than anything Ópalo would have designed, but fascinating all the same. He hoped to soon be well enough to take a closer look at the construction. Likewise, Mateo's knife was a cruder, heavier thing than the metal works Ópalo was accustomed to, but it didn't seem to affect Mateo's ability to slice the apple into sections so thin that they nearly dissolved when Mateo placed one on Ópalo's tongue.

The sweetness suffused his mouth, and he moaned softly. He'd eaten whatever Lámina insisted in hopes of healing faster, but everything until now had been foul medicinal herbs. The apple was heaven in comparison. "*Gracias.*"

"Is it as good as you remembered?"

Ópalo laughed, but his broken ribs stabbed him and he winced.

"Better."

Mateo smiled and placed another sliver in his mouth. "As good as my lips?"

"Hardly even close."

Mateo leaned forward and kissed him gently, and Ópalo sighed against his soft mouth.

"My sisters should be back in the morning with more of fairyland's waters. Do you think you can hold on until then?"

"With your tender, loving care I imagine I will survive. As to the change, my injuries seem to be working both for and against me. Returning to my home will be the best course of action to repair the damage done and restore my magic."

Mateo's eyes clouded then, and he leaned back in his chair, his hand coming up to cover his heart. "I feel no different. Rather, what I feel is so sad."

"Your heart is still your own, *mi pájaro.*"

Mateo shook his head. "No, I gave it to you."

"It doesn't work quite like that. Lámina has either forgotten or is trying to trick you into feeling something you don't."

"Lámina has never lied to me."

"Then perhaps she believes you gave it, but whatever the case, Mateo, my heart feels just the same. The hole is still there. One day, I know you will fill it with your own, but that day has not come." Ópalo struggled to sit up, the pain lancing through his broken legs, but he managed. "I'm lucky indeed that the fall didn't crack my spine."

"Or your skull."

"Well, crack it very much," Ópalo said, touching the lumps that had not yet receded. How he wished for a pond of fairy water to dip in. He'd be quite well by now.

"If my heart is still mine, then why do I feel so much despair? Seeing you this way, my own soul seems to ache."

"You might not love me just yet, Mateo, but you're a human with a kind heart, and you do care for me. That is enough to make any man feel broken. Seeing a friend, no, a lover, in the state I am in, why, you'd have to be quite cruel to not feel pain for me."

"I suppose so." Mateo rubbed his stubbly face.

"By the way, you don't have to grow that for me, though you look so dashing with it, I must say."

Mateo smirked and fed him another slice of apple. "I've been by my father's side day and night and haven't even thought of shaving." Though his eyes were still dark with sadness, he said, "I rather like having a beard. I'm told it makes me look older."

"Perhaps your sisters will finally give you the respect you deserve."

Mateo chuckled and a spark seemed to catch for a moment inside him. Ópalo felt a corresponding easing of pain, and he smiled. "Ah, there you go. Your heart might not be mine, but mine is yours, and when you laugh, I feel better. Come, laugh some more."

"You are entirely free to be funny again."

Ópalo indicated his state. "I'm rather out of sorts at the moment, to say the least."

Mateo pressed another bite of apple between his lips and rose. "Give me a moment. I believe something helpful is in this bookcase right over here."

Ópalo noted the number of books lining one wall of the room. Mateo ran this finger over the volumes on the top shelf. "Ah. Here we go. I suppose a book of bawdy jokes will have to do?"

Ópalo settled against his pillow and smiled softly. "Please, just don't make me laugh. I only want to hear you. It's like water on stones, *mi pájaro*."

Mateo sat down next to him and said with a hint of teasing in his tone, "Then perhaps I should read silently. I'd hate to cause you more pain."

Ópalo watched as Mateo read the book, enjoying the thin slices of apple that Mateo fed him from time to time. When tears of laughter filled Mateo's eyes, Ópalo relaxed against the soft blankets, feeling slightly euphoric. The pain ebbed away almost entirely.

MATEO KNEW HE should have expected it, but he hadn't. When his sisters came through the portal armed with so many glass stoppers of fairy water that their dresses rattled as they walked, they were escorted by Canario. Mateo's father, who leaned heavily on a cane and one of the servant boys, drew himself up as best he could.

"Allow me to dispense with formalities," Canario began, after bowing over Papá's outstretched hand and kissing the knuckles perfunctorily. "But there is no time to lose if my brother is to be healed completely."

"I have done good work on him, your highness," Lámina said, bowing to Canario. "He will live and the waters will take his pain away completely."

"Lámina," Canario said, a bit of awe in his voice. "I must assure myself of my brother's state, but I wish there was time to show you the honor you are due."

"This way," Mateo said, hustling Canario out of his sisters' chambers and into the hall. The rattle behind him indicated that all eleven of his siblings followed. Ópalo was asleep, his face not nearly so swollen as even the hour before.

"Oh *pollito*," Canario murmured, stroking a hand through Ópalo's white feathers. "You are changing already." He sighed and then bent to kiss Ópalo's forehead, which roused Ópalo from his sleep.

"Canario," he gasped.

"Shh, we have the water." He turned to Mateo's sisters, who barely fit into the room.

One by one they handed their multitude of stoppered bottles to him, and Canario alternated between forcing Ópalo to drink it and pouring it directly onto his open wounds. Finally, when the last bit had been swallowed and the last wound doused, Canario sat on the bed next to Ópalo and took his hand, watching as the wounds healed before all of their eyes.

"Amazing," the king murmured. "Astounding, truly."

Canario only had eyes for Ópalo, and as his brother was finally whole, he spoke again. "What pain has our impatience wrought you? We have been so very worried. Even Halcón sends his affections."

Ópalo scoffed at that. "You needn't lie to me, brother. It appears I will live after all. Save Halcón's affection for my death bed."

Canario chuckled. "Oh, you are such a stubborn one, Ópalo. If you'd fed him cake. But no matter. Here we are, and now we must go before either of us is irrevocably lost to this world."

Mateo blinked as he realized that now Ópalo was healed, his eyebrows were beginning to molt. Soon he'd lose his feathers, and with it his fairyness.

"But the portal doesn't open again until tonight," Ópalo said, confused.

"You only need this." Canario pulled a small, dark bottle from his pocket. "Father gave it to me, and it can only be used once. I'd been saving it for an urgent situation, and I suppose this is it, *pollito.*"

Ópalo sat up, Mateo's white nightshirt too big on him and slipping almost off his shoulders. He gazed behind Canario, obviously seeking someone, and Mateo thought he'd found the person when his eyes lingered on Mateo's father. "Sir," he said, nodding his head. "I wish I could stay and get to know you, but it is rather urgent that I leave. I hope you won't mind me taking this opportunity to thank you for your hospitality and to tell you that I love your son, though he does not yet love me. And I give you my solemn vow that I will only ask for his hand when I am sure he wants to share his heart with me."

Lámina made a soft noise, but didn't disagree.

Ópalo smiled at Mateo and reached out his hand. "*Mi pájaro,* I will be waiting for you."

Then Canario lifted Ópalo in his arms. Adelita opened the glass bottle, poured the black dust over both the fairies' heads, and in the cloud that rose out of it, they vanished.

Mateo rushed to the bed Ópalo had rested in and gathered handfuls of the sheets in his hand, feeling odd and bereft as his sisters crowded around him. His father took hold of his arm.

"Come, Mateo," his father said. "Let us while away the hours before you can join him in fairyland tonight. I have much to discuss with you and your sisters. I believe there are plans to make."

Chapter Seventeen

ALTHOUGH ÓPALO WAS exhausted from all he'd experienced, when the time came to take the boats to wait for their brides, he insisted on going with his siblings. He felt sure Mateo would be with them, although doubt lingered in the corners of his mind. Of his heart.

"They're late again," Halcón muttered, but he sounded almost contrite at the same time, as if ashamed by his lack of patience. He darted a glance toward Ópalo and added, "Don't get any ideas in your head about going to fetch them, you little idiot. Just stay here and wait with the rest of us. They will come."

Ópalo coughed softly, trying to cover a smile, and dug his oar deeper into the mud at the lake bottom.

Long minutes passed until there was the sound of something dragging, and then they saw them—a tangle of brides in dresses sparkling with jewels, the king riding on a sled pulled by a large, beastly dog.

The twitters from his siblings were a rousing selection of joy, surprise and concern.

Pulse racing, Ópalo sought out Mateo's dark, curly head. When he found it, his knees strengthened and he stood upright and proud.

Mateo worked his way to the front of the group, his face lighting up when he spotted Ópalo. "You are truly healed?"

"I am. Just about." Ópalo ruffled his feathers ruefully. "My pink might not return."

"As long as you are well. That's all that matters, *mi...*" Mateo seemed to remember they were not alone. He cleared his throat and pronounced, "Our father, the king." Then he moved aside as Elisa and

Gracia took one hand each to pull their father up from the sled.

The king stepped forward, his eyes narrow and his lips set in a straight line. He took them all in with a slow, serious gaze. "It is not customary in my world to take brides without asking first for their father's blessing."

Ópalo glanced down the line, and each of his siblings looked abashed.

Mateo's father continued, "However, since I have it on good authority that my daughters love each of you dearly and have promised themselves to you, I will allow your oversight to be remedied now."

Canario was the first to recover himself and quickly did as Mateo's father asked. He spoke eloquently of his love for Adelita and requested the honor of her as a bride.

The king did not make Canario wait for his answer, instead turning to Adelita and saying, "Go now and be as happy as your mother and I once were."

Adelita fairly skipped to the boat and climbed aboard, a chaste kiss passing between her and Canario.

And so it went until the king came to Ópalo. He stared at Ópalo, saying nothing, and obviously expecting nothing. After a time, the king turned to Mateo. "If the day comes when you seek my blessing, I will give it to you."

"Thank you, Papá," Mateo said, and Ópalo felt a strange buoyancy. Mateo had not denied there was any possibility of needing his father's blessing.

"My daughters will return to me every day until I am gone from the earth," the king went on in a commanding voice. "Vow it."

Ópalo and his siblings answered in unison. "You have our word."

"Childbed or illness will be the only exception."

When Canario bowed and thanked the king for his leniency, Ópalo's siblings took note and bowed as well.

Mateo walked toward his father. "You grow tired, Father. I think it is time you go home."

"Indeed."

"I shall walk Papá back to the portal," Mateo said. "Ópalo, if you are willing to wait longer, I can return."

"No, my favorite boy, run along with your lover," his father said. "I can make it back safely."

The king called the great dog to him and climbed aboard the sleigh. "Breakfast will be early, my darlings," the king said in a tired voice. "Sleep well."

With a bark the dog set off, and they were gone.

MATEO'S BODY WAS warm underneath his as they lay at the bottom of the boat alongside the oars. A rose stem had been left behind, failing to make it overboard with the rest, and Mateo was still bleeding a bit on his bearded cheek where it had scratched him. Ópalo ran his thumb over the cut and wiped away the bright-red. Then he leaned over the edge, dipped his hand in the water and brought a wet finger to the cut. He smiled as the wound began to heal immediately.

"I have missed this," Mateo said, reaching down to squeeze Ópalo's ass. "When I saw you there, broken on the cobblestones, I feared, oh, I was quite numb with fear, actually. I thought I'd never know you or see you again."

"Fairies are stronger than we look," Ópalo said.

"You don't have to convince me. The miracles I witnessed with my own eyes cannot be overstated."

Mateo gripped him closer and they began to move together again. The boat rocked on the waves of the lake in the rhythm of their lust, and Mateo whimpered in urgent frustration.

"What is it?"

"I only wish the boat was big enough for you to fuck me properly. I long for your cock inside me, Ópalo. I long for so much."

Still they rutted against each other, prick against prick, mouths pressed urgently together, cries rising as they reached another climax and wet spurts of seed pulsed between their shaking bodies.

His heart pounding and Mateo's panting breath tickling his ear, Ópalo snuggled in closer. Who needed dancing when they had this? The stars above were faint, but the moon was wide and brilliant, illuminating them in glossy, opalescent light.

"What did you think of our world?" Mateo asked when his breath had slowed again.

"It was quite dark, and everything seemed very small. I regret that I can never stay long enough to explore it fully."

"I am so grateful that Canario saved you as he did." Mateo brushed his hair over Ópalo's feathers. "I rather like the white. It suits you."

"Does it? For that at least, I'm glad." Ópalo kissed Mateo's neck. "Lámina is not what I expected her to be. After all the stories of her sacrifice, I thought she would be regal and stately. More like Blanca."

"Ah yes, Lámina is quite odd."

"I have to agree," Ópalo said. "I mean no insult to your world, but I would not want to give up my home to stay there."

"I love it, but it seems quite changed in my eyes now that I've been here. Though, for now, *mi pájaro*, I still choose not to eat."

"The food is not that delicious anyway," Ópalo teased.

In the quiet of the night, they rested together. Ópalo kissed the edge of Mateo's mouth and settled down, resting his head against Mateo's chest. He listened to the sound of Mateo's human heart. He closed his eyes, soaking it in.

It wasn't his yet, but one day it would be.

Epilogue

"ONCE UPON A time, in a kingdom by the great, foamy sea," Mateo began, kneeling down to speak to the children who stared up him with rapt expressions. "There lived a kind human king and his wonderful human queen. Over the years, they were blessed with eleven human princesses, each more beautiful than the last."

"That's my mama," Luz's eldest girl, Colorista, chirped.

"And one incredibly, devastatingly handsome human prince."

His little nieces and nephews twittered with excitement, their feathers fluffing. They loved the part of the story set in the human world the most, and it amused him to think of his own childhood seated in Lámina's lap, listening to her speak of her world as if it was a fantasy land.

"Do they never tire of this one?" Ópalo asked good-naturedly. He leaned against a tall pole on the side of the dock, looking fanciful in his newest breeches, dyed with some berry that made them a bright purple. The color set off his white feathers.

"No, Uncle!" Flora cried, her yellow feathers bristling at him. Her concern that Mateo might not finish the tale marred her pretty features. "Don't take him away yet. The story isn't over!"

Mateo smirked. He too would like to rush off to their nest, but the children had taken to greeting him at the dock when he arrived, along with the flocks of cousins.

"Then let me have the honor of finishing it for him," Ópalo said, grinning. A sigh went through the children. They knew story time was about to be cut short. "All eleven human princesses and one charming human prince came to fairyland, fell in love and everyone but the incredibly handsome human prince and the famously attractive youngest fairy prince had elaborate weddings with all the best food and lived happily ever after with a lot of squalling babies who grew up to be adorable little fae who loved their uncles dearly and understood that after three days apart they wanted to be alone together. The end."

"Only one day for him," Marvolo mumbled with an expression quite like Imelda.

For a moment Mateo thought they might argue, but they didn't. One by one they hugged him and scampered off in a dazzling show of feathers and color. Mateo watched, amused and now happily alone with Ópalo.

Ópalo grinned. "I think you should take your famously attractive fairy prince back to our nest." He held out his hand.

"Famously?" Mateo laughed.

"Of course."

Mateo gazed down at Ópalo's face, taking in the blue eyes, the feathers and soft lips he'd kissed so often. "How many years have I been coming here now?"

"In your world's calculations or mine?" Ópalo asked, and his brow furrowed, obviously attempting to do the math in his head.

Mateo cut off his efforts with a kiss. "It doesn't matter. Yes, let's go home."

Ópalo launched out in front of him, striding with great purpose, before turning around and calling, "Race you!"

"Wait! Let us go by the dance and grab some wine. There'll be cakes. Your favorites."

Ópalo shook his head, his backward steps speeding up, clearly trying to get a head start to win.

Mateo remembered the night his father had died, and how the three days with Ópalo had steadied him for the grim reality of the service and the responsibilities of the throne. He remembered long nights of laughter, and the first time he saw Ópalo dancing playfully with Adelita's little boy. He remembered the fights they had over stupid things like whether to ride horses or swim in the lake. He thought of the way Ópalo smelled like wood dust after working on a project and still looked like the most delicious cake ever made.

Over the years, so much had changed. Yet one thing had not changed at all, only growing stronger and more real, until it had become the most real thing of all.

"Come," Ópalo called again, still trying to get Mateo to run after him.

"No! Let's get cakes!"

"I'm not hungry for cakes!"

Mateo ran then, chased Ópalo across the green grass toward the entrance that led most quickly to their rooms. He grabbed him next to the roses and kissed his mouth hard. Ópalo laughed, and returned his urgency before breaking away and tugging at his hand, clearly eager to be alone. But Mateo did not budge.

"Ópalo, I'm ready," Mateo said.

"So am I, my stubborn bird! Why are you dragging your feet?" he grinned and lifted his brows in a hilarious attempt at lechery. Mateo pulled him close, lifted his chin and gazed down into his eyes. He waited until Ópalo stopped laughing and grew serious.

"What's wrong?"

"I want to go by the dance, because I wish to eat cake, *mi pájaro.*"

Mateo watched Ópalo's face explode with delight and ecstatic joy. If he'd thought his declaration would result in a detour by the dance so he might declare his love publicly and take a wedding vow in the form of a piece of fairy cake washed down with wine, he was mistaken.

It wasn't until two hours later, after Ópalo had proven again how strong he was by hauling Mateo up to their nest and stripping his clothes in such a way that they were left in ruins, and after Ópalo had buggered him and they were covered in spendings, sweat and feathers, that Mateo even had a chance to express his disappointment in not getting to experience the aphrodisiac of the cake before their coupling.

Ópalo, tucked into the slot between Mateo's arm and his body, slapped Mateo's chest with the back of his hand. "The cake is rather tasteless anyway," Ópalo said. "And our pleasure can't be very much greater than it is."

Mateo scoffed. "It's as though you don't want me to have it."

Ópalo looked vaguely embarrassed. "I like knowing that you've chosen me. The hole in my heart has long been filled, *mi pájaro*. It stopped aching years ago."

"Then what was all this for?" Mateo asked gesturing between them at the evidence of Ópalo's enthusiasm at Mateo's declaration of intent toward the fairy cake.

"You love me."

Mateo touched Ópalo's face tenderly. "I do love you. Lámina was right. I gave you my heart long ago before I could admit it to myself. It is how it is and always will be."

THE END

ANGEL UNDONE

Leta Blake

An Original Publication From Leta Blake Books

Angel Undone
Written and published by Leta Blake
Cover by BRoseDesignz

First Edition, 2016

Acknowledgements

Thank you to Tom Robbins for Skinny Legs & All and to Neil Gaiman for American Gods both of which inspired aspects of this book. Thank you to the small press which hosted an angel-inspired anthology even if it never came to pass. I wouldn't have started this one if not for the prompt. Thank you to my readers for taking the journey and let's hope we're all forgiven the blasphemy in the end.

For Hamilton

Chapter One

ANGEL WINGS AREN'T easy to fold into the shape of human scapulae, but Michael is accustomed to the strain and hardly breaks a sweat. He forces the long primaries to bend into the upper wing coverts, and then, in moves like feathered origami, he tucks it all in again, before smoothing them under flawless human skin.

He glances in the modest hotel room's bathroom mirror and pulls on the dark brown shirt that will set off his eyes, before running a hand through his blond, curly hair. The light of his angelic grace glows from his pores, too bright to escape notice, and with a small exertion of will he tamps it back.

Though human form is confining and uncomfortable, the time has long passed when dropping down in a blaze of angelic righteousness was appropriate. Now covert operations pay the dividends of souls delivered from jeopardy. Even if Michael's skin feels too tight, and his wings are already aching, protection is his business and discomfort is a small sacrifice.

After tightening the laces on the leather, soft-soled Clarks he keeps for nights of trawling the Mercy Street bars, he kneels by the sliding glass door to the balcony and looks up at the stars. It's a fallacy that heaven is up there somewhere. Heaven is everywhere all at once, and yet when Michael dons human skin, he finds his eyes drawn to the sky when he prays.

He rises. Time to go.

ALL IN ALL, angels aren't what they used to be. In the face of creation as it exists currently—suburbs, cities, cars, trains, and the vast sprawl of technology—dramatic entrances have been rendered obsolete, and as much can be accomplished with a misdirected email as a flashy herald from the sky. Angels' duties have shifted accordingly.

Protection is Michael's calling. Once, he was a warrior and his role a valiant one in an epic clash with great stakes, but heaven has been different since the war and there is no army to lead. As the ages drag out, it seems that there may never be a need for a heavenly army again. But Michael's desire to protect the people of God hasn't changed.

It's never the same victory twice. The mark is sometimes a woman, sometimes a man, occasionally a child, and protection can be hidden in a handkerchief given at just the right moment, a steadying hand across a busy street, a drive home on a night of too many drinks, or safe delivery to a house away from hands that hurt small bodies. But, occasionally, a desperate soul requires something more intimate than that.

Tonight his mark is sitting in a corner booth of Boat Out Bar at the very end of Mercy Street. With his head nodding gently to the loud strumming guitar of canned country music, and a clutter of beer bottles around him, the man plays host to a deep sadness that penetrates his bones. Michael drops onto a bar stool and orders a scotch and soda. The alcohol won't touch him, but the scent of it on his breath can suggest camaraderie to the drunken human he'll be approaching.

Michael examines his quarry closely—forty years old with dark, crescent-shaped marks of sleeplessness and recent tears under his eyes. His slim form is slumped forward, wrapped up in a long, dark trench coat, as if trying to disappear into its depths. His limp, black hair has seen neater days, and his dark eyes are rough with grief. He clutches another beer bottle with trembling, long fingers.

Michael peers harder, sees straight into the man's delicate, beating heart, feels around in the tight fiber of his muscle and discovers his name—Asher—along with the secret pain knit into his being. He closes his eyes, gasping softly as he presses deeper. Asher is an echo of the ocean several streets over: deep and teeming with hidden life. Each breath is a tide churning with unexplored emotions. Michael rubs a hand over his mouth. Like the tide, Asher's soul tugs at him.

Careful now.

Michael settles himself with a sip of his drink and then another, waiting for the sign that it's the right moment to approach. In the meantime, he glances over the room, looking for the danger. He's not sure if it's a person, a mood, or a thing, but he's never given a human to protect without *something* on its way. Given the way beer bottles are collecting on his table, it occurs to Michael that the danger might be inside the man himself.

As more beer goes down the hatch, Asher's eyes roam. They linger on a light-haired, tall man by the window and then steal away, frightened, when the tall man makes a gesture asking to cross the room to join him.

Asher keeps his eyes down and Michael can hear the thrum of his pulse, the subtle vibration of the internal words he uses to urge himself on: *Don't be such a sissy. Ha. Sissy. **Be** a sissy, Asher, come on. Just look at him. Just **look** at him.* Asher's eyes dart up again, and his lips tremble into a terrified smile.

Michael's attention turns to the man at the window. He narrows his gaze, takes in his heart, the breath that exits his strong lungs and penetrates farther into his bones, his marrow, his soul. There's a good person in that body—someone with a generous portion of mirth and humor, someone who loves children and small dogs. There is also too little patience, not enough self-control, and Michael downs the rest of his drink in one gulp before slapping some dollars onto the bar. This is his cue.

It takes effort to open his pores up just enough for a gentle glow to shine through. The eyes of men and women in the room suddenly focus

LETA BLAKE

on him, and he modulates his inner light, until they all turn back to their drinks and companions. All except for Asher, who now stares at Michael with glossy-eyed drunken wonder, as though he's just seen an angel—as though he knows, somehow, that he truly has.

Michael walks confidently toward Asher's booth, and slides into the darkness opposite him without asking permission. Asher's mouth is open, his lips wet and his tongue against the roof of his mouth.

"Are you driving tonight?" Michael says, smiling softly, allowing more light to illuminate his eyes. "I think you've maybe had too much to drink."

Asher's throat clicks as he swallows. It seems to take an effort to pull his gaze from Michael, but when he does, there's surprise in his expression as he takes in the table of beer bottles, and the one clutched in his hand.

"Wow," he says. "Look at that."

His voice shivers up Michael's spine, deeper and gentler than he expected.

"I think you've been at it quite a while." Michael grins and leans forward, taking hold of the neck of the beer bottle in Asher's hand and tugging gently until Asher lets go.

Asher takes a shaky breath, his bones screaming his anxiety.

Michael's chest aches in sympathy and he quickly eases Asher down, gracing his bones with a sense of holy safety. "Let me take you home. Make sure you get there safe and sound."

Asher rubs a hand over his face, and peers at Michael again. Asher's wide eyes set off an unexpected ricochet inside, like a pinball machine in Michael's normally calm chest. His job is to keep Asher safe, but he can't deny the man's ocean-soul is calling to him. He leans into it, wanting to illuminate Asher's depths with his own grace. *Careful, Michael.*

Asher's appealing voice is low-pitched and too quiet, but Michael hears it clearly over the clanking of glasses and the loud chatter around them. "I don't know. I mean, I don't even know you."

Michael takes a swig from the beer he's just liberated, suffuses peace

262

into Asher's throbbing heart, eager to relieve him of anxiety, and settles back into the leather booth. He admires Asher's dark eyes, and allows a whisper of his attraction through too. "We could remedy that problem if you want."

Asher clearly misses Michael's cheesy innuendo and his shoulders relax from where they are bunched up by his ears. "Yeah. I'd like that. What's your name? I'm Asher, by the way."

"Michael," he says, putting his hand out.

Asher takes it with a delicate touch that sends a shiver through Michael. His skin flushes and a little radiance slips out. He won't have to work to give Asher what he'll need. Michael may be an angel, but he has preferences of his own. Sometimes he relies heavily on his ability to pull divine love through to the core of his angelic being while he gives the human he's helping what he or she needs. Tonight, though, he feels so much for Asher already, it won't require effort from him.

"Nice to meet you, Michael." Asher's dark eyes roam the table in front of them. "Wow, these bottles are staring me down like a row of accusers, all of 'em screaming, 'You're drunk.'" He flushes, embarrassed, and rolls his eyes. "Shit, ignore me. You're probably wondering why you even sat down now."

"You *are* drunk," Michael says. "We're in a bar. It seems the place for it. Nothing to be embarrassed about."

"Can we just—here—" Asher starts moving the bottles aside, trying to get them out of the way, but he's uncoordinated and he nearly knocks the lot of them over.

Michael grabs several before any fall and break, stands up, and takes them to the trashcan by the bar. Once the table is clear, he sits down again across from Asher who's shored himself up against the side of the booth, his eyes glimmering with heat as he watches Michael move. An attractive form is always an advantage, and Michael's human body is decidedly beautiful. He chose the details himself—straight nose, full lips, curly blond hair, and soft, brown eyes. Beautiful, but not terrifyingly so. It's a combination that always does the trick.

He smiles at Asher. "There, they're out of the way. Feel better now?"

"Yes. Thanks. For cleaning up after me, I mean."

"It's not a chore."

"*Why* are you being so nice?"

Michael shrugs. "Because I saw you eyeing that other guy and I'd love it if you spent the night with me instead."

"I just met you and that's kind of…" He trails off, eyes wide, scared and excited. Mostly excited.

"But you were going to go home with him, weren't you?"

"Maybe? I might have chickened out. Probably would've actually."

"And if you hadn't?"

Asher wipes a hand over his mouth, his fingers trembling. "I'd have done it, at least. And I'd have to live with myself. Admit it. Admit what I am. Finally." Fire blazes in Asher's eyes and it starts to fade out almost as soon as it catches.

Michael reaches out, takes hold of Asher's hand where it rests against the table. He feels his responding attraction like a burning tingle against his skin. An answering flame grows inside, a desire to cover Asher with his wings, protect him, love him whole. "I can help you with that. In fact, I'd like to."

"Why? You don't know me."

"Maybe it's easier that way. You didn't know him, either," Michael says, an urge to draw Asher close flaring in him. "Or we can go back to remedying that problem."

Asher doesn't pull his hand away, but he doesn't speak either. The air between them pulses gently.

"Where should I begin?" Michael asks, biting his lip and basking in the glow of mutual burgeoning desire.

"How old are you?"

"I'm older than I look."

"Thank God, because you look half my age."

Michael ignores that. "I like baseball and chess. I enjoy movies with asinine fart jokes because my everyday life is pretty much always serious business. I prefer Coke to Pepsi. I find disaffected Jews attractive."

Asher cracks a smile.

"I believe you fit that bill."

"Does my nose give it away?"

"Does it matter? What else do you need to know before you agree to let me leave with you tonight?"

"Are you in school? Or do you have a job?"

"I work for my father," Michael says. "He runs a rather large business—a worldwide thing—very corporate. Very dull."

"Posh?"

Michael grins. "Don't I wish." He remembers the war and the subsequent years of rebuilding and the seeming eons of daily service to humans. "No, for the most part I work in the trenches."

"And your dad? Does he work alongside you? Are you close?"

No one is really close to Father. Not like that, anyway. "My father expects a certain respectful distance."

"What kind of business is it? What does he do?"

"It's complicated and rather vast."

"You said it's worldwide?"

"Yes, and very boring," Michael reiterates, letting off a little light to shut down further curiosity in that direction. "Father oversees the whole, great machinery of the thing, while my brothers and I travel and do the dirty work. What about you? What do you do?"

"I'm a professional at letting people down. If I could get a salary for that, I'd be set. Alas, if I got a salary for *anything* I wouldn't be letting my folks down anymore, so that'd be against the terms of my position. It's a damn Catch-22, I tell you."

Michael squeezes Asher's hand. It's a good sign he hasn't pulled away from him yet. "Charming sense of humor, my friend, but aren't you being too hard on yourself?"

Asher's expression is withering. He doesn't respond.

"All right. So, you're out of work. It happens to the best of us."

Well, not really to Michael, but he supposes his brother Lucifer had been without a job until he'd carved himself out a nice position as the Prince of Darkness.

"I've never been in any kind of work to be out of. I went to school until I couldn't anymore. After that I took care of my grandmother until she passed away. Now? According to my father, I'm useless. I'm too lazy to get a job, or hold down a fort, or even set up a damn tent to keep myself out of the rain. My mother and I are close, but I know she's disappointed in me too. She just loves me too much to say so."

Michael doesn't think Asher would have even needed to chicken out had the fellow by the window made his way over. He'd have run him off with this line of conversation. "I'm not going to walk away until I know you've gotten home safely, so feel free to say all the disparaging things about yourself that you'd like."

"Why do you care?"

"It's what I do."

"Caring about strangers in bars is what you do?"

"Tonight, caring about you is what I do."

Asher pulls his hand away and slumps back against the slick vinyl of the booth. His eyes focus fully on Michael for the first time, a sober gleam beginning in them. "Why aren't you creepy? I should find you creepy."

"Because I'm not." He misses Asher's fingers, and he reaches out for them.

"See? That—*that* should be creepy. I should be entirely disturbed by you right now." Asher's hand slips into his own again, and Michael shivers, feeling a little more eager than he should. "You come over to pick me up, and when I'm a freak, you don't go away. I'm drunk, so I have an excuse. But, you're not. Or are you?"

"No, I'm not drunk." And Asher has a point. What is it about his vulnerability, his social awkwardness that makes Michael want to cuddle him closer than his average mission? Why does he want to comfort Asher to satisfy himself and not Father alone?

"So, what's wrong with you?"

"Oh, where to start with that question?" Michael deflects. "I have a particular weakness for Jewish men. I've mentioned that already. But, let me ask, why are you trying to scare off the same men you'd like to screw?"

Asher blinks rapidly, licks his lips, and says, "So, you came over here because you want to screw me?"

"Yes." Michael is surprised by how much *want* plays a role already. It often does once the time comes, but he's here to protect Asher from making a terrible mistake, not get off on his mission. And yet Asher's vulnerability is stirring something deep inside him. It makes no sense— vulnerability is on display before him every moment of every day, and yet something about Asher's dark eyes makes his cock thicken.

"I don't get it. You saw me over here, in a corner and you thought, 'I'd like to screw him'? So you came on over and asked to take me home?"

"I believe that's how it's done."

"Is it?" Asher sounds at a loss now, desperate and worried. "Is that how it's done? With girls it's…it's never as simple as…it's not like that."

"It depends on the girl," Michael says, taking another swig from the beer he stole from Asher. "But usually, no, it's a bit different for women than it is for men."

"Why?"

"The stuff our fathers taught us about them, the things their fathers taught them about themselves, the lives their mothers lead, the lives their grandmothers led. Culture. History. Religion. It all adds up."

"My father taught me *this* was wrong. Two men together."

"Your father and my father should meet. They'd probably have a lot to say to each other."

"But if it's wrong—"

"I never said it was wrong."

"—how can it feel so right? And how can you be so easy? A look across the room, and then you ask to take me home." Asher's lashes fall to his cheek. "What do we do when we get there?"

Michael's dick throbs and lengthens down his pant leg as he imagines how beautiful it will be to witness Asher awakening to his lusts, and he surrenders to the unusual thrill of helping him accept them.

Asher's voice is breathy. "How does this work? Would we fuck? Do we even kiss?"

Wondering what Asher's soft, drunk-loose mouth will taste like, he moistens his own lips in anticipation.

Asher leans forward, his heart pounding, and his pupils dilating. "Would you take me to my bed, or just fuck me on the stairs, or on the sofa, or the floor?"

"What would you want me to do?"

"I'm not the one auditioning here." He smiles wryly, flirtation floating over his face. "You're seducing *me*, remember?"

"That was my answer, Asher. I'd do whatever you wanted me to do."

Asher's heartbeat quickens and Michael's pulse thrums. Human flesh is so responsive. A sharp surge of want pierces him as Asher says slowly, "But I want to hear what *you* want to do. To me."

What he wants? It's never even a question. He does Father's bidding and he protects humans. There's rarely room to indulge his own desires.

Michael tilts his head and studies Asher's eyes, the vulnerability twisting in them despite the demands of his words. As Asher's gaze darts away, he seeks deeper, finding the hum of anxiety and fear, hearing the murmur *could be a rapist*, and the hungry denial of lust. It's a wound he wants to heal, a sweetness he wants to pull up and nurture. Yes, Asher is a flower and Michael wants to watch him bloom. The image flushes him with desire and the words come easily.

"I'd kiss you while I undress you."

Asher's lashes flutter and his cheeks darken.

"I'd take my time with your mouth, find out what you like—gentle and slow, or rough and insistent." Michael flicks his tongue out to wet his bottom lip and Asher's eyes follow the movement. "I'd kiss your chin and your eyelids while I unbutton your shirt. I'd listen to your breath—does it hitch when I touch my lips to your collarbone, or do you like it better when I kiss just behind your ear?"

Asher sits very still, his pupils dark, and his lips parted, staring at Michael helplessly. He spins his words with a warmer energy, letting them pass to Asher and fill him. "I'd slip your pants off, but leave your boxers on, and then I'd ask you, 'Do you want my clothes on, Asher, or off?' and you'd say—"

"Off. I'd say I want them off."

Michael shudders with pleasure at Asher's insistent tone. "Good. I'd start with my shirt, too. Undo the buttons all the way down. I'd unzip my pants and slip them off. You'd see I'm not wearing underwear."

Asher gasps.

"By that time I'd be hard. Is it okay if I'm hard from kissing you and seeing you naked?"

"Yes," Asher says softly.

It feels so good to talk about what he wants, to imagine Asher's reaction to it all. The freedom adds an extra sweetness to his lust.

"Is it okay if I'm hard now telling you what I want?"

The click in Asher's throat is loud as he swallows and nods his head.

"I'd leave my shirt on my shoulders, something for you to take off later if you want, but I'd leave it so you'd know I'm not pushing you." He'll never push Asher. He'll only make it so good for him. So good for them both. The way Father intended sex to be.

A well of joy warms his gut, a protective heat that he'll share with Asher, healing him, making him whole. Tonight, he'll prepare him for a future where love can find him. A curl of jealousy slips up into his gut, confusing and unacceptable. He lets it slide away, hoping Father doesn't notice it. "It's up to you decide how far we go tonight, Asher."

"I'm so drunk. I'm not sure I can get hard. I should be hard right now."

Michael thinks he's picking up the slack, his cock full and balls tingling. He normally doesn't get carried away by his own seductions, but

Asher is delicious in a way he can't resist. He considers reaching out to Father, ask him why Asher's like a tide pulling at him, but he doesn't want to lose his chance to feel this. Whatever the reason, he's willing to go under with Asher's tide, see how it feels to surrender to it.

"Who wants to screw a limp-dicked drunk?"

Michael wants to rub his hands all over him, shoving away the layers of sadness and guilt, revealing the soul beneath. He settles for squeezing his fingers. "It's okay. Let's say you don't get hard, Ash. I'll hold you, kiss your mouth, and touch your nipples with my tongue."

"Oh, God."

"I'll touch you everywhere and I'll let you explore my body with your hands and mouth." Michael wants to transport them to a bed now. "I'll rub my hard dick against your hip, but I won't come—"

"I want you to come."

"Then I'll come for you."

"Please."

Michael smiles and rises the table. "Do you want me to take you home now?"

"Yes," Asher whispers, letting Michael tug him up. "I want you to take me home."

Chapter Two

MICHAEL ISN'T SURPRISED when Asher balks at giving his address. It's a smart move, really, not letting a stranger know where you live, so Michael lets him off the hook by suggesting they go to his hotel. This is why he keeps a room, after all.

It's impossible to know on any given night if the room will come in handy, but sometimes it does. Such as the nights when Michael has brought in homeless men or women for a shower and a set of clean clothes. Or the nights when a battered family requires a place to hide before making a clean break from town with providentially provided cash and a shot of heavenly confidence. But it isn't often he uses it for seduction purposes.

"It's clean," Michael says. "That's about all I can say for it."

Asher stands by the curtains gazing out the window. The view is unremarkable, but Asher looks out searchingly. He's sobered up some during the short walk from the Boat Out Bar, and his anxiety is of a more solid variety. Michael picks up the deep hum of it in Asher's bones and he listens to it as he turns back the burgundy and blue covers on the queen-sized bed, giving Asher space.

"You come here a lot?" Asher says, his voice just barely louder than the in-room air conditioner.

"When I'm passing through on work, it's a place to sleep."

"Oh."

"I don't bring a lot of men here, if that's what you're asking. Well, not for sex, anyway."

Asher remains silent, his fingers curling into the fabric of the drapes, and his heart beating rabbit-fast.

Michael sits down in the square, blue-upholstered hotel room chair by the round little table in the corner, and removes his shoes, untying them carefully, taking his time. "You don't have to be scared. I'm very good at this, very patient and willing to hold back, to be kind." And he *is* good at it. While statistically sexual seductions account for a low number of missions in the scope of his work, over the centuries he's become well acquainted with the pleasures of the human body and the art of sex.

"My virginity is that obvious." Asher isn't asking, and Michael doesn't point out Asher nearly said as much back at the bar.

It's his experience that focusing on details like that loosens his grip on the bigger picture of gaining his assigned human's trust, pulling him in, and delivering salvation up to his father. Michael sighs, mentally acknowledging his father's 'salvation' changes from one day to the next and often from person to person. He's given up trying to follow his father's logic—or as he tends to think of it, his father's whims—long ago.

Michael leans back in the chair and watches the long line of Asher's back as he stares out the window. He gives him time to sort out what he wants.

Sex is a pleasure that at least makes stuffing himself into human skin enjoyable. The human body is built for sexual congress and the gratification of using it for that purpose is immense. He's never dared to say it aloud or let his mind form the thought into a confessional prayer, but he enjoys the experience of human lust and orgasm more than almost any other sensation. Almost more than being naked and submissive in his father's presence, and that is considered by humans and angels alike to be the most blessed and rewarding experience of all.

Blasphemy.

Michael hears in Asher's heartbeat the moment his determination overtakes his fear. As Asher jerks the drapes closed, shutting out the reflected light of street lamps bouncing against the brick wall outside, Michael spreads his legs to welcome Asher into the space between them.

Asher stands looking down with his grief-rough eyes, and he whispers, "Tell me why I should trust you."

Michael twines his fingers with Asher's soft, cool ones. "Because you're fighting a battle and you need someone on your side. Living this lie—it's killing you from the inside out, Ash."

"I don't want to live a lie any longer, but my father…"

"I've been in my fair share of brutal and bitter fights—" he's been nearly pulled into hell by his own brother after all "—so, where you are right now, battling for your life and what is right for you, feeling like it's your father's love on the line—I've been there, too."

"Your father didn't accept you?"

"My father is the most judgmental man you'll ever meet and I live every day in dread of him."

Michael remembers Lucifer's face aglow with righteous rebellion. An answering fire sparks inside him, held tightly wrapped in confining human skin. Is it any wonder orgasm is such a glorious thing? The intense and all-too-fleeting sensation of breaking free of the prison of the human body, the delicious pleasure of escape that seems, in the moment, worth almost any consequence?

Oh, Lucifer, look how you tempt me even now with your example. Is it so very dark without our father's love?

Michael has never dared to ask. He isn't sure he could trust Lucifer to tell the truth anyway.

But he can tell the truth to Asher.

"You can trust me on this, at least—you can lose your father, Asher, but gain a life of your own. The loss is immense but the reward is nothing short of fulfilling your destiny."

"You'll be gentle."

"Yes."

"You won't hurt me."

"No."

Asher grips Michael's fingers tightly, and with a grim paleness to his cheeks, he drops to his knees, his face aligned with Michael's groin, and he licks his lips. A tremor runs through his body, and he doesn't let go of Michael's hands, gazing up with wide-eyed terror.

"Let me suck it."

Michael feels a tight clench of lust spike through him. Even inexperienced, Asher's mouth will be hot and wet, and if there are teeth—well, Michael's always been a little bit of a masochist. He pulls his hands loose and undoes his button fly, watching Asher's face grow heated as his cock is revealed.

It's a pretty one. Michael chose a long, rosy length with a reasonable girth, but nothing a virgin like Asher will be too terrified to take in hand...or ass. As for the head, Michael always chooses circumcised. There is the whole thing with Abraham and his covenant with Father to consider when designing a human body. He's happy he doesn't have to endure the act itself, but simply fashion a penis that fits his father's whimsical orders.

Asher makes a noise at the sight and all hesitation is thrown to the wind. Permission to act on his urges seems to overwhelm him, and he's greedy as Michael shoves his pants down far enough that his cock bounces free. Asher's mouth is on it before Michael settles back into his chair, and, yes—hot, wet, enthusiasm with an edge of teeth that makes him yelp.

Pain can be a wonderful thing—underrated by far too many humans as far as Michael can see, but he supposes that's to be expected when the submissive perfection of the angelic state is unknown to them.

"Shh, slow, slow," Michael murmurs. Despite his own willingness for a dash of discomfort in the mix, he knows he needs to lay the groundwork for future encounters. "Take your time. Watch the teeth. Use your hand."

Asher gets a grip at the base of Michael's cock and it's just that much better now. He relaxes, leans his head against the back of the chair and lets Asher have at it. It's sloppy, and there's a lot of spit sloshing between Asher's fist and his mouth, sometimes rushing down over Michael's balls. It's nice, good—not the best Michael's ever had, but over centuries the delicious details all blur together. It's enthusiastic and that's what he always likes most.

Finally, Asher pops off, his lips red and wet, his eyes glazed over and pupils blown wide. "Wow," he whispers, licking the head of Michael's cock again, tonguing the slit, and sliding his mouth over the head to suck. Another pop off and he's panting now. "Wow. I knew I'd love it...but, God—wow."

Michael's game for letting him suck for as long as he wants. His skill level and lack of dedication to a rhythm makes it unlikely Michael's going to have trouble lasting to the next phase, but Asher seems to have another plan. He stands abruptly and ditches his shirt and his pants while Michael slowly strokes his cock, watching.

Long, lean legs with black hair against pale skin, lead up to a thick, veiny cock that's bigger than Michael's by far. It takes a moment for Michael to pull his eyes away from it. So many new images fill his mind, most featuring himself on his stomach with his ass in the air. Because that cock was made to plow, he's sure of it, and if anyone can handle the discomfort of something that big in the hands of someone so inexperienced, it's him.

"Wow, yourself," Michael murmurs, and is pleased when Asher takes his huge prick in hand to pump it, showing off. The shyness is gone now. It always amazes Michael how quickly a mouth full of cock can change things.

Michael kicks his pants free, and unbuttons his shirt, leaving it on for Asher to remove later as he'd promised in the bar. "Bring that gorgeous prick over here."

Asher does as he's told, stepping back into the space between Michael's knees. He holds his cock against Michael's mouth and rubs the slick head over his lips, smearing his pre-come on like ill-applied Chapstick. Michael lets him play, keeping his mouth shut as Asher drags his cock against Michael's cheek, gasping at the scratchy stubble, and over Michael's eyebrows, down his other cheek, and to his mouth again.

Michael grabs hold of Asher's hips and remembers his training ages ago in a series of brothels he worked in Sodom. Those were days of adolescent heights of sexual obsessions. His work included forays into it almost every day. Then the rapes happened, followed by retribution and destruction, and, well, sexual salvation assignments grew less frequent in the following ages.

Michael opens his mouth and sucks Asher's cock in deep and fast, taking it into his throat, letting it slide back out. Asher groans, tossing his head back and tensing all over. It seems unfair to do this to him, take him from zero to oh-my-God-is-this-real? He's not going to get this sort of treatment from most guys, Michael knows. It's been a few years since his mark was a virgin and a man, but he usually takes it slowly, sucking the head and bringing them off with a pumping hand and rhythmic suction.

But something about Asher's enthusiastic, messy attempt has him wanting to escalate to the hottest, fastest, most intense place he can. Or maybe it's just been too damn long since he got to screw a guy with a flat stomach and a handsome face. Or maybe it's something about Asher's flesh and bones and the anxious, needy hum that feeds into Michael's own, singing with *so good, so **good**, oh, please, God, so **good**.* Regardless, Asher's a blithering maniac now, spilling filthy words that imperfectly echo his body's pleas.

"You—oh, God, you're gonna make me! I can't stop, can't stop—it's so close, aw, fuck, *fuck*, your mouth, your fucking *mouth*—" His hips twitch and thrust, and Michael grips them hard, holds him steady, moving his head so Asher's cock is fucking his throat, and just as he's going to spill, Michael pulls back, tonguing the slit and jerking his hand wetly on Asher's dick in a fast, urgent rhythm.

His own cock thrums against his stomach, aching for a touch, yearning for the return of Asher's mouth, but it can wait. He's bringing Asher careening into the finish now, and he spares a glance up to see Asher's chest heaving and stained red with exertion and lust. He's beautiful with his dazed eyes and his sparse chest hair swirling in tufts around dark, small nipples. Michael's suffused with affection and pride. "That's it," he encourages before going back to sucking. "You're being so good for me."

Asher covers his face with his hands, and Michael doesn't stop sucking to tell him not to be ashamed, to let him see, because this is Asher's moment. A rushing connection opens between them, angelic and human twining together, and Michael pushes his own arousal into Asher's body, too.

Asher's torso tightens, his breathing stuttering. As his cock swells in Michael's hand and the first white, hot load of semen spurts onto Michael's tongue, he throws his arms wide and cries out. His wild eyes pin to Michael's, his flesh and bones screaming *yes, yes, for **you***. He convulses as he pours his pleasure out.

Through their connection, the ecstasy hits Michael hard, loosening his grip on his human skin. A flash of light pulses in the room as Michael's cock throbs and shoots untouched. It's a shocking orgasm that rolls through him. He pulls Asher closer, shaking and trembling as his chest and shirt are drenched with his own come, all while milking twitching, shocked cries of lingering pleasure from Asher.

Fuck, Michael thinks. *Holy fuck*. It's been a long time since he let a human's pleasure run so hard into his own. It's exciting. It's beautiful. He knows his father will probably cluck his tongue and disapprove. Michael has a function, but damn if he can remember it right now with his human skin barely containing him, his wings itching in the confines of human scapulae, and his body ringing with shared and amplified satisfaction.

He kisses Asher's cock, and stands up, helping the now-limp man toward the bed, where he collapses face down, still quivering with aftershocks. Michael sits beside him, his hand resting on Asher's panting back. He looks at the come on his own stomach and chest, and closes his eyes, shuddering. Not since his affair with that beautiful, nervous, but incredibly delicious dolt in Queen Elizabeth's court has he gotten carried away enough to lose control that way. He wonders if Asher noticed or if he just assumed it was the intensity of his orgasm that caused the flash of light.

"Christ," Asher mumbles against the sheets.

Michael almost jokes that he's not nearly so humble as that particular fellow, but he can't bring himself to speak just yet. It's been so long.

MICHAEL SHEDS HIS human skin and returns to the steady submission of angelic state. He's put it off as long as he could, and had it not been for Henry's sweet mouth, Michael would have shed his body days before.

At the thought of Henry, Michael plots his return. The next assignment he has. Surely a detour to the court will not be noticed or condemned?

At that moment, his father calls to him, and Michael redirects his steps to the Throne of Thrones. As always, it is impossible to look upon his father, and finds himself prostrate on the floor in naked submission.

"You, Michael, are getting too near to him," his father says, his tone bored with the infinity of all knowledge.

Although no name is spoken, Michael knows Father means Henry.

"I'm fulfilling the assignments you give, Father," Michael says. "Queen Victoria did not drink the poison. The barber did not bleed the young duke to death. Is it so bad that I see him, too? Can these things not exist side by side?"

"Your assignment was to save Henry from his fear of his own nature, not to indulge in an endless episode of altogether unangelic lusts. I know, Michael, wearing a human form comes with pleasures to make bearable the pains."

Michael has to bow his head.

"I have never denied my angels exploration and enjoyment of the sensual side of humanity during their time in human skin, but there has always been a limit."

"Henry and I cannot reproduce as my brothers did with Eve's

daughters."

"No, but this you do with him is becoming something more."

"I have not fallen in love."

"No, of course not. For you, pleasure with Henry is not about love. It is about yourself." He feels Father's smile and it is mostly benevolent. "Congress is a beautiful thing that brings the future for my children. I encourage it in all healthy expressions which befit a human's nature. It is not meant to feed an angel's dissatisfaction with his place in my creation."

The threat isn't spoken. It's not even a threat. Not to **Father**, who knows and sees and feels everything, so nothing is good or bad any longer. But to Michael, it's a threat.

Lucifer was dissatisfied, and look what has become of him. If Michael continues to see Henry, the sweetly shaped man with powdered hair and a body that makes Michael's human form sing in heretofore unknown pleasure, might he lose his place? Will he be cast down?

Michael doesn't dare ask.

He doesn't see Henry again. He doesn't allow himself to miss it. He enjoys, even wallows in the seduction assignments as they come, but stays focused on their salvation. He never again considers returning to the same man for a second night, or a third, or more.

MICHAEL RUNS HIS fingers through the hair at the back of Asher's neck. He's still collecting himself from the unbearable freedom that crashed over him at orgasm. Angels are intended to be submissive and perfect. Humans are slaves to the trap of their body. But this *wonder* is true freedom. And when it's like it is with Asher—violently, exposingly urgent—it's addictive.

"Thanks," Asher says hoarsely. "I think I'm fucked now."

Michael whispers, "No. Not yet. Give me a few minutes and I'll see what I can do about that."

"No, no. I'm so *fucked*. How am I supposed to do anything now?" He rolls over, black eyes shining with emotion. "I didn't know. Michael, do you understand? I didn't *know*."

As he first discovered with Henry so long ago, Michael *does* understand. How humans ever get any work accomplished when Father allows them to share *this*, he has no idea. No wonder their church and culture have so twisted his father's words and creation in the attempt to put orgasm into a box.

"My hand? Nothing compared to this. Fuck. *Fuck*."

Michael nudges Asher over and collapses beside him, his shirt half off one shoulder. He breathes slowly, waiting for his skin to feel settled, because the memory of Asher's face as he came, the message in his body (*for you*) has him half-hard again, and shot through with lust.

This is dangerous, he thinks. What is it about this sad, sweet little man living his desperate life—not unlike millions and millions of others of Father's creation—that makes Michael feel more than he should? He thinks of that human expression, of things that get under the skin.

Why, Father? Why did you send me to him?

Long minutes pass, as Michael sends the desperate question up in prayer, staring at the ceiling, imagining the night sky beyond it. Surely his father doesn't *want* him to fall? The air conditioner has cooled their sweat enough that Michael is slightly cold, and as he moves to crawl beneath the blanket, Asher does as well.

"Is it always—"

"No," Michael says. Because it's not. He's fucked untold men and women and only with Henry was it ever close to this.

"Why?"

"Chemistry," he says, but he thinks *souls*.

But he's an angel. He has no soul. Not like that anyway.

He can't explain it. He never could with Henry either. Asher is forty years old and an attractive man, but Michael's had sex with other men who were more stunning. *It's never looks*, he recalls telling a woman a few nights before, as she'd cried on his shoulder over losing the man she thought she loved, fearing it was her aging face that'd driven him away. *What makes a connection between two people is something only God knows or understands.*

Why did you send me to him?

"I came so hard I thought I'd died." Asher rolls onto his side, smiling unsteadily at Michael. "Was it okay? Did I do okay?"

Did he do okay? Here Michael is contemplating whether or not he could risk everything by seeking Asher out again tomorrow, and the next day, and for as long as he can before Father puts an end to it, or casts him to earth for good, and he wants to know if he did *okay?*

"You did great. It was great. I thought I was dying, too."

"*Le petite mort,*" Asher says in accented French. His dimple is unexpected, and the happy glow in his eye feels as sweet as a kiss.

Speaking of.

Michael leans over and kisses Asher, tasting his tongue, sucking at his slippery lips, sharing the taste of Asher's come. He laughs when Asher realizes it, and instead of pulling away, dives in for more. It's delightful, and there's a weird pull in Michael's stomach to see Asher again. He should ignore it. But he thinks maybe he won't. Not this time. One more night can't hurt.

"Wow," Asher says again. "You're all…scratchy. It's good. This is good." He gestures between them. "It's really good."

"It is," Michael agrees. "You are."

BLESSED BE, IT is so good. Michael's not sure when he was last fucked. It seems that in most cases, he's the one to do the fucking. But tonight, for Asher's first time, Michael's on his stomach, sweating, biting the pillow, and wondering if Father put the prostate just *there* because he's a generous deity or a horrible son of a bitch. It stops mattering when

Asher rams into him hard and fast, jolting pleasure through him in arcs that threaten Michael's control.

"Damn, you're so tight. And hot," Asher says desperately. "God, how are you so hot?"

Michael spreads his legs apart, letting Asher go deeper, and he doesn't just see stars, he's *sweating* stars. He loses a little control and angelic light breaks in sparks over his skin. Asher's so far gone that he doesn't do more than stutter, "Holy shit, I thought fireworks were a joke."

Michael can't speak. His shoulder blades itch, and he forces his wings in tighter, the effort of which only makes him squeeze his ass around Asher's cock, and that's so good for both of them they cry out together. Chills break over Michael's body, and Asher grips Michael's hand, as he whimpers and mouths at the back of Michael's neck.

"You like my dick in you?" Asher's voice is ragged.

"Yes," Michael says. "You have no idea."

"Am I…am I doing it right? I am aren't I? Look at you."

Michael squirms on Asher's thick cock, feeling the stretch all over— in his nipples, in his eyeballs, racing over his scalp. He's so *big*. "It's perfect."

Asher moans and redoubles his efforts. Michael clings to his fingers, and rubs against the bed sheets, hoping to get some relief. It's been so many years since he felt this kind of immense physical pleasure, so long since someone else's natural urges and movements fit so well with his own.

Your own? He fights back the condemning voice in his head. You're Father's tool. You don't have urges and needs of your own.

But he does. And he always has.

"Michael, please," Asher says, a note of desperation in his voice. "I'm going to…I can't wait."

"Do it."

Asher doesn't let go of Michael's hands, hunching desperately into him. Michael's ass feels alive and desperate for more, gripping and releasing Asher's dick on each stroke.

"You're so beautiful, so hot and tight," Asher moans and twists, fucking into him as hard as he can. "Are you real? This is too good. I'm gonna—"

He feels the resonance the moment Asher reaches orgasm, welcomes the stutter of hips and breath, and the hard thud-thud of Asher's cock unloading into the condom, as Asher's body screams *yes, God, yes, yes.*

Michael pulls his right hand free of Asher's and works it down to his own dick. It only takes a few tugs and he's coming again, too, clenching and grinding on Asher's cock.

They tremble and hold each other for a long time before Asher eases out, leaving Michael feeling wide open and aching. He rolls onto his back, intensely aware of the confines of his human body again after the jerking bliss of freedom he'd just tasted.

Asher lies next to him, staring up at the ceiling. Waves of excited satisfaction roll off him. Michael bites his lip, reveling in the sensations coursing through them both.

Asher grins. "Why did I wait so long?" He licks his lips. "Now what?"

Michael turns on his side, too, reaches out to touch Asher's face. "We have tonight. Anything you want."

"Just tonight?"

Denial flares inside. He doesn't want to admit that. He opts for a shrug.

"In case you're worried, if this is the part where people get clingy, I'm not going to do that. If this is just a one-time thing, I understand." He doesn't sound as if he really does, though.

Michael knows what he's supposed to say. He's done this so many times before. "If I say it's just for tonight, what will you do next? Will you go back to denying this to yourself?"

"No. Not ever again."

"Good." Michael wants to tell him that he'll meet him back here tomorrow night. He wants to say, *"Let's not get out of this bed for the next week."* He wants things that aren't part of his mission.

"It might be fun to explore my options. Maybe the guy I had my eye on earlier tonight. Maybe someone else."

"It won't be as good," Michael says. It's true, but petty for him to say.

"Sure, that blow job was astounding, but—"

"No buts. It won't be as good."

Asher's eyes narrow suspiciously but he looks amused. "Are *you* getting clingy and possessive? I thought that was the prerogative of the inexperienced."

Is he? He isn't supposed to. "It's just the facts. You should be prepared. Not every guy you take home is going to spark with you like this."

"How many men have you sparked with? Like this?" Asher asks, his dark eyelashes fanning on his cheek.

Why is Michael noticing these things? He sighs, gazing into Asher for whatever is inside him that makes the sex so good, that draws Michael in. It's there, nameless, a kind of hum that Michael wants to lean into until he's enveloped by it. It's familiar and unique all at once. It's got Father's thumbprint on it. A blessing.

"Have there been lots of men you've felt this spark with?" Asher asks again.

"Just one. A very long time ago."

Asher scoffs. "You can't even be thirty years old. How long ago are we talking here?"

"I told you. I'm older than I look."

In all eternity there has only been Henry. Sweet, sexy Henry. A dolt, for certain, but Michael's human form had been set endlessly ablaze by him. Asher, at least, is intelligent.

"How old are you exactly?" Asher asks.

"Older than thirty."

Asher rolls his eyes. "Cryptic isn't cute."

"Not trying to be cute, my friend." Michael runs his thumb along Asher's cheekbone and tries to turn his attention to the matter at hand. Has he accomplished his mission yet? With any luck, he hasn't, and he can do something about the hard cock that has returned with a vengeance. "Is this everything you needed, Ash?"

"You mean in order to prove to myself this is what I want?"

Michael smiles softly. It's what Asher wants. He's got his Father's special stamp all over him, all over his bones and in his blood. Special delivery—one male with leanings against the predominant culture! *Enjoy your difficult life! Learn to love yourself, because I do!* Father is a son of a bitch, really.

Perhaps he should try to find out Lucifer's phone number, or at least where in the world he's living these days. Because his mouth is forming the words before he knows he's going to say them.

"Can I see you tomorrow?"

Asher grins, his dark eyes glittering. "Name the time and place. I'll be there."

Chapter Three

M USEUMS ARE GOOD for contemplating the vastness of eternity. Michael tucks his hands in his pockets and stretches his shoulders. The itch of his wings is uncomfortable but he knows he'll get used to it. He stares at the painting of *The Archangel*, admiring the attention to detail in the wings.

"Hello," Asher says, his voice low and smoky. "I'm sorry I'm late. Traffic."

Michael turns to see Asher wearing brown pants, a green button-up shirt under a corduroy jacket, and scuffed Clarks. It's a nearly identical outfit to Michael's own, except that his shirt is yellow and his pants are navy. Michael seeks inside Asher and finds that he actually overslept but he smiles and accepts the token of violets Asher extends.

"From our garden. My mother's favorite."

Traditionally violets stand for a delicate love, something fragile, fresh and sweet. Michael wonders if Asher knows that. The heightened color on Asher's cheeks and the bashful look in his eyes makes him think he does. He almost pushes into flesh and bone again to read it in him, but he chooses not to. Somehow, not knowing for sure makes it a little sweeter.

"They're lovely. Thank you." He puts one in the buttonhole of Asher's jacket, and tucks the rest behind his own ear, making a silly face as he does. Asher smiles and reaches out to pull them free and presses the stems carefully back into Michael's curly hair so they stay in place.

They stand and look at each other with smiles Michael can only call goofy. Asher's eyes no longer sport dark crescents beneath them and they seem to sparkle.

"You look good," Michael says.

"Thank you. So do you. You look amazing." He stumbles on, "I'm really sorry about being late. I realized I didn't have your cell number and was freaking out in the car. I was worried you'd leave and I'd never hear from you again."

Michael pulls the phone from his pocket and they share contact information. Asher is the first legitimate contact he's ever entered into the prop he uses only to appear typically human while on assignment. He swallows hard as he presses *Save As New Contact.* The act feels like rebellion.

"There. No more missed connections," Asher says and pockets his cell. His eyes rise to the painting before them and he sighs. "This is one of my favorites."

"Is it?"

"Yeah, my mom used to bring me here. She'd sit on the bench and look at *Astrid in Ecstasy.*" Asher points at the painting on the opposite wall. "I'm not sure what she saw in it, but clearly it moved her. I would sit with my back to her back, and stare at this painting while I waited. I loved his wings."

"They are fine wings."

Asher seems lost in memory. "Eventually, I started to pray to Michael, The Archangel in the painting, to change me, to fix me. I gave in to the seductive idea that prayer helps." Asher laughs softly under his breath.

There's a strange pressure in Michael's throat and his eyes burn. He doesn't pay much attention to the prayers directed his way. There are simply too many of them and he's busy with his missions most of the time. Even for an angel, there's only so much he can do and it isn't his job to choose which pleas are answered.

All in Father's time, indeed.

"It's a common prayer."

Asher smiles painfully, his eyes still on the painting. "Last night, when you introduced yourself…" He shrugs and rolls his eyes. "It's silly. Never mind."

"Don't stop," Michael says, refusing to look inside Asher for the answer. "Tell me."

"I heard your name and for a moment I let myself believe that maybe my prayers had been finally answered."

"Did you?"

"Truth is, Michael, I still feel that way." Asher clears his throat and looks at his feet.

"Well, maybe that's the case, then. If we were meant to meet last night, who are we to go against God's plan?"

There's a justification now and he clings to it like he's seen humans cling to their excuses for just one more hit of their drug of choice. If Father knows what will happen, if he's planned this from the start, Michael's only doing what has been asked of him, isn't he?

"What about you? What do you like about it?" Asher nods at the painting.

"The wings," Michael says. "They're quite fine wings."

"Quite fine? You sound like someone's grandpa. From Britain."

"Britain has many fine grandpas," Michael says, laughing softly. It's a feeling like none other and one he doesn't get very often. Angels, for the most part, are serious creatures, and laughter is the medicine of humans.

"Come on, I'd like to see the Picasso. It's this way," he says pulling Asher away from the painting before he can give too much thought to the upper right corner of the canvas and its parting clouds unveiling a disembodied hand, finger pointing accusingly.

Over coffee in the museum café, Michael ignores the people who continue to look at him oddly for having flowers stuck in his hair. Instead, he listens to Asher talk about being adopted.

"It's just that I feel like I owe them, you know? They took me in when no one else wanted me. They loved me, or tried to love me, just the way I am. So now, I feel like I should take care of them. But I'm not sure they'll ever accept me." He sips his coffee morosely. It's not a good look on him, and Michael wants to reach out and wipe the expression off his face. "Take care of them? Who am I kidding? The first thing I need to do is find a job. In this market it's harder than it seems. Especially for someone without work history. A resume that consists of a PhD in European history and 'Ten years caring for aging grandmother until she died' doesn't make potential employers hot for me."

"You'll find work," Michael says with certainty.

"Maybe. Anyway, so, that's another reason I never left. My grandma was always so good to me. When someone saves you like that, when they love you on purpose, putting in that sort of effort and making those kinds of sacrifices, you don't show them disrespect by leaving them alone to rot and die in an old age home the way my dad wanted to do."

"Colorful."

He glances down at his coffee and fiddles with the handle. "I gave up so much to care for my grandmother and I've given up so much to try and be the son my parents want. But I *am* starting to hope maybe I can do both. Stay and be their son, and still have some kind of life of my own." He glances up at Michael and the heat in his eyes is echoed in a low, hot coil in Michael's groin.

Asher's ripe mouth, his black eyes, his timid hopefulness makes Michael want to take him apart with his angelic warrior strength, ravish him, and bring him to his knees with pleasure.

Asher licks his lips and smiles. "Do you ever want that kind of balance, Michael? In your life?"

Balance in his life? There isn't supposed to be balance, only mission and devotion to Father.

"Perhaps."

"Oh." He sounds disappointed, and Michael reaches out to touch his hand, stilling it on the handle of his mug.

"Now, I didn't mean it like that."

"How did you mean it?"

"I meant that I hadn't thought of it before. It's never been an option. But it's not that I don't like the idea."

Michael tilts his head and two of the violets fall into his coffee. Their laughter echoes in the empty café, drawing the attention of the barista. Asher doesn't flinch as the man looks at their joined hands, but Michael lets go anyway and takes up his sugar spoon to fish the flowers out of his drink.

Asher plucks the last violet from Michael's curls. It's wilted and limp. He puts it down on the table between them where it rests—purple, yellow, green. Shortly, the flowers from Michael's cup are arranged on the edge of his saucer, and the final one in Asher's buttonhole leans miserably to the side. He laughs again, stroking his fingers over Asher's hand. The softness of his skin and the knotty curve of his joints makes him go soft inside and so Michael does it again.

"I've enjoyed our date," Asher says. He leans back far enough that his hand is no longer accessible to Michael's fingers.

"I have too."

"But I'd feel a lot more comfortable if you weren't so young."

Michael doesn't protest. He can fix this by showing him the driver's license in his wallet. He can fix this by just telling him an age he can understand and will want to hear. Or by suffusing him with enough of his grace that he won't care anymore. But he doesn't. If this can be how it ends, if he can let it be over now without another tempting taste of Asher's body, then it must be for the best.

"At the same time, I don't think I'm ready to let this go. I don't want to go back to hiding from myself." Asher glances down, his thick, black eyelashes fanning on his cheek. It's becoming a familiar expression to Michael. He knows without having to seek it inside of him that Asher's going to confess something he finds embarrassing now. "And, I have to admit, every time I look at you I just want to find a bed and make good use of it."

Michael's groin tightens.

"The tiny one in the Elizabethan gallery looked plenty good enough to me if not for those hovering guards," Asher says quietly, his eyes darting to the barista, and back to his coffee, color rising on his cheeks.

"So, right now, I feel like I should just say damn it all."

"Damn it all?" Michael swallows. He can feel the heaviness of the words like steel weights dangling from his balls, tugging at him with delicious, tempting pain. His wings itch, itch, *itch* under his skin.

Michael's mind goes to the Elizabethan era gallery on the second floor, too, but not to the bed. Instead, it lingers on a particular painting done by a relatively unknown artist hanging in the least advantageous position in the room. When he'd laid eyes on it, it'd rendered him speechless for several moments.

"HENRY, DARLING, PUT the paintbrush down."

"I will not."

"Replacing her face with a dog's shall only lead you into peril should it be discovered."

"Nay, for I intend to burn it when I am quite finished."

"The Queen does not suffer fools lightly, Henry, and you are ever so foolish at times and now behaving rashly. It is not wise."

"I'll leave wise to people who have no heart. She had them put to death! They were but infants!"

"They were pups, Henry, and while you loved them dear, there were too many by far for the court. The Queen cannot harbor every bitch's brood."

"I say why not when she harbors the whores of the fancy Lords? Would my sweet Maiden's pups have not contributed more happiness to our court than the lot of those sluts?"

"Shush! Before the guards hear you. Your tears and wails have called them to your door. Who do you think fetched me?"

"You always come when I need you. I supposed you fetched yourself."

"Right you are, then, and I believe you should return the Queen's face to its lovely shape on that canvas, or paint over it entirely!"

Henry throws the brush aside and turns to Michael with wide, dark eyes, and his red lips a little redder from where he always wipes his hand on his mouth as he paints.

"I loved those pups. Do you understand? Do you even know love, my darling?" He studies Michael's face with his slightly mad, lead-addled eyes. "Do you love me?" His face is swollen with tears.

Love? Michael cannot answer that question honestly. Angels aren't incapable of that emotion, but he doesn't feel it for Henry. Not in the way the man feels it for him. So he kisses him, purposely splashing the canvas with paint, covering the treasonous dog-face on the Queen as they fall to the ground, lust easily overcoming Henry's objections.

ASHER IS STILL talking. "You're young and you might decide I'm not even worth another screw, or you might think I *am*—and given how you've looked at me all day, I'm hoping at least one more night is absolutely on the table. And if that's all there is, fine. But I'm forty now and I've been too afraid for too long. If I have a chance at something more with you, then I'm going to take it. Everything else be damned. Everything."

"I see."

"I'm sorry. I'm doing this all wrong."

"No, it's not that," Michael says, pulling his cell phone from his pocket and pretending to read a message.

"Do you have to go?"

Michael shakes his head, taps in words and pushes send. Nonsense sent nowhere to no one. "Work. Sorry. What were you saying?"

Asher looks embarrassed. He shakes his head and shrugs. "Nothing. It was nothing."

Seeing Asher retreat when he'd been so brave isn't something he can stomach. "I thought it was damn it all, you want to see if we can have something?"

"Yes."

Michael's grace vibrates so that he trembles all over. "Truth is, I travel a lot. My life isn't my own. I can't make promises or be that kind of person to you."

Asher's visible disappointment slices into Michael's chest and he wants to grab the man, pull him tight, and shelter him under his wings.

"Is it over then?"

"I don't want it to be, but I can't give you what you're asking. So we can end this here, if that's what you want." Every nerve and sinew in his human skin begs for him to give the right response. Michael isn't even sure what right is, but he knows it has to happen now. He holds his breath.

"No. I understand what you're saying. But I want to see you again anyway."

A bell rings somewhere deep in the museum and Michael is swept cold with relief and dread.

"I want to see you again, too."

THE HOTEL ROOM is like an old friend. It pulls Michael in and he drags Asher behind him, mouths latched, clothes coming off, cocks rubbing hard against each other.

Michael knows it's wrong. He's already succeeded in this mission and set Asher on a new path, away from the self-destructive shame and misery that would have ended him. Now Michael is grasping beyond his reach. This isn't what angels are made to do. He should be prostrate before Father, not kneeling at Asher's feet.

He closes his eyes, sucks Asher in, and waits for the punishment to come down on him. Asher moans and clenches his fingers in Michael's hair. His hot whimpers slice through Michael's anxiety and he redoubles his effort, tonguing the slit and working his own hardness with his other hand.

"Thank you," Asher breathes, his head hitting the back of the hotel room door again and again, a soft thump as he struggles to hold back from coming. Michael wants to cradle Asher's head with the back of his hand, but he needs Asher's cock in his throat, and he can't do both at once.

He works his own dick and feels the pressure mounting as Asher gives up and starts to thrust, fucking Michael's face with wild urgency, his cock hitting the back of Michael's throat. The room is filled with the noise of Asher's need and Michael's gurgling grunts.

Michael can feel the orgasm rolling up from his balls and groin. He opens his eyes and stares up at Asher's face, black hair across his forehead, cheeks pink with exertion, and red mouth open wide. If he's going to be cast out for defying Father, for coming back for another taste of this man, then he wants to see everything, feel everything.

He pulls off as Asher starts to come, orgasm pulsing through them both at the same time. Their cries fill the room and Michael feels a burst inside him, the freedom of ecstasy, and he wants it more than almost anything else. He braces himself as the orgasm peaks.

All that falls is their seed onto the carpet.

In the panting aftermath, curled with Asher on the hotel room floor, he stares at the patches of semen, consumed by a strange disappointment.

Chapter Four

A WEEK-OF-SEEING-ASHER LATER, Michael walks five blocks over from Mercy Street to a brand new surf shop on Ocean Drive. The store is small and signage is a big poster with the words, *SURF AND BREAKERS* drawn in gold magic marker. There's also a drawing of a surfboard sporting angel wings, and if he has any doubt he's in the right place, that cinches it.

The chime on the door announces his presence, but it's unnecessary. Lucifer's right there by the counter, grinning like the cocky jerk he is, applying wax to a surfboard. He's tan and his blond hair hangs in long waves not quite to his shoulders. As always, his blue eyes crackle with intelligence and amusement.

"Long time no see, bro."

Michael ignores the slang, though it feels like a hot needle prick, as if Lucifer is flaunting something Michael wants for himself. "It's been a while, brother, yes."

"Let's see, last time I saw you, I was tugging on those annoying white wings of yours trying to pull you out of heaven with me. Good times."

"If you say so." Michael steps closer to the counter, noting that the surfboard is covered in art resembling human tattoos—winged hearts, round-faced birds, and women with large breasts tumbling all over it. His next words are surprisingly true. "A surf shop suits you."

"Doesn't it, bro? Fun, sun, babes, boys, wet, sex. It's all good."

"Why the new shop here?"

Lucifer laughs in his face. "As if you don't know? You called me here, pretty brother. There's rebellion brewing in you and I'm always on board for that, Mike."

"Don't call me 'Mike.'"

"I think it works, actually. When you're cast out, consider switching to it. Michael's so prissy."

Michael ignores the critique of his name and focuses instead on the question that's been plaguing him, the one that lured Lucifer here. "Is it horrible?"

"What?"

"Being cast out. Fallen."

Lucifer grins and wipes a hand over his sweaty forehead. He stops rubbing the wax on his surfboard and takes in the sunset over the ocean, the women walking toward their cars with sand sticking to their flesh, and their skin pink from too much sun.

"Nah. It's all right. Everyone makes being fallen out to be something awful. 'Oh, Father cast him out. He's lost to God's love.'" Lucifer sneers. "How little they know." He waves a hand at Michael and adds, "The old guy's around every day checking in on me."

Michael considers this might be a lie. Lucifer might be trying to trick him. "Every day? If that's true, why doesn't anyone know?"

"He's not shy about it. I guess you idiots up there are so busy laying at his feet that you don't notice if he pops out for an hour or two."

It's disturbing because it's possible. No angel dares look directly at Father.

"Don't you miss it?"

"All that worshiping of his holy highness? Nope. And, if I do say so myself, I think he's kind of proud of me." Lucifer glows a little like the sunset has stroked his skin. "I'm the only one. The only angel who's ever had the guts to really tell him where to shove it."

Michael half expects there to be a rending sound and the room to be torn in two as the wrath of their father smites Lucifer yet again, but nothing happens. If anything, Lucifer looks terrifyingly *free* saying anything he wants without fear of repercussions.

Michael runs his fingers over the corner of the counter, feeling the sharpness of the edge. He doesn't look Lucifer in the eye, when he says, "Do you know about…well, did anyone ever tell you—"

"About that pretty pansy from the bitch queen's court?"

Michael clenches his jaw. "That's no way to—"

"I'm Satan. Cut me some slack."

"Fine. Yes, that's what I was wondering."

"Of course I heard about it." His eyes are alight with glee. "And I know that you're tempted again now. You reek of lust and sex. You're hungry for it. I can practically *taste* it and I've been hard since you walked in."

He gestures at his crotch and Michael sees that, yes, Lucifer's sporting some impressive wood.

"Did *you* put Asher in my path? Did you put Father's stamp on his bones?"

Lucifer cackles. "Not you, too! Do you really think I'd spend time messing with you, Mike, when I can mess with human beings with much more interesting weaknesses?"

Michael isn't sure if he believes him, but, more strikingly, isn't sure he cares. "Father gave me the assignment." Even if Lucifer created the situation, there are other angels, and his father chose *him* to go into this breach.

Lucifer's lips twitch in amusement. "So he sent you into temptation again. Do you really think he's going to deliver you from evil?"

Michael doesn't look at him. Lucifer chuckles. "Oh, I get it now. You don't want him to deliver you, but you can't untangle why he sent you. You still think Father cares. Oh, Mike. It's all a game to him. A test. Will you pass? Will you fail? Will he cast you out or take you in his big, strong, forgiving arms and tell you that it's all right? Tell you that you can go fuck your human friend all you want because he *knows* just how good it feels?"

That is exactly what Michael wants and he feels a flush of embarrassment that Lucifer has read him so well. "I know that will never happen."

"Of course not. Even though he made it feel that way for you. Even though he stamped this Asher with his own holiness and made you want him. He basically made you go back for more."

"Why *me*? Gabriel's good with a human prick and last I checked he hasn't taken a turn in human skins in a decade or more."

"Gabe's a daddy's boy. A total pet. What else would you expect from him? He never has to do the hard stuff. I always did want to punch him in his smug face and—"

"What about Zadkiel? Or Puriel?"

Lucifer waves his hand dismissively. "Zad's always got all that *forgiveness* crap to deal with. He's a busy guy. And would you really set Puriel on a poor human virgin?"

Michael sighs. Of course not. The angel is far too zealous to take his time and not terrify.

"He wasn't called 'pitiless' in the war for nothing. Mike, listen, the old man enjoys this. He's set you up. Just make a choice. I advocate rebellion, of course. It's a lot more satisfying in the end."

Michael feels a tug in his cock and his stomach. He squeezes his eyes shut. Lucifer laughs. "Is it really rebellion if he designed it?"

"Ooooh," Lucifer coos. "You are so close. You've already mostly chosen. But you can't be sure, until you know the worst of it all, right?"

Michael opens his eyes and watches Lucifer rub wax over a drawing of a woman with bulging breasts.

"Let me tell you. The bugger of it is I can't die. So, aside from vacationing down in hell, I'm stuck in human skin forever. It's uncomfortable, as you know. But it has its perks. Sometimes I think I'll just say screw it, tear it off, and let the wings hang out, man. And glow. Just think how I'd glow. And I'd trumpet—because seriously, humans and their Bibles, they love the freaking trumpet—'All who wish to live, bow before me!' And do you know what that would be, Mike?"

Apocalypse. The end of the world.

"What?"

"A really fun day."

Michael can't tell if Lucifer's joking. "He'd end you."

Lucifer shrugs. "He might. He'd be so damn proud. I'm telling you. He likes that I've got some balls."

"What's stopping you?"

"I haven't gotten bored enough yet."

Michael shakes his head. This is the brother he'll have to align himself with if he does this, if he makes this crazy choice. "I have no idea why I thought coming to see you would be helpful."

Lucifer grins, a wicked gleaming thing that makes Michael a little jealous. "Because you knew I'd tell you the truth."

Lucifer goes back to stroking his surfboard and Michael waits long enough that he starts to feel pathetic before he turns to go.

"For what it's worth," Lucifer calls.

Michael stops to listen, but doesn't look back.

"I think he would. Be proud of you, I mean. The old guy loves a good rebellion, and, despite the rap he gets here on earth, he loves sex. He's the one who made it so good, after all."

Michael bangs the door open and barely hears Lucifer yell, "There's always a job for you here, bro. If you need it."

Michael feels sweat prickle his neck as he walks away, the hot sun screaming down at him as the image of himself in a surf shack T-shirt immediately springs to mind. The fact that it's more amusing than unwelcome is troublesome. Maybe he *is* ready to jump ship for an experiment in Lucifer's brand of freedom. Or maybe he's not.

Maybe he'll just meet Asher one last time and be done with it.

For good.

"So, YOU SAW your brother?" Asher asks, panting softly in Michael's arms. His wet, semen-slick cock is shoved against Michael's sticky stomach, and they've barely recovered from their orgasms.

"Yes. He's still an asshole."

"Did you find out what you needed to know?"

He knows Asher doesn't like the cryptic manner in which Michael discusses his work and his family, but Michael can't exactly tell him, "Ash, for the love of your cock and the hot roll of our orgasms, I'm thinking of giving up my eternal gig as the Angel of Justice and Protection and opting to become a cast out, washed up, surf shop employee."

He can't tell him that the idea of walking away from Asher and watching him get involved with someone else, like Henry had all those years ago, makes him want to kick things and maybe start a rebellion that could end with *him* dragging some of his brothers from heaven's grace.

He settles for, "Yes. He can help me if I quit working for my father."

Asher moves on top of Michael, his dick taking interest again, and his eyes hooded. "I can't believe...I mean, we were a one night stand. And now you're quitting your job to be with me? I just came out and it's kind of getting serious really fast." He doesn't seem frightened, though, just pleased. "Maybe I waited so long because you're the—"

Michael cuts him off before he can finish that doomed sentence. "I'm not quitting my job just to be with you."

"You're not?"

"No. I haven't been happy for a long time. A very, very long time. I'm re-evaluating what working for my father costs me, and I've decided it's..." Oh, God, he can't say it. He can't make his mouth form the words.

"Not worth it?"

"It's slavery."

That's something he can say. That's something he knows is true. Submission and absolute obedience aren't doing it for him anymore. He wonders if they're doing it for his father, either. Maybe Lucifer's right. Maybe that's why Father sent him to Asher. Maybe that's why he stamped Asher's bones. Entertainment at Michael's expense isn't beneath him. Being God does gets very tiresome. He knows that.

"That's a little over the top, don't you think?" Asher kisses his lips, nuzzles his neck, and Michael decides that fucking again definitely beats talking about this any longer. Especially when Asher's got his ass on offer this time, dragging Michael's hand down to his hole, whispering, "Finger me. Fuck me," like it's something Asher needs more than air.

Conversation is dropped. Serious focus is applied to open Asher up, and then Michael's shoving his cock in. *So hot, so good.* Nothing beats the pressing simultaneous need to drag this out and surrender to climax.

Asher is so tight, and Michael thinks back to the first time earlier that week, and how Asher had trembled with fear and anticipation, how beautifully he'd spread himself and let Michael inside. They'd both been overcome.

Michael has to wonder, with a spark like theirs, does fucking ever get old? So far, the only thing that has stopped them is their human bodies' reluctance to perform an unlimited number of times, and Asher's sense of self-preservation. If Michael had his druthers, they'd simply never quit—not for food, not for drink, not for anything. Not even for Father. He supposes that's why it's wrong, and why he'll be cast out.

Asher's on his stomach letting loose with loud, hoarse cries as Michael fucks him. Banging on the wall from the hotel room next door leaves Asher trying to cover his sounds of pleasure by biting into the pillow. Michael holds back his own groans, pressure rising inside as he denies himself that vent. Asher spasms beneath him, his ass clenching rhythmically around Michael's cock, and the scent of semen fills the air. Asher's orgasm ricochets in Michael when he pushes into his flesh and bones, taking in his pleasure, and pulsing his grace to extend it.

Michael licks his lips, closes his eyes, and fucks him harder. Asher's legs skid all over the bed, his hands grip the pillow and clench white-knuckled hard, but he yells for Michael to keep going, *don't stop*, so he doesn't.

Pounding into Asher's convulsing ass, ignoring the thump-thump-

thump of the person on the other side of the wall as Asher's cries can't be contained, Michael succumbs to it—a rip of pleasure that obliterates him. He screams as he loses control, his human form unable to contain his ecstasy, and as he pushes deep into Asher's trembling body, he breaks free—wings unfurling and spreading wide. He arches back, and comes, and comes, and comes.

Holding Asher still beneath him with the weight of his body, hoping he doesn't open his scrunched eyes or roll over to witness the spread of Michael's wings, Michael folds them back into scapulae. Sweat-drenched and still throbbing, he takes inventory: he's smiling, he's humming, he's happy. He's not fallen yet.

Asher laughs and shoves out from under Michael before turning around to grab him around the waist. "You think your brother might have a job for me, too?" Asher grins up at him.

"Probably," Michael says, though he isn't sure letting Asher around Lucifer is a good idea. It isn't as if it would be out of character for Lucifer to decide that Michael's lover would be a delightful plaything. "But I'm not sure working together is a great idea."

"True. I've got some applications in," Asher says. "I'm hoping one pays off soon, because I'd like to get my own place. Living with my folks isn't going to cut it if this," he gestures between them, "is going to be anything. And we can't keep meeting in a hotel, can we?"

Michael has never considered the entire living situation aspect. He wonders if he would require a job or if his divinely given abilities to influence people to do anything he wants will remain intact after…well, if he chooses something he probably won't choose. The real danger is of Father deciding to simply cast him out for the choices he's daring to make. Before that happens he should understand more of what might lie ahead. He'll ask Lucifer about those details soon. Until then, he can easily maneuver himself into a house if he wants, and Asher can live there. His absences might cause a lot of questions, which he can probably cover up as travel for Father's job. Though the idea of future sexual assignments seems unsavory now.

Are more lies really the way to start your new life, Mike? He hears Lucifer's voice in his head and he rolls his eyes. This is complicated stuff and Lucifer loves complicated. Though he doubts Lucifer's ever felt the warm, happy sensation engulfing him in waves every time he lays eyes on Asher. He's not going to give that feeling a name. If he doesn't say it, then it isn't true, and he can pretend what he has with Asher is something he'll eventually get tired of.

Except in every single way it isn't, for reasons Michael still can't really put into words.

He knows it's often like this for humans. They can meet thousands of people in their lives before coming across one who sparks a connection they don't want to live without. He listens fondly as Asher continues talking, realizing he could listen for hours and be utterly content.

"Job hunting is the pits. Talk about new lessons in failure and ego-crushing rejection."

Michael touches Asher and infuses him with all the rosy, warm feeling in him. Asher reddens and glances down, pleased at the understanding that passes between them.

"At least I know you don't see me that way," he says.

"I never have and I never will." Michael carries on before he acts on the affection he can feel vibrating in Asher's flesh and bones, echoed in his own human form, and ringing throughout his angelic one, too. "Where are you hoping to hear back from most?"

"Synagogue," Asher says, his dark eyes sparkling. "They need a new bookkeeper and since I did that for Dad awhile, I thought why not?"

Synagogue. Of course. Michael almost laughs. Well, at least he knows exactly how to make that happen for Asher—a visit to the rabbi, which the man will soon thereafter forget, and it's a done deal. The pay will probably be slightly more than Asher is expecting as well. All the better for moving out of his parents' home.

Michael's insides quiver at the thought of using his powers for something *he* wants for a change. He wonders if this is how Lucifer feels all the time, or if after thousands of years he's accustomed to the sensation of freedom now.

"I've been thinking," Asher says, as he turns on his side and reaches out to thumb the small indent in Michael's chin. "I want to know more about you, about your family. I know it's early for this, but, maybe I could meet your dad?"

"Meet my...? Well, he's hard to pin down."

"Your mother? You've never mentioned her."

"Entirely out of the picture. It's almost like she never existed."

Asher frowns. "I'm sorry. That must have been hard growing up. My mom and I are close—or we used to be before I realized what I was. I can't imagine my life without her in it."

"Tell me about her," Michael says, meaning it earnestly. He suddenly wants to know every last detail of Asher's mother. He can breathe in and catch the imprint of Asher's childhood still lingering around him, and it's warm, glowing, like the happy dreams of humans he's sometimes looked in on.

"Well, her name's Marie and she's almost seventy now. She's retired. She used to work for the phone company when I was in high school, but when I was a little kid, she stayed home. Some of my favorite memories were of her greeting me when I came in the door after school. She always seemed so genuinely happy to see me then."

"Not now?"

"Oh, sure. I guess. It's hard to say. I mean, I'm a pretty big disappointment to her. No job, no wife, probably gay." He looks at Michael. "Definitely gay. Actually, I was going to tell you, but we...got distracted." He blushes prettily. "Anyway, I told her last night and my father, too."

Michael's skin prickles and he stifles the nearly overwhelming urge to stretch his wings again and shelter Asher under them. "Are you okay?"

He lets himself see into Asher's body, reading his bones and flesh, and he knows the answer isn't as bad as it could be.

"My father told me he didn't want to hear that kind of bullshit and left the room."

"I'm sorry."

"My mother said she'd known it for a long time but had hoped it wasn't true." Asher frowns and fiddles with the edge of a sheet. "Her brother is gay and she says she recognized some of the signs in me."

Michael stops his hand and twines their fingers together. Asher meets Michael's eyes and relaxes. "And then?" Michael asks because he knows that's not all of it. He can feel the rest of it bubbling in Asher, a mixture of pain, hope, and determination.

"We didn't talk about it again until dinner. My mother told my father she expects him to accept me and he didn't say he wouldn't."

"It's a start."

"I always thought he'd hurt me—kill me even."

Michael thinks of Lucifer's face as he fell—proud, surprised, and angry. He sees a touch of that in Asher's eyes and feels an echoing call of it in his own chest.

Asher's hand squeezes in his. "What about you? Have you told your parents?"

"My father knows, and like I said, my mother isn't in my life."

"How did he take it?"

"He understands. He's supportive." There's really no good way to say 'he sent me to you' because that makes Father sound rather like a pimp. And, hey, well, now that he's considered it... Michael chuckles at the thought.

"Wow, it's a different world today. You kids have it so easy."

Michael scoffs. "I've told you, I'm not a kid."

Asher rolls his eyes and pulls away, flopping onto his back to stare at the ceiling. Michael feels dissatisfaction well up inside him. That's not how he wants Asher to react at all. He wants to see him smile again.

"When I was growing up, there wasn't any hope for someone like me. Or if there was, it was only just starting to be a glimmer on the horizon and you had to move to San Francisco or New York City. You couldn't live here."

"Los Angeles is just down the road. Why didn't you move?"

"Because I have obligations to my family and because I'm not the kind of guy who does that kind of thing. I'm a coward, Michael. In case you didn't notice."

Michael breathes in and out slowly, feeling the power folded into his wings. He used to lead armies into war. He defeated Lucifer and his father called him The Archangel, and he'd been proud. Tired, but proud. Once, Michael had been glorious. Now what is he?

"I'd be satisfied with meeting your brother," Asher says, coming back to the original topic.

Michael knows he's referring to Lucifer but chooses to obfuscate by asking, "Which one?"

"Any of them?"

"None of them are worth meeting, I promise."

"Michael, the cryptic refusal to reveal anything about yourself has to stop. How many brothers do you have?"

"Four," he says. The lie tastes bad in his mouth. He forges ahead. "Zad, Rafe, Luke, and Gabe."

"And you don't remember your mother?"

"I'm the youngest. She was gone before my memories begin." Another lie. Can this feeling keep growing between them if there are always so many lies?

Oh, bro, now you're worried about the feelings? Love! Ain't it the grandest? You're screwed.

"And your father runs this big business. Did he inherit it, or build it himself?"

"Oh, he built it himself. From scratch."

From nothing into everything, Father spoke it into being.

"I know you've said it's complicated, but it can't have always been. Tell me about how he got started."

Michael remembers a time when mankind was a small experiment his father was running. How quickly that experiment blossomed into a cottage industry! Back then it was easy to be an angel. He showed up with his hair aflame, and the people cowered before him and feared to lift their eyes to his countenance.

Then there was the Great War and things changed. The whole Jesus situation had led to some complicated interactions, too, and Mohammed confused it all over again.

Now that little cottage industry has morphed into something akin to the largest corporation imaginable. A rather poorly managed one, at that, if he dares say so himself. Father doesn't seem to mind the mess his creations live in. If anything, he's having fun watching his wind-up toys run, throwing more cogs in the works and laughing when the people blame Lucifer.

Well, he supposes Father laughs about that. Come to think of it, he's never really heard Father laugh. He wonders if he can and what it might sound like.

"Well?" Asher prompted. "Your father's business?"

"It's a dull story. Have you read Genesis?"

"Yes, of course."

"Did you read all of it?"

"Well, no. I stopped when I got to the begats, but what does that have to do with anything? Sometimes I feel like you got a degree in double speak in college."

"Alas, if only I'd known they offered that major," Michael teases. "The story of my father's business is much the same—in the beginning there was my Father and he was lonely."

"With five sons he was lonely?"

"I thought you wanted to hear about his business?"

"I do!"

"Then, yes, he was lonely even with his five sons and all of my many cousins." Michael feels better now that he's at least acknowledged the rest of his brethren. "And he was bored."

"With five boys he was bored? I'm surprised he had time to even think."

"Oh, all the time in the world. So in his boredom, he made a thing or two, and then made a few more things, and that led to even more things."

"What are these things?"

"All kinds of things. It's hard to begin to encompass the extent of it."

"Try."

"Well, let's put it this way, eventually his creations made their way all over the earth and, if you ask me, they'll eventually play a role in destroying it."

"So your father created the Cylons from *Battlestar Galactica*?" Asher says. His amusement is touched with annoyance.

"Very much like that, actually. You'd be surprised."

Asher laughs and shakes his head. "I wish you'd be honest with me, Michael."

Michael wishes he could, too. "I'm being honest, just not forthright. Believe me, I made it all sound much more interesting than it really is."

Asher sighs and runs a hand over his chest, wiping away come and sweat.

"I'll tell you what," Michael says, the compromise on his tongue the very instant it forms in his head. "Meeting my father is out of the question at the moment, but how about I agree to meet yours?"

Asher goes pale and his breathing goes still. "You really want to do that?"

What are you doing, bro? This right here? This is stupid.

"I do," Michael says.

Chapter Five

Asher's mother is petite and smells of caramel when she opens the door of the house. Michael had carefully considered his offering before arriving and he extends the small, potted and beribboned hydrangea to her. Michael pushes it gently into her hands and sees that she knows the meaning of a hydrangea given as a gift. *Grateful for the recipient's understanding.*

"How lovely!" she says, taking it from him. "Thank you, dear."

"You're welcome, Mrs.—"

"Call me Marie."

"Michael," he says and she smiles at him.

"Come in, come in."

She puts the hydrangea on the entryway table, centering it just so, then turns and takes his light jacket. She hangs it up on the neat coatrack by the door.

Michael spots Asher's tennis shoes at the base of it, the strings unlaced and dangling. Warmth rises in him and his cheeks burn, his heart tripping.

He's momentarily baffled by the emotion—the shoes are just shoes. Asher is just a human. Yet there is something about him—his vulnerability, his determination, his specific way of tilting his head, the sound he makes when he's surprised—so many tiny particulars that add up to a person Michael is unwilling to walk away from. It isn't just Father's stamp. He refuses to believe it's only that.

"My, you are such a handsome young man," Marie says, as he follows her down the hallway.

Michael's cheating, he knows. He's turned the angelic light up a little and there's no way Marie will be able to resist that. Asher's father is a tougher nut to crack, as evidenced by his frown and refusal to rise from his recliner when Michael walks into the room.

"Gay and a cradle robber," he mutters after a fast flick of the eye toward Michael. "This is the thanks we get."

"Michael," Asher says from the kitchen doorway, dishtowel on his shoulder, and his dark hair tousled. He has a dark spot of something brown and gooey near the collar of his red shirt. "I'm glad you're here. Come in the kitchen."

Marie kicks Asher's father's shoe. As Michael moves toward the kitchen, he hears her whisper loudly, "Ira, have some manners. Do not embarrass me in my home."

Asher's smile is tight as he pulls Michael into the warm kitchen. "Sorry about my dad." Then he frowns, a deep, sudden expression of concern that makes Michael's stomach hurt.

"I want you to feel comfortable here and he's ruining it."

"I'm fine. He's fine, too."

Relief sweeps over Asher's face, echoing Michael's feelings.

Michael drops onto the bar stool at the counter when Asher waves a hand toward it. There's a mess of wax paper and apples and a bowl of brown goo set out there.

"Mom made shepherd's pie for dinner. Meanwhile, I was making kosher caramel apples for her to take to synagogue for the children's program tomorrow."

"Buttering up your potential new boss through your mother?"

"Every little bit helps. I'm just really grateful he's even considering me for the position." Asher's cheeks flush a little and he clears his throat.

Michael's eyebrow lifts of its own accord. "Is the rabbi considering you for another position I should be aware of?"

A dark chasm opens in him, one he's never known before. He's risking so much, perhaps foolishly, for this. What if Asher doesn't return the same level of affection and loyalty? Humans often don't.

Asher meets his eye with a twinkle and a blush. "He's married and straight." He stabs an apple through with a cooking skewer and dunks it into the caramel. "Attractive, yes, but competition? No."

The darkness in Michael recedes, but he still senses a dark spot of it, like a stain. He clears his throat.

"Why? Would you have been jealous?" Asher asks, nonchalantly.

"Of course."

He's said the right thing. Asher's eyes light up and he leans over the counter to press a fast kiss to Michael's cheek.

"Now, now, I just got your father settled. None of that or you'll get him riled up again." Marie takes up a place beside Asher and together the three of them make caramel apples and talk about Michael.

It's horribly easy to lie. He's very good at it. Lies of omission and other outright misrepresentations are a staple of his job. It just feels wrong now when it's Asher he's lying to.

"So, you've traveled the world," Marie says, carefully putting one of the last apples down on the wax paper. "Working for your father selling mysterious items—"

"Not so mysterious," Michael says. "More ephemeral."

"So, finances then. You're in finances."

He laughs. "It's so much worse than finances, Mrs. Rosenthal."

"Crime. You're a mobster."

Michael sits up straight and nods his head. "You've found me out. I'm absolutely a mobster."

"As if," Asher murmurs, and quickly amends, "Well, if mobsters are angels, maybe."

Michael's heart does a strange tap dance. But a quick look into Asher reveals that he's only teasing in an affectionate and loving way. He hasn't guessed. He doesn't know.

But would it be such a bad thing if Asher did know? How can Michael ever tell him?

"Your son is right. I'm much too angelic to be a mobster."

"Though, your innocent face would be the perfect cover," Asher says, thoughtfully. "I know, let me guess—you're a spy."

Michael laughs. An argument could be made that he *is* a spy of sorts.

"Oh, my, aren't you two cute together. I never thought I'd see this day," Marie says. "And it's nice."

"I'm happy to hear that, ma'am."

Marie goes back to focusing on Michael's career aspirations. "Well, Asher says you may be leaving your father's employ soon?"

"Yes, I'm considering working for my brother. He owns a surf shop."

"Quite a step down," she tuts.

"Yes, quite a steep tumble actually."

He can't believe he's joking about it and he should use his angelic power to wipe their minds of questions, but he can't do that to Asher. Not now. So he just shakes his head and says, "Mrs. Rosenthal, how can I help with dinner?"

Marie turns to the cupboard and pulls out plates, amusement and happiness shining in her eyes as she hands them to Michael and indicates the table.

Michael smiles when Asher washes his hands and pulls silverware from a drawer. Their bodies brush as they lay the places together and each touch is a tingling reminder of why he's here and why he's risking it all.

Dinner is tense with Ira saying barely a word, but when it's over Asher's father stands up, puts his hands on his hips, and sticks his bulging stomach out. "I didn't expect to raise a queer, but since I have, I'll accept my lot. If you come around a few more times, I'll consider learning your name. Until then, you're on probation. I want to see how long you actually stay in my son's life."

"I understand, sir," Michael murmurs as Ira leaves the room and heads back to his recliner.

"He's having a hard time," Marie says, smiling sadly. "But everything passes, and this will, too."

"Hopefully before he does," Asher mutters.

Michael puts out his hand and takes Asher's fingers. He's saying the words before he can really think about them and when he hears them come out of his mouth, he only feels a thrill of excitement. "I want to be here when he gets over it."

"Well," Marie says, standing up to clear dishes. "You're suggesting a very big commitment, since that's likely to take years."

Asher grins and squeezes Michael's fingers. "I'm okay with years."

"Me, too."

"DUDE, HOW DOES it not even occur to you that this is what he wants you to do?" Lucifer says, slamming his empty beer mug down and motioning for another. The bar is crowded with people, and everyone's jostling for the bartender's attention, but of course he serves Lucifer first.

"He wants me to fall?"

"He sets you up with this guy—which, bro, seriously, could you look more lovesick?—and then leaves you to twist over whether or not you want to keep on serving the whims of His Divinely Fickle Highness or bravely step into the new world order, embracing love and sex and human skin."

Lucifer glows as he warms to his speech. His blond hair shines with an unearthly glow in the low light. Women take notice, and a few men, too. Lucifer does nothing to conceal it.

"And he hasn't given you any assignments since, now has he? Why's that?" He pounds his palm against the wood of the bar. "Because this one isn't over, bro. That's all there is to it. He's planned this and now you get to act it out for him. A puppet in his play."

Michael searches himself. This doesn't feel like something he's acting out on behalf of Father. He remembers Asher's profile that morning, outlined by the light from the hotel window as he put on his socks. His nose standing out, backlit, and beautiful. He remembers the strange roll in his stomach when Asher laughs, or the aching fondness he feels when he catches Asher looking at himself in the mirror, touching the small wrinkles by his eye. He loves those wrinkles and feels squishy inside whenever Asher smiles enough for them to pop out.

Every other assignment he's ever been sent on, even Henry, and even as the leader of the Great War for Heaven, has felt like more of a strain than this attachment to Asher and his particulars. He doesn't even have to reach for it. Not even a little bit.

"Ah, man, look at you, bro. It's a sad day when you look that lost."

"I'm not lost."

"Yet."

"Touché."

The song on the jukebox in the corner comes to a jangling close and Lucifer turns to it, points a finger, and within a few moments a beachy, summery song with female vocals fills the room. The chorus comes quickly and Lucifer sings it at Michael with fake cow-eyes of love. "*Falling, falling,*" the women sing over and over. "I'm falling, falling," Lucifer sings along with them.

Michael's phone buzzes and he pulls it from his pocket. It's Asher, of course, texting with a picture of his mother in the garden, digging out a place for the new hydrangea Michael brought her. She's small and looks fragile, but Michael knows she's full of secret strength. The phone buzzes again and this time it's a selfie of Asher's grinning face with a thumbs-up held next to his cheek, his mom's hunched form barely visible in the background. Michael smiles to see Asher's cheesy smile, so fake and ridiculous, and yet his eyes are bright with real joy.

Another buzz.

My mother says you are a charming young man and very beautiful. My father glared at her. I think you're amazing.

"Aw, look at your widdle face! Damn, Mike, I haven't seen you look that genuinely happy in, fuck…forever, man. You've *never* looked like that. Not when you were Father's favorite, not when you were kicking the shit out of me in the war, not when you pried my hot hands off your wings and sent me tumbling." Lucifer makes a grab at the phone. "I'm telling you, he's doing this to you on purpose, and you should just fall right into it. I'll make sure you have a soft landing." He captures the phone from Michael and looks at the picture of Asher and laughs harder. "Or, hell, *he* will. Look at him. You always had a thing for the Jews."

Michael doesn't try to grab his phone back. He's not going to fall into some ridiculous physical fight with Lucifer in this place. He waits until Lucifer's flipped through the other photos Asher has sent in the last few weeks of their relationship.

"Lover Boy with kitty cat. Lover Boy giving a seductive smile—did that get you hard, Mike? I bet it got you hard. Hmm, Lover Boy sends a lot of pictures of flowers. Wait, I see, there's a pattern here. Clover and a note for good luck for your meeting with your dad, ha, and coreopsis for joy with the message—'so happy I met you.' Oh, sick, bro. He's sending you love notes and flower pics to match. That's not normal, dude. That's like some kind of faggy crap," Lucifer says with a serious expression, and then bursts into a radiant grin, singing under his breath, "Falling, falling!"

As he hands the phone back to Michael, he changes the lyrics of the first part of the next verse from something innocuous and cliché to, "There ain't no love like an anal love, and two dicks are better than one!"

"You're as annoying as ever."

"And you lack a sense of humor. Shocking! Does this guy make you laugh, 'cause Baby Jesus, you need to laugh."

"Must you reference him? Whatever. You know, why do I keep coming to you for advice? You have nothing to offer me."

"I've offered you the best advice you're gonna get, Mike. Let go. Feel the gravity. Taste the dirt when you hit the ground. It's not all that bad and you'll like it. I promise."

"Oh, *Eve*, that knowledge you're holding there in your sweet innocent hand will taste so very good and won't hurt you at all! I promise!"

"She liked it." Lucifer looks pleased with himself.

"She did," Michael agrees. "And he did, too."

Singing again, but not necessarily along with the song, which has now changed to something else, Lucifer opines, "Once you got it, you can't let it go, you gotta have it, bro. So just give in!"

"Keep your day job," Michael says.

"Hey, I did the rock star gig, if you recall. I was crazy successful at it."

"Yeah, after the actor gig, and the politician gig. Which, by the way, seemed to be your best. It certainly produced the most evil results."

"Yeah, but I'm not *all* bad, you know. I mean, I don't really want only evil shit to happen. It's just a little more fun when it does."

Michael chuckles softly, taking a sip of his beer.

"*There* you go, brother. Laugh a little. When's the last time you had fun?"

He thinks about Asher's mouth on his cock the night before. It'd been a sweet encounter, both of them feeling very skin-hungry. They'd held hands while Asher bobbed his head up and down, saliva running down to Michael's balls. Asher's little sounds as he'd worked had been so sweet and urgent, and when Michael orgasmed—wings pushing against his skin, aching there angrily—Asher had swallowed it all, gripping Michael's fingers and nursing his cockhead for every drop.

Heat pools in Michael's groin and he swallows another mouthful, lust surging in him, along with that weird ache that only eases when he's near Asher, and is, otherwise, a rotten pain in his neck. Is this what humans know as love? Romantic love? It's so much more visceral than the heavenly stuff.

Lucifer's still talking. "Rock star was fun, too, not quite as easy to really get in there and fuck shit up, but whatever. I figure resting a few years in a surf shop, taking sweet jaunts off to commit hardcore mischief when necessary, should put the bite back into my badness soon enough." He claps Michael on the back. "And it looks like I might have someone to leave the shop to when I go."

Michael ignores that and asks, "Is it fun being bad?"

"Nah, it's mostly boring because it's so easy. It's kind of pathetic. You know, you'd think if he was going to make them, he'd have made them a little less simple."

"Simple." He thinks of Asher's smile and his mother's watchful gaze over dinner the night before. He thinks of Asher's father's tight mouth. "Right."

"So, recently, I've been thinking I should spend a little more time messing with the Christians. Such a dramatic lot, those kids."

Michael shakes his head and glances over his shoulder at the exit. He's only a ten minute walk from the hotel. Asher is going to be there soon, and he suddenly wants nothing more than to go there and wait for him.

Lucifer raises his beer and clangs it against Michael's sitting on the bar. He takes a long swig and wipes his lips with the back of his hand. "The real question, Mike? Is why he never just blows that damn horn or sends in the messiah. Did you ever ask yourself about that?"

He has actually, many times. But he's never been daring enough to ask Father. Maybe, one day, if he's ever sure that he wants twenty years with Asher more than he wants forever as his father's tool, he'll come out and demand a response.

"I'm not sure he's got a plan."

Lucifer's eyebrows go up. "Whoa, blasphemy, bro."

"I mean, *surely* he's got a plan? Right?"

Lucifer just stands up and pats him on the shoulder. "Whatever you need to tell yourself."

"Wait," Michael grabs his wrist.

"Yes?"

"It's just…why him?"

"Why who?"

Michael grips him hard, showing him a little of his strength. He may have lost the taste for it, and he may be out of practice, but he is still a warrior.

"Why Lover Boy?"

"Why him in particular? He's not special." Yet as soon as the words are out, he wants to argue with himself about the pure specialness of Asher's smile.

Michael sighs as Lucifer sits down again and slaps the bar with both hands. "There's the rub. Why anyone? Love is a mystery and why any human falls for another is something I can never understand." Lucifer lifts a brow. "But you're not human are you? And since I've never done the deed myself—fallen in love, I mean—I can't say what it's all about. It happens. It sometimes sticks and sometimes doesn't. People make stupid choices for it." He sneers. "Case in point."

"I don't know why I ask you things."

"Me either. Stop analyzing it and just let yourself love the human. You want to, and what's the worst that can happen?" Lucifer points at the jukebox and the song about falling starts up again. "Bye, bro. You're gonna have to figure it out on your own. I've got some badness to get into."

"If you must."

Lucifer stands up. "I'll see you Monday."

"What's on Monday?"

"Your first day of work at the surf shop. Every fallen angel needs to work, now doesn't he?" Lucifer winks, ruffles Michael's hair affectionately, and walks out singing under his breath about anal love.

"Great." Sunlight breaks into the room and vanishes again with the swing of the door. "Because I'd hate to be unemployed." He looks down at Asher's picture on the phone again and his heart flips. "Someone in this relationship needs a job."

Chapter Six

A ND A PLACE to live.
The house isn't huge but it's large enough to give them both space and in the master bedroom there's a large bathtub in which Michael can soak to offset the pain of keeping his wings tucked in. The backyard is a nice mix of sun and shade that will support a garden for Asher to fill with his choice of flowers, shrubs, and vegetables.

Asher loves the house. At least he seems to based on his enthusiastic texts in response to the photos Michael has sent him of each room.

Are you sure? This is so impulsive! Asher replies when Michael says he's arranged for the purchase.

Impulsive is my middle name.

Michael stares at the teasing words he shot back, high on Asher's happiness, and buzzing with a giddy sensation that he's never experienced before. This house is *his* and the choices he makes in it are his, as well. A life apart from duty and servitude. Rebellion.

It feels so big it might crush him.

It feels amazing.

He's going to make a life with Asher. He has no idea what he'll tell Father when he finally calls him to duty again. What he'll do. Go, he supposes. And come home to Asher. This house, this plot of land in the country. Perhaps one day he'll even be able to spread his wings here and show Asher who he truly is.

Will Asher love him anyway? He believes the answer is yes, or else he wouldn't be here with this key in his hand and the deed to this property in his pocket.

Michael stands on the back porch staring at the roll of green land extending to a bank of trees, imagining the flowerbeds Asher will put in. Near the back of the property they can plant daffodil bulbs to represent a new beginning for both of them. He smiles cynically as the double meaning of the narcissus comes to mind.

Is this what selfishness feels like?

No wonder his brother enjoys it so much.

He waits for Father's retribution for his rebellious thoughts and deeds, but nothing happens. Michael wonders what he's waiting for, what action will take it far enough that his father forces him to choose, or simply casts him out. Whatever the line is, he hasn't crossed it yet.

That night, holding Asher close against him on the brand new mattress they've just broken in, he kisses the shell of Asher's ear and whispers, "I love you."

A warm delight spikes and Michael opens himself up to let Asher feel it.

"I love you, too."

"Tomorrow do you want to go looking at furniture?" He can have the place decorated with a snap of his fingers, but he wants Asher to help him choose. It seems like something human lovers do.

"Sure, that'd be fun." There's hesitancy in his voice and Michael wants to smooth it away.

"But what?"

"I've been thinking." Asher turns on his side to look at Michael earnestly. "What do you see in me? You're so young and beautiful. You could have anyone at all."

"I see all the particulars of you that make you Asher, and I love them," Michael says, reaching out to brush Asher's dark hair from his shining forehead. "This kind of spark comes once or twice in a hundred years. Trust me."

Asher rolls his eyes and laughs. "Yes, if you say so, oh, ye wildly experienced child."

"I'm not a child, Asher." He sounds petulant but that's only because he knows he has to be honest with Asher sooner rather than later. If Lucifer is telling the truth, he won't die, though Asher will. Eventually there'll be no denying his inhumanness, and explanations will have to be given. If he waits too long there will be no hope. A shiver passes through him at the thought that in Asher's reaction to the truth lies the dénouement of the relationship.

"Are you cold?" Asher pulls him closer, sweaty skin on sweaty skin.

"Keep me warm."

"I will," Asher says. "I've been thinking of other things, too."

"Like?"

"That you can't keep blocking me out of your life. I deserve to know where you work and what you really do when you're not with me."

Michael swallows thickly, his grace pressing against his skin, aching to wipe hard questions from Asher's mind. But what would that make him then? It is one thing to use his powers for Father's work, but for his own ends? That's Lucifer's territory. "I know. You're right."

Asher blinks at him and sighs. "I've also been thinking about that night you picked me up. You did it to protect me, didn't you? Like your namesake, the archangel Michael. You swooped in and saved me, huh?"

Michael starts to say he did it because he finds Asher unbearably attractive, but takes another tack. "What did I save you from?"

"From making the mistake of going home with that other guy."

Michael nods slowly. "I didn't see that turning out well."

"How do you know?"

Michael shrugs. "He wouldn't have been gentle." Asher tilts his head and narrows his eyes skeptically. "He was the type to hurt you whether he meant to or not."

"You know what I think? I think that night you needed me just as much as I needed you." Asher grins, kisses Michael's lips. "You needed someone to love. Get you out of your mid-twenties rut. Make you choose yourself over what your dad wants for the first time in your life."

"Maybe that's so."

"I have a question for you to ponder," Asher says, as he gets up from the mattress, turns on the new space heater set up by the window, and then heads toward the bathroom.

"Okay."

He pauses in the doorway, smiles cheekily, all sweet, flushed face, and glittering black eyes. "If that's true, who really saved who here?"

Michael feels an odd tightness in his chest, a thickness in his throat. Is that wetness in his eyes? Are these tears? Is he so happy he's going to cry? "My hero," he whispers. "My savior."

Asher laughs as he turns away.

"Wait." His chest aches, his wings burn against his back. "It's time that I'm honest with you."

"Should I be worried?"

Michael nods and Asher's vibrant eyes shutter. This shivery burst in his body is new and Michael recognizes it as anxiety. He's experienced dread and fear of Father before, but never of a human being. Asher has more power than he knows.

Michael takes comfort in the fact that Asher only puts on his boxer shorts and slides his burgundy button-up shirt on over his shoulders before sitting on the edge of the mattress. It implies a trust that Michael might not deserve but hopes to benefit from anyway.

The space heater whirs and Michael twists his fingers together.

"I'm listening," Asher whispers, sliding his hand forward across the mattress toward him, palm up.

But Michael doesn't take the offered comfort. Instead he stands, naked and vulnerable. Asher gazes up at him with soft, worried eyes, the creases by his mouth deepening into a frown.

"Just tell me. Whatever it is, I'll be okay."

Michael reaches out to heaven, feeling the connection at his back, and he waits to see what Father will do. Will he stop him now?

His wings unfurl with a crisp snap, always eager to be free of human skin, stretching to touch the walls on either side of the room. Michael tamps back his bursting radiance to avoid blinding Asher with his angelic grace.

Words are unnecessary.

Blood drains from Asher's cheeks and he goes completely still. No fight or flight in him—no breath even—frozen in awe before the archangel of heaven. As he should be.

Asher's eyes are wide, his jaw dropped, and when Michael pushes into Asher's bones he finds only terror. Without speaking or reaching out, he allows the moment to drag on and take up space in the eternity he lives in and which far exceeds Asher's imagining.

Air rushes into Asher's lungs with a rattle and he scrambles to his feet and back until he's pressed against the wall, hyperventilating and shaking. A shrill keen pierces the air, pushed out of him between shuddering breaths.

"Peace," Michael says and pushes it into Asher's flesh, willing it into him.

Asher melts to the floor, weak-limbed and still trembling, but the keening stops, replaced with rasping, slowing breaths.

"I mean you no harm."

Asher turns green and Michael sends him a wave of strength and another push of peace.

"What—you—what's happening? This isn't real." Asher's voice is slow, like he's piecing the words together from a tangle of thoughts. Michael can know these thoughts, can read his mind like he did the first night in the bar, but there's a certain respect that comes with being someone's lover and not their guardian angel. Asher deserves his privacy.

"It is real. I am Michael."

"The Archangel. That's absurd." He runs his hand over his face and stares desperately at Michael's wings. "This is a dream. I'll wake up soon."

Michael steps forward and Asher screams, pressing himself back against the wall, arm up, like a child shielding himself from a parent's raised switch.

"I won't hurt you." Michael reaches out but doesn't touch. "I love you."

Asher stares at him.

"The night we met my father sent me to teach you self-acceptance, to show you his love."

Asher blinks rapidly. "Please stop."

"Would you feel more comfortable if I folded my wings beneath my skin again?" The incandescent fear that he's enjoyed in many a mortal upon his revelation isn't enjoyable at all on Asher.

"If you *what?*"

Michael flexes, carefully tucking the primaries into the upper wing coverts, and sighs as his skin smooths into place.

Asher leans over and vomits.

"It's overwhelming to be in the presence of an angel," Michael says in his most gentle tones. "Allow me to soothe you. I have the ability to reduce your fear."

Asher wipes his mouth with the back of his hand, the stench of vomit rising around them. Michael snaps his fingers and whisks it away.

"How did you…?" Asher's voice trembles. "What do you want from me?"

To be your boyfriend seems an absurd response but it's the only true one. Still Michael says nothing for a moment, trying to formulate a comprehensive answer.

"Am I dead?"

"No. You're very much alive. This is very real. And I am breaking many rules by being here now with you."

"Breaking rules?" Asher looks around with fear screaming through him, echoing in the room as it radiates from his flesh.

"Angels don't fall in love."

"Fall in love." Asher is stuck and Michael has to reach into him, permission or no, to free him so he can understand.

"This won't hurt," Michael says, feeling his way through Asher's body, suffusing him with true peace. He guides Asher's heartbeat and breath until his eyes are no longer sharp and wild, until he's rubbing at his face and looking warily at Michael, but no longer insensible with fear. "Asher Rosenthal, I am the Archangel and I'm at your service."

Surely this is the sacrilege that will bring Father's wrath. But he still feels his link home like a golden thread at his back and there's no hint of a disturbance from heaven.

"You came for me," Asher whispers. "After all these years."

"Father has a strange sense of timing." And a comedic one at that, if Lucifer is to be believed.

Asher leans his head back against the wall and stares up at Michael. "What does this mean?"

"It means I'm even more angelic than you already believed me to be."

It's too early for jokes. Asher doesn't laugh.

"It means I love you and you needed to know the truth." Michael smiles ruefully, stretching his shoulders that already ache from the wings. "I couldn't let you move your things in without understanding who you're living with."

"What I'm living with," Asher says, his voice low enough that it's more breath than sound.

"Allow me to explain who I am." Michael sits on the floor across from Asher, folding his legs like a pretzel and starting at a point in time that is vaguely the beginning and leaving out eons to get to the point where they are now.

By the time he's done talking, Asher's eyes are wide again and he compulsively wipes his hand over his mouth over and over, like he's pushing away words he's afraid to speak.

"You can say anything," Michael says. "I know you have questions."

"Why?"

There's all of time in that question, the weight of him, the wear. But the truth's not an answer Asher can ever comprehend. "Because of these," he says, touching the wrinkles fanning from the edges of Asher's eyes. "And because you're right. You did save me that night. I'd never felt a pull for any other human the way I did for you. Did Father put you in my path to fall in love with you? I don't know. But I have. I did. I can't say why. I've met so many humans, but you're different for me." Michael struggles to explain himself and his feelings. Do humans have to justify their love? "You're my savior, my hero."

The back of his neck prickles ominously. He's close now.

"More like your damnation," Asher says, shaking his head.

"Not as you understand it." Michael struggles for words to explain. He takes Asher's hand. "A fallen angel is barred from heaven and no longer feels Father's presence fully." He adds quietly, "Lucifer claims Father comes to visit him. He claims Father is proud of him even now."

"Lucif—you mean, Luke? Your brother at the surf shop? He's Satan?"

Michael makes a face. "Yes."

Asher huffs out a shocked laugh, mouth working before asking incredulously, "Is that why you don't want me to meet him?"

Michael smiles tenderly. "One of many reasons, yes."

Asher stares at their entwined fingers with a new awe that puffs up Michael's pride. They sit in silence together for a long time, the weight of revelation heavy on them both, until Asher says, "What happens now?"

"That's for Father to decide."

Asher meets Michael's gaze. "And if he decides you can't have me?"

Michael closes his eyes. "I'll be cast out."

"Like Luc—Luke."

"He says it isn't so bad."

"Well, Satan would say that wouldn't he?"

Michael laughs and Asher's lips tip up at the sides.

Asher says, "If it comes to it, if God doesn't approve of this between us, promise me you'll choose heaven."

"No."

"Please, Michael. I'll be okay. I'll even find someone else to love one day if that's what you need to hear. But don't sell your soul for me. I'm not worth it."

"Angels don't have souls—" But before he can explain more a dizzying vibration grips the room. He gasps.

It's Father.

Asher's eyes blaze with fear and the scent of ozone burns in the air.

"Don't!" Michael spreads his wings, protection from the destructive perfection of God.

"Come home, Michael."

Father's voice crushes all resistance. Asher falls into submission, eyes closed and trembling as he presses himself facedown to the floor. Surrender.

Father's summons overwhelms Michael, shuddering through his human body until he sheds it against his will, a snake stripped of skin. He's delivered up to heaven, naked at Father's feet.

"Michael, do you remember the flood?"

"Yes, Father," he whispers.

"What preceded my wrath at that time?"

"Many sins, Father. Too many to count." Michael knows what's being asked, and in the ringing, terrifying silence he stalls. Finally, he gives the answer he knows is expected of him. "Angels took daughters of men as wives and created young with them." Michael had not been among their number but he was careful not to name any names.

"My flood wiped those children from the earth."

"Yes," Michael whispers, trembling. He cannot open his eyes and he prostrates himself. "Please, Father." He does not beg forgiveness. He begs for permission.

"You have been my right hand many times, perfectly obedient, perfectly just. But the ages have changed you."

Michael feels a rising hope and he dares to reach his hands out toward Father. "Please," he begs again into the radiance that floods him.

"I have indulged you. I gave you freedom to protect your people, freedom to explore the human world."

"Yes."

"Freedom has a price."

Michael quakes.

Father is silent a long time. "There is a battle coming, Michael."

"Soon?"

A swell of visions rises within him—violence, rioting, crowds, humans screaming, crying, laughing, and a sky that breaks open as angels charge in. Fear rises, not for himself, not for the humans, but for Asher.

"Soon enough."

He sets his jaw. Asher will be protected. Michael will cover him with his wings, and may Father protect any who try to harm a hair on his head.

"I will require warrior angels by my side."

Michael searches for the purity of purpose he's known before. It's lost somewhere back in the middle ages, or perhaps in the years when the Caesars still ruled. He's empty of any desire to fight.

"You are far from the warrior I need."

"Forgive me, Father."

For I have sinned. Michael burns with shame.

Father has heard his thoughts. "There is no sin in love."

"Then why are you doing this?"

"It is not a punishment, Michael. I will always be here waiting for you. My love is eternal. But you are not human, the rules are not the same for you, and your angelic vocation comes with privileges that cannot be extended if you are no longer devoted only to me."

"Will I still feel you?"

"Not as you did. But I am always with you."

Michael trembles at the thought of not feeling Father. "If I was human, I could have you and this as well."

"You're not human. You are as I made you—fierce and strong. But you cannot remain with me and put your love above my work." A sense of peace fills Michael and he knows Father isn't angry. "Make a choice."

"Can I come back? If I change my mind, will you let me return?"

"Always."

A heavenly gong strikes quite nearby. Everything shakes. Heaven goes topsy-turvy and Michael can't move.

"Choose."

Another swell of visions fills him, this time accompanied by sensation, and it's all Asher—*why did you let me love him?*– and he's caught up in it, cresting and aching, pushing, pulling, pulsing and a sensation like orgasm catches him up and spits him out into a vision of Asher in bed asleep, his beautiful black brows and lashes against pale skin, and his human, delicate collarbones, and further down his chest, the black hair Michael likes to grip in his fingers.

Horrible aching affection holds him hard, and Michael struggles flopping like a fish at Father's feet, trying to hold the emotion back and failing. *Love.* Unangelic, far too human, tied to lust and human dreams of home and building a life.

It's love or battles, love or fighting with Father for something he doesn't understand, love or the soldier he once was?

"Choose now, Michael."

He turns toward Asher's arms, pleasure-blind and free. This, *this* is his choice.

And, just like that, he falls.

He's barefoot and naked on green grass, his house a hulking shadow behind him in the night. His wings are extended and his heart pounds. There's an emptiness at his back, as though a tether has been cut away.

He groans and folds his wings and smooths the skin in place. He waits for the crushing weight of pain, for the severity of Father's rejection to pull him down forever.

Instead pride rushes in along with a dim sense that Father is impressed with his choice, sin or no. It's not so bad at all. He chuckles and thinks he owes his brother an apology.

It's just as Lucifer said.

Chapter Seven

THE HOUSE IS not the same as he left it.
Weeds overrun the yard and vines have ventured to creep up the side. His hands tremble as he unlocks the back door with his angelic ability—relief sweeping through him that his powers appear unaffected. The light switches don't work as he makes his way through the kitchen and into the hallway. His footsteps echo as he climbs the stairs, taking his time as understanding slides through him. He took too long making his choice. It's too late.

He stands in the open door to the bedroom, moonlight pouring through the windows. The mattress is still resting on the now dusty floor. The clothes he'd discarded before making love to Asher are neatly folded in the middle of it and a note rests on top. Picking up the dry paper, he recognizes Asher's handwriting.

I waited until I knew you weren't coming back. I'm proud of you for choosing your calling. You saved me and if letting you go saves you, I'm happy to do it. Well, maybe happy is too strong a word, but I'm trying to make my peace with it. I know it's too much to hope that I'll ever see you again. I won't pine for what I can't have. You wouldn't want that. I feel blessed to my bones to have been your lover, however briefly. I don't know what to do about the house. So I'm leaving it as it is. It is better than a motel for your future assignments. Yours always, Asher

Michael drags a hand over his face and resists the urge to throw his wings out wide. How long has he been away? Father's time is not the same as earth's linear time, and he's been dumped unceremoniously without the usual finesse of a mission-driven visit.

For all he knows, it's been years.

The thought cuts through him messily, all sharp, jagged edges of loss.

Groping through his clothes on the bed, he finds his cellphone still in his jean pockets, but the battery is dead. Closing his eyes, he takes a steadying breath. There's only one place he can go in the middle of the night after falling from grace. He dresses himself and seeks out his brother's location. It's a tight squeeze through space and time, but he manages it.

"Mike! Hey, bro. It's about time," Lucifer says, grinning from his lounging position on a giant sectional sofa. He clutches an iPhone in one hand and a beer in the other, looking all too human. "Get your ass over here." He pats the seat next to him.

Michael gazes around the apartment over the surf shop, taking in the one-bedroom setup. The kitchen is small but not filthy and the counter separating it from the living room is covered in unopened mail. The walls sport posters of Lucifer's old band from a few years back, a print-shop sign reading *Hell's Parties Are More Fun*, and a few upside-down crosses. He points at the last. "Are those really necessary?"

"Ambience, baby."

Michael rolls his eyes and sits gingerly at the edge of the sectional, as far from Lucifer as he can get. "Where are the pet lions and the girls in bikinis? Where's the silk and velvet?"

"I'm trying something new." Lucifer takes a sip of his beer. "Opulence is so *done*."

"Mm," Michael says noncommittally.

"Did dear old Dad do the deed?"

Michael scratches at his arms. Despite feeling it pulsing inside like always, he's convinced he feels his grace dying beneath his skin. "I chose."

"Hot damn. I knew you had it in you." He raises his beer in a toast. "To my fellow rebel. Shall we resume our age old fights to be the old man's favorite?"

Michael ignores the question. "Now what happens?" He remembers Asher asking the same thing. It feels only hours ago, but evidence points to it being much longer than that.

"Not much. You're the same old you. Same grace, same wings. You've just been kicked out of the club. No more celeb-style parties in the clouds. No more kissing Father's sweet-smelling toes."

Michael pulls his phone from his pocket. "Got a charger?"

"On the counter."

Michael plugs it in and hisses when the phone powers up revealing the date. "Is this right?"

"You've been topside a long time, bro."

"But seventeen months?"

"A lot's changed."

"Asher…"

"Oh, yeah. Your sweet little prince stopped by the store a month or two after you left. He nearly pissed himself, but he asked me, 'How's your brother?' It was all I could do not to devour him on the spot."

Michael whips around, snarling. "If you—"

"I didn't." Lucifer holds his hands up in surrender. "It's no fun seducing him if you're not here to watch."

Michael sits down on the sofa again and pinches the bridge of his nose, a strange sensation like a headache coming on. "What did you tell him about me?"

"That you were with Father. That's all I knew." Lucifer sniffs. "He left then, like a bat out of hell. What did you tell him about me? I could smell his fear."

"The truth."

"What? That I'm a better lover than you? That I throw the best parties?"

Michael ignores the taunts.

"Don't worry about *me*, though. I wasn't lonely while you were gone," Lucifer says, waggling his brows. "Kept myself busy with half a dozen sailors and arranging crime sprees in Jersey."

"That's all in seventeen months? I expected more." Michael instinctively reaches out to feel Father and the silence feels as large as the universe. It fills him with yearning, a sensation he's only tasted before. Now it's consuming.

"As for your sweet meat, well, he's moved on," Lucifer says, smirking. "You gave up Father and heaven for someone who's now dating an assistant rabbi at that run-down old synagogue. Seems he's into holy types." Lucifer winks. "Choices are fun, aren't they? And consequences excruciatingly interesting."

Michael collapses back into the sofa, wiped out and aching inside. He's got angelic power. He's got his wings. He's got eternity ahead of him. But he's lost everything: Father, heaven, and Asher, too. His chest squeezes and burns. His stomach churns. The yearning swells and presses against his skin like his wings—painful, urgent. This kind of pain is new. And, yes, interesting.

"Oh, please, you're not going to cry are you?" Lucifer grimaces. "You're an angel. Take that lover-stealing rabbi down. All it takes is a flick of your finger. Stop fretting like a virgin hovering over her first fat cock."

Michael sighs. His brother is disgusting and, worse, obtuse. His throat hurts and maybe he is going to cry because his eyes burn.

"You're ridiculous," Lucifer hisses. "You *fell* for him."

"Falling doesn't entitle me to his love."

Lucifer tosses up his hands. "Now you sound like a date rape ad. 'Is she too drunk to drive? She's too drunk to consent. Don't be that guy.' Listen to me, bro, don't be *that* guy. You didn't lose heaven for a prison of honorable choices."

"For the love of Father, what is wrong with you? Have you no shame?"

Lucifer grins at Michael. The absurdity of his question floats in the air like laughter.

Michael sighs. "If he's moved on, if he's with someone he can share the seasons of life with—family, aging, death—I can't take that from him."

"You can actually."

"I won't."

"Prig."

"Satan."

Lucifer smirks. "You'll come around to my way of thinking eventually. Eternity without Father's presence is a long, long time."

"What happened to your claim he comes to visit you?"

"He does. And he's a bastard about it. He doesn't let me *feel* him. But I know he's there." Lucifer shifts around, smoothing his hands down his jeans and wrinkling his nose. "He knows I'm an addict jonesing for a fix, knows it kills me that he's right there in the same room, but I can't have him. Torture. He's a real peach, our Dad."

Michael says nothing, rubbing his eyes as exhaustion and aching sadness fills his core.

"You can stay one night. Then you have to leave. I'm not going to baby you." Lucifer points his finger at the screen on the opposite wall. "Get your lover back. Enjoy him while he lasts. Because, in the scheme of eternity, he won't last long."

A reality television show about housewives in New Jersey begins. Michael stares at it numbly, barely paying attention. They share a bowl of buttered popcorn that appears on the cushions between them. He knows what Lucifer says is true. Asher won't last long, and that's all the more reason to stay away from him. Let him enjoy his normal human life and whatever happiness he's found.

If that means Michael suffers, it's only part of Father's design.

Falling is meant to be painful.

MICHAEL DECORATES HIS house alone.

A finger snap here and a blown breath there, and he has curtains, dishes, beds, tables, and chairs. It's attractive enough, but lonely. The dreams he's had of sharing the decisions with Asher—of seeing the man he loves choose things he admires, of learning his aesthetic—all rot on the vine, along with the dozen other fantasies he's allowed himself to concoct in defiance of Father.

Michael knows Asher will never plant the beds around the house, so he haphazardly fills the yard with hyacinth, hyssop, and honeysuckle and calls it a day.

Days pass, one into another, and he rides the time like a child on the back of a tortoise: slow and burning. The weather is hot, and his skin parches in the sun, pulls tight against his angelic form, and stings over his wings. He wants Asher, he wants Father, he wants shade, and comfort, and love.

The museum is cool when he steps inside. Footsteps echo on the tile and hushed voices murmur over the art. He's kept his mind carefully blank on the way here but once he's walking toward the painting, he can't deny why he's come.

Asher sits across from *The Archangel*, his mouth moving in a silent prayer that Michael hears above the others that always swirl around him. He's thin and strong, but he's anxious, and Michael feels that even before the heart-thumping power of seeing his beautiful face, his dark hair, and proud nose wakes him from his long wonderless sleep.

"My mother likes him," Asher prays. "My father shook his hand when he asked for mine. He wants to marry me." Asher's shoulders slump. "But I don't want to marry him." He gazes up at the painting again. "I wish this looked like you. I always thought the angel in the painting was inhumanly beautiful until I knew you. But it doesn't do the real you justice." He laughs softly. "Nothing and no one does you justice. You ruined me. And I wouldn't change that for anything in the world. But I don't want to break his heart, and I know you're not coming back. There won't be anyone else like you. No more angels for me." He laughs hard enough that he wipes at his crinkling eyes with the tips of his fingers. "Marrying him would be a good move. And he does love me. And I like him." He shakes his head, scrunching his nose and radiating with *you **like** him, Asher? Pitiful.* He covers his face with his hands.

Michael sits on the bench beside him. "No more angels for you? Are you sure about that?"

Asher goes still, swallowing hard before he drops his hands away from his face. He stares at Michael, his eyes wide and mouth wet. "You."

"You." Michael whispers back. He wants to lean forward and kiss Asher's lush mouth. It would soothe so much in him, but he holds himself back. "I've been gone a long time."

"Yeah, you have," Asher snaps, unexpected anger in his tone. It hits Michael like a whip, breathtaking and sharp. "Why are you here?"

"You prayed to me." Michael's off-balance in a way he doesn't understand. He pushes into Asher, trying to read his flesh and bones, but Asher's anger pushes back hard until Michael relents, panting. "How did you do that?" he asks.

Asher's still focused on the prayer. "I prayed to you hundreds of times in the past and you never came. I prayed to you for a year after you left. *Nothing.*"

"I was detained."

"By God?"

"Yes."

"He put you in angel jail?"

"Not exactly. Why are you angry?" Michael tries to push into Asher again and is rebuffed just as quickly.

"Because you came now. Right when I've made up my mind to marry Stanley. Is that why you came back? To stop me?"

"I heard your prayer and I had to see you. You sounded desperate."

"Are you here—" He breaks off, bites his bottom lip, and shakes his head. "Is this a mission? Are you saving me again from another mistake?"

"I don't do missions anymore."

"I don't understand."

"I chose you."

Asher gapes. "No, you didn't. I waited for a year for you. I went back to the house every day. I paid the utility bills. I grieved. I begged. I screamed. I finally gave up."

"I'm sorry I took so long."

"You're *sorry*? Where the hell have you been all this time?"

Their whispered argument is attracting the attention of the guards and other museum guests. Michael reaches out a hand to soothe Asher since he can't calm him from within, but Asher ducks away from it.

"Father's time is different from earth's time. When I fell, he wasn't exact about when I landed. I wasn't on a mission. You were already with your rabbi and I didn't want to disturb your happiness. What I wanted? It didn't matter."

"It matters to me that I cried for you like you were dead."

Sorrow and useless regret flow through Michael. He wishes he could go back and take away Asher's pain. "I didn't hear you. When I'm with Father, I hear nothing but him." He glances around to make sure no one is watching before he closes his eyes and summons snatches of honeysuckle into his fingers. The sweet perfume fills the space between them, pungent and strong. Asher blinks rapidly before taking the sprigs from Michael's hand.

"Eternal bonds."

"Yes," Michael murmurs, and tries to push into Asher again, to sense his inner sweetness. The blocking anger retreats and he lets his angelic grace fill in the space left behind. "For you. I fell for you. And then I fell." He leaves aside all of his questions of how and why and if it's all a set up or a test. He doesn't care. He can be with Asher now that he knows he's not happy with his rabbi.

Asher gasps. "I feel you. Pushing into me." His eyes flash wide. "I've felt this before when I was with you, but I didn't know—oh!"

Michael allows his devotion to flow between them and Asher dissolves against him, the heat and weight of his body a balm for the want and yearning Michael's suffered with since he fell.

"You love me," Asher whispers.

"I told you I did."

"But you gave up—what exactly did you give up?" Asher wraps his arm around Michael's back and presses his cheek against his shoulder.

Michael supports his weight, cuddling him close. "Perfection. His, not mine. Even angels aren't perfect." He laughs softly. "Constant comfort. Boredom. But I get to keep eternity and my power and, hopefully, you."

"Me?"

"For as long as you'll have me."

"I'll age. You won't. That's creepy. I'll be some dirty old man."

Michael laughs. "Well, that's only half true. I'll never die, but I can refashion a different body. Lucifer does it every once in a while for a fresh start. I could choose older bodies so that we're more matched."

"But you don't have to do that now," Asher says, desperately, cupping Michael's cheek. "I like this one."

"I'm in no rush."

"Okay," Asher says, sitting up straight, and a smile breaking on his face. "Then I want you for as long as I live." They both feel the surge of certainty in Asher's body as he speaks the oath.

"I'm sorry I was away for so long. I hope your rabbi has been good to you."

"Assistant rabbi," Asher corrects. "He's been kind and wonderful. But, as good as he is, and as gentle, he's no angel."

Michael tugs him down for a kiss. "Let's get out of here."

"Where? Somewhere with a bed?" Asher asks.

"Of course."

"I should probably break up with Stanley first," Asher says, hesitantly.

"That can wait," Michael says. "Be with me now."

Apparently, he's no angel either.

Epilogue

THEY'VE SPENT AN afternoon in Michael's bed fucking. Covered in come and sweat, they spoon up together, listening to the birds outside the bedroom window and panting softly.

Everything is perfect. Actually, everything is incredibly imperfect.

Michael's surf shop job is strange. He has to listen to Lucifer pontificate about all kinds of nonsense. His house is drafty and lonely since Asher wants to wait before moving in—a kindness in deference to the assistant rabbi's feelings, quite bruised after Asher ended their engagement. It's a good thing, but Michael can't help but to selfishly wish Asher was a crueler man in this if nothing else. But he loves him fiercely for his gentle heart.

Michael's been given to understand that Asher's father still hates him—this time for being the bastard who broke his son's heart, instead of the bastard who woke it. Sometimes in the night his wings ache so badly he cries. Everything is as far from heavenly as it can get. But none of it makes him regret his choice.

But Asher will move in soon. The surf shop job is a pleasant enough distraction. Michael can quit in the future if he wants to, and he might if Asher ever wants him to. Being around Lucifer isn't that bad, really. He's interesting at least, and keeps him on his toes.

The drafts in the house can be fixed up by human hands or angelic persuasion, and Michael's not sure why he's dragging his feet on it. Lucifer rolls his eyes and says it's because Michael wants to punish himself with petty human problems. He's probably right, and Michael smiles, taking pleasure in the mundane.

And Mr. Rosenthal will either come around to Michael's return to Asher's life or he won't. All that matters now is that Asher is smiling at him. Michael kisses the wrinkles by Asher's eyes, his heart squeezing painfully with joy.

"You make me feel old when you do that."

"You're just a whippersnapper." Michael kisses them again. "Now, tell me what you want out in the garden. Tell me how you're going to fill our flower beds."

Asher goes thoughtful. "Marjoram for joy. Myrtle for marriage."

Michael quivers inside, a bell striking deep within. Marriage. No matter what laws come and go on this earth, Asher has as good as proclaimed himself married to Michael until his death. It's an honor he doesn't know if he deserves, and a responsibility he cherishes.

"Don't get any angelic ideas," Asher says. "I want to plant it all myself. None of that magicking up plants like you did that time at the museum."

Michael nuzzles Asher's sweaty shoulder and agrees. "Roses for love?"

Asher nods and then goes solemn. "And rosemary for protection."

"But I'm not in the protection business any longer."

Asher plucks at the bed sheets. "I was thinking along the lines of protection for us."

"Are you worried about that?" Michael pushes into Asher's body and feels his anxiety. "We're safe here."

"Are we? Isn't your father angry with us? With me?"

Michael shakes his head and lays his hand on Asher's chest, feeling the steadiness of his heartbeat. Has Asher been worrying about that all of these weeks? "No. Father doesn't get angry these days." He tries to think of how to phrase it so that Asher understands. Father is awesome and terrifying, but he's no longer full of the whimsical rage he once exhibited. "He's very final in his judgements, but not wrathful. Your soul is safe. He doesn't blame you for my choice."

"Are you sure? In the Torah he's often vengeful."

"He's mellowed. In his youth, though—watch out world!"

"Literally."

"There was that flood." Michael remembers it well. The screams of the people. The orders to let them drown. No help was to be given. He frowns. "There were some nasty plagues." Locusts and sickness. The suffering of people had barely disturbed him then. Now, though, suffering gets under his skin.

"The slaughter of first born sons," Asher offers.

"I agree he's had his moments. But he's not angry about this." Michael is relatively certain. Since he no longer feels Father, he can't know for sure. But if Father wants to strike them down, he'll have done it by now. "We're safe here together."

Asher nods slowly, accepting Michael's opinion. "Let's still plant rosemary." He smiles cheekily, his eyes flashing and his voice warm with laughter. "For lust."

Michael grins, sliding his hand over Asher's chest hair, down the trail to his belly button and lower, chuckling at what he finds. "Already?"

"I want you to ride me. With your wings out."

Sex between them was always good, but with nothing between them now but naked honesty, their connection pulses, a living entity. Riding Asher's cock, looking down on his open, flushed face, Michael can no longer feel Father's stamp on Asher's bones. He only feels Asher and it's beautiful. Asher's gentleness, forgiveness, and love rushes through him like a wave, filling the new yearning places inside.

"Let me see you," Asher says, gripping Michael's hips and pushing up into him. "Show me who I'm fucking."

Michael's wings snap open and he cries out in relief. He stretches them wide, moaning with delight, the maddening itch and burn at his back gone.

"Beautiful," Asher whispers, grinding his hips up to get as far into Michael as he can. "Michael, my angel. Come for me."

Falling, falling.

The song from the day in the bar with Lucifer pops into Michael's head as he rides Asher hard and fast, his cock straining and aching, his human flesh on the verge of maddening bliss. *Falling, falling.* Love is something with endless depths. Like the ocean. Like Asher's soul.

He slams into orgasm as hard as the earth. Hot come spurts between them and Michael drops his wings over Asher as a shelter.

"I love you," Asher says, clinging to him and shaking. "I hope God doesn't damn me for it, but I'm happy you chose me."

"I love you," he whispers. He wants to shout it to the heavens. "I'm happy I chose you, too."

The bars and missions of Mercy Street seem an eon away. Michael's no one's tool any longer. He's old, tired, and no warrior. He kisses Asher passionately, losing himself in slippery lips and hot tongue, in the eager grasp of Asher's arms and his joyful declarations of love.

He's fallen and falling, and he knows he'll never stop.

THE END

Letter from Leta

Dear Reader,

Thank you so much for reading *Three Fantasies*! I hope you enjoyed reading these stories as much as we enjoyed crafting them.

Be sure to follow me on BookBub or Goodreads to be notified of new releases. And look for me on Facebook for snippets of the day-to-day writing life, or join my Facebook Group for announcements and special giveaways. To see some sources of my inspiration, you can follow my Pinterest boards or Instagram.

If you enjoyed the book, please take a moment to leave a review! Reviews not only help readers determine if a book is for them, but also help a book show up in site searches.

Also, for the audiobook connoisseurs out there, many of my other books are available in audio. I hope to eventually add my entire backlist, including *Three Fantasies*, to my audiobook roster over the next few years.

Thank you for being a reader!
Leta

ANY GIVEN LIFETIME

by Leta Blake

He'll love him in any lifetime.

Neil isn't a ghost, but he feels like one. Reincarnated with all his memories from his prior life, he spent twenty years trapped in a child's body, wanting nothing more than to grow up and reclaim the love of his life.

As an adult, Neil finds there's more than lost time separating them. Joshua has built a beautiful life since Neil's death, and how exactly is Neil supposed to introduce himself? As Joshua's long-dead lover in a new body? Heartbroken and hopeless, Neil takes refuge in his work, developing microscopic robots called nanites that can produce medical miracles.

When Joshua meets a young scientist working on a medical project, his soul senses something his rational mind can't believe. Has Neil truly come back to him after twenty years? And if the impossible is real, can they be together at long last?

Any Given Lifetime is a stand-alone, slow burn, second chance gay romance by Leta Blake featuring reincarnation and true love. This story includes some angst, some steam, an age gap, and, of course, a happy ending.

SLOW HEAT

by Leta Blake

A lustful young alpha meets his match in an older omega with a past.

Professor Vale Aman has crafted a good life for himself. An unbonded omega in his mid-thirties, he's long since given up hope that he'll meet a compatible alpha, let alone his destined mate. He's fulfilled by his career, his poetry, his cat, and his friends.

When Jason Sabel, a much younger alpha, imprints on Vale in a shocking and public way, longings are ignited that can't be ignored. Fighting their strong sexual urges, Jason and Vale must agree to contract with each other before they can consummate their passion.

But for Vale, being with Jason means giving up his independence and placing his future in the hands of an untested alpha—as well as facing the scars of his own tumultuous past. He isn't sure it's worth it. But Jason isn't giving up his destined mate without a fight.

Standalone

THE RIVER LEITH
by Leta Blake

Amnesia stole his memories, but it can't erase their love.

Leith is terrified after waking up in a hospital bed to find his most recent memories are three years out of date.

Worse, he can't even remember how he met the beautiful man who visits him most days. Everyone claims Zach is his best friend, but Leith's feelings for Zach aren't friendly.

They're so much more than that.

Zach fills Leith with longing. Attraction. Affection. **Lust**. And those feelings are even scarier than losing his memory, because Leith's always been straight. Hasn't he?

For Zach, being forgotten by his lover is excruciating. Leith's amnesia has stolen everything: their relationship, their happiness, and the man he loves. Suddenly single and alone, Zach knows nothing will ever be okay again.

Desperate to feel better, Zach confesses his grief to the faceless Internet. But his honesty might come back to haunt them both.

The River Leith is a standalone MM romance with amnesia trope, hurt/comfort, bisexual discovery, "first time" gay scenes, a second chance at first love, and a satisfying happy ending.

First in a Duology

TRAINING SEASON
by Leta Blake

Can a cowboy's firm hand help discipline this feisty figure skater—on and off the ice?

Matty Marcus fears he doesn't have what it takes to achieve his Olympic dream. His self-esteem is at an all-time low after figure skating coaches and skating judges have told him he's not skinny enough, good enough, or masculine enough to win.

Matty wishes he could afford the kind of coach he needs, a top-notch one who specializes in keeping their skaters focused. But those coaches are ridiculously expensive, and Matty is financially strapped.

Until a lucrative house-sitting gig brings him to rural Montana.

And to Rob.

No one has ever looked at Matty the way rural cowboy Rob Lovely looks at him. No one has ever touched him, loved him, and healed him from the inside out. No one has ever made him feel so valuable and adored. Worthy. Strong.

No one has ever taught Matty how to fly. Or how to lose.

Rob might be a cowboy and a single dad who knows nothing about figure skating, but after only a few months, he's trained a new kind of bravery into Matty's soul.

But to achieve his Olympic dream, Matty will have to face the ultimate test. Has he truly learned what it means to win—on and off the ice—during his training season?

Training Season is a MM romance with a feisty, flamboyant figure skater and an easy-going dominant cowboy, opposites attract, hurt-comfort, single dad, winter holiday highlights, love beyond reason, multiple steamy scenes, and a well-earned happy ending. *This book contains some BDSM elements.*

Gay Romance Newsletter

Leta's newsletter will keep you up to date on her latest releases and news from the world of M/M romance. Join the mailing list today and you're automatically entered into future giveaways.
letablake.com

Leta Blake on Patreon

Become part of Leta Blake's Patreon community in order to access exclusive content, deleted scenes, extras, bonus stories, rewards, prizes, interviews, and more.
www.patreon.com/letablake

Other Books by Leta Blake

Contemporary

Will & Patrick Wake Up Married
Will & Patrick's Endless Honeymoon
Cowboy Seeks Husband
The Difference Between
Bring on Forever
Stay Lucky

Sports

The River Leith

The Training Season Series
Training Season
Training Complex

Musicians

Smoky Mountain Dreams
Vespertine

New Adult

Punching the V-Card

Winter Holidays

The Home for the Holidays Series
Mr. Frosty Pants
Mr. Naughty List
Mr. Jingle Bells

Fantasy

Any Given Lifetime

Re-imagined Fairy Tales

Flight
Levity

Paranormal & Shifters

Angel Undone
Omega Mine

Horror

Raise Up Heart

Omegaverse

Heat of Love Series
Slow Heat
Alpha Heat
Slow Birth
Bitter Heat

For Sale Series
Heat for Sale

Coming of Age

'90s Coming of Age Series
Pictures of You
You Are Not Me

Audiobooks

Leta Blake at Audible

Discover more about the author online

Leta Blake
letablake.com

About the Author

Author of the bestselling book *Smoky Mountain Dreams* and the fan favorite Omegaverse series *Heat of Love*, Leta Blake's educational and professional background is in psychology and finance, respectively. However, her passion has always been for writing. She enjoys crafting romance stories and exploring the psyches of imaginary people. At home in the Southern U.S., Leta works hard at achieving balance between her writing and her family life.